**Jenny Roberts** was born in Bridlington and runs the Libertas! Women's Bookshop in York. Her first novel, *Needle Point*, was published by Diva Books in 2000. This is the sequel and she is currently working on the next book in the series.

Visit Jenny's website at www.jennyroberts.net or mail her at mail@jennyroberts.net

# Breaking Point

## JENNY ROBERTS

First published 2001 by Diva Books
an imprint of Millivres Limited
part of the Millivres Prowler Group
116-134 Bayham Street, London NW1 0BA

A catalogue record for this book is available from the British Library

ISBN 1 873741 58 8

Cover illustration and design by Andrew Biscomb

Printed and bound in Finland by WS Bookwell

# Acknowledgements

Every author I've met in the last year has insisted on telling me (often several times) that the second book is the hardest one of all to write. So I am particularly thankful for all the help and support I've received whilst working on *Breaking Point*.

Firstly, I am indebted to all those who have contacted me to say how much they enjoyed *Needle Point*. When you're stuck in front of a screen and have (literally) lost the plot, it helps to know that your readers enjoy what you do.

Thanks to Anne in London for advice on the legal profession and for commenting, in particular, on Becky's role; to Chris in York for his help; to the Humberside police for talking to me about their work; and to Roger Forsdyke for reading the first few chapters and putting me right on various points of police procedure. If any mistakes remain then they are mine rather than theirs.

Thanks to Jackie in Calgary who read the first draft and provided an invaluable perspective on the improvements that were needed; to my friend Ann for special help; and to Kirsty, who helped me source essential information on various animal rights campaigns. I respect and support the law-abiding work undertaken by animal rights campaigners. Thanks also to Helen Sandler, my editor, for her encouragement and advice; and to Andrew Biscomb, for the cover.

My acknowledgement to Line One, who really did provide the e-mail addresses for both Magda Swinson and Cameron (please don't e-mail them – they aren't there!).

Bouquets to the team at Libertas! – Nic, Chrissy, Ann, Denise and Joan – who kept the wheels turning at a very busy bookshop for months, leaving me free to write. Without them...

Finally, my greatest thanks have to go to my partner Ann, whose life has sometimes been seriously disrupted over the year, and who has borne it all with fortitude, total support, constructive advice, encouragement and love. This book is for you.

*Note: Line One and Freeserve are registered trademarks.*

*To Ann*
*Love has never been so sweet...*

# One

Easter Monday. 8.15 am.

The juggernaut swept past in a shroud of dirty spray and dissolved into the greyness ahead, leaving me wet and miserable in its wake, straining to see ahead as I picked my way along the near-deserted road on my Harley.

I felt lousy. My holiday had ended suddenly after the row with Hellen and my mood, already black, had been made worse when the ferry was diverted across the Humber. Now the weather was slowing me down and soaking me to the skin. It would be a relief to reach the Humber Bridge and leave the coast and fog behind.

I dropped down a gear as a big road sign loomed out of the mist, and approached the junction for Barton with a feeling of deep dread. I'd forgotten that the road went past here, within a mile of my mother's nursing home. I'd promised to visit her so many times, and if I had an ounce of decency I would turn off and do it now. But I didn't. I just looked straight ahead and carried on down the hill, hoping that the bad feelings inside me would go away.

For a moment I was so buried in myself that I lost my bearings completely. Then, as I strained my eyes to see ahead, the grass verge gave way to a crash barrier, and within seconds I was driving under the enormous south gantry of the Humber Bridge, which towered through the mist, disappearing far into the sky above me.

The bridge is massive – more than a mile across – and in that weather, I soon lost track of how far I had crossed. I could just make out watery headlights on the opposite carriageway and I knew that, by now, I must be high over the estuary. But the fog was so thick that I could see no more than ten feet in front and, at the speed I was going, it would be several minutes before I reached the toll booths on the other side.

Most of the ferry's container traffic seemed to have passed me by now. I was alone, just me and my machine, cut off from the rest of the world. So the sudden flash of headlights and the high-pitched screaming of a horn sent my head reeling in panic and my bike veering towards the crash barrier. Instinctively, I pulled back onto the straight and held the machine steady as the dark blue MGB Sports shot through the gloom beside me, water cascading off its soft-top, carbon dioxide spiralling out of its twin exhausts. It was going too fast, maybe 60 mph against my 10, its headlights ricocheting off the mist, the blare from its horn dropping to a lingering whine as it shot ahead of me, disappearing into the blanket of grey.

My heart was pounding now, my head exploding with anger. Fucking idiot! I gunned my Harley and gave chase, picking up the thin grey outline of the car again as it careered back and forth across the road ahead of me. For a few seconds I felt marginally better. But even if I caught it there was nothing I could do. So I dropped my revs, slowing back to a safe speed, breathing deeply, calming down. One crazy driver was enough. Slowly, my heartbeat returned to normal.

The fog was even more impenetrable by the time I picked up the sombre warning from the foghorn on the mid-channel buoy. I slowed down to a crawl now, peering through the gloom, keeping close to the crash barrier and praying that no other idiot would come up behind me at speed.

And thank God I was going so carefully. The MGB which had passed so recklessly was slewed across the road; its doors hung open, its headlights shining out into a wall of fog. I braked and pulled into the side, cursing the irresponsibility of the driver, as another juggernaut, its horn blaring, its lights flashing angrily, sliced through the air beside us.

I ripped off my helmet, shaking in shock. Of all the stupid, dangerous things to do…! I pulled my bike onto its stand, switched on the trafficators and ran to the car. Empty, the driver gone. Fucking stupid, irresponsible idiot! I leant quickly into the passenger side, switching on the hazard warning lights, and closed the doors, then climbed over the crash barrier at the side of the road to seek the relative safety of the cycle track below.

It was a crazy thing to do. If I'd been more clear-headed, I would have got back on my bike and driven to the toll booths with a warning. But by now I was wound up and, despite my anger, concerned for the driver of the car. The bridge has more than its fair share of suicides. It was hard not to come to the obvious conclusion.

So I made my way carefully down the steep metal ramp onto the wide cycle track alongside the carriageway and shouted out: "Hello. Are you all right?"

The mist seemed to close in around me, shutting me in and muffling my voice, like I was shouting into a cardboard box. I yelled a second time and stood very still, listening, searching the gloom all along the low railings at the edge, half expecting to see someone sitting on them, preparing to jump. Wondering what I would do. Wondering what I would say.

And then, as the mist swirled around me, I heard her scream, some yards along the track. It was faint, muffled by the blanket of fog, but unmistakably desperate. I shouted back and as she screamed again, I hurried towards the sound, my heart thumping.

It was just then that the mist began to part ahead of me. And, for a second, time froze.

She was no more than ten yards away, at the very edge of my vision – a mere shadow, struggling against the railings. Struggling frantically against another, bigger shape. Kicking out with her feet, twisting her body. Fighting to stay on the bridge, to stay alive. Holding onto the railings, floundering in mid-air. And slowly, inescapably, being forced over the side.

"Hang on!" I heard myself screaming, momentarily petrified by fear, but unable to ignore her plight. She screamed again as the fog closed in around them. Then something inside me took over and I was running. The big bridge seemed to give beneath my feet as I propelled myself forward, my boots splashing through the water on the cycle track. As the mist cleared a second time, I saw the man glance towards me, a scarf covering his face. I hoped to God he would run.

But, instead, quite calmly, he pulled a knife out of his coat, flicked it open, and brought it up, hard, into her stomach.

The screaming stopped. The only sound as I ran those last few yards was my own feet, pounding through the tunnel of fog all around me, thumping through my head. I didn't know what I could do or how I could stop him. All I knew was that I had to try.

I was almost upon him as he plunged the knife in a second time. I hurtled into his stomach, shoulder first, before he could pull the weapon free and use it on me. Together we crashed violently backwards, tumbling onto the rough wet track. He grabbed for me with his big hands and I rolled away, giving him the chance to run again. But he hurled himself after me, grabbing my neck and throwing me heavily, crashing and tumbling, along the pathway. Then he turned back to his victim. The woman made a desperate attempt to stand before he got to her. Her face was wreathed in terror. Moaning, whimpering, she collapsed again as he neared, flailing her arms, trying to hold him off.

I struggled to my feet, breathless, my belly churning, my heart thumping. But I was too slow. Before I had taken a single step he stabbed her twice more as she lay on the ground.

I stopped in my tracks as he turned and rose to his feet again, the bloody knife held out in front of him, the scarf wrapped right around his face. His flat cap was pulled down low so that I could see nothing of his eyes. He was around six feet tall; wearing a long black raincoat. And he said nothing. Just stared at me from under the cap. A panther cornering its prey, trying to mesmerise me with fear. I looked back as calmly as I could, trying to figure a way out, scared, more than anything, by his lack of reaction. He'd just stabbed a woman four times. Yet there was no passion, no anger, no panic in his body language.

A cold shudder ran down my spine. I backed off and opened up an exit for him again, hoping he'd run this time. Still he showed no emotion. Just looked at me and then glanced over his shoulder at the body by the railings. She looked dead, but I guess that he wanted to make sure, to get her out of the way, into the river. He took a step back towards her, keeping his eyes on me. Behind him I saw the briefest of movements from her broken body. She was still alive. I could run and leave her to him. Or I could try and stop him before he finished her off.

I didn't really think about it. I took two steps towards him, my body angled, my hands at the ready, trying to remember the few jujitsu lessons I'd once taken.

He seemed to understand that I wasn't going to give up, and glanced from me to the woman and back again. If he picked her up, I would go for him. He couldn't heave her body over the railings and hold me off as well. Heartened by his hesitation, I took another bold pace towards him, even though I was breaking up inside. He studied me through the scarf, pointing the knife right at my belly, his eyes a band of darkness.

"Go away!" I screamed. "Leave her alone!"

He glanced at the apparently lifeless body behind him. Then he nodded his head slowly, backed away and disappeared into the mist.

I watched him go. My limbs were putty as I ran across to her. She was slumped on the ground, her left arm twisted awkwardly behind her, her right hand stretched out towards the railings. Wet mist clung in pearls to her mauve rain-jacket, her blue jeans were sodden and her hair was matted against her face, her lips blue. She was lying in a small pool of water which was slowly turning pink as it ran in rivulets across the tarmac and over the side of the bridge, dripping into the estuary a hundred feet below. She opened her eyes and tried to lift her head, her lips moving soundlessly; her expression a mixture of fear, agony and disbelief.

I put my hand beneath her head and held her steady as she fought painfully for each breath. "It's OK, he's gone," I gasped, trying to sound strong and comforting whilst my own heart still pounded with fear. "Take it easy. Don't try and speak. I'll get help."

She grabbed my arm, and a rasping noise came from her lips. "No, please..." She croaked with great effort, pulling me closer.

"Please..." Her eyes were big and desperate. "Important... file... M... Swinson... at line one..." She coughed, blood spilling out onto her lips. "Please, tell Joanna... Whittling... no one else..." Then she fell back.

I held her in my arms, panicking. "What do you mean?"

She looked up into my eyes again, alarmed; swallowing painfully and gulping air after each word. "E-mail... Please... help us... only Joanna."

It was her e-mail address: mswinson@lineone. There was something in her e-mail box she wanted me to pass on.

"But... How do I open your e-mails?" I asked. "What's the password?" She closed her eyes, wincing at the pain.

"Benjy... two..." she coughed again painfully, her voice becoming weaker all the time, "five... six." She breathed.

"Please... tell... no one else... Promise," she demanded, grasping my arm.

I looked back into her desperate face. "I promise," I answered, heaven help me. "But where is she?"

"Urgent... Thursday." She gasped, staring into my eyes, her breath growing shallower by the second. Then she lifted her head, and with all the energy she could muster, she whispered something that sounded like 'ice'. But it was more of a gasp than a word, almost imperceptible. Then her eyes closed and her head fell back heavily in my arms.

I pulled out my mobile and dialled 999. The bridge vibrated noisily beneath my feet as traffic thundered past on the carriageway, and I swore in dismay when I had to repeat the message a second time. By the time I put the phone away, the woman was lying quite still, her breathing almost indiscernible. But she had a pulse. She was alive – just. They'd better be quick.

I put her into the recovery position and made sure her airways were clear, then opened her jacket and tried to stem the flow of blood with my scarf. But the bleeding inside, I guessed, would be a lot worse, and there was nothing I could do to help that. Her only hope was the paramedics. At least the traffic from Hull was light today; even in the fog, they might make it in time.

I took off my leather jacket and covered her as best I could. The blood was already seeping through my scarf, turning the white silk a deep red. I desperately wanted to make it all right for this stranger who had asked me for help, but there was so little I could do. Even if I'd saved her life a few minutes ago, she looked like she might die now.

As my own terror receded, my eyes filled and my body started to shake. I'd seen too much of death lately. It was still barely eight months since my sister, Carrie, had been murdered. That was bad enough, but then, when I'd gone over to the Netherlands to find out why, I'd lost another good friend to the thugs in Amsterdam. The fact that justice had prevailed didn't really help. Loss is loss. I'd coped. I still was coping. But that didn't make them come back. I hoped, for the sake of her loved ones, that the woman next to me would beat the odds and survive. I also hoped that I could find her friend, whoever she might be, and pass on the strange but urgent message.

Whilst I waited, I gazed around me, trying to occupy my mind. This was a bleak and hostile place. Nothing but the cold sea below and the swirling, wet mist all around us. My shirt and jumper were sodden with rain and I no longer knew whether my shaking was delayed shock or severe cold. So I wrapped my arms around myself in an effort to keep warm and wondered: what had happened to her? She didn't look the type to get into this sort of trouble. She can't have been more than thirty years old; slightly smaller than me, perhaps five-foot-seven, with shoulder-length fair hair. She had been... Hell, I was already thinking of her as dead. She *was* good looking. Warm, friendly face. Casually dressed, but in expensive clothes. A plain shoulder bag. No make-up or jewellery. She looked like a woman who was comfortable with herself.

The man who attacked her had been cold and unemotional. This wasn't a domestic, that was for sure, nor did it look sexual. Her bag was still by her side, so it hadn't been theft either. What did that leave? Unpaid drugs bill? Gambling debts? Maybe, but then she looked too much like a good, clean-living woman. I thought again about her urgent plea, "Important... file... M... Swinson... at line one," and wondered what the hell the file was. One thing was certain. The man who had tried to kill her was no ordinary thug with a knife.

I knelt down by her side. Whether it was sensible or not, I'd just made a promise. She'd given me the password for her e-mail file: Benjy 256. I'd promised to pass on the contents to her friend. More than that, I'd promised to keep the information to myself. I shuddered again.

Cameron, what are you getting yourself into? Someone has just tried to kill this woman and here you are promising to deliver a message for her. You must be crazy.

Probably. But what else was I supposed to do? Tell a dying woman to get lost?

I glanced around me and listened to make sure that I was still alone. Then, feeling like a thief, I leant across and picked up her bag, flicked open the leather clasp and peered inside, sorting carefully amongst the make-up, tissues, spare tampons and the other oddments with my fingertips, looking for an address book, or anything that might identify her friend. But there was little else except a purse. I pulled one of the tissues carefully out of the packet and picked up the purse with it, worried, somehow, about leaving fingerprints. Inside there was nothing more than loose change, a few notes and several credit cards. And the confirmation that this was indeed Magda Swinson.

Just then, and with some relief, I heard a voice. A man's voice. "Anyone down there?" he shouted from the road above.

I returned the purse to the bag and laid it back on the ground, shouting back, urgently. "Yes, come down quick, we need help."

When he appeared out of the mist he was a small man with a big frontage; someone who obviously appreciated an all-day breakfast and a few pints.

"You all right, love? What's happened to your friend? Is she ill?" His rounded East Yorkshire accent sounded reassuring, safe. It was just good not to be alone any more. And, quite suddenly, I felt tearful.

"She's been attacked. Stabbed." I stuttered, looking up at him and shaking now with emotion. "There was a man... he's run off... that way."

He crouched down beside me, white as a sheet, and swore under his breath. "Is she dead?"

I shook my head. "No, but she's barely breathing. I've called the ambulance. About five minutes ago. I wish they'd hurry up."

A cyclist stopped, a younger man in bright yellow waterproofs.

"What's up?" he asked, getting off his bike.

All-Day Breakfast, the initial shock receding, stood upright again and took charge. "There's been an accident. There's a mobile up in my cab. Do us a favour mate, and dial 999 – get the ambulance and the police here, whilst I stay with this lady."

"It's all right," I reassured him, standing up myself and producing my phone, "I told you, I've already done it."

"Better just ring again anyway," he nodded to the man in yellow, "better safe than sorry, eh?" The cyclist grunted in agreement and turned to go up the steep slope to the carriageway. "Oh and while you're at it," he shouted, "there's a couple of blankets behind the passenger seat. Bring them down, will you? We need to keep this poor woman warm if we can." He looked at me and my soaking jumper and shirt. "You look petrified, love." He took his jacket off and draped it round my shoulders. "Here, put this on for now. You look like death yourself, don't want you catching a chill, do we? You want to go and sit in the cab?"

I looked down at the woman sprawled on the wet ground, her eyes shut, her mouth hanging slightly open, the water dripping down off my jacket and then onto hers and mingling with the pool that she was lying in. Though I desperately wanted to get away from the horror of it all, somehow I was reluctant to leave her. "No, it's OK, thanks," I replied firmly. "I'll stay here until the ambulance arrives."

By now there were a few people fussing around, but not knowing what to do. The lorry driver crouched down by the woman again, scratched his head, then looked at his watch. "I wish they'd hurry up."

So did I. I felt awful. After a lousy few days and an awful journey back from Amsterdam, all I'd wanted to do was to get home to York and forget Hellen. Now, I felt bad because this woman had been hurt so much... Bad, I guess, because I hadn't been able to stop him.

The police arrived first. Two typical traffic cops, the sort you would grovel to on any motorway in the country. But, for once, the face of authority was comforting. For once, it felt good that someone who knew what they were doing was taking control. One of them dispersed the few onlookers and started to tape off the area, the other was kneeling over the woman and talking into his radio. We were moved back. The paramedics arrived a few minutes later and soon she was in the ambulance and on her way, sirens going full blast, lights flashing. Maybe she was going to be all right after all. Maybe. Maybe not.

More police arrived. One of the uniformed men took the lorry driver to his squad car straight away, and, whilst I stood back numbly watching them get on with their scene of crime work, I felt a tap on my shoulder and turned around to face a plain-clothes officer.

"Excuse me, miss, I understand that you were... witness..." The man's voice trailed away and his mouth dropped open. "It's Cameron, isn't it?"

I didn't remember him straight off. He was older and, out of uniform, he looked more mature. The fresh-faced eagerness of the young copper I had known years ago was tempered now with both age and experience. He'd just come out of police college at the time; I'd just started work as a drugs counsellor, and we met regularly in court.

"Jimmy!" I spluttered, the memory quickly returning. "Jimmy Wilson!" I was equally surprised, and pleased to see him again – especially just now. "I'm sorry. You look different." I shook my head and momentarily forgot everything else. "I didn't recognise you at first."

"Well, you look just the same, Cameron." He smiled, standing back, the fine lines around his eyes crinkling with pleasure. "How are you?"

"Well... not so good at the moment," I said ruefully, coming back down to earth and glancing across to the place where her body had been. "I'm cold and a bit shaken."

"I'm not surprised, love." He squeezed my arm. "You'd better come with me. I need to take some preliminary details from you."

I followed him up the steep ramp to his car, which was parked on the side of the carriageway. I'd always liked Jimmy. Of all the cops I'd ever met, he had an uncommon warmth and humanity about him. And, all those years ago, we had found ourselves drawn into a sort of professional friendship. I guess he would be pushing thirty now. His face had filled out and he'd put some weight on, but he still looked good with his full head of wavy brown hair, his strong, angular, clean-shaven chin and those sharp green eyes of his. I preferred him in the jacket and slacks too, the formality of uniform had always seemed slightly at odds with him. He could be gay. He'd never said, and I'd never asked. Or he could just be a really switched-on sort of guy. It didn't matter, I just liked him.

"So how long have you been in CID, Jimmy?" I asked, sliding into the front passenger seat of his car.

"Nearly three years now," he replied, starting the car and letting it idle, so that the heating came on full and hot, cascading over my cold, wet clothes. "I was made up to sergeant last year." He looked kind of proud.

"That's great." I smiled, meaning it too. "The police need more officers like you, I'm glad you're appreciated."

"Yeah," he laughed. "I remember. Coppers aren't generally your favourite people, are they? Still, I enjoy the life. Whatever you think, they're not such a bad bunch... Anyway," he started, suddenly remembering he was on duty, "enough about me, are you all right?"

"Yeah, I guess." I smiled back as best I could. I suddenly felt very tired. "Just a bit shaken that's all – and very cold and wet. Thanks for the heat."

"Part of it's shock, Cameron. It's quite normal. You need to sit quietly for a while, get warm." He leant back and grabbed a blanket from the rear seat. "Here, put this round your shoulders, it'll help." Then, when I had settled myself down and the shivering was finally abating, he pulled out his notepad. "Right love, sorry to be so formal, but I have to ask you a number of questions. First, can you give me your full name and address. Then I'd like you to tell me exactly what happened."

I sighed and gave him all the details. I was glad it was Jimmy I was telling, but for all that, I was beginning to feel really dejected. Adrenalin withdrawal, perhaps. Or maybe I was just becoming resigned to the hassle that I knew would follow, once this preliminary was over. I watched as he wrote everything down in his little book and I chose my words carefully, keeping it factual and relevant. I couldn't decide what to say about the message the woman had given me. It could be important evidence and, if I had any sense, I would tell him about it now. But, then again, I'd made a promise. A promise to pass the details on to this Joanna Whittling, and no one else. Maybe I would bide my time, at least until I knew what was in the file she'd mentioned. I could always tell them later.

"So you've just got back from Amsterdam. What were you doing there?"

I told him about my holiday and my early return, thinking angrily that I wouldn't have this conundrum if Hellen hadn't been so fucking obsessed with her career. The first few days had been perfect. Then she'd started on at me, about giving up my job and moving to Amsterdam. That was when it all began falling apart. A few days later she said she had to go back on duty and frankly, that was the last straw. By then I'd had quite enough of a relationship with a cop.

Sergeant Wilson looked up from his notebook, his eyebrows arching slightly and a faint smile crossing his face. "You're in a relationship with a police officer! Cameron, you never cease to amaze me!"

"I *was* in a relationship with one," I corrected him. "Yes, well… It was just as big a surprise to me," I added, feeling wretched at the very thought.

"Well, maybe you need someone to keep you in check. Or have you calmed down these days?"

"Yeah," I responded, not wanting to pursue this subject any more. "I'm the very model of a responsible citizen now."

"I hope not." He smiled back, good-naturedly. "Heaven forbid, that you of all people, should be that boring." I tried to respond with a quip and a smile, but somehow the joke had worn thin and all I could manage was a shrug.

We eventually finished going through everything and Jimmy left me in the car whilst he went off to see his boss. It had seemed odd, sitting there, going over the attack, giving details to someone I used to know quite well. But then, the whole morning had been bizarre. And I guessed it wasn't over yet. Thinking about what I knew of police procedure made my spirits fall even lower.

By now there were official vehicles parked all along the carriageway. Traffic police, their yellow and blue neon insignias shining through the grey morning; panda cars; unmarked CID vehicles; a scene-of-crime van; and, in the sky, the rattle of a police helicopter, hovering overhead. All the paraphernalia of modern detection. The outside lane of the carriageway was emptying, as the last of the traffic on the bridge drove past. Behind me stood the MGB, still skewed across the road. Somewhere just behind it was my bike.

After a few minutes, Jimmy returned, looking apologetic. "Like I thought, he wants to interview you properly, Cameron. I'm sorry, that means you'll have to go into Hull and make a full statement. I assume that's your motorbike?" I nodded, expecting the worst. "Don't worry, we'll take care of it for now, love. You stay here where it's warm."

"Thanks." At least my clothes were drying out and my limbs warming up. "I don't suppose there's any point in objecting."

He smiled back. "None at all. You don't know the half of it. The Guv'nor will probably close the whole bloody bridge. We have to be certain that we don't miss anything." He hesitated, then he delved into his wallet and pulled out a card. "It's been really nice seeing you again, Cameron, in spite of the circumstances. Maybe when you've had a chance to recover, we could meet for a drink; have a proper chat." I nodded and smiled back, as he wrote his home number and his mobile on the back of the card. "Give me a ring when you're ready and perhaps we can arrange something."

"Yeah, I'd like that," I answered, meaning it.

"One more thing, Cameron..."

"Yes?"

"Go easy when they interview you. You were the first on the scene and they'll be thorough with their questions. I know what you're like. Just don't take it personally OK? Stay cool, love."

He must have seen the look in my eyes as he opened the car door to get out, because he hesitated before he closed it behind him, and stuck his head back inside. "I'm talking as a friend now, Cameron. Don't make waves. Go easy on yourself. All right?"

I nodded back at him. "Yeah, OK, Jimmy. I'll be as good as gold."

He grunted and threw me a dubious sort of smile as he slammed the door shut.

I sat by myself in the car for another half-hour. Maybe I deserved all the hassle. Maybe it was divine punishment. If I'd made that right turn at Barton; if I'd called in to the nursing home like I should have... I sighed, suddenly angry with my own self-pity. If I hadn't been on the bridge, the woman would certainly have died. At least now she had a chance – however slim.

I hoped she would survive. She must have been in that swerving, high-speed car, with her attacker. She must have been so frightened, so distressed, knowing that there was nothing she could do to get away from him. I wondered again about the e-mail file and whether that was what he was after. It seemed all too likely.

The mist was starting to clear now and I could just make out the vast stretch of water beneath us. The traffic had stopped completely, meaning the bridge really had been closed. Down to my left the area had been cordoned off and some of the scene of crime officers, dressed in their white boiler suits and slippers, were combing the ground, depositing various bits of detritus and blood samples in evidence bags. A police photographer was recording the scene. And, a few yards along the road, the MGB was being put onto a low loader. My Harley would be next.

A genial face appeared at the car window and I wound it down. "Sorry to keep you waiting so long, madam. I'm Superintendent Peter Warren from CID. I'm really sorry to delay you, but I'm afraid I'm going to have to ask you to make a proper statement." He paused to blink a few times. "Naturally, we're treating this as a serious incident and we need all the help we can get. Don't worry about your bike, we're taking care of that." He smiled sympathetically. "I expect you could do with a nice hot cup of tea as well. We'll get you to our interview suite at Coltman Street – it's much more comfortable than the station – then we can get the police doctor to give you a quick once-over, ask you a few more questions and then, perhaps, get you on your way."

I nodded as pleasantly as I could. Like Jimmy had said, there was little point in objecting.

Still, I had a strange sense of foreboding all the same.

# Two

As I changed, I studied myself in the full-length mirror. To say I didn't look good would be an understatement. My grey eyes, normally dark and strong, were tired and anaemic. My face was drawn, and the skin around my mouth was beginning to sag. I felt and looked like a wet rag. I'd voluntarily agreed to go through all the routine procedures when I arrived here: fingerprinting; scrapings from under my nails; samples from my hair; a swab for DNA analysis – all of them, as the charming superintendent had explained, needed to eliminate me from the scene. The police doctor had examined me and pronounced me shaken but not stirred. I was the centre of attention and it felt lousy.

I'd even agreed to let them keep my motorcycle leathers so they could eliminate some of the fibres and particles on the victim. They were filthy anyway and, though I loved them dearly, it was a blessed relief to get out of them. My bag of clean clothes and dirty underwear was searched and passed back to me. Big of them. As I pulled on my spare pair of black jeans, white T-shirt and grey jumper, I thought again about what I'd done. I'd made a promise to a woman I didn't know. I'd withheld information at the scene of crime. Now, as I slipped into my black leather bomber jacket, I was contemplating doing it yet again, this time in a much more formal interview.

Cameron. What are you playing at? What on earth are you getting involved in? Why don't you just tell them everything – wash your hands of the affair and go home?

In all honesty, I didn't have an answer to that. I still don't. All I know is that, every time I tried to reason it out, her face came back to me. Desperate, fighting for breath, as she spelled out the e-mail address, her password, and the name of her friend. I could still feel the tight grip of her fingers on my arm as she pleaded with me not to let anyone else know about it. I could still see the earnestness in those eyes. Whatever was in that e-mail, it mattered like hell to her that only Joanna got it.

The message apart, I couldn't believe how co-operative I was being. Maybe it was guilt at not telling them everything. Maybe it was the comfortable surroundings, here in the 'Vulnerable Victim Suite'. Maybe I really had taken Jimmy's advice to heart and was making it easier for myself. I suppose that if the police want something, they usually get it anyway, so it's easier to make at least some pretence at co-operation in the first place. All the same, I wasn't particularly happy about it all. I'd been so looking forward to going home. Now, even when they'd finished with me, I knew I couldn't do that. I'd made a promise. I had to find Joanna Whittling. I had to deliver that message.

It was already mid-morning and I guessed there was little chance of leaving here for at least another hour. Friendly witness or not, I knew they would be thorough with their statement-taking. They had to be – one slip with procedure and an entire prosecution could be lost. And, whatever my feelings about them, whatever my disquiet about not telling them the whole truth, I did want them to get the man on the bridge. So, when I came out of the medical room, I settled back into one of their easy chairs, and waited.

It was encouraging to see how much the approach to crime against women had changed. OK, so there was still a long, long way to go; but this room was paying a lot more than lip service to traumatised and frightened victims – or witnesses of violent crime like me. Pastel walls, passable pictures, a nice carpet, table lamps, a settee and two squashy armchairs. It was warm as well – and it smelt good. Which was more than could be said for the average police station. There was a pay-off for them too. They'd probably get a lot more information in these surroundings than in the formality of a normal interview room.

It was working on me, anyway. I was almost asleep when the door opened and Superintendent Peter Warren came in with a woman colleague.

"Hello again, Miss McGill." He beamed, shaking my hand. "Sorry to keep you waiting so long. These procedures are tiresome, I know. This is Detective Sergeant Moore, she'll be sitting in on the interview." He sat down in the other chair directly opposite. She smiled at me formally and sat on the settee to my left.

"First of all, Miss McGill... oh, do you mind if we call you Cameron?" he enquired tentatively. "It's not so formal is it?"

I nodded. Slimeball. Police procedural technique number one: put the victim or witness at ease. Make the interview seem as much like a friendly chat as possible. Except, he hadn't invited me to call him Peter. Already, I could feel my hackles rising.

He smiled officiously. "Thank you for your co-operation this morning, Cameron. I know that you must want to get on your way and that all this is a nuisance but we needed to make sure you were unharmed, as well as eliminating some personal pathology from the scene of crime. We treat all violent crime seriously, my dear, but of course, we're particularly concerned by assaults against women."

I nodded, resigned to the formal interview, and waited for them to continue. He was in his forties, a ruddy-faced man in the standard grey suit, not very tall, carrying little weight, with a pleasant enough, but practised demeanour, thinning brown hair and a propensity to blink rather more than was normal. His colleague was younger, perhaps twenty-eight or twenty-nine, smaller than me, neatly dressed in a skirt and jumper with sensible shoes. She had an attractive oval face and big brown eyes, which didn't need the eye shadow she had so carefully applied. She played with strands of her short blonde hair, before settling down, her notepad resting on her knee.

Inevitably, I thought of Hellen and how easily I had succumbed to her charms last autumn. Six months on, and I still wished that it could have worked out. The irony was massive. Apart from my dead sister Carrie, I had spent my entire life avoiding emotional intimacy. Then, when I finally dropped my defences and fell in love, it had to be with a fucking cop. It had to be with someone who was already married to her career.

The sergeant inserted a new tape into the machine at her side, pressed the button and stated the date and time mechanically towards the artificial plant on the table between us. "Interview with Cameron McGill. Present: Detective Superintendent Warren and Detective Sergeant Moore."

She turned to look at me now. "I have an obligation to tell you your rights before we begin. OK?"

"Yes," I responded, a little impatiently. She was attractive in much the same way as Hellen was and that irritated me. "Is this going to take long? I really want to get on my way."

"Well," she replied impassively, "that's up to you, Cameron. We just want to go carefully through the events of the morning in as much detail as possible. We are videoing the interview and audio taping, as you will gather, but I don't want you to worry about that." She paused, watching me. "This is a voluntary statement, you understand. You are free to leave at any time. And you may have a solicitor present if you wish."

She looked at me and waited. I shook my head. "I don't want my solicitor here. I don't mind telling you what happened. But, please, can we get on with it?"

Warren leant forward in his chair and made a few preliminary blinks at me. "We'll be as quick as we can, Cameron, I promise. Now, there is one more thing – a formality, that's all it is. Before we start, I need to caution you: *You do not have to say anything. But it may harm your defence if you do not mention now something which you later rely on in court. Anything you do say may be given in evidence.* Do you understand the caution, Cameron?"

A shiver ran right through me. It was lousy English, but I got the drift very well. 'Don't withhold evidence, Cameron, or you'll pay for it later.'

"Yes," I said. "I understand."

He beamed over at me, either unaware or unconcerned about the increasing blackness of my mood. "Just a formality like I said. Now, tell us exactly what happened this morning."

I sighed, keeping my cool. The more co-operative I was, the sooner they would let me leave. I went through the whole thing for the second time, trying to cover everything. I told them about the car driving at speed; I described how the man had been threatening her when I arrived at the scene; how it seemed like he was trying to throw her off the bridge, how he'd stabbed her when he saw me. I told them how he nearly attacked me as well but then walked off; and how concerned I was about the victim – my feeble attempt at first aid. They sat quietly, listening. I guessed the questions would come after I finished. They did.

"Cameron," Warren spoke first, "can we be quite clear about this? Have you ever seen the victim before?"

I shook my head.

"The interviewee is shaking her head." DS Moore could irritate me without even trying.

"What about the man?" Warren continued. "Were there any identifying features? Did you see his face?"

"Sorry, Superintendent. Like I told you, his face and head were completely covered by the time I got close. All I can tell you is that he was around six-foot tall and medium build. He wore a long black raincoat, a black scarf around his face, a dark grey flat cap pulled over his eyes and black leather gloves. His shoes were well polished, black brogues."

"Did he speak? Did you hear his voice?"

"No." I sighed. "I'm sorry."

"Any identifying traits then? Such as the way he walked. Any mannerisms?"

"No, nothing. All I can tell you is that he was quite cold, calm and totally unemotional the whole time. He took his time. He showed no trace of panic at any point."

"And the victim – what did she say to you?"

I didn't even hesitate. I didn't stutter, stammer or go red in the face. I'm one of the most honest people I know. But, just then, I was the world's number one liar.

"Nothing, Superintendent." I looked at him as casually as I could.

"Are you absolutely sure?" He leaned forward, blinking at me.

"Perfectly," I replied, glancing up at him. Sometimes I think I should have my head examined.

Their faces were both expressionless. For all the comfort of the room, for all their forced friendliness, it still felt like an interrogation.

It was.

Moore leant towards me. "We have a statement from the lorry driver that you were kneeling next to the body when he first saw you."

"Yes, of course." I gasped, unable to believe the inference she was making. "I was concerned about her, watching over her."

There was silence for a few seconds, then she brought her face closer to mine. "The lorry driver seems to think that you might have just stabbed her."

My stomach turned and my head started pounding. This was the last thing I had expected.

"Well he's wrong." My voice came out hoarse and dry. I breathed slowly, deeply; trying to stay calm; trying to stem the panic that was already tightening my chest. Some kind of friendly chat this was turning out to be.

"What is this?" I demanded, recovering both my voice and a little composure. "I'm a witness. Your only witness. Why would I want to attack someone I don't even know?"

The sergeant chipped in again then. Her eyes were cold, like granite. Maybe she did need the make-up after all. "You still dealing?"

I froze, shocked and speechless.

She leant back against the settee contemptuously and smirked. "Come on, Cameron, we know all about your conviction."

Fuck. I wasn't going to just sit there and take that sort of abuse, whatever Jimmy Wilson had said. "Sergeant, I'm here on a voluntary basis – you said so yourself," I countered, struggling hard to remain civil. "I've had a crappy morning. I nearly get run off the road. I stop my bike and prevent a murder. I do all I can to help you with your enquiries. And you have the gall to bring up a fifteen-year-old record!"

"OK, Cameron, just relax." Warren soothed.

"Relax!" I spat back at him, losing it now. "How dare you! How dare you treat me like some sort of fucking criminal!" I stood up, furious, ready to leave. "Just for the record, I was twenty at the time and if you'd checked the records properly you would know that I was a user, *not* a dealer."

Warren blinked at me calmly. "Sit down, my dear, we're not accusing you of anything."

I glared at him, feeling betrayed. Somehow I had been in the right place at the right time and now they were hassling me for it.

"Cameron, please…" Warren motioned towards my chair.

"All right, Sergeant," I growled, sitting down again. "I can see that you've done your homework. But I don't have anything to do with hard drugs now – and, if you're inferring that I'm somehow mixed up in this because of them… well you're wrong." I slumped back in my chair. "And, if you check properly, you'll find that I've spent the last five years helping other users clean up. So don't you dare insinuate that I could have anything to do with this attack."

Warren looked at me in his practised, civilised way. "Cameron, please calm down. It's not that we don't believe you. But we have to be careful. You have a record and we have a responsibility to investigate thoroughly. You can help us by just answering the questions. No one is trying to trap you, my dear."

No, like hell they aren't.

"Superintendent," I replied coolly, trying desperately to gain some control, however small, over the proceedings. "I am not 'your dear'. Please don't patronise me."

He stared at me impassively and blinked some more. The sergeant, meanwhile, was getting into her stride.

"When the car passed you at speed, you said you were very angry." She put her head on one side. "What did you do next?"

"I told you, I speeded up to follow it, then thought better of it. I was very annoyed, it was very foggy and the car was going too fast."

"So you chased her?"

"Yes, but only a little. Then I slowed down again. I know what you're getting at, Sergeant. No. I didn't chase her, stop her and then have a row. I don't do road rage!"

"Well, you seem to see it as an option, otherwise, why would you mention it?"

"I can just see where all this is leading, that's all," I replied petulantly.

"Well, I'm putting it to you that you did 'do road rage', Cameron. That you were so angry at her driving like that, that you went after her, had a heated argument and ended up assaulting the woman."

"Well, you're wrong!" I cried, really rattled now. She leant back against the settee, a satisfied look on her face, apparently pleased at my angry response. Jimmy Wilson was right. Sometimes I just wish I had more control.

"One more thing, Cameron," Warren asked, ignoring my tantrum. "Do you know, or have you ever had dealings with, any animal rights activists?"

I looked at him, stunned this time at the unexpected question, replying more calmly. "No, I haven't. Not as far as I know – why?"

"Have you ever attended an animal rights protest?"

"No, never," I said, puzzled.

He looked at me sceptically, then across at the sergeant. She nodded almost imperceptibly. Then Warren studied me in his practised, civilised way again. "Cameron, I want you to try and understand something. You've been through a lot this morning and we would very much like to believe all that you've told us. But, as I'm sure you will understand, we have to be careful."

He sighed and pursed his lips before continuing. "I'm sorry but, at the moment... Well, let's just say that there are a few too many question marks around you." He smiled his reassuring smile again. "Much as I'd like to rule you out of the frame, I'm afraid I can't. There's more than enough evidence to suggest that you could have been involved in the assault and, until we can be sure, I have a duty to detain you for further questioning."

I could feel the blood draining from my face as he spoke.

"Let's face it, Cameron," he continued, looking me up and down, "you don't exactly look like a shrinking violet. Short hair, leathers, a big bike... Some people would believe you capable of violence..."

I gave him the death stare. What is it about dykes that scares some straight men so much?

"However, be that as it may, the evidence that we have at the moment points in your direction." He paused and looked into my face, his eyes quite still for the first time. "But be thankful for small mercies. At least she's not dead – not yet anyway."

Bastard.

"She's not dead, Superintendent, because I stopped him killing her."

He looked at me stonily, all his charm now gone, and I fell back in the chair. It was all I could do to hold back the tears. Fuck them. Fuck them all. I'd finished with the woman I loved, ruined a holiday, had a rotten journey home, almost certainly saved a woman's life and spent nearly three hours 'helping the police with their enquiries'. Earlier I couldn't have conceived how my day could possibly get worse. Now I knew.

Warren stood up and faced me. I looked across at Moore. She was still seated, her gaze impassive.

I knew what was coming now, and it was the last thing I needed.

"Cameron, I'm sorry, but on the evidence I have, I am obliged to detain you. I must make it quite clear that I am not charging you at present, but I am arresting you. You will be detained in custody so that we may interview you further. I have to caution you, once more." He recited the words again as if they were some kind of a mantra. "Do you understand the caution?"

I nodded. This time I hadn't heard a single word. I just felt sick inside.

"Please reply in words for the tape."

"Yes, I understand," I croaked, through a mouth that was as dry as the desert.

"We will leave here shortly, Cameron. You will be detained at Hessle Police Station for a further interview. You are, of course, entitled to legal representation and you may make a phone call to your solicitor if you wish, or we can contact the duty solicitor, if you prefer. In addition, you may make a second phone call to contact a friend or relative to advise them of your situation."

"Thanks," I replied. "I have my own solicitor. I'd like to call her now please."

As I picked up the phone to dial, I felt more nervous and vulnerable than ever. I knew a lawyer I could trust, and I knew she would come over from York straight away, even though it wasn't a work day. I even knew where she would be on Easter Monday. What I didn't know was how to break the news to her.

The phone rang six times before she answered.

"Hi Cameron," she breathed. "Sorry, I was outside, tidying up the garden. How nice to hear from you! How's Amsterdam? How's Hellen?"

Hearing her warm, friendly voice made my throat go even drier and my eyes even wetter. I tried to speak but couldn't.

Becky, as ever, was instantly perceptive, her soft Liverpudlian accent rising and falling as she spoke again. "Cam, what on earth's the matter? You in trouble or something?"

"Becky," I managed, swallowing hard, "you just wouldn't believe it."

# Three

It didn't take long to get from the uneasy comfort of Coltman Street to the drab formality of Hessle Police Station. And, even though I'd been through the procedure fifteen years before, I still wasn't prepared for the bleak feeling of impotence that you get when your freedom is taken away from you.

We entered the station from a secure area at the rear and I was handed over to the custody sergeant, an older man who was politely brusque and official. I stood before the stainless steel counter and waited as he put on his spectacles and turned his VDU to face him.

He spoke to Sergeant Moore first. "What are the grounds for arrest?"

She spoke slowly, deliberately, outlining the scene on the bridge, the fact that I was found leaning over the body and the other details that led them to suspect me. Every word rang icily in my ears, sending a tremor of despair through my whole body. I couldn't believe that this was really happening.

He tapped the details into his computer, logged all my personal information and told me my rights all over again. Then he listed and bagged my money and valuables. I heard every word he said and I signed the form he gave me; but somehow, I wasn't quite there. The whole procedure was vague and distant, like someone else's bad dream. It seemed that, whatever I said or did today, things could only get worse.

They put me in the juvenile cell next to the custody sergeant's desk. A concession of sorts, but that didn't make the cold, sterile room any more comfortable. There was no toilet, just a slatted bed built into the wall, stained cream walls, a dull red composite floor, and a small patch of daylight that had to fight its way in through a panel of glass bricks. It smelt. Disinfectant on the high notes with a trace of something less pleasant underneath. But still, it was probably better than the grown-up cells.

Lunch arrived early, soon after I got there – an unexciting vegetable bake which I picked at and eventually left. The desk sergeant had assigned a woman officer to me who looked in through the flap from time to time. She was brusque and matter-of-fact. I had to ask her to take me to the toilet. Humiliated, stripped of both my freedom and my self-respect, I was trapped by a justice system I was supposed to be helping.

Fuck them all! I was glad I'd kept the message to myself.

It was nearly 12.30 when the lock on the door rattled, and Becky – beautiful, round-faced, glowing Becky – walked in. As the door slammed shut behind her, she paused to look at me.

Her light blue eyes are what you notice first. Soft but striking. She uses them well: for holding attention, and, some believe, for peering deep into your soul – Becky is a tough person to lie to. She's my age, thirty-four, but born seven months later in March – an Aries; shorter than me by two inches at five-foot-six, and a little rounder all over. She dresses casually – jeans and a sweater – unless she's in court, when she'll maybe wear a trouser suit. But even that does little for her professional image. Her eyes apart, her warm country face suggests that she might be a carer of some sort, whilst her hair, short, blonde and spiky – and her manner – marks her out, unmistakably, as a dyke.

Becky doesn't look like anyone's idea of a criminal lawyer.

But appearances can be deceptive and her gender, her features and the softness of her voice hide a toughness that ambushes clients and adversaries alike. For all her softness, Becky grew up in one of the roughest areas of Liverpool with a docker father who was fierce in his opposition to the Establishment. Maybe that's why she's opted to work for a firm that specialises in legal aid for the last seven years. At work, she's hard-nosed, tough and very good at her job: the police and the courts, all over Yorkshire, have come to respect her.

But right now, the woman I saw before me was just my friend and I got up at once and fell into her arms.

"I'm sorry I've taken so long, flower, the traffic was crap!" she breathed, as she squeezed me tight. "Bloody bank holidays, you can't move for people going shopping!" She pulled away a little and took my face in her hands. "You OK?" When I nodded sheepishly, she laughed gently and shook her head from side to side.

"God, Cam, what are we going to do with you, eh? I don't know, love, you do seem to get yourself in some sticky situations." Her smile faded to a look of concern as she stroked my face. I turned away, trying not to let her see the strain that was tearing away at my insides.

"It's all over with Hellen, then?" First things first.

I grimaced. Becky seemed to understand without me needing to say a word. "Yes... I finished with her yesterday."

I sat down on the bed and tried to avoid her eyes.

"You had a row?"

"Yeah. A big one this time," I said, talking to the floor. "She's just so tied up with her fucking work, Becky. I go all that way and she goes back on duty after just a few days. Like I wasn't there."

She sat down next to me. "She cut her holiday short on purpose?"

"No, not exactly." I studied the laces in my boots. "All leave was cancelled, there was a big political rally... But it's not the first time. It always happens."

"Always?"

I couldn't hide the bitterness in my voice. "The same thing happened in February when I went for a weekend."

"Well, that's only once, flower. Maybe it's just bad luck. But she is a police officer. It does happen, Cam. I'm sure she didn't do it on purpose. It's the same for lawyers, and lots of other people.

31

Sometimes the job gets in the way."

"It's not just that… There's other things as well. She wanted me to give up my job," I said, floundering now.

"Why would she want you to do that?"

I turned and looked at her. It was much easier to deceive myself than Becky.

"Because she wanted me to get a job over there."

"Ahh," she nodded. "Now I understand. She's getting serious."

"No, it's not just that…" I blustered.

"Cameron, are you running away?"

I pulled my jacket around me. "No. 'Course I'm not. I was just happy with the way it was, that's all. Apart, that is, from her obsession with the Politie."

She put her arm around me and pulled me close. "It's all right, love. I understand. I know you find it difficult. We had our moments as well, remember?"

"It's not that, Becky…" I didn't want to talk about it. About then, or about now. "It's just that we're different. We want different things, that's all."

She gave me a knowing look and backed off. "Is she upset?"

"I don't know. We were shouting at each other and I stormed out. I guess she is. I feel terrible about her, Becky, but there's nothing I can do. It's over and that's it."

She gave me a sad look and stroked my head. "Are you sure this is what you want?"

My eyes filled up and my anger crumbled into tiny pieces. I could hide my true feelings from almost anyone. But not from Becky.

"Oh Cam. What are we going to do with you?" She took hold of my hand and squeezed it. "Maybe you can still be friends?"

"Yeah, well, maybe," I replied, pulling myself together. "That's what I wanted all along."

"Well, it takes time, Cam. She'll have to adjust. But if she wants to, she will… *We* managed it all right, didn't we?"

I nodded and hugged her.

"And now you've jumped from the frying pan into the fire," she said.

I dropped my arms dejectedly to my sides and shook my head. "Becky, I don't know what's happened to me today. I haven't done anything except stop a woman being killed – and put my own life on the line in the process. This is all so bloody stupid – and unnecessary." Now the tears were running down my cheeks again. This time I wasn't sure if they were out of anger, frustration or distress. Probably all three.

Becky pulled me close again. "Come on, Cam," she soothed, "it'll be OK. Now, tell me the full story, from the beginning."

A good lawyer is worth her weight in gold, but even Becky can't work instant miracles. So we had to go through the full routine again and I had to retell the day's events for a fourth time. I still hadn't mentioned the message – not even to Becky. I didn't want to compromise her in any way – and at this point I just wasn't sure what the rules of disclosure were for solicitors.

Warren and his sergeant went over much the same ground with their good-guy/bad-guy routine. It was wearing a bit thin now and I was becoming cynical over every question. Becky, soft and lovable as a friend, was transformed into the tough professional. We'd been lovers around the time when I got busted for drugs, and it was her determination, and my sister's, that got me out of the mess then. In the last few years, I'd seen her in court defending some of my clients – users who were usually making a deal with the courts over rehab – so I knew how good she was; but I'd never seen her in a situation like this, and it was both reassuring and slightly odd to have her represent me.

We sat around a table in the bare, windowless interview room; Becky and me on one side, the sergeant and the superintendent on the other; with the irritating background hum of the air conditioning as a backdrop. Becky made sure I only answered when I should and put the two cops quietly but firmly in their place when one of them – usually Moore – resorted to speculation and innuendo. She shot down all their attempts to goad me with my ancient record, telling them – and me – that it was irrelevant and, more to the point, inadmissible. I wanted to cheer her. Why didn't I think of that?

When we got to the end and the tape had been turned off, she took over.

"Superintendent, I know that you are only doing your job, but I really must object strongly to the way my client has been treated."

He smiled using every ounce of his fake charm and blinked twice at her. Sergeant Moore looked daggers. "I thought you might, Miss Williams..."

Becky interrupted. "*Ms* Williams please, Superintendent."

He paused for just a second and the sergeant rolled her eyes. Then he continued, smoothly. "I would rather expect you to stand up for your client. But this is a serious crime and you must appreciate that I would be failing in my duty if I didn't pursue it with all due vigour." He blinked a few more times and leaned slightly towards Becky. "You must agree – er, Ms Williams – that, since your client was found leaning over the victim, with the woman's blood on her hands, I have good reason to treat her as a suspect."

Becky's softness had evaporated now and her voice was hard, confident. "No, I don't agree, Superintendent. For a start, where's the murder weapon?"

"We're searching the river for it at this moment."

Becky raised her eyes to heaven. "Not good enough! Your evidence against Miss McGill is wildly circumstantial. My client was innocently making her way home when she saw a stationary car in the fog. She acted responsibly by switching on its hazard lights and then trying to find the driver, who she thought might be attempting suicide. She had only just arrived back in the country; it was her who phoned the police; and it was her who wrapped her own scarf around the woman's wounds and kept her warm with her own jacket.

"Does that sound like the actions of a murderer to you? There is a perfectly adequate explanation for both the blood on her hands and the fact that she was kneeling by the victim. The only evidence you have against Miss McGill is the groundless supposition of a lorry driver who saw my client helping the victim and jumped to the wrong conclusion." She shook her head and looked at the senior officer with contempt. "Come on, Superintendent, you know as well as I do that if you sent this lot to the CPS, they would send it straight back."

The sergeant said nothing but the sullen look on her face spoke volumes about the way Becky had neatly sidelined her. Warren, though, remained unperturbed to the last. "You may be quite right in everything you say, but nevertheless, I do have reasonable cause to suspect. Your client has been properly arrested on suspicion of assault and our enquiries are proceeding with all due diligence. I have every right to hold her."

Becky leaned back in her chair, smiling slightly now. "I would dispute that, Superintendent. You have no grounds whatsoever for detaining my client at the present time."

She paused, softening her voice. "I know that you will be making further investigations, and that you will be awaiting the results of forensic tests in the next few days. If you continue to hold my client, we shall all have to appear in the magistrates' court within the next thirty or so hours. If that happens, we both know very well that, on the evidence you have, the court would find in my client's favour. Wouldn't it be infinitely more sensible to release her on police bail now, pending your enquiries?" She smiled. "My client isn't a thug, Superintendent. Don't you think, in the circumstances, that bail would be a better option, rather than me advising my client in two days' time that she has a case against you for wrongful imprisonment?"

Warren nodded quietly. His composure was unchanged, but there was a tired look creeping into his eyes. "Give us a few minutes." He and Sergeant Moore left the room.

I looked at Becky, impressed, but she shook her head and laughed modestly. "I just scared them with my haircut." Then, more seriously, "I think you'll be OK, Cam. They really haven't got enough against you to risk charging you and, if they keep you here for too long, they're going to have to justify detaining you beyond the thirty-six hours. My guess is that they would rather let you out on police bail and re-detain you, if necessary, for the remainder of their thirty-six hour limit once they get the full forensic."

I tried to speak but she held her hand up. "I know what you're thinking, but there won't be any other forensic evidence they can use against you. Look, Cam, the only fibres and prints they will find in the car are going to be consistent with you leaning in and turning on the warning lights. That's good, that corroborates your statement and de-molishes their silly notion of road rage. They may trace the knife, but that's not going to count against you, as you didn't handle it. And, even if the victim tests positive for drugs, so what? They won't find any evidence on your bike or in your clothes... will they?" She stopped suddenly and raised her eyebrows.

I shook my head and smiled. "No, Becks, no way. I wouldn't risk bringing any dope back, and you know I'll never touch hard drugs again."

"Good, so even if the victim is positive, they can't pin anything on you. Oh, and all that about your record – it was a wind-up, by the way. They were trying to get a reaction from you."

"So what's with the police bail?"

"If they agree, you'll be free to go, but they'll impose certain conditions."

"Like what?"

"One will definitely be that you go nowhere near the victim. Another that you don't leave your home area without notifying them. They must be able to contact you if they need to. They might ask you to report daily to a police station, but I would doubt it. They might also insist they keep your bike, but I would fight that."

Becky was right and within half an hour we were walking out of the station's front door towards her car. The only condition of my bail was that I didn't try and make contact with the victim – now fighting for her life in intensive care – and that I should be available for interview at all times. They took Becky's details. They also took my passport, but that was fine, I guess. I wouldn't be needing it again for some time. The good news was that they let me have my Harley back.

Once outside in the car park, I gave her a big hug. "Thanks Becks, you're a wonder." I breathed, feeling the relief coursing through every vein in my body. "You don't know how much this means."

"Oh, I think I do." She smiled.

"Mmm, well... I don't know what I would have done if you hadn't been able to come," I admitted, glancing across at my Harley over the other side of the car park.

"You can't wait to get back on that bike, can you?"

"No, you're right, Becky, I can't." I shrugged as nonchalantly as I could. "I thought I might spend a few days here in Hull, since I'm still on holiday. See a bit of the area. Is that OK? You don't mind looking after Tibby until the end of the week?"

I knew I'd blown it when, instead of replying, she just nodded silently. Her expression was studied, thoughtful, but her eyes were sharp and they were looking right through me.

"I'll see you later then." I smiled, turning to go, hoping that I could get away before she asked me any more questions.

Fat chance. Becky had hold of my arm and before I knew it, I was facing her again. "Cameron," she began, her voice deep and ominous, "you know very well that I don't mind looking after your cat for a few more days. But I do mind a lot when you start being evasive with me."

"What, me?" I responded innocently.

"Come and sit in my car for a few minutes," she growled. "I need to talk to you."

Oh shit. Now the real interrogation was about to begin.

# Four

"You can't put it off indefinitely, you know, Cameron."

I feigned incomprehension. I might be feeling better now, but I could do without this.

"Come on, Cam, you know very well what I mean," she said, a little sharply. "I know you can't wait to get away from me, so that you can avoid the subject... You passed Barton on the way here. You must have thought about her."

Jesus!

"Yeah," I admitted, sourly. "I thought about dropping in. But, well... you know..." I shook my head and pulled a face.

"She's dying, Cam!"

I nodded awkwardly. "Yes, I know. I spoke to the doctor before I left for Amsterdam. I meant to set off early and call in before catching the ferry."

Becky raised her eyebrows. "And?"

"... And I pissed around at home until there wasn't time."

Silence.

"So?" Becky wasn't going to let me off the hook.

"So, I'll come back and see her soon... I promise."

She leant back in the driver's seat and gave me that come-off-it-Cameron-you-must-think-I-was-born-yesterday look she does so well. I turned and stared hard out of the window at the car park.

"Cameron, she's your mother, for God's sake! You might never have got on with her, but she's still your mother."

Damn you Becky, why can't you just let things be?

"Look love, I know you're having a really bad time, what with Hellen and all that's happened this morning, but if she dies, and you haven't made up, it will plague you for the rest of your life."

"Yeah, all right!" I conceded, irritably. "But it's not that easy. I haven't seen her for years. What would I say to her?"

She glared back. Admittedly, as excuses go, it wasn't the best.

"Becks, she's always hated me," I whined, trying to justify the neglect to myself, as much as to Becky. "She's been out of her mind since I was little... And, anyway, what the fuck do I say to her about Carrie?"

She leaned over and stroked my arm. "You don't have to say anything, love. She probably won't even remember you. Just be there. Just be with her. That's enough... Look, go and see her today, whilst you're in the area."

I nodded, disconsolately. Damn Becky. She was always doing this to me, acting like a surrogate conscience. Of course I should go back across the bridge and see my mother. If I didn't do it whilst I was here, I never would. But that didn't make it easy. It had been no effort for Carrie. She and my mother had always hit it off. But me? I looked out of the window again and blew my nose.

"OK Becks, I give in. I'll go," I conceded reluctantly. "But not today. Tomorrow maybe. I'm in no hurry. Like I said, I'll hang around the area for a few days. I'm not due back at work for another ten days."

I should have known better than to think she was going to leave it at that. The smile on her face faded, and she put her head on one side, eying me up. Maybe I can manage the odd lie to the police without a second thought. But Becky? I've never quite acquired the knack.

"Cam... What – are – you – up – to?"

I tried to look away but her eyes followed me. I could feel them burning right through into my thoughts.

"You won't like it."

"Try me."

I squirmed in my seat and bit my lip. "Yeah, well... There's something I... something I didn't tell you in there... Something I didn't want the cops to know about..."

Her face went all serious then, her eyes the darkest shade of blue they've ever been. Staring at me. Waiting.

"Thing is, Becky..." I wriggled inside, feeling like a naughty schoolgirl.

"Yes?"

"Well... Before she passed out, Magda Swinson asked me to pass a message on to a friend. A confidential message. To someone called Joanna Whittling."

I winced inside, waiting for her reaction, but she just stared at me numbly as I rambled on with the story of the e-mail address and the password. As I recounted Magda's words and described the desperation on the woman's face, Becky's eyes grew bigger than ever.

She turned on me then, cutting off my self-justification in mid-sentence. "You're damn right you should have told me, Cameron! More to the point, you should have told the police!" I flinched. "God, you are so stupid sometimes. Arrogant, pig-headed! Don't you realise that withholding something like that could land you in big trouble if you're charged? Didn't you listen to the caution?"

I coloured up. I hate being told off. I hate Becky telling me off. "Becky, I promised her that I would only pass the message on to the person she intended it for. I didn't have a chance to discuss it with her. She passed out, remember?" I spluttered. "I couldn't tell the police. Besides, after the way they treated me, why the fuck should I?"

She looked hurt. "Well, you could at least have told me, for God's sake, I'm your lawyer as well as your best friend." She ran her fingers through her hair.

"That's why I'm telling you now," I said, trying to make up. "I just thought that if I told you at the station, you might be obliged by law to pass on the information to them."

She shook her head at my ignorance. "Everything that you tell your lawyer, Cam, is subject to complete confidentiality. But you should have told me. How the hell can I advise you properly if you withhold information like that? Of course, I wouldn't pass anything on without your say-so. But, Jesus, I could at least have told you how badly it might affect your defence."

"Well," I muttered, "I still wouldn't have told them. So it's academic."

She snorted derisively. "Huh, not to the police it isn't. Cam, this could be important. It could give them a lead on the case."

"Sure, and it could also get me in deeper. They didn't believe me when I said I didn't stab her. Why should they believe me when I say she gave me a message? Besides, the woman was desperate that no one else knew about it. I don't know what the file's about, but there has to be a reason for that. Whatever you might think about me withholding evidence, I want to know what's in it before I tell anyone."

She sat staring over the steering wheel, fuming quietly. I'd said all I had to. Maybe I should have told her earlier. Maybe not. But, regardless of that, I was sure that I was doing the right thing.

"So how are you going to find this woman? This Joanna Whittling. Did she tell you who she is? Where she lives?"

"She didn't have time, Becky," I replied through gritted teeth. "She was fighting for her life, for God's sake."

She folded her arms across her ample bosom and gave me the look. "So how are you going to pass the details on, if you don't know who she is, or where to find her?"

"I don't know, Becky." I snapped. "I'll have to find her somehow, won't I?"

We glared at each other for a few seconds. Then, as I looked away, she spoke again, more calmly this time. "Really, Cam, you can be so difficult sometimes. You know that? You've changed, you know. Since your sister died, I mean."

"I don't think so!" I answered huffily. "You always accuse me of being 'difficult' when you're angry with me." I tried to make it sound light and good natured, but I failed on both counts.

"Yeah, well you are. So no change there," she muttered. "That's not what I meant. You're still the same infuriating person that I've always loved, but now, somehow – since last autumn in Amsterdam – you seem to enjoy looking for trouble."

"Not really," I replied, puzzled.

"Yes, really, Cameron. Before Carrie died, you would have just walked away from something like this and left it to the police. But now, you're letting yourself get involved at the drop of a hat." She shook her head in despair. "It's not sensible, love. You don't know what on earth you're getting into. You're already a witness to a murder. Someone may already want to get at you for that. Now, by keeping that message secret, you could have put yourself in even more danger." She sighed. "Not to mention the possible legal consequences – you'd better just pray that they don't charge you!"

"You're blowing it all out of proportion, Becky."

"Am I, Cameron? Am I? You worry the hell out of me. You know that? You only escaped death by the skin of your teeth last year in Amsterdam. Now you tell me you're getting involved with something else – and this time it's not even personal!" She paused and looked straight at me with those big pools of blue. "You're getting a taste for this sort of thing, aren't you?"

"What sort of thing? I was just given a message to pass on – I didn't bloody well ask for one!"

"Oh come on, Cam! You know very well what I mean. You were a really good drugs counsellor a year ago but, since you got back from Amsterdam last autumn, you've found it harder and harder to get yourself to work each day. There's no wonder Hellen thought you might want to move."

"That's just life, Becks," I replied, off-handedly. "Most people find work hard. Most people just have to put up with it."

She stared at me and I looked away. Shit, I hate confrontation.

"It didn't used to be like that, though, did it? You used to love your job. I think that in some perverse way you enjoyed that episode in Amsterdam. Investigating, getting around, tasting some excitement. I think it was some kind of a renaissance for you. It must have been. Because here you are getting involved all over again!"

I shrugged. "It's just a message, Becks. You're over-reacting."

"Yeah, maybe," she breathed dismissively, "but anyone else would have let the police sort it out."

We sat for a few minutes more in silence. Then she relented and leant across, taking hold of my hand. "Cameron, I know you too well to think that I can talk you out of this. But you've got to start looking after yourself. It really is time you settled down again."

She sighed heavily, pointing a finger at me. "Look, if you're determined to pass this message on, then get it done quickly, see your mother and come home. And don't take any risks, OK?"

She looked at her watch. "I've got to get back to York, I'm on duty at the Women's Centre later this afternoon and I need to feed your blessed cat before that."

She squeezed my hand and looked into my face, still disapproving. "Please take care, love. Don't take any risks, will you?"

"Yeah, OK. I promise."

She smiled lopsidedly then, unable to stay angry with me for long. "And see your mother!"

I screwed up my mouth. "Thanks Becks, you're a real friend."

She snorted. "Huh, I'm a fool! I should take you back to Hessle and make you tell them what you've just told me. But, instead, I wish you well."

"I appreciate it. Thanks."

"Well, just you take care, all right? I love you. I want you to be safe. No heroics, OK? No repeat of Amsterdam. And Cameron…"

"Yes?"

"Be very careful, you're still on bail. Keep away from the hospital and ring me tomorrow to let me know how you're getting on – I want to know that you are all right… Oh, and I *will* expect a progress report on the visit to your mother."

Sometimes Becky gets right up my nose.

## Five

I felt sick as I watched Becky drive out of the car park. I was glad to be free but, though I hadn't admitted it to her, I was as worried as she was about the danger I might be in. And scared even more about the police. The last thing I wanted was to spend the next twenty years in jail.

But worrying would get me nowhere. The sooner I found out what was in that message and passed it on, the sooner I could clear my name and get back to something like a normal life. So I pushed my concerns to the back of my mind, swung my rucksack onto my back, sat astride the Harley and turned on the ignition. The engine roared to life and, as I pulled out onto Hessle Road, I began to feel more like I was back in control.

The drive into the centre was along one of the wide, tree-lined dual carriageways that characterise this sprawling, curiously self-contained provincial city. The fog had lifted completely now and, for once, the sun was out, warming my back; shining brightly on the pussy willow that was beginning to blossom from the trees on the central reservation. I used to come here as a child sometimes, to stay with my aunt. Now I still visit from time to time, because I like it. A lot of people make snide remarks about this city – not least, some of the people who live here – but I have a soft spot for Kingston-Upon-Hull.

My affection for the place is all about its weirdness. Architecturally, it is a mish-mash of styles, a complete paradox. If there ever was a plan, it must have got lost after the extensive bombing in the war – it's such a jumble. As the dual carriageway gave way to the city centre roads, I passed an engineering yard, right on the fringes of the centre, surrounded by a housing estate; then, following the main route round to the shops, a modern glass-fronted building standing next to a huge, ugly, retail shed; and to my right an elegant old building looked down its nose at the multi-storey car park next door. I smiled to myself. In any other context, the mixture of opposing styles would be offensive but somehow Hull carried it off – like a dotty old aunt who you love for her foibles.

I drove along Ferensway and past the run-down entrance to Paragon Station and then turned left near the bus terminus and pulled into the surface car park. Like so much else it looked out of place in a modern city centre; like an old bomb site, taken over temporarily as a car park. But it had been here for years, makeshift and basic. Like I say, Hull is a funny place. Maybe I like it because it is odd, because it is different, and because it doesn't ever seem to know where the hell it's going. A bit like me, maybe.

It was early afternoon and the streets were full of bank holiday shoppers enjoying the spring sunshine and the sales. This was the latest Easter I could ever remember but even so, until today, the weather had seemed like winter. Now, as I walked across the main road and then set out towards the shopping centre to look for a computer bureau, it was good to see the sun again.

I'd been thinking about the message, and about the woman it was intended for, ever since the ambulance arrived. If I'd been stabbed like Magda Swinson – possibly dying, caught up in pain and shock – then I wouldn't waste my breath passing on details of something petty or irrelevant. The file – whatever it was – must be really important to her. And to someone else too. The more I thought about it, the more certain I was that the attack and the document in the woman's e-mail file must be connected. So the first thing I wanted to do was find out what it was about.

I found a small bureau in a side street, just up from the station. About ten computers with the new flat screens were arranged neatly on five tables, each back to back with another. Six people, all of them in their teens or twenties, were sitting at the state-of-the-art consoles, so absorbed that they barely looked up when I walked through the door.

The counter was to my right, up three steps in a small recess. I thought it was unattended at first, but once I'd reached the top step I saw a figure hunched on a seat behind, buried deeply in a magazine called *Computing Wizard*. I coughed politely to attract his attention. Normally I know enough about computers to get by, but today I needed a second opinion. I needed to know that my grasp of e-mail mechanics was right. I hoped he could help.

I coughed again, more loudly this time, but it wasn't until I spoke that he actually noticed me. And when he finally looked up and put the magazine aside, the first thing he did was sneeze very loudly, spraying a shelf full of mugs with his germs. Good job I wasn't thirsty.

I stood back. "Bless you," I said.

"Pardod?"

"Sorry, just an automatic response. A sneeze was one of the symptoms of bubonic plague."

He looked at me like I might be a few bits short of a megabyte.

"What cad I do for you?" he asked, struggling to pronounce all the consonants without the benefit of a nose. I must try and curb this sudden desire to wind him up.

"I'd like to use one of your consoles and I'd like some help please. But not necessarily in that order."

He looked up at me pathetically and brought the back of his hand across his sore, flaking nose. Apart from the health risks, he looked like just the anorak I needed.

"Cub this way," he intoned, shuffling out from behind the counter, down the steps and across the room, indicating one of the free consoles. I sat down in front of it and he grabbed a nearby chair, sighed heavily, coughed twice, sniffed, and finally sat down just a tad too close. I slid away a little. The last thing I needed this week, on top of everything else, was a cold.

"You wod to dow how to ude it, I suppode."

"No, it's OK, I know how to use a computer. What I want to check up on, is how e-mails actually work."

"Dad's eady." He sniffed. "You oped de e-mail prograb like dis..."

"No," I shook my head patiently, reaching into my jacket pocket and handing him a wad of clean tissues, hoping that I could get through to him before he stopped breathing altogether. "That's not what I meant either."

He looked bemused and blew his nose, "'Scude me," then walked back to the counter and reappeared a few seconds later with a Sinex nasal spray which he proceeded to squirt up each nostril. A few more sniffs, a good blow, and he started breathing again, almost normally. Just like in the Vick advert.

I tried again. "It's the mechanics I'm interested in." No reaction. "Look, let's say, someone sends a file to a friend of mine. They would address an e-mail to her private e-mail address, attach the file to it and click on the SEND button. Right?"

Vick nodded.

"OK, so they send the e-mail. Where does it go from there? Exactly?"

Ah! Now he was with me. His eyes lit up and when he spoke, his nose was working again too. "It would go from their computer, to their ISP –"

"Hang on!" I stopped him. "You're talking more clearly now... but I don't recognise the language. What's an ISP?"

"Oh, sorry." He coloured up, absent-mindedly wiping his nose on his hand again. "Everyone who uses the web or sends e-mails is accessing a worldwide network of computers which are switched on permanently and are linked to each other. Yeah? Now, nobody's computer is connected directly to that network, so everyone – including businesses – has to use one that is. Yeah? This is what they call an Internet Service Provider – an ISP. It's just a big computer which is permanently connected to the web and which acts as a sort of gateway into the worldwide network."

"What, like Freeserve or Line One?"

Vick blew hard into another of the tissues and wiped the mucus off his face with a second. "You've got it!" he croaked.

I hope not, I really hope not.

"So," I continued, "if this person sent an e-mail to my friend, it would go from their computer, through the phone lines to their Internet Service Provider." He nodded. "Then that computer would route it on though the network to the ISP that my friend uses, which, let's say, is Line One."

"Yeah. Simple, see."

"Then Line One would hold onto the e-mail until my friend logged on through her home computer and collected it."

"Yeah." He smiled, relieved that our conversation was over, and started to get up.

"Just hang on a minute," I cautioned, and he slumped back down with a sigh. "What if this person had sent this e-mail to my friend and then, for some reason, my friend couldn't get to her computer – say she's ill or something. In hospital. But she needed the file urgently – what would she do? Could I pick it up for her?"

"Yeah. She'd have to give you her user name and her password and then you could pick it up off your own computer or one of these here. You want me to show you? What's her e-mail address?"

I looked at his germ-infested hands and decided that I didn't want them anywhere near the keyboard that I was about to use. "No, it's OK, just tell me. I think I know how anyway, I just want to check."

He shrugged. "It's easy. You just log onto the web. Her ISP will have a website, so you just key in their address. Yeah? If it's Line One, for instance, you would key in www.lineone.net. Yeah? And then press return. Their page will come up on the screen, and when it does, you just key in her password in the box provided and then click the e-mail icon. Then the screen will take you to her mailbox." He coughed. I'd better be quick. The spray was wearing off now. Soon his nose would be closing down again.

"So I click on any e-mails in there and read them. What happens then?"

"As long as you don't erase them, they stay there until she picks them up from her home computer – when she gets out of hospital, that is."

"And if I erase them from the website now, they're deleted from the server and all trace of them will disappear?"

"That's right, cad I go now?" He was deteriorating again.

"All right, last question. What about other people accessing her mailbox like this?"

Vick looked at me through his watery-red eyes as if I was some kind of alien and answered with more patience than I guess I deserved. "They can't access it, not without her password."

"So any message held by her e-mail provider – say Line One – is absolutely secure."

"Er, not necessarily..." He hesitated. "It would be secure as long as she hadn't keyed her password permanently into her home computer. If she'd done that, like most peoble do, then anyone could access it frob dere just by turning it on."

"So a burglar could break in and access it."

He threw me a peculiar look. "Yeah, bud why would he want to do dat?"

"I dunno. The thought just occurred to me, that's all..." I shrugged. "Thanks for your help."

He stood up suddenly and began wriggling his nose and blinking rapidly. "Dat's fide, no probs. Excude me, I'm going to sneede." It was a close run thing, but he'd reached the confines of the counter before he exploded again.

Good. Magda Swinson had given me her password and her address, so I had everything I needed to pick up that message. I was just a few keystrokes away from knowing what all this was about.

I clicked on the worldwide web icon and waited until the bureau's home page appeared. I keyed in *www.lineone.net* into the address box and pressed return. The screen went blank and after what seemed like an age, the colourful Line One home page appeared with its features, adverts and interactive choices. I keyed in the e-mail address she'd given me – *mswinson* – in the user name box and then *Benjy256* in the password box, pressing return and holding my breath as the computer searched Line One's site.

A new page appeared with the message '*Welcome Magda*' and I breathed easy. I was in the right file, that much was certain. Now I clicked on the e-mail icon and the screen went blank again, replaced a few seconds later by Magda's inbox which contained just one e-mail with no title. I clicked again on that and the e-mail opened up. My heart sank a little as I saw it. There was no wording at all, no explanation. But there was an attachment with it – a file, an unnamed file. I clicked on that straight away, holding my breath as the screen went blank again and the computer started to load the file from the Line One server. It took a few seconds, it was big.

As I waited, I thought this could be the moment when I would find out why she'd been attacked. But I was wrong. When the attachment opened, it was long – nearly thirty pages long. But it told me nothing. Instead of words, every page was covered in small boxes, numbers and symbols. Total, incomprehensible rubbish.

I cursed and waved at Vick, who was busy rearranging chairs and clearing rubbish away from some of the other consoles. I saw him roll his eyes just before he ambled over.

"You see that?" I said. "How can I turn it into English?"

He scratched his head and sniffed deeply, then, as I moved well out of the way, he moved up to the keyboard and fiddled about for a good ten minutes, copying the file into other programmes, trying foreign language formats and technical software. In the end he sighed heavily and shook his head.

"It must be encoded. Typed on some special software," he said nasally, smiling mischievously now. Suddenly I'd gone up in his estimation. "I don't know what you got dere, love, bud someone doesn't want it read by any Tob, Dick or Harry."

"Or even by any Sarah, Doreen or Harriet," I corrected him, poker-faced.

He coughed and sniffed again, bemused; tried to laugh; failed; then sprayed his nose again before continuing. "Er, yes... but, anyway, if you want to read it, you'll hab to find the software first – and that might be difficult. Some big companies hab deir own. It stobs peoble like you and me finding out their secrets."

"Yeah, I can see that," I said. "Thanks."

I settled back in the chair, defeated but thoughtful, as he retreated once again to the safety of his counter and the comfort of *Computer Wizard* magazine. The file could be anything. Anything at all. The fact that it was obviously confidential didn't help me much. I still didn't know what it was – or why it had been so important to Magda Swinson. And why it might have cost her life.

I clicked back to the e-mail itself. From what Vick said, if someone else got to her home computer, they might be able to access it from there. I should transfer it somewhere safe. I didn't think it was a good idea to send it to my own e-mail address, so, whilst I was on the Line One site, I set up a brand new address called u.n.known@lineone.net (password: Tibby) and forwarded the e-mail and the file over to that. Then I deleted the original from Magda's mail. For now, the file was safe and secure.

I leant back in the chair. I still didn't know what the file was about. Or how Magda Swinson had known it was in her mailbox. But there was one clue, on the heading of the e-mail: the sender's name. The file had been sent from somewhere called GME Technologies. And, more interesting still, it had been sent that morning, at 7.45 am.

That was just forty-five minutes before Magda Swinson had been stabbed.

Hull's Central Library was just round the corner from the internet café in Albion Street. Not the marbled Victorian building that I'd expected; it was more 1960s than 1860s with its red floors, beige walls and a rather plain staircase which took me up to the reference section on the first floor.

I felt uncomfortable the minute I walked through the door. It was quiet, like libraries should be. There were a few students preoccupied with their books, a couple of older men buried in the daily papers and a woman scrutinising a shelf of large books at the far end. But the woman on the desk peered over her glasses at me the moment I came in, nudging the man who was sitting next to her, following me with her eyes as she whispered conspiratorially to him. Then he looked up and stared as well. I know that I probably looked dishevelled, I suppose that I look like everyone's idea of a lesbian, but I couldn't imagine why they should be so interested. By the time I reached the shelves crammed with telephone directories, I couldn't stand it any longer and I turned, pointedly, and stared back at them until they turned away.

Jesus, people are so rude!

I was disappointed that the trip to the computer bureau hadn't given me any clues as to where I might find Joanna Whittling, or even who she was. Becky had been right, it probably wasn't going to be easy to locate her. But I had to try, and the local telephone directories were probably as good a place to start as any.

I pulled out the one for Hull first and then searched others for North Lincolnshire, the Yorkshire Coast, York, Doncaster and Lincoln – everywhere within travelling distance. Whittling isn't a common name and there were only three entries in the whole lot, all of them outside Hull, and none with the right initial. I scratched my head. If she was married, then one of them might well be hers. On the other hand, she could be ex-directory. So I made a note of the numbers and rummaged around on some more shelves until I found the voters' list. If she lived around here, then her name and address would be listed. But it wasn't. In fact there appeared to be no one of that name living in the whole of Hull.

That left me with my one remaining lead to the whole affair: GME Technologies. They had no website – I'd already checked that out at the bureau – but there was an entry for them in the North Lincolnshire directory. The business, whatever it might be, was located back across the river, in Barton on Humber.

I walked out past the desk again, feeling exposed and eager to get out. The two librarians were looking at a newspaper now, but they continually glanced up at me. When I looked back from the top of the stairs, they appeared to be having a discussion. I sighed and shook my head. Maybe they don't have lesbians in Hull. Maybe I've suddenly grown two heads.

I tried the three telephone numbers as soon as I got out onto the street, hoping against hope that one of them would solve my problem and lead me to Magda Swinson's friend. But no such luck. The first number – a Lincoln one – was switched to an impersonal BT answering service, the second in Goole didn't reply, and the third – a number in Hornsea – answered but told me there was no one called Joanna at that address.

The planets must be particularly bad for Virgos today. I still couldn't understand why all this was happening to me. All I'd tried to do was save a woman's life. You'd have thought everyone would have thanked me for that. But instead, I'd been treated like a criminal myself, locked up in a cell and only released because I had a good lawyer. On top of all that, the knifeman, whoever he was, could easily come after me next. I was the only witness, and I couldn't imagine why he hadn't killed me when he had the chance.

Back on my bike in the middle of this odd city, I felt increasingly trapped by a promise that I should never have made. Becky was right.

I was arrogant and pig-headed. I should never have promised to find Joanna Whittling in the first place. And even if I had, I should never have lied to the police about it.

But it was too late now for regrets. I *had* lied. I *had* promised to find Joanna Whittling. Somehow I had to keep my word and extract myself from the mess I was in. At the moment, the only link I had between Magda Swinson and the file was GME Technologies. I'd never heard of them. I didn't know who they were, or what they did.

But at least I knew where they were.

It wouldn't be dark for hours – maybe if I went back over the river and found out more about them, I could pick up some kind of lead.

# Six

The Humber Bridge looked at its most beautiful in the late afternoon sun – a long, shining platform hanging in mid-air, carrying traffic across the wide expanse of dirty grey water between Lincolnshire and Yorkshire. As I left the toll booths and drove under the big northern gantry of the bridge, I gazed across the river to Barton, nestling on the opposite shore. And Becky's sermon about my mother came back to me, flashing images of my childhood into my mind.

My parents had been here on the bridge when it was opened by the Queen in 1981. They'd been telling me for months how it was the longest suspension bridge in the world, how it was an engineering triumph. As if I cared. In his capacity as a Very Important Person, my father had seemed to get invited everywhere and the official opening of the bridge was no exception. I was sixteen at the time and already committed to the Revolution, so they didn't take me with them. I might have said something very obscene about the monarchy in front of all my father's Very Important Friends. Another missed opportunity.

We never found it easy to talk, my mother and I. Even when I was little. Even when she was sane. And it got harder as the years passed. As she had become more withdrawn, more clinically depressed, I had become more angry. For just a brief moment, when I was eighteen and my father died, we had become closer. Relief at his death was probably the first thing we ever had in common. But even that didn't last long. For her, there was only Carrie. Even when she was at her most depressed, she still had time for my sister. Now that Carrie was dead, it seemed like she might have given up. Perhaps that was my fault. Perhaps I should have made some effort to be there instead.

Halfway across, my thoughts were interrupted by the continuing activity on the other side of the road. I slowed down and looked over, at the two police vehicles still parked on the inside lane: the mobile incident room. Brightly coloured plastic tape marked off the area where Magda Swinson had lain in a pool of pink water. Bleeding. Maybe bleeding to death.

I wondered whether she was still alive. And for the hundredth time, I wondered what she'd got involved in – what she'd got me involved in. And what the fuck I was going to do about it all.

Once over the bridge, I took the first slip road off the dual carriageway and tried to concentrate on finding my way – turning left and heading down the hill into the small market town, past rows of postwar semis and well-kept suburban gardens, until I reached the more traditional buildings near the centre. Quiet, uncomplicated Barton. Sitting on the banks of the Humber, rich agricultural land behind it, marshes on its seaward side. The last time I'd been here was with Carrie, when my mother first went into the home. It was years ago now, but the place hadn't changed. Nor had my memories and, as I passed the bottom of Whitecross Street, a shiver ran down my spine as I recalled that my mother's nursing home was just up the hill.

It was a big old house with a modern extension and beautiful gardens; kind, overworked staff; and the awful stench of old age and urine. Now that I was her next of kin, they rang me regularly with reports on her declining health. Since Carrie's death last year, I was her only living relative. I had the power of attorney, I paid the bills. I suppose they assumed that I cared about her. I wished I did. I wished I could.

I put her out of my mind again and pulled in to the side of the main street to ask directions to the GME site. There had been no address in the phone book, just the name and town, and I didn't know where to start. The first person I asked – a woman – looked at me mistrustfully and shuffled off. I put it down to the fact that I hadn't removed my helmet and took it off before asking again.

The next person, a man, seemed to know. "They're on the outskirts, love," he said, looking me up and down, "but if I were you I'd stay away. There's all sorts of funny people round there." Then he was off before I could ask him more.

After another two unsuccessful attempts, I gave up, got off my bike and went into a small grocer's shop further up the road. I'd hardly eaten all day and I felt sickly with hunger and, I guess, with anxiety. So I bought a plain bread bun and, whilst I was there, asked the young, post-punk shop assistant where I could find this business that no one wanted to talk about.

She reacted immediately.

"Yeah, I know 'em." She screwed up her face in disgust. "Animal testing place, it is. Killin', that's what they do. You know, dogs, mice, rabbits – poor little mites, locked up in cages with nasty things in their eyes. Shouldn't be allowed." She looked me up and down. "There's a protest camp there – that where you going?"

"A protest camp?"

"Yeah. A bunch of animal rights people. Quite a few of 'em. Been there for a year or two now."

"Is that why nobody would tell me where it was?" At last, someone I could relate to.

She laughed. "Yeah. People round here don't like 'em much. Come to that, they don't like the firm much either. Huh, folk are dead stick-in-the-mud round here. Boring buggers, all they want to do is draw their pensions and die. The people at that protest camp: they really freak 'em out."

"Well, I'd like to go and see them. How do I get there?"

"Easy, love. They're down by the marshes – Fisherman's Paradise

I calls it, on account of all them blokes that go down there on a weekend and sit dangling their hooks in the ponds. Seems like a daft waste of time to me. But then again, if you live round here, I suppose even that could seem exciting."

"Yeah, well I never fancied fishing. Bit like watching paint dry."

She laughed again and drew me a map on the back of a paper bag, with graphic illustrations of marshes and ponds and trees and woods. Then she sold me a double roll of Andrex. "There's no public lavatories out there, love. Best be prepared." Some people just make me smile.

I followed her directions, driving out of the town on the other side until I hit a junction with a small road winding off to the left where I turned, following it round a long bend until, according to my map, I was moving along parallel with the estuary.

It was no more than a country lane really; long and straight and, even at this time of the year, quite pretty. Shrubs and trees lined the sides, overhanging the road, forming a kind of shady tunnel with dappled patterns of sunlight painting the road ahead of me. The hawthorn was already in full leaf, other trees were beginning to come to life as well and, every so often, a clump of blackthorn broke the greenery with its early white blossom. There were no houses now, nor fields. But there were lots of big signs and entrances – each one announcing a different fishing pond. And through the scrub at each side of the road I could see rushes and flashes of bright light where the sun was reflecting off the water.

The road was just about wide enough for two cars to pass and had clearly been resurfaced and widened slightly within the last few years. I drove along slowly, watching out for the entrance, not quite believing that any business would locate itself in such an unlikely place. It was nearly half a mile before the marshes on my right gave way to fields. But the long, straight road still stretched ahead of me – and, approaching in the distance, was what looked like a police car.

On impulse I pulled quickly into a fishermen's car park and stopped behind the cover of a hawthorn hedge to watch. There were actually three cars – all, presumably, coming from the direction of GME Technologies and the protest camp. Two were police cars and the third was an unmarked vehicle driven by the woman who had interviewed me this morning, Detective Sergeant Moore.

I waited until they were out of sight and then pulled out into the road again, relieved that she hadn't seen me. The ponds on the right gave way to green fields but those to the left grew increasingly bigger, until I was driving along the side of a small lake which stretched for nearly a quarter of a mile, covering the whole area between me and the distant sea defences at the edge of the estuary.

I was about two-thirds along its edge when the road ran out, turning into a narrow grassy path that continued along the water's side. But a new tarmac road led off to the right up a small hill between open fields. There were no signs, no people, but, as I parked my bike and began to walk up the small road, I could see and smell the wood smoke, spiralling up into the air from above the brow.

I suppose I expected to find a polished high-rise building, with a big entrance and a gatehouse where security guards checked everyone in and out. In the event, when I got to the top of the road, all I found ahead of me was an assortment of tents, maybe seven or eight, in different shapes and sizes. There was an old ridge tent, sagging in the middle and green with algae; several hoop tents, their brightly coloured material now lack-lustre and faded after months in the open; a couple of frame tents, bigger than all the others and, beside them, two small caravans, both old, both hand-painted, one in dark green, the other a bright yellow with flowers stencilled all over it, both looking like they wouldn't last another winter. They were all nestling quietly on a wide patch of grass verge on the right-hand side of the road.

Smoke rose from a fire somewhere in amongst them, and handmade banners, painted in red, were slung across the sides of the caravans and between makeshift poles near the tents. 'GME ARE MURDERERS', 'STOP THE KILLING', AND 'CRUELTY IS NEVER JUSTIFIED'. My heart jumped as, quite suddenly, I found myself smelling and feeling the atmosphere at Greenham again: those angry, heart-warming days when so much seemed to matter to so many. I was glad to see that there were still people who cared about important issues; cared enough to camp out on rough grass verges, defying authority through the miseries of the British weather.

Just beyond the encampment, the road gave way to a cattle grid with a stout field fence on either side and what was obviously some kind of entrance to private land. There where SLOW signs by each gatepost with a notice beneath warning of speed ramps. More chillingly, another large sign warned: 'KEEP OUT – GUARD DOGS – DANGER OF INJURY'. A whiteboard leaning against the fence, on my side, urged in red marker pen, 'TURN BACK NOW – DON'T GET BLOOD ON YOUR HANDS'.

Standing just inside the field, on a tarmac pitch by the road, was a long-base Land Rover, complete with roof-mounted spotlights. Two uniformed security guards were leaning against the radiator, two very pissed-off looking Alsatian dogs lay at their feet.

Beyond them, the road continued across the field for maybe two hundred yards where it was met by a high brick wall which extended around the research site beyond. It was about a hundred yards wide at the front, almost, but not quite, hiding the range of buildings behind. Large brown double doors in the centre of the wall, at the end of the field road, marked the way into the place. Mature woodland stood beyond on all three of the other sides, shielding it from public view across the flat Lincoln'shire countryside.

GME Technologies looked like a huge fortress under siege.

I was taking all this in when there was a loud whistle from the field to my right and I turned as I heard a car approaching at speed. A woman's voice shouted loudly, urgently, from amongst the tents, "Scramble!" And a big grey Saab shot over the top of the hill, just brushing my arm, as I careered to safety on the grass verge.

By the time I regained my balance, the car was already crossing the cattle grid and a knot of people – mostly women – were in its wake:

shouting at it angrily, waving placards and banging on the sides and roof as it slowed down to cross the grid. The two guards were already making for the gate, the dogs straining at their leashes, their teeth bared. Then, once the car had disappeared across the field, the protesters continued shouting their abuse at them. Above the din I could hear one of them more clearly – one of the men – now standing defiantly, halfway across the entrance, jeering at the security men.

"Come on then! Have a go if you want!" He beckoned them with his hands. When the guards turned and walked away, he shouted after them, before turning back towards the protesters.

"Fucking clowns!" he muttered as he reached the others. When he saw me, he carried on straight through the group of eight women and one other man, down the road towards me.

The others turned and watched as well, weighing me up. They were a rag-tag group of people, dressed for the cold in torn, knotty fleeces, faded khaki parkas and battered weather-proof jackets. They had scarves wrapped around their necks, gloves on their hands and various kinds of headgear from baseball caps to woolly knits. One of them, an older woman, her long grey hair blowing in the breeze, strode behind the man, towards me.

I felt cold and strangely vulnerable as I went to meet them.

The man reached me first. He was in his early thirties, tall and thin, dressed in an old army camouflage jacket and wellingtons. He wore a brightly coloured knitted hat over his shaved head and he stopped right in front of me. He was close enough for me to smell the tobacco on his breath – too close – peering at me through narrowed eyes.

"What do you want?" he demanded, with no trace of welcome in his voice.

I shifted my feet and shrugged, meeting his gaze, as the woman came up behind him. "My name's Cameron. I've just come along to say hello."

He reached out his hand and tugged at my leather jacket, making his point without saying a word. I shivered uneasily and pulled my scarf up round my neck, looking straight back into his thin, weather-beaten, unshaven face.

The woman laid a friendly hand on his shoulder and looked at me quizzically. "We've not seen you before, dear, are you local?"

She was probably in her sixties, wearing a big fleecy grey coat and a long red scarf. A woman who wouldn't have looked out of place at any of the protests that I'd been involved in during my youth: solid, dependable, committed. She put me instantly at ease.

"No, I'm not from round here," I answered, ignoring the man. "I was in the area and I just wanted to come along and see you."

"Why now?" he asked. "Why this morning?"

"Oh come on, Charlie!" She put her arm round his shoulders and gave him a squeeze. "Don't let them get to you. I'm sure Cameron is perfectly harmless."

He glanced at me suspiciously again. "Yeah, probably. But we should be careful, Elana. You know what they're like. They'll do any-thing to trap us – specially now."

I stepped back. "You think the cops have sent me?" I asked, laugh-ing contemptuously at the absurd notion.

Elana looked at me disapprovingly. "It's not as silly as you might think, my dear. We've had the police here nearly all day. There's noth-ing they'd like better than to get rid of us. We're a thorn in their side at the best of times. But now... with this stabbing on the bridge..."

"Well, I don't think you need worry about me," I sighed. "I'm their chief suspect. The cops arrested me this morning. I can tell you, I don't like them any more than you do."

They both stared at me with their mouths open.

"But I didn't stab her."

Elana recovered first. "What's your name, girl?"

"Cameron... I told you, Cameron McGill."

"So it was you!" Elana gasped. "You're the woman they arrested for attacking the scientist? We heard it on the radio. What happened?"

"Sorry?" I asked. "She's a scientist? You know her?"

"Yeah." Charlie's mouth turned down at the edges. "She works over there, in the laboratories. Magda Swinson's her name. She's one of their main people. She's scum, Cameron." He looked at me now with new respect and it wasn't particularly what I wanted. "As far as I'm concerned, if you'd killed her, I'd be forever in your debt."

"Oh, be charitable, man," Elana scolded, taking her hand off his shoulder. "Whatever sort of work she does, Charlie, she doesn't deserve to be attacked like that! For goodness sake! We, of all people, are supposed to have respect for life."

"Well, whatever they're saying on the radio, I didn't kill her, I promise you," I said. "I just stopped someone else doing it. Then when I gave a statement to the police, they arrested me." I snorted bitterly. "Like I say, I have no particular affection for them."

"Well, you're very welcome here, my dear." She smiled, inviting me to follow her back to the tents. "Come and sit down by the fire and get warm, you look perished. It chills the bones out here, even when the sun is shining."

I followed both of them, past one of the caravans and through into a small clearing among the tents where a camp fire was burning brightly, in the centre of the makeshift village. Everyone turned to look as I sat down next to Elana on the plastic sacks that were spread out around the fire. They were weighing me up, some smiling, others just watching, reserving their judgement.

"This is Cameron, everybody," she said brightly. "And I want you to make her very welcome because, like us, she's not having a very pleasant day." More of them smiled now as she explained who I was and about my problems with the police. Then she went round the circle introducing everyone.

"This is Stella." She nodded at the big-boned woman on my left with long straw-coloured hair tied back in a single pigtail. "Next to her is Sandra." The younger woman with a delicate, pale face and long shiny hennaed hair smiled broadly. She was sitting next to Lou, another young woman, with piercings and bright orange hair cut Ziggy Stardust style. Beside her was Jean, in her forties with a weather-beaten face and short salt and pepper hair, the same colour as mine. She didn't smile, just looked across non-committally. Opposite me was a woman called Beano, well built and dykey-looking, smiling slightly, smoking a roll-up. On her left, two women, probably in their early forties, sitting close together. Jude and Annie. Obviously a couple, obviously enjoying each other's company. The only other man there, Len, was more relaxed than Charlie, around thirty with long brown matted hair, clean shaven and wearing a red baseball cap back to front. He was over by a makeshift table, pouring boiling water into a big teapot.

Introductions over, Elana turned to me again. "You must forgive our less than friendly welcome, my dear. We mean no harm, but you might realise that there are all sorts of people who would prefer us not to be here."

"It's OK. I understand. I've never been to an animal rights protest before, but I used to go to a lot of demos in the eighties. I know what it's like."

Everyone looked relaxed now. The fire was blazing in front of me, and it felt good to be warm again after the cold journey across the bridge. Len brought me a mug of tea and I accepted it – and the welcome that it signified – with gratitude.

One by one, they asked me questions about my morning and the attack on the bridge. I was pleased they were friendly and, even though I really didn't want to talk about it, I told them how I had stumbled upon the attempted murder and managed to stop the man from killing the scientist whom they disliked so much. I told them about my arrest. But I said nothing about the words that Magda Swinson had spoken. I needed their help, but as I sat there, I had no idea of how to broach the subject.

Annie took her eyes off her lover for just a moment to ask. "So how did you find out about us, Cameron?"

I smiled back. It was nice that this couple felt safe here, it made me feel better too.

"Well, strangely enough, it was the police. I'd never heard about GME or about your protest. It was when the cops asked me if I'd had any contact with animal rights activists that I started thinking – it seemed like a trick question at the time." They all laughed. "I guess now I can understand why they were interested. I didn't know she worked at GME. Now I can see what they were getting at. I guess that, in the circumstances, you'll be almost as suspect as I am."

"More suspect, Cameron," Charlie shouted across from behind the women. "They might have arrested you, but we're the ones they'd like to lock up. They just haven't any evidence, that's all." He grunted cynically. "But they're working on that, believe you me."

"He's right," Len chipped in as he walked past after distributing the last of the tea. "There's nothing they'd like better than to pin the attack on one of us. That way they could really discredit our protest. Maybe even get rid of us. They've tried just about everything else. That's why we're a bit careful with strangers today. Can you blame us?" He patted me on the shoulder – a sort of apology. "Anyway, it's nice to see you, love. Regardless of the circumstances."

"Thanks. You had me worried at first, I must admit." Most of them laughed, but Charlie didn't look so amused. The guy probably wouldn't trust his own mother.

"So how long have you been here?" I asked Elana, wanting to move the conversation on, away from me.

She laughed ironically and sat back on her haunches. "It seems like for ever, Cameron. But actually it's nearly eighteen months since we set up a permanent camp. Before that it was mainly weekend protests. A few of my women friends started it. I came and lived here then – the dark green van, that's mine. Then Charlie and Jean joined soon after. It's not easy here, like I say. But, I can tell you, we're going to stay till those immoral bastards over there pack up and go home. You can be sure of that."

A murmur of agreement went round the group and Lou, the young woman with the orange hair, nodded her head towards Elana. "She's being too modest. Elana's the one who really got this protest going." She looked across at her with admiration. "Whatever she might say, she's given up everything to be here. A lot of us just come and go, but she's always here, always fighting. She's a real inspiration."

The woman coloured up. "Oh come on Lou – you know I just enjoy good company and the outdoor life." The others hooted with playful derision at her modesty and I smiled. It was good to be back amongst committed, political women. They weren't all that different from those I'd met on the Common. Boisterous, feisty, edgy and warm – all at the same time. I looked across at Charlie, sitting out of the circle on his own, and wondered if the presence of men in the group was a help or a hindrance. For sure, the dynamics would be different and probably not always constructive.

I sipped my tea. It was hot and sweet and scalded my mouth in the pleasurable way that hot tea does. It was exactly what I needed. The atmosphere too had warmed and I felt more welcome.

"I'm sorry about my leather jacket and boots," I confessed, blushing slightly as I glanced across at Charlie. "I guess you don't really approve."

"Well, maybe we should just throw you out, instead of offering you tea, love." Stella grinned and poked me in the ribs with her elbow. I was glad she was joking. "As long as you're against animal testing, you're welcome here, Cameron," she continued reassuringly. "What you wear is up to you. It's true, most of us don't wear leather, but we won't condemn you for that. Will we folks?"

There was a general murmur of agreement, then a short silence. I looked around wondering how much I dare say. They seemed OK. Even Charlie was looking more relaxed about me now.

"So, tell me about the woman who was stabbed. You say she works over there – what does she do? In fact, come to that, what do GME do?"

"She's one of their top researchers, Cameron." Elana looked depressed at the thought of the big laboratory just across the field. "It's all big business. They talk about serving the community, but really, they're only interested in making money. And they don't care how they do it. Money and amoral men –" she snorted, shaking her head sadly "– that's a powerful and poisonous combination. It's even sadder when women start to work with them.

"Still, the movement's been fighting people like them for decades – and we'll keep on doing it until we win. Years ago they were using animals to test cosmetics and tobacco. For the moment, quite a lot of that has stopped. So we've made some progress – now, at least you can buy products that you know haven't been tested on animals. But we still have a long way to go. They're still testing pharmaceuticals, oven-cleaner, food additives, disinfectants, fertiliser – that kind of thing. The greed of men really seems to have no boundaries." She looked across at Charlie and then back at Len. "Though I'm glad to say that there are honourable exceptions."

Jean spoke up now. Looking serious and intense. "It's horrible, Cameron. GME and companies like them are killing off millions of animals every year. But it's us who are seen as the trouble makers – their cruelty is actually sanctioned by the authorities." She paused, calming her anger. "And scientists like Magda Swinson just don't seem to care. It's nothing less than legalised torture and it needs stopping." She looked at me meaningfully. "By whatever means necessary."

Charlie got to his feet, backing her up. "That's what I keep saying Jean, but no one listens, do they? It's no good us just sitting here talking. The whole situation's getting worse by the day. We need more direct action. We've got to get at the bloody researchers more – without them, this place can't function…"

"Yes! Great!" It was Lou, shouting across at him now. "You go threatening people and breaking their windows, then when one of them is attacked, we become prime suspects. Can you tell me how that helps us, Charlie? 'Cos I can't see it."

"Just calm down, you two." It was Elana again. "We can talk about this later. Right now, Cameron wants to know what's going on over there." Charlie opened his mouth to speak again, but the look she gave him shut him up instantly.

Lou told me more, a little sulkily at first. "Charlie and Jean believe in taking direct action against the scientists and technicians. It's not a point of view we all endorse. But Charlie's quite right when he says things are getting worse, I agree with him there. I used to be a science student, studying genetics until last year... I dropped out 'cos I couldn't hack it any more." She ran her fingers through her hair and sighed. "The thing is, the same people who were making money by testing products on animals have discovered the new science in the last year or so. Now I'm not saying all genetic research is bad..."

"Well you should be, Lou!" Stella interjected.

Lou looked across at her. "I'm not going to get into that argument with you again, Stella," she said calmly, and then turned back to the rest of us. "The fact is that there can be, and is, some ethical research. Look, take Vitamin E deficiency," she said, defensively. "A Third World NGO has developed a rice that contains Vitamin E. It's cheap, produced by a non-profit making trust, and is potentially capable of saving millions of lives in the Third World..."

Stella was nodding her head derisively. "You believe everything you're told, love, don't you?"

Lou coloured up and cast a fierce look at her. "All I'm saying is that those rich capitalists that have used animals to make money in the past are exploiting genetics now. Whatever the benefits of the new science could be in the right hands –" this was aimed at Stella who shook her head sadly "– the use of genetics by big business is danger-ous." She looked around the group which had fallen silent. "Not con-tent with putting innocent animals through hell by pasting their eyes with chemicals, ripping them apart, giving them cancer... and all the rest, now, Cameron, with genetic engineering, they're playing God and cloning freaks."

"So that's what's going on over there, is it?" I asked.

"Yes, it is." Jean prodded the fire angrily, sending sparks and smoke spiralling into the air. "You know what we're talking about here, love – pigs with human-compatible hearts, sheep that are manufactured so that they produce vaccines in their milk – that sort of thing. They say it's for the benefit of mankind… Huh, well they're right – it's for the benefit of the mankind that runs big business."

"Yeah I've heard of it, of course," I interrupted. "You mean like Dolly the Sheep…"

"You got it, Cameron!" Stella raised her cup to me. "Everyone knows about Dolly the Sheep. And a lot of people agree with it if it can help save lives and ease pain. But what they don't realise is the danger this poses to the balance of nature, not to speak of the danger to human society."

"I'm sorry, I don't really understand much about cloning."

"Well, the principle's quite simple." Lou sat forward on her knees, eager to explain. "In simple language, what happens is this. They take some pure cells from the animal they want to clone and grow them in laboratory conditions until they have a good supply. Then they transfer the cells to a minimal media. That's basically a solution that allows the cells to live, but makes them revert to a quiescent state –" She smiled and shook her head at the technical term. "Sorry! That's a condition where they're ready to use. You with me so far?"

I nodded. I was glad she was keeping it simple.

"Then they get an unfertilised egg from another female animal of the same species – lets call her Sally the Sheep – and carefully remove the nucleus. This means that all traces of Sally's genes are removed. The egg becomes an empty receptacle. Right?

"OK. Then they implant one of the previously grown cells – one of the cells from the animal that is being cloned – inside the coat around the egg. Then they electroshock the egg and, if it's done properly, that fuses the egg and the cell together."

"So then you have an egg which contains only the genes of the animal that you are cloning," I asked, concentrating hard.

Lou smiled. "Yes, that's about the sum of it. After that they have to repeat the same process over and over again with more eggs – you need a lot because most of them won't survive. Then they allow what are basically embryos to grow and divide a few times by putting them in a suitable growth media."

She paused to make sure I was taking it all in. "Finally, after all that, the embryos are implanted in another animal of the same species – the surrogate mother. She's really no more than a living incubator. None of her genes are in the foetus. And that's that. All they do then is cross their fingers and hope that the foetus they've manufactured goes to full term."

"And then you have a clone – like Dolly?"

"Yeah that's right." Stella's voice was cynical. "If you're very lucky! Lou makes it sound simple, but it fucking isn't. It's being done all the time now, with all sorts of animals. But in order to get a result they have to do it over and over." She looked at me intensely to see if I'd got the message. "Meaning, love, that for every 'success' there are hundreds, possibly thousands, of failures. And both the surrogate mother and the foetuses are expendable. It's a like a weird, sick game, Cameron. Frankenstein come true!"

"And GME specialise in that?"

"Yes, dear." Elana looked depressed. "And it's very worrying. More than ever it's really important to protest outside businesses like this one. It's not just the animals. That's horrible enough." She sighed heavily. "What really worries all of us as well is that the same process is easily transferable to human beings."

The rest of them murmured in agreement.

"You mark my words," she continued. "If we don't stop them cloning animals, before long, someone, somewhere will have produced the first human clone and then the floodgates will open."

"But they'd never be allowed to!" I objected.

"Huh, that's what I thought!" Lou retorted. "But things are moving slowly and relentlessly in that direction. They're already talking about it seriously in the States and in Italy. Besides, even before the law changes here, people will be doing it. There's too much money at stake. The first company to perfect human cloning – provided they get away with it – will make a fortune!"

"Think of all the rich, middle-class couples who can't have children!" It was Jean again. "Think of all the money to be made with Designer Babies!"

Elana looked sad. "She's right, Cameron. We might disagree amongst ourselves about the best way of stopping it, but none of us have any doubts about the evil they're playing with." She looked down, fidgeting with her hands for a moment, then when she turned to me again her face was filled with dread and sorrow. "The first thing I think of is the Nazis, and their eugenics programme. They were obsessed with racial purity and with producing the perfect race. This really isn't any better, my dear. I lost both my parents to the death camps when I was little. The last thing I want is to see any sort of animal being selected – especially human ones."

A deep silence fell over them all. I really didn't know what to say to the woman by my side. Whatever anyone might think of her or the others, there was no doubt that their objections to GME and other companies like them were based on deeply held beliefs. And though I could see some of the medical arguments, if I had to come down on any one side, it would be theirs.

"I really hope you are successful," I said, feeling chastened by everything I'd heard. "Thanks – I never understood the implications before."

"Well, you do now, love!" Stella looked at me ruefully. "Just go out and spread the word. We need all the help we can get."

"So, are GME part of a big conglomerate, then?" I asked.

Stella shook her head cynically. "It's the same old story, Cameron. GME is owned by a holding company in Switzerland. Heaven knows who's behind these people now. They were quite small until a year ago, then they expanded rapidly, building new laboratories and animal compounds – and their high walls and big gates. It's obvious there's heavy money involved, and that their research has gone big time. We know it's genetics. We know it involves animal experimentation. We also know that there are a lot of deaths – the knacker's wagon comes several times a week. But, we don't have a contact on the inside, and, until we do, we'll never really know exactly what's going on."

"So are you going to come and join us, Cameron?" Lou looked at me, wide-eyed and appealing.

I shook my head. I was enjoying their company. And I was getting an education, but I was still unsure of how I was going to phrase the question I had to ask.

"No, I'm sorry Lou, I can't stay – I'm just passing through. I have to get back to York in a day or two." I hesitated. If they knew of Magda Swinson, then they might know the woman I was looking for.

There was only one way to find out. I couldn't leave here without asking. At least they were friendly; the risk was worth taking.

"Actually, you might be able to help me. I'm trying to find someone – a woman, she's called Joanna Whittling."

I saw Charlie react at once. His face changed to the same expression of acute distrust as when we first met.

Elana's face fell. "She a friend of yours, Cameron?" she asked with an edge to her voice. The others who had been talking amongst themselves went quiet.

"No," I rejoined firmly. "I've never met her. I just want to contact her, that's all."

"Well, you'd better not expect any help from us!" Charlie stood up, his voice crackling with anger. But this time, the disapproval seemed almost unanimous. He pointed a finger at me threateningly. "If you ever want to come back here, Cameron, then you'd better stay well away from her. You hear?"

"Fine," I retorted, rattled at being told what to do, especially by him. "I hear you, Charlie. But since I don't know the woman, you might at least tell me why you dislike her so much."

Elana turned to me, speaking evenly, but with an intensity in her voice that betrayed deep hatred and concern. "Why do you want to find her, Cameron? Tell us that."

I shook my head. "It's confidential, I can't say." I was in an impossible situation. "All I can tell you is that I need to find the woman to deliver an important message. I don't know her, I don't want to know her. All I want to do is find her and pass it on."

Silence.

I looked around the circle. The smiles had faded, the attentiveness had dissipated. Lou was looking across at me sympathetically but most of the others were drifting off, not wanting to get involved. Elana got up and touched me on the shoulder, before she turned to go. "Leave it, Cameron. You seem an all right sort of woman. Leave it. Don't get involved with these people." Then she too walked away and disappeared into one of the tents.

Lou smiled at me sadly and set about preparing a meal.

Charlie threw me another unfriendly glance and turned to go.

"At least you could tell me where I can find her," I shouted at his retreating back. He froze for a second. Then he turned, an expression of disgust on his face.

"We don't know where the fuck she is, Cameron. And, believe me, woman, even if we did, we certainly wouldn't tell you."

## Seven

Everyone had moved away, like I was infectious. Like Joanna
Whittling's name was some kind of evil incantation. Nobody would
say why, but they hated her. And, by association, they didn't like me
either – or trust me any more. I would just have to find another way.
Though it escaped me what that might be.

I started my bike and drove back along the marshlands road towards Barton, feeling lost and dejected. The sun was fading now and
the road through the trees was as gloomy as my mood. My brain was
working overtime, trying to figure out their reactions. I felt sore. But I
felt confused as well. Just when I thought I might be getting somewhere, my search for answers had only produced more questions.

If Magda Swinson worked at GME, if she was one of their key researchers, like everyone at the camp said she was, then why would
anyone there need to send an important e-mail to her? And, come to
that, how did she know about the e-mail anyway – if it had only just
been sent to her? From what Vick had said at the bureau, I knew that
she couldn't have collected her e-mails that morning from her home
computer, otherwise the message would never have been available on
the web page.

Then there was Joanna Whittling. A woman whose name alone
was enough to provoke anger and distrust at the camp. Who the hell
was she? And why did they hate her so much?

That morning, when I'd made the promise to Magda Swinson, it had seemed like a kindness. But now, I wasn't so sure that I liked what I'd promised to do. Some animal rights activists may be extreme, Charlie amongst them, but there was nothing wrong with their values. And knowing that the message had originated at an animal testing laboratory, I wasn't so sure that I could go along with just delivering it. Especially when, even in Elana's terms, both the woman who'd asked me to do it and the recipient were so suspect.

When I left the camp, I'd almost made up my mind to drop into the nursing home and get the visit to my mother over with. But now, sitting on my bike at the bottom of Whitecross Street, my mind was too full of other things. I needed to talk to someone about the predicament I found myself in, to ask for advice. But there wasn't anyone I could talk to, was there? I couldn't face ringing Hellen. Becky was against the whole thing anyway, and I didn't want another lecture. And Jimmy Wilson? Well, I daren't even mention my plight to him. However well we had got on back in York, he was still a cop.

I took off my helmet and ran my fingers through my hair, trying to quell the anxiety by looking around for some distraction: teenage boys across the road, laughing, pushing and jeering at each other; a mother and daughter chatting happily as they walked up the hill, arms weighed down by plastic shopping bags; men and women on bikes, in cars, a decorator's van, all probably on their way home from work; a couple holding hands. It was all so normal. It all looked so comfortable. It all made me feel so isolated.

A small voice inside my head whispered that I could just walk away. It would be so easy. No one would ever know. Walk away, you'll never see Magda Swinson again. Forget Joanna Whittling. Forget the e-mail file. Just go home, it said. Just leave. Right now.

I parked the bike and pushed my helmet and scarf into the box on the back, undid my leather jacket and set off towards the town centre. Another voice inside my head was more accommodating. Have a drink, it said. A really strong one.

It was still early and the first pub I found was empty except for two men sitting on high stools at the bar. They both turned to look at me as I walked in. But instead of turning away again, as even small-town people usually do, they kept staring, then looked meaningfully at each other. I ordered a Campari and tonic from the woman behind the bar and stared back at them until they gave up. By the time I sat down, they were having a detailed discussion with the barwoman as well – glancing over at me all the time. Just like in the library.

I ignored them as much as I could, staring into my angry red drink, wondering where to go from here. I was deep in thought when a woman stopped just inside the door and looked across at me, meeting my eyes as I looked up. Then she strode across to the bar and waited whilst her pint was pulled.

She'd been at the camp – a dyke, I was sure – sitting back from the others, saying hardly anything, but listening and watching. When I'd said the dreaded name, I had seen the reaction on her face. It had been different to the others. She wasn't appalled. She hadn't even looked hostile. The look in her eyes had been more of surprise and interest, even excitement.

She chatted easily with the two men at the bar, but glanced over her shoulder at me, making it plain that she wanted to talk to me. Then she exchanged a few last words, picked up her pint, and strolled across.

Her shoulders rolled from side to side as she walked, an action that, in a man, might have registered as arrogant. But with her it smacked more of insolence. The I-don't-fucking-care-what-you-think-of-me gait of someone who knows just exactly who she is and doesn't care whether anyone else approves or not. And the rest of her body echoed those same sentiments. Her hair, thick and black, was cut short, shaved to almost bare skin at the sides and back, but full and curly on top with a small unruly quiff that bounced up and down as she walked. She wore a single earring – a small gold cat that hung carelessly from her right ear – and she had a wide, generous mouth, turned up naturally at the edges, deep brown eyes that illuminated her round, rather battered-looking face, and a crooked sort of nose that could almost belong to a prize-fighter.

She smiled as she approached and held out her hand. "Hiya." Her voice was deep and throaty, her grip firm and strong. "Thought I'd lost you for a minute. I saw you sitting on your bike out there in the street, then suddenly you'd split. I'm Beano, by the way. Remember? I was at the camp just now." Then she sat down on the other side of the small table and took a big mouthful of beer.

She looked like a GI gone wrong. A large khaki jacket hung from her shoulders, swinging open as she sat down, revealing a dark green T-shirt which, loose-fitting as it was, still did nothing to hide her ample breasts and bulging stomach. Her trousers were over-sized, faded green combats with pockets everywhere, gathered at the waist with a thick brown leather belt which held a mobile phone and a canvas pouch. She looked at me intensely and pulled one leg up to rest on her other knee. Her trouser bottoms were gathered at the ankle, above what had once been beige Caterpillar boots. Leather boots.

"So you're the woman on the bridge, eh? The one who is, quote: 'helping the police with their enquiries', unquote." She pronounced the last bit in an approving posh accent, as she dug around in her pouch to extract a tin of tobacco and some papers. "They're talking about you behind your back all the time on the local radio, Cameron, I thought you should know. You're becoming quite a personality."

I grunted, remembering Superintendent Warren and his accusations all too clearly. "Yeah, well, like I say, whatever the police have told the media, it wasn't me who stabbed her," I said ruefully. "I was just in the wrong place at the wrong time."

"Or the right place." She smiled – a real broad, friendly grin. "You don't look much like a killer to me."

"Thanks." I smiled back, I liked her already. "They didn't seem to take to me very much at the camp, though."

"Yeah!" She chortled. "You went down a real treat, didn't you?"

"Mmm. I never realised what impact a name could have."

"Well, you chose well, Cameron," she remarked jauntily, lighting her fag and taking a deep drag. "Joanna Whittling, I can tell you, is some kind of spook as far as the protest is concerned. She used to run the research place until a year ago. They see her as a serial animal killer." She inclined her head, looking thoughtful. "I guess they're right. No one who really cares about animals could be involved in something like that."

My spirits lifted. At last, someone who was helping. Someone who was willing to talk. "So what happened? Why isn't she there now?"

"Ahh! There are two versions. My fellow protesters would argue that she was one of their early successes. Charlie, Jean and their predecessors hounded her mercilessly. Ringing her at work, ringing her at home, protesting outside her house, putting unpleasant things through her letterbox – you know, all the routine stuff. Then, one day, about a year ago, she simply gave up. She'd had enough. She sold out and quit."

"And the other version?"

"Mmm. Well, other people say differently. They say that her husband died – and the group of bankers that were backing them wanted out, once the boss-man had fled his mortal coil. The company was getting through a lot of cash and needed more – and quickly, if it was to stay in business and continue its research. The original backers weren't too keen on that, apparently. The company wasn't anywhere near a breakthrough. So anyone investing even more money would be taking a huge gamble. To cut a long story short, word is that they sold out to a foreign consortium – for peanuts. Furthermore, the story continues, our Mrs Whittling was surplus to their requirements so she got the big E before it all went through, without getting a bean."

She took another swig of beer, wiping her mouth with the back of her hand. "So… choose the version you like best, Cameron. I know which one I believe."

She sat back and I watched her for a moment. She looked like she might be an animal rights activist, but there was something else about her. Something that didn't quite fit. "How do you know all this, Beano – you been at the camp a long time?"

She shook her head. "No, only came across at the weekend. From Manchester. But I'm nosy. I get talking to people and listen a lot." Then she eyed me reproachfully. "Also, I don't just leave when things become difficult – like some people." She took another drag and leant back in her chair, swinging onto the back legs. "Oh they're all right, back there at the camp – just a bit leery, that's all. You can't blame 'em for that, though, can you? Nobody wants 'em there. Not GME. Not the cops. Specially not the council. They're all waiting for an excuse to diss 'em."

She looked across at the bar, returning the stares of the two men until they turned their backs on us. "Some people can't deal with difference. So they assume that anyone who isn't like them is going to be violent, on drugs, dangerous or dishonest. That's why they're all so pissed off with the hassle today. Sooner or later, the cops are gonna get 'em for something. Just like they tried to get you. We're untidy, Cameron, we get in their way."

I swirled the ice cubes and the remains of the Campari around in my glass and nodded in agreement, before finishing it off. The pungent liquid filled my head with its aroma. The gloom was lifting. This woman fascinated me. But she also worried me a little.

"What I want to know, Cameron, is what you are doing here?" She stuck her head on one side and eyed me up again, knitting her brow. "Why are you so fucking interested in Mrs Whittling?"

I smiled to myself. So that was why she'd followed me. "Like I said, Beano, I just have a message to deliver. That's all."

She leant back in her chair again. "Uh, if you want to know where she is, you'll have to do better than that." She grunted, stubbing out her cigarette. Then, after a pause: "It's to do with the stabbing, I suppose."

Her face was too eager. I didn't know who she was, or why she was so interested in me, but her curiosity was making me very uneasy.

"I can't tell you anything else. It's confidential."

"But it has something to do with Magda Swinson?"

For a big woman who gave all the appearance of being a slob, her eyes were bright, searching. I could almost feel them piercing my brain, dissecting my innermost thoughts. I shifted uncomfortably, determined to hold my ground, but feeling myself slipping, inch by inch.

"It might do, but I'm not telling you any more, Beano, I can't."

She shrugged. "You want another drink then?"

I shook my head. Oh no! I'm not going to let you work on me.

"No, thanks. I'd better be going. Things to do."

She took another sip from her beer, relaxed, as if my departure was of no consequence. "Yeah, well, you take care, Cameron. I don't know what you're on at, love, but be careful. It can be nasty out there."

"Yeah, OK, Beano. See you around maybe."

"I wouldn't doubt it for a moment," she said, smiling a little too confidently over the top of her glass.

I was glad to get out of the woman's clutches. She obviously had a knack with getting people to talk. Direct but friendly, inquisitive but open. I knew that if I'd stayed, I might have said too much. And, however much my instincts told me she was all right, I just couldn't take that chance.

I was heading back to Hull again. There seemed little point in staying around Barton. The camp was openly hostile, Beano openly inquisitive and the spectre of my mother was lurking around every corner. Tonight I needed some space. Time to think. Time to decide what to do next.

At least I knew who Joanna Whittling was now. But I still didn't know how to find her. More to the point, I still didn't know if I wanted to.

Crossing the bridge, I swallowed hard as I approached the spot where it had all happened and, inevitably, thought about Magda

Swinson and the e-mail file. A message from one animal abuser to an-other. At least that was what I was supposed to believe. I wondered how she was – if she was still alive. She was still critical when Becky and I left the police station. She could easily die. She might be dead already. They'd be straight on to me if she was... Then, I'd be on a murder rap. And if Warren found out that I'd withheld evidence as well, I would be really sunk. No one would believe a word I said, and I'd be charged before you could blink.

So, if she had died, I would have heard from them already, right? A message on my mobile. A squad car coming up behind me at speed, its blue light flashing. A hand on my shoulder whilst I ordered a drink at the bar. I was still free, wasn't I? The traffic around me was quiet, my mobile silent. OK, then maybe she's still alive.

Night was falling now, and a cold wind was blowing across the river, working its way through my jeans and inside my jacket, making me shiver. The seductive voice in my head had gone too – washed away by the equally cold wind of reality. I'd made my choice when I lied to Warren.

At least I still had my freedom – for now. I still had time to find out what the message was about, and if it was that which got Magda Swinson stabbed. I had a chance to try and find out who really stabbed her, a brief opportunity to clear my name before it was too late.

OK. So stop whingeing and get on with it.

I paid the toll and came off the bridge, swinging right at the big roundabout up the road, and heading down Boothferry, back into the centre of the city. She would have visitors. She must have relatives or friends who would be concerned about her. People who knew about her life – people who might know about her ex-boss. It shouldn't be difficult to find her. There was only one major A&E hospital in the city centre, the Hull Royal Infirmary.

But it was risky. My bail conditions were clear. If they thought I was trying to get to her, I'd be back in jail. If Becky knew I was even thinking about it, I'd be in even bigger trouble.

But you're not trying to see her, are you? Maybe you can't go to the hospital and try to make contact. But you *can* go to the hospital and ask how she is. And your bail conditions don't say anything about talking to any relatives or friends, do they?

Not a mention.

But Becky did specifically say that I must keep away from the hospital...

But what she *meant* was keep away from Magda Swinson.

Yeah, you're right, you know. You're damn well right!

## Eight

I was there within ten minutes, pulling into the large visitors' car park across the road from the shabby high-rise building, weaving my way through the rows of cars, looking for a motorcycle parking bay. But it was peak visiting, and every available space was taken, so I headed back towards the entrance and pulled the Harley onto the wide pavement to one side of the barrier. This would have to do. A parking ticket was the least of my worries.

Daylight was almost gone now, the bright sunlight of the afternoon replaced by the dirty orange glow of the sodium streetlights all around me. I sat down on my bike, idly watching the traffic as it drove in and out of the car park, thinking about the risk I was taking, and getting cold feet to match my cold legs. What if the police found out that I was digging around? What if they saw me in the hospital? Maybe I should ring Hellen, ask her advice. No, bad idea. Or Becky – admit that I'm scared and that I don't know how to get out of this.

Yeah, sure. And have her tell you how stupid you are for getting involved in the first place? How you should cross your fingers, trust the system and walk away from it all?

It was true. I was stupid. Stupid for making a promise that was nearly impossible to keep. Stupid for putting myself in danger from both the legal system and the man who had stabbed Magda Swinson. But it was too late to change anything now.

I sat there for a few more minutes thinking about Joanna Whittling. Then I remembered the telephone numbers from the library and my spirits rose a little. I still hadn't spoken to two of them.

I pulled out the piece of paper and the mobile, and punched in the first number. A man answered this time, but he'd never heard of anyone called Joanna. Wrong number, he said. The same thing happened on the second call and I stuffed the phone back into my pocket and stared out across the road towards the hospital forecourt. There wasn't going to be an easy way out. I was going to have to go into the hospital. I was going to have to see if I could find someone she knew.

Traffic had been coming and going along the road between the Infirmary and the car park all the time. I'd been idly watching it as I dialled the two numbers. Now, as I got off the bike and locked it, I noticed the blue Astra again. I was sure it had driven past once already. But it wasn't so much that. It was the driver: a big man with a shaved head. I didn't see his face, because he turned away when he saw me looking.

As the car drove back to the junction and out onto the main road, I realised I was becoming paranoid. Cars were coming and going all the time. And if someone turned away as they passed, well so what? Maybe he was looking for someone over by the hospital. Maybe he was avoiding someone coming through the entrance behind me. I stuck the rucksack back on my shoulder. Maybe I'd had enough today. Next thing, I'd be hallucinating.

I took the pedestrian crossing over the road, skirted the flower booth and the newsagent's kiosk in the forecourt, and walked in through the main entrance of the Hull Royal Infirmary.

There was nothing very royal about the place. Once upon a time, perhaps back in the brave new world of sixties architecture, it might have seemed impressive. Now it was merely depressing, like a lot of the NHS – slightly seedy and severely underfunded. It was clear that, whatever money there was, it had to be diverted into patient care. The staff here, like everywhere else, would be coping as best they could whilst the buildings around them deteriorated. I shivered at the awful thought of being ill in such a place. There was precious little 'feel-good factor' left here.

Visitors were coming and going at the end of the big lobby, and, further along, a middle-aged man was leaning against the information desk looking fed up. There was no one there to help him, or me, so I leaned against the desk as well, and waited. A few patients came down the stairs to my left from outpatients, and there were a few more in the raised seating area at the far end of the lobby, waiting for their ambulance home.

A woman in an official-looking blouse, more M&S than NHS, appeared after a few minutes with a form. She smiled at me reassuringly, then went into a huddle with the man as they filled in the details. His unkempt moustache twitched every time she wrote something. I waited as long as I could, but my boredom threshold is so low that it's in danger of tripping me up sometimes, and I decided to try and find intensive care all by myself.

The list of wards by the lift didn't mention it, so I asked a passing nurse if she could direct me there. She frowned and said that they normally only allowed relatives in – and even then, it depended on the circumstances. I looked down at the floor and, in a quiet voice, explained shakily that my brother had just been admitted. She told me to go to the third floor.

I stayed in the lift when the doors opened, scanning the lobby for a police presence. When I was sure it looked safe, I approached the nurse behind the desk. She smiled gently when I said I was a friend of Magda Swinson's.

"I'm sorry, I can't let you see her. We're not allowing any visitors at present. But she's been in theatre earlier and undergone emergency surgery. It went very well but she's still critical, and unconscious. She has stabilised though and we're very hopeful. Try not to worry too much. We're doing all we can."

I shuddered at the thought of her, all wired up, surrounded by every kind of machine and monitor. I was pleased to be spared the sight. I'd seen quite enough of her pain and suffering earlier in the day. Besides, I don't like hospitals. Just the smell of them makes me ill. I'd spent too long in the one in Amsterdam last autumn, nursing my wounds and coming down off that weird cocktail of narcotics. This place brought it all back. That and the memory of Hellen, creeping into my hospital bed like a redeeming angel.

I shuddered inside and my eyes started to burn. Why did I keep thinking of her? Why did I have to keep remembering? It's over, Cameron. You don't need her.

"Do you mind if I stay a while?" I asked. "I feel a little faint."

She looked concerned and indicated some seats. "You're very welcome to sit down for a while. That's your friend's mum over there, I don't know whether you know her. Would you like a glass of water, perhaps?"

I said I would be all right. Magda's mother was sitting by herself in the middle of a row of chairs against the wall: a grey-haired woman in her sixties with her head hanging down and her shoulders sagging. As I sat down, she looked up and did her best to smile, her eyes glazed with anxiety. I smiled back as kindly as I could.

"It's a to-do," she said, tugging at a small tear-stained handkerchief in her lap.

"You have someone in the ward?" I asked, knowing the answer and hating myself for intruding.

She nodded sadly. "My daughter." She was trembling, her red, swollen eyes filling with tears.

"I'm so sorry," I replied inadequately, feeling the shockwaves of her grief in the air all around me.

"She's always been such a good girl..." she sobbed, shaking her head. "Never been in any sort of trouble, always worked hard. A real credit... Then... this." She blew her nose, then looked down into her lap, crushing the hanky between her fingers. "It's not safe for anyone on the streets any more..."

"Do you want to talk about it? It's all right if you do," I said, telling myself that I might be helping her by listening, but feeling a fraud all the same.

Her face was drawn and white. "She was mugged, love. Stabbed as she drove over the Humber Bridge." She looked into my eyes, appealing for an answer. "Who would want to do such a thing... to my Magda?"

We sat in silence for a few minutes, me looking down at my hands, Magda's mother staring into space, as if unable to comprehend what had happened. After a few minutes, she spoke again, her voice strained and loaded with disbelief.

"I thought she was safe in Hull. London's so violent these days. I was pleased when she left home. I thought... a nice car, a good job, a house in a nice area, on the edge of the city..."

"You've travelled up today?"

"Yes, love... this morning, as soon as they rang me. Her father... died two years ago. I don't know what I'll do if... She's unconscious you know, she might never come to." She brought her handkerchief up to her mouth in a desperate effort to control her emotions. But the tears were already running down her cheeks and her body was shaking with grief. I felt like the worst sort of heel.

"I'm sure she'll be all right," I comforted, squeezing her arm.

"Has she got friends – a husband perhaps – someone who will look after you, put you up for the night?" Cameron, sometimes, you are the lowest form of life.

"No." She shook her head. "The police have been very nice. They've made arrangements. She doesn't seem to have any friends, doesn't Magda. Except for work. That's all she ever talks about. Her job. The new cures that she's working on. She's such a kind girl..."

She looked up as the lift door opened, and I froze as a uniformed policeman walked out. I buried my head in a magazine, praying that he wouldn't come across. But he didn't even notice us, just walked past the nurses' station and on into intensive care without a second glance.

"They've been wonderful, have the police," she said, turning back to me again, as a woman officer left the ward, walked by with the same disinterest and took the lift down.

"And so they should be too," I murmured, squeezing her arm, and getting up to go. "I'm sure everything will be all right. Try not to worry."

I couldn't bring myself to ask her about Joanna Whittling. However much she might be able to help, I couldn't put her through any more pain. I felt quite bad enough already, and there had to be some boundaries, some respect for decency. So I left, still appalled at the way I'd used her, walked across to the lifts and angrily punched the DOWN button.

The lights above all four doors were flashing as the lifts shuffled busily between the floors of the high-rise building. The first was full when the door opened, and I stood back. The second was little better, but the people inside shuffled back self-consciously to let me in, and I joined them, feeling uncomfortable and hot amongst the knot of unfamiliar bodies. I looked down, avoiding eye contact, empty inside. I needed to be alone, out in the open; not here, in a lift full of sweaty strangers.

Her grief had brought it all back: last September, the day when Carrie's body was found in the canal. The day when I was asked to go back to Amsterdam to identify her. The day I lost my sister and began the journey that led me to Hellen. I'd lost them both now. One to Karst and his gang, the other... Well... As the lift doors opened I pushed my way out, fighting for air, into a vestibule that was seething with visitors: mothers and fathers; brothers and sisters; children and friends, spilling from every lift, on their way home after visiting their loved ones. I felt excluded, all alone in a city where I could trust no one.

I fought my way through the crush and out into the main lobby, where I slumped against the wall and blew my nose, trying to compose myself and move my mind onto something else – something I could cope with.

It was then I realised I was being watched.

She was loitering close by, near the entrance to the lifts; a young, attractive woman. Mid-twenties, with the 'petit gamin' look; the kind that the media still pushes so hard. But she looked good all the same, with her nut-brown shoulder-length bob, neatly combed, and just a trace of make-up on her angular, delicate face. She wore a simple mauve shirtwaister over her slender body, with a beige raincoat thrown carelessly on top and a patterned navy and cream scarf around her neck. There was a rolled-up newspaper under her arm.

And she couldn't take her eyes off me.

It was just like the library, and the pub in Barton. I hate it when people stare at me, and I moved off again, wondering what it was about Hull. I pushed my way through the noisy crush, across the lobby towards the exit, forcing myself to look straight ahead and pretend she wasn't there. But I could sense that she was following me.

"Excuse me," she shouted rather breathlessly, catching me up, "can I have a word with you?"

Funny how time seems to freeze at particular moments, when your emotions are exposed and raw. Funny how, at times like those, your mind can process a whole range of detail in a fraction of a second.

The noise around me seemed to still, and I knew she recognised me. It might have been her eyes. They were a deep emerald green, and just then, they were big – very big indeed. Or it might have been her face. It always amazes me just how many expressions a human being can fit onto one face at any given time. And hers carried a wide assortment: disbelief, concern, hesitation, sadness and surprise.

My panic stilled for the moment, I could only manage one – confusion.

"I'm sorry, you probably think I'm ever so rude..." She spoke earnestly, but her voice was light, almost musical and she laughed, self-conscious and sad, pushing back her fringe as she spoke. "Are you... er... Cameron McGill?"

I nodded cautiously. "Yessss... I am. Do I know you?"

She looked quickly around us and then bit her lip. "No, you don't know me. You've sort of... met my friend though... And... and I really need to talk to you."

I screwed up my eyes, trying to work it out, my head spinning, thinking that maybe she was an ex of an ex.

Then she unrolled the newspaper under her arm and passed it over to me, her hand trembling ever so slightly. I took it, puzzled, and the front page headline came up to meet me.

'*Amsterdam Heroine Arrested in Bridge Stabbing.*' I recognised the picture of Magda Swinson at once but the picture of me next to it was not a flattering one – I'd seen it before, last November. It had been taken by a news agency whilst I was still recovering. I looked tired and weak; incapable of lifting a teacup, let alone stabbing anyone. I raised my eyes from the paper, and looked into hers. Now my face must have been playing a range of feelings too. Shock, despair, anger, panic...

The girl with the emerald eyes smiled weakly, and I read on:

Cameron McGill, the woman who so bravely exposed an Amsterdam drugs racket last November, has herself been held for questioning over a serious stabbing incident which took place early this morning on the Humber Bridge. The victim, a young research scientist called Magda Swinson, is now fighting for her life in Hull Royal Infirmary. Doctors say her condition is still critical and that she has not yet regained consciousness.

McGill, a drugs counsellor from York, and the sister of the late Carrie McGill, the investigative journalist murdered in Amsterdam last year, was picked up this morning at the scene of the crime on the Humber Bridge. At the time of going to press, she was still being held. Superintendent Warren, the senior officer in charge of the investigation, told reporters that, whilst they suspected it could have been a road rage incident, and a woman was helping them with their enquiries, they were not yet in a position to press charges and were continuing with their investigation.

The victim, Magda Swinson, aged 28 and unmarried, is an accomplished genetic scientist who works for GME Technologies on the south bank of the Humber, near Barton.

Marcus Stantonwell, the chief executive of the company, which specialises in medical research, told the *Hull News* that they were extremely shocked by the attack. "Magda has always been a dedicated employee, working tirelessly for the good of the community. This is a tragic situation, which has shocked and appalled us all. We sincerely hope that the police will catch the assailant soon and that Miss Swinson will recover fully."

The vicious attack comes after more than a year of protests by a small number of animal rights activists outside the company's premises. Speaking for them, a man who gave his name as Charlie said: "Whatever our feelings about the work which Magda Swinson was involved in, we can only say how upset we all are over this incident. However, since it has nothing at all to do with our protest, we shall continue to oppose the wholesale mistreatment and slaughter of animals at her employer's premises."

*Closed bridge causes holiday traffic chaos – page 3.*
*The woman who exposed the drug racketeers – page 5.*

I handed the paper back, my stomach churning.

"You can keep it," she said.

"I'm not sure I want to," I sighed. But I took it anyway. Now I understood why I had been stared at today. Now I realised how lucky I'd been, not getting spotted on the wards. It was one thing to 'help the police with their enquiries', quite another to have my face splashed sensationally over the front page of the local evening tabloid.

She put her head on one side, weighing me up. "So, you're free then?"

"Yes. And I didn't do it. Who are you?"

"I'm Angel – and I believe you."

I relaxed a little, but only a little. "I'm glad someone does. You must be a journalist?" I asked, cynicism creeping back into my voice.

"No," she said, shaking her head. "No – I'm Magda's ex-girlfriend."

## Nine

Twelve hours ago, I'd been an ordinary person on my way home from the ferry. Now I'd been transformed by the local tabloid into an infamous knifewoman.

I stuffed the newspaper into my pocket and ran out of the hospital, round the corner and across the road to my bike. I rested my head on the saddle and closed my eyes, trying to deal with the nausea in my guts and the shock that was jangling through my brain. When I looked up, she was standing beside me.

"Are you OK?" she asked, placing her hand tentatively on my shoulder.

"Of course I'm not OK," I snapped, straightening up and glaring at her. She shrank back and I instantly regretted my outburst. She knew Magda. She was the only lead I had. However tied up I was in my own feelings, I couldn't afford to alienate her.

"I'm sorry." I breathed deeply, shaking. "I've no cause to shout at you. It's just... well, I've had a shitty day."

"You think I haven't?" she countered, more patiently than I deserved, holding me with those eyes.

"Yeah, I'm sorry." I blew my nose and stared out across the car park. It felt better out here, away from people.

She stood fiddling with her shoulder bag, waiting for me to calm down. She must be upset. How would I feel if it was Hellen?

"When did you find out about her?" I asked, trying to keep the tremor out of my voice.

"Not till I saw the newspaper hoardings this afternoon." She swallowed hard and closed her eyes tight for a second or two. When she opened them again and attempted a smile, I patted the bike seat, inviting her to sit down next to me. She hesitated for a second, and then turned and lowered herself onto the small, narrow seat. Our bodies touched.

I could feel her through my clothes. I could sense her moving, breathing, as she pressed against my arm. I shuddered inside and tried to make space between us: half of me scared by her closeness; half of me clinging to the comfort of her warmth.

I started to get up, worried by the sudden intimacy. She laid her hand on my knee and restrained me. "It's all right, Cameron. Stay where you are. Just rest for a moment, there's no hurry."

I sat down again and breathed in, trying to get a hold on my emotions, trying to relate to her situation, rather than mine. "You found out from the paper? That's a terrible way to get the news."

"Yes, it was." She dabbed her eyes with a tissue and then blew her nose.

"You've been to visit her then? I didn't see you in there."

She shook her head sadly. "They wouldn't let me in, Cameron. I went into intensive care, maybe an hour ago, but they don't allow visitors. Only close relatives. They said she was too ill; that she'd just come back from the operating theatre. Maybe, if I'd been a relative or partner..." She shrugged and looked down into her lap, as she thought about it. "I did catch a glimpse of her through the open door though. She's on a ventilator, all wired up to machines, with tubes in her mouth and up her nose... Ugh! it was horrid seeing her like that."

She stared into space for a few moments.

"There was a copper with her," she said.

"Yeah, I know, I was there when they changed shifts."

"They must think he's going to have another go."

"Who?"

"The bloke that stabbed her."

"Oh, they probably just want to ask her a few questions when she comes round," I offered reassuringly, not believing a word of it.

"Well, I dunno, Cameron." She shifted her body against mine, sending a tingle down into my belly. "The nurse said she'd lost so much blood that she'd gone into a coma. She said it could be days, even weeks before she came round." She shook her head in disbelief and wiped her eyes with the back of her hand. "Poor Magda."

"Yeah. Her mother's distraught. She thinks she might not make it."

"Her mother?" She frowned.

"Yes, her mother," I repeated. "She was sitting in the waiting area. Didn't you see her?"

She hesitated, like she was momentarily thrown. "... No. No, I didn't... I've... er... never actually met her mother. Besides, I was only in there a minute or two."

"Well then, that explains it," I responded, matter-of-factly, watching her eyes. She hardly blinked. But that mild panic had been strange.

We sat quietly for a while, side by side on the bike seat. She seemed a nice woman: someone I could get on with, who might be able to help me. Someone I could talk to. I wanted to ask her if I could see her again but I wasn't quite sure how to phrase it. She might think I was coming on to her.

I watched the cars streaming past us out of the car park, people going home after visiting. Some of them would be relieved that their loved ones were all right, others worried and anxious. My mind went back to Magda's mother, sitting all alone in the waiting area, and I thought again about her daughter and the file. There had to be a connection. And since I was the only one who knew about it, I had to do something for all our sakes. If Angel had known Magda, then she must at least have heard of Joanna Whittling too. Whether she thought I was coming on to her or not, I had to see her again. I had to ask her.

But before I could get the words out, she turned to me and touched my arm.

"Can I ask you a favour, Cameron?" she said quietly.

I nodded.

She bit her lip, staring at the ground. "I don't want you to think I'm being forward or anything... But the thing is..." She took a deep breath, looked straight at me, and blurted it out: "Will you come home with me for a while, Cameron? I'd really like to talk to you."

I looked away for a moment, thrown by the immediacy of her invitation. It was music to my ears, but I already felt bad about questioning Magda's mother. I didn't want to take unfair advantage with Angel as well.

I turned back to her. "I'd really like to see you again, Angel. But maybe it's not a good idea to invite me home with you. You don't know me. Why don't we go somewhere safer, more public – a café or a pub perhaps?"

She shook her head despondently. "We can't, Cameron. Your face is all over the papers. Someone might recognise you – and I saw how you reacted back there." She was right: wherever we went, I would imagine people were staring, even if they weren't.

"Besides," she continued, "I might bump into someone I know. And right now, I'm not ready to cope with that either."

"Well, maybe we could meet tomorrow?"

"Please, Cameron," she implored, her little girl's face looking at me in the most appealing way. "I need to talk tonight... It would mean a lot. I've been hanging around the hospital lobby for ages because I don't want to be on my own... Not this evening."

I hesitated, and was instantly lost.

"Look," she said, capitalising on my indecision, "you drive to my house – I'll give you directions – and I'll get a taxi. Then we can have a drink and a chat." She smiled reassuringly and touched my arm. It felt nice. I guess I needed some company as well. "It will do us both good. We can help each other."

That was exactly what I wanted her to say. It was probably true. When I agreed, she beamed back at me, explaining the way to Hessle village and to her house. Then she was gone, off to find a cab, looking like everything was all right with the world.

I watched her go, shaking my head in disbelief. But it was a normal enough situation: we were both upset over the attack, both lonely, both frightened of the outside world. It was natural that we should be drawn to each other. She would want to know what had happened this morning, I wanted to ask her about her ex-girlfriend. Quid pro quo. Two people who needed each other.

But it felt surreal all the same. It was lucky I'd bumped into her like that. Magda's mother had said her daughter didn't have any friends, that she was too tied up with her work. Maybe she was mistaken. Maybe she didn't know her daughter was a lesbian.

Still, I'm never too sure about coincidence – especially when it keeps happening. There was a blue Astra behind me again, a few cars back. An Astra like the one that had kept driving round near the hospital. It had been there since I left the city centre. I knew because I had seen it follow me as I pulled out from the Infirmary.

I kept one side of my brain on the car and thought about Angel with the other. She seemed nice enough. Feminine. Attractive. But she puzzled me. When I'd shouted at her – after I ran out of the hospital – her eyes registered something close to fear. Then it passed. It seemed strange that she trusted me so much, so soon – enough to invite me back to her house. I could be anyone. For all she knew, I could be violent, I could have stabbed her ex. Yet here I was driving to meet her, in Hessle, at her home. It didn't seem like a sensible thing for her to be doing.

And just then, glancing back in my mirror, I began to wonder just how sensible it was for me.

I turned left off the main road, and down around the centre of Hessle, just like she'd said. The Astra was keeping well back, but it was still there, shadowing me around the winding, narrow streets of the old village. When I finally turned left into May Blossom Road, it carried on past the end and round the corner out of sight.

Maybe I was just being paranoid.

Angel's road was a pleasant cul-de-sac, a mixture of old and new houses, nestling together in a quiet area of Hull, close to the banks of the Humber. You would need some serious money to live there, where you could watch the traffic as it shuttled over the distant bridge every minute of the day and night. Angel's house was halfway down, set back a little off the road. It was a cottage, exactly like the ones you see in old pictures – right down to the wild-looking garden in the front and the rambling rose growing over the stone porch. Not the sort of place you would expect to find in the middle of Hull – and not at all the sort of place I would expect her to live.

I drove through the gates like she'd told me to, across the pea gravel drive, and waited. She wasn't far behind. And when the taxi drew up a few minutes later, I wondered if she might have reconsidered. I hoped not. I liked her and I was hungry for some company and relaxation. She paid the driver and walked across the gravel, beaming at me as if we were old friends.

"Are you sure you want to invite me in?" I asked, hoping for the right answer, but checking all the same. "You don't know me. I won't be offended. I could be dangerous."

She looked straight at me without a hint of irony in her voice. "Believe me, Cameron, I know dangerous when I see it, and it isn't you, love."

Inside, the lounge was bigger than I expected – and cosy: a mixture of old world and modern, liberally sprinkled with houseplants and post-impressionist prints. She knelt by the old brick fireplace and flames leapt up around some fake logs, slowly filling the oak-beamed room with the warmth and glow of what looked and felt like a real fire.

"Sit down." She smiled sociably, but still a little edgy. "A drink?"

"Thanks," I said, taking a seat on the ample chintz-covered settee in the centre of the room. "Campari and tonic if you have it. Beer if not."

"Campari?" She glanced sideways at me, screwing up her nose in the most attractive way. "Campari, Cameron? What kind of a drink's that?"

"It's bright red, and most people say it tastes like medicine." Not everyone appreciates my favourite drink.

"And does it?" she asked.

"Yeah..." I admitted. "I guess it does a bit."

"Ughh!" She made a face and smiled fleetingly. "Beer then. OK?"

She poured a Carlsberg into a long glass and passed it to me. Then she excused herself, saying she needed the toilet, and disappeared upstairs.

Whilst she was gone, I got up and looked around. I didn't know who Angel was, or what she did for a living, but for someone so young, she seemed to be doing well for herself. The room was expensively furnished and neat. The shelves on either side of the chimney breast were well stocked with books: cookery and history on one side and various kinds of fiction on the other. No lesbian books. Nothing political. It all looked very straight and very middle class.

I listened for any sound upstairs and, when there was none, went across to the dresser and opened the doors in the cupboard below. They contained tablecloths, coasters, a sewing kit – all the things I'd have expected to find in Angel's house. Then I tried the two drawers.

The left-hand drawer was no different: stationery items, stamps, a few packets of sweets, an old tobacco tin that contained a packet of Golden Virginia tobacco, some papers and some dope. Again, exactly what I might have expected. But the right drawer was different. It contained a miscellany of items, many of which looked out of place in her house: a packet of men's linen handkerchiefs, two tie-pins, shoelaces, and four packets of foreign rolling tobacco in bright blue plastic packets, called BlauBerg.

I heard Angel's feet above me and returned to studying the books.

Surprisingly, amongst the fiction, there were a few about real crime: a book detailing some particularly gruesome murders, complete with photographs, one on the modus operandi of major criminals, and a third about organised crime.

I was thumbing through the last one when she returned, her face radiant, and came across to stand beside me. She was smiling pleasantly, relaxed, her mood much better. That's when I should have noticed the signs. Me, of all people.

Instead, I held up the book. "This yours?" I asked in astonishment.

"No, of course not, silly!" She chortled. "Most of the books are my brother's. He's away at the moment. He's a business consultant; I keep house for him. He's into that sort of thing."

I smiled back, and sat down on the settee with my drink. She had an explanation for everything. "It's a lovely house, how long have you been here?"

She poured herself a neat whisky and sat down next to me, her legs crossed tidily, like they teach you in deportment classes. Close enough for me to smell her perfume, but not so close that we touched. "Oh, only about a year, it's rented. I've lived with Martin for a lot longer though. It's convenient and his work takes him all over, so I see a bit of the world. We've lived in Paris and Berlin... all over the place." Her voice sounded like she was thrilled at the life. But her eyes told a different story.

I took a mouthful of beer, as she lit a cigarette. "You said you needed to talk to me, Angel. Why?"

She shrugged her shoulders, unhappiness crossing her face. "Because you were there when she was attacked. Because you probably saved her life. Because I'm upset and I want to know how it happened." She bit her lip and lifted her eyes up to mine. Little girl lost, again. "I thought you might like some company too. It must have been hard for you today. You were really stressed back there at the hospital."

"Yes," I said appreciatively, raising my glass to her. "I must admit that it's really nice to relax for a while."

She smiled, a warm, full-faced smile. "I'm glad you came."

So was I. But I would have to take her word that she was Magda Swinson's ex. That she was lesbian. She didn't advertise her sexuality at all, like so many dykes do, including me. She was very chic, and almost middle class, but somehow not quite. There was more than a touch of streetwise experience there as well. Cute though. Good looking, intelligent, sharp as well. But, as we sat there together, I was increasingly getting the feeling that she was trying to lead me. She'd made all the moves to get me here. Now it seemed like she was positioning and repositioning herself, giving me opportunities that I'd rather not have. Under normal circumstances, it might have been tempting. But not today and not with her. I was far more interested in what she had to tell me.

Besides, I was still trying to work her out. There were too many contradictions in her behaviour. For a start, she didn't look the type who'd befriend the woman suspected of stabbing her ex-girlfriend. I felt like I was missing something.

"How come you trust me?" I asked, letting my puzzlement show. "As far as you know, I could be guilty. It really could have been me who put the knife in."

"No chance, Cameron!" She laughed lightly at the silliness of the notion and stubbed out the half-smoked cigarette. Then she got up from her seat and walking across to the sideboard. "I know it wasn't you," she said, looking back over her shoulder. "For a start, you didn't even know her. And I don't believe that stupid story about road rage either."

I followed her with my eyes. She looked good. "I can assure you that there are plenty of others who would have a real motive." She pulled open the left-hand drawer and took the tin out before returning to her seat. She sat closer this time, so we were nearly touching. "Anyway, Cameron, you seem like one of the good guys to me. I thought so from your picture in the press. Now I'm quite certain."

"You have a nice line in flattery, Angel. But there's a certain

Superintendent of Police who would definitely disagree with you."

"Yeah, well, maybe he would," she said, lifting the lid off the tin and holding up a generous lump of almost black hashish, looking at me meaningfully. "But then, I don't reckon people like that. How about you?"

"I have my reservations," I replied.

"Mmm, after today, I bet you have, Cameron." She took the packet of Rizlas out of the tin, pulling five papers out and starting to assemble them.

"The thing is," she continued, sprinkling some of the Golden Virginia along the papers, "I know that Magda has made a lot of enemies in her time." She grunted. "Don't get me wrong, she's a nice woman, but a little too tied up in her work."

"That's more or less what her mother said. She's a research scientist, isn't she? Lots of scientists are workaholics."

She shook her head. "That isn't what I mean," she said, holding the resin over the flame of her lighter. "She's a workaholic all right, but the reason she makes enemies is because she's a genetic scientist. She experiments on animals."

"Yes, I know."

The sharp, fruity smell of the dope was drifting past my nose now. Amsterdam... The squat café... coffee bars... long relaxing nights... Hellen.

I swallowed hard, putting her out of my mind. "What exactly does Magda do?"

"Like it says in the paper, she works for a firm in North Lincolnshire, GME Technologies, just over the bridge. They specialise in genetically modified organisms; but with animals, not plants." She sprinkled the resin on top of the tobacco. "Cloning, that sort of thing."

"And the enemies she's made. They're the animal rights protesters, I suppose?"

She wet the edge of the papers with her tongue and rolled the joint between her fingers and thumb. "Yeah, there aren't a lot of them. Most just picket the main gate." She paused and tore off some card to make a roach, rolled it between her fingers and slipped it into the end of the papers. "But a few of them are pretty wild –" she tapped the joint on the tin and twisted the end "– even violent. Threats, bricks through windows... that sort of thing." She lit the end and took a long drag, holding the smoke in her lungs and closing her eyes.

Charlie was one of them, no doubt. And Jean, maybe.

After the second toke, she passed the joint to me. I should have said, 'No thanks, Angel,' but I didn't. It had been a difficult day and I needed something to help me wind down. A few drags on the joint would do no harm.

"So what are you saying?" I asked, pulling the heavy, acrid smoke deep into my lungs and holding it there a while before breathing out again. "Are you saying you think it was an animal rights protester that attacked Magda?"

"Probably." She moved very close to me, so our bodies were touching. By the third drag I could feel my muscles relaxing and my head taking on a warm, soft, comfortable glow. "I can't think of anyone else who would do it. And I know they threatened her." I passed the joint back and she drew on it a few more times without speaking, her eyes closed as she enjoyed the sensation. Then she held it out to me again and continued.

"I kept telling her to be careful, but she was so damn passionate about her work. She wore her career like a fur coat, Cameron, and flaunted it in front of all the wrong people."

Probably not a good move, I had to agree. Shit, but this stuff was really good.

"It only takes one person. Somebody with a grudge, someone who gets a little too angry. There are plenty like that in the animal rights movement. Look... I don't agree with animal experimentation..."

Yeah, good. I was beginning to wonder...

"But there is a limit. Some of them are no more than terrorists."

She shook her head with conviction. "I just know it was one of them who attacked Magda. She said they had already threatened her – told her to resign or face the consequences. Uh, she wouldn't, of course." She threw her head back in disapproval. "Told them to fuck off!"

I took another long drag and offered the butt end to her, but she waved it away, letting me finish it off.

Yes, even though I didn't know her at all, the way Magda had fought on the bridge had given all the appearances of strength. And even if I didn't approve of the work she did, I still admired her courage. I leant back against the settee, and took a swig of my second beer, straight from the bottle this time.

Angel leaned against my shoulder and looked up at me with her big emerald eyes. "Did Magda say anything to you?"

"Like what?" I asked, bells – slightly muffled bells – ringing in my head.

She shrugged. "Anything. Anything that might give a clue to who had stabbed her."

"She mentioned a name," I said carefully, aware of the effect the dope was having on me – and aware too of Angel's closeness, the smell of her perfume, the soft warmth of her body. "I heard her say a name, that's all – Joanna Whittling – is she a friend? Do you know her?"

She thought for a moment and then, surprisingly, shook her head. "No, the name doesn't mean anything to me."

"Are you sure?" I asked in disbelief.

"… No, she never mentioned her… What else did she say?"

"Nothing," I lied. Even with the dope caressing my brain, I was disappointed. From the few words that Magda had managed to say, I had been certain that she knew Joanna Whittling well.

"You sure, Cameron? She must have said more than just a name."

"Not another word," I answered.

Angel looked downcast for a moment. But for someone who had smoked half a joint and drunk two whiskies, she was acting a lot sharper than me. Or maybe it was the effect of the dope on my perception.

Whatever she'd put in the joint was strong, really strong, and I was already having to concentrate very hard to take in what she was saying.

"I'm really worried, Cameron," she confided, leaning into me. "Those people will stop at nothing. I'm really scared for her."

I put my hand on her arm, reassuring her, but already struggling to remember what the fuck our conversation was about. "I'm sure it will be all right, Angel," I muttered. "The police are with her now – no one can harm her...

"How long have you known her?" I asked, trying to keep with it.

"Almost a year. We met in the Polar Bear when I first came to Hull. Neither of us was out, we were both sort of drifting around, scared of who we were. We got talking... and, well, one thing led to another. It was great. We spent a lot of time together in there. It was just about the only place she felt safe."

"So what went wrong?"

She smiled wistfully and finished her drink, before pouring herself another generous measure from the bottle at her side and passing me a beer from the supply on the floor. "Oh, what you would expect, I suppose. She was desperately scared of being outed, what with the animal rights lot and everything. Said that it would be the end of her career. That she might be blackmailed, that she would be fired... That's why she would never let me meet her mother." She shook her head and her hair shone in the soft light, framing her face. "We split after a few months. I kept in touch, but it wasn't ever going to be the same."

She turned her head towards me, her eyes sharp and enquiring. "Cameron, she must have known who attacked her. Are you sure she didn't say anything?"

I shook my head. Shit, I wanted to tell her. I needed to tell someone. And she knew the woman. Even if Magda Swinson's message was confidential, it would surely be all right to let her, of all people, in on the secret. She could help me. It seemed so obvious. And yet, there was still something inside me untouched by the alcohol, the dope and the closeness of her body. Somehow, through all the fuzziness inside, I heard myself insisting, again, that all Magda had said was the name.

Angel leant into me some more, her small breasts pressing against my own, unmistakably inviting me to try something. The light, honey-like fragrance on her skin had already begun to envelop me. For a moment, I was captivated: dazzled by her slender, vulnerable body, enchanted by her sweet child-like face, and drawn dangerously into her spell.

I thought about Hellen: how for months, I'd been faithful; how I'd denied myself so many opportunities, because I was happy just with her. It didn't matter now. I was free. I didn't need to hold back. Our faces moved closer and as her lips parted, enticing me, drawing me towards her, I almost fell into those deliciously wet, emerald eyes.

Before I knew what was happening, we were in a deep embrace, our tongues exploring, her hands roaming freely over my body. God, it felt so good. Too good.

Stoned as I was, I thought back to Magda Swinson lying on the bridge, like she was dying, her mouth moving slowly, painfully. Suddenly, this closeness with Angel – her ex-girlfriend – seemed quite wrong.

"I'm sorry, Angel. This isn't right. I can't," I muttered, pulling away and hating myself for it.

"It's all right, Cameron," she whispered, holding on to me and nibbling my ear, "we're not doing anything wrong. A little love-giving, that's all. We both need it. It doesn't have to go any further."

She was right. I did need it. And it was nice – very nice. The warmth of her body, the softness of her touch and the fragrance of her skin: they were all working on me; making me feel good, relaxed and safe again, after a day filled with horror and frustration. I let her pull me down onto the settee, taking comfort in her arms, enjoying the sweetness of her warmth.

"Was it awful?" she asked, kissing my neck.

A shiver of desire ran through me, mingling with the memory of those dreadful few minutes on the bridge. "Yes, it was. The man was vicious. He was trying to throw her into the river. She was hanging onto the railings for dear life. Then he just pulled out a knife and stabbed her... There was nothing I could do, Angel."

"Oh, poor Cameron." She stroked my head, comforting me, pulling me closer. "Did he go for you as well?"

"No he didn't," I said, and wondered again, even through the dope-induced haze, why he'd spared me.

"Mmm, but did you see his face? Could you identify him?"

"No, nothing, not even his eyes." I snuggled into her soft, inviting neck, pushing away her hair and kissing the scented skin. I was tired of answering all her questions. Why did she keep on asking more?

"You didn't see anything at all that might help to find him?"

"No, I've told you," I replied distractedly, stroking her belly. "His face and eyes were covered. I wouldn't recognise him again if I bumped into him tonight."

"Good," she murmured, and I looked up at her, into a face that seemed strangely pleased. She saw my puzzled expression. "It's good that you can't identify him, Cameron. It means that you're safe." She smiled at me and shifted down, against my breast. I could feel her warm breath through my T-shirt, the softness of her lips against my nipple. I sat up again, drunkenly trying to get my feet onto the ground, telling myself that I shouldn't be doing this, and taking another swig of beer as my Common Sense argued with my Libido. Angel draped an arm around my neck and rested her head dreamily against my shoulder.

Shit, let them fight it out, I was enjoying myself.

"And all she said was the name of that woman?"

I breathed in sharply, to stop myself blurting out the rest.

She gave me a look, sensing that I was on the verge of saying more. And waited. Her eyes connected with mine: inviting, warm, sympathetic. 'Let me help,' they said.

"She gave me a message, Angel," I confessed. God help me. "An e-mail address and a password. An e-mail address that contains a file. An important file which I promised to deliver to the woman she spoke of – Joanna Whittling."

She pulled me close, running her fingers lightly across my thighs. "I still can't remember her mentioning anyone of that name, Cameron. Have you had a look at this file? Do you know what it is? Does it explain why Magda was attacked like that?"

"I must be going," I said, standing up shakily. In amongst the dope and the alcohol and the passion, Hellen kept fighting her way into my mind: her familiarity, her smell, the way she always knew what turned me on. "I've had a long day. I need to find a hotel."

"No, Cameron, don't go, please," she pleaded. "Stay with me – for a while at least."

She pulled me down onto the couch and pressed her body against mine, finding my mouth and kissing me deeply.

I pulled away. "Angel, why are you asking so many questions?" Things were getting out of hand. I'd never intended that we would go this far.

"Cameron, I was in love with her once. She's still a dear friend. I just want to know everything, that's all. I want to help her." She nibbled at my ear, whispering. "I want to help you, as well."

Hell! I ran my fingers over her back as she played with the nape of my neck. Shockwaves of passion were exploding all over me now and the tiny voice of reason was fading fast. It seemed so obvious. Of course she wanted to know – of course she wanted to help.

"Did you read the file, Cameron? Did it say anything that might help?"

She moaned as I brought my hand up and across her belly, cupping her breast. Her body arched slightly as my fingers brushed the nipple through the fabric.

"Did you?"

"No, I didn't!" I gasped in frustration, wanting to forget about everything but the passion of the moment. "Forget the bloody file, will you!"

She drew back, her lips trembling with passion. And I smiled, feeling warm, excited – ten miles high.

"You can stay the night if you want."

I nodded. Fuck Hellen. "Yeah, I'd like that. But no more questions, OK?"

She smiled again, her eyes animated. I slipped the dress off her shoulders and unclipped her bra. She pulled off my vest and buried her head in my breasts, running her lips over my skin and teasing my nipples; leaving me gasping for air, making me wet. I slid my hand up her bare legs and inside her briefs, caressing her belly, stroking the damp hair below it with my fingertips.

"Wait," she said, "I need the loo first."

I sighed and rolled away from her. "Hurry up," I groaned. "I can't wait."

"Me neither. I won't be long."

As she disappeared up the stairs, I leant back on the settee, aroused now by alcohol, dope, and by her – drunk three times over. My need to question her was a distant memory; her curiosity over the file, somehow unimportant.

It may have only been a few minutes but, in my stoned mind, she seemed to have been gone a long time. I followed her up the stairs, thinking she might be waiting for me in the bedroom. But she wasn't, so I made for the bathroom, where the light was on and the door slightly ajar. She jumped when she saw me and instinctively tried to hide the needle, and the cord which she was just releasing from around her arm.

She looked more like a schoolgirl now, caught smoking in the toilets. But I didn't care. "You ready?"

She smiled, pleased that I wasn't angry. "You want some smack?" she asked, holding up the syringe, her eyes sparkling.

"No." I staggered through the door, taking the needle off her and putting it by the washbasin. "I want you."

I took her slender, almost weightless body in my arms and she groaned in response, tearing at my jeans, then running her fingers down over my belly and into my briefs, tantalising me, making me cry out for more.

Then we were lying naked on her bed, devouring each other with our mouths, my hands roaming across her breasts, across the soft skin of her belly, and down. She groaned loudly, pulling my body close to hers, so close that I could hardly breathe.

"Fill me, Cameron," she cried urgently, "fill me up."

I slid two fingers in, waiting for her to do the same with me. But her hands were on the bed frame, holding on. Her body arched up and she began to shake wildly.

"More! Give me more!" she screamed. "Take me...! Fuck me... Harder!"

I pushed in a third and then a fourth finger. Still she shouted out for more, her face wreathed in a mixture of pain and ecstasy. I eased in my thumb as well, till my whole fist was inside her.

"Yes!" she screamed, more in pain than pleasure. "Go on... Go on."

I didn't know whether it was me or her. But right then, my euphoria dissolved. This sex, which had started out so well, was becoming too violent, too one-sided. There's a point where even the most enthusiastic fucking can begin to seem like abuse, and suddenly I was stone-cold sober. My passion had evaporated, my willingness to service her like this was spent. I withdrew my hand and rolled onto my back.

"What's the matter?" she asked, moving onto her side, her eyes betraying a mixture of puzzlement and anger.

"I can't do it," I replied, not knowing what else to say. "I can't do it. I'm sorry, I should never have stayed."

She fell silent then: the barren, spiteful silence of rejection.

"I'm sorry," I repeated, trying to smooth things over.

"You should be!" she spat back. "Some fucking butch lesbian you turned out to be!"

I winced. I shouldn't have encouraged her. I shouldn't have let it get this far.

We both lay there for a while on our backs, staring at the ceiling. I felt like shit. I'd had a hard enough day without her abuse. I know full well that one-night stands never work, yet I'd allowed myself to get involved, to be led along by someone I didn't even know – and on the strength of the last half-hour, someone I didn't want to know any more.

I got up off the bed and got dressed, as she continued to sulk.

"You inject a lot?" I asked, annoyed that I hadn't spotted it earlier.

"That's my business, Cameron," she replied sharply.

"Yeah well, you should be careful. You look like you're shooting up too much for it to be just recreational."

She grunted and got out of bed, grabbing a dressing gown and putting it on. "I'll see you to the door."

I followed her, angry and hurt. My head ached from the sudden come-down. My body felt heavy. I was tired and irritable and I couldn't take any more.

"Don't bother, I'll let myself out," I snapped, petulant on the outside, while inside, my emotions were going through hoops.

When she slammed the door behind me, I couldn't remember all that I'd said earlier. But I could remember that I'd talked about the e-mail address, the password and the file.

I shook my head as I got back on my bike.

Cameron, why did you do that? What in heaven's name were you thinking of?

## Ten

As I drove back up May Blossom Road, I was still beating myself up for being so stupid. But by the time I was riding along Hessle Road towards the city centre, I was reasoning it out a bit more. I suppose I couldn't blame Angel for wanting some answers. If one of my friends – one of my ex-girlfriends – had been attacked and hospitalised, then I would have been exactly the same. I would want to know every detail. Wouldn't I?

But, however understandable her curiosity might have been, I still had an empty feeling inside. I'd done the one thing that I'd promised Magda I wouldn't do. I just hoped Angel would treat my confidence with respect – in spite of the way we'd parted. Maybe she would. But the thought made me uneasy. She wasn't the woman I'd taken her for. All evening I'd been drawn to her. I liked her. Yet, when it came to intimacy... I felt almost abused by the way she'd behaved in bed.

But was it her – or was it me?

Whether I liked myself for it or not, I'd found myself comparing Angel with Hellen from the moment we started to get close. A little voice at the back of my head, ticking off the pluses and the minuses of every touch and every kiss. Hellen won by streets. How could she fail to?

I was driving into the city again. I don't know why. I hadn't even thought about it. All I knew was that I had to find somewhere to sleep, a hotel room where I could lock the door behind me and find some solitude. I needed to recharge after all the shit of the day.

It was nearly ten o'clock. As I drove along the big dual carriageway, I could feel the wind nudging me towards the kerb as it swept in from the sea and through the city, penetrating everything with its salty dampness.

And there was something else. Since I left the village, the blue Astra had been dawdling innocently in my wake, about a hundred yards back. The same car. It had to be. And driven by a man.

A cold tingle ran through my body. I'd been the only witness. For some reason that I couldn't fathom, he'd let me go, at the time. Now, maybe, he was looking for an opportunity to get me on my own.

For a moment, I thought about making a run for it: accelerate, leave him behind, get out of the city. But if he was the killer, he wouldn't leave it at that. Thanks to the tabloid, everything about me was public knowledge now: the city I lived in, my job... even my sexuality was pretty clear from that photo... If he didn't get me tonight, he would be waiting for me tomorrow, or the day after.

The car stayed on my tail as I drove into the city. It followed me as I turned left up Ferensway. And it was right behind me by the time I drove under the run-down frontage of Paragon Station. I pulled into the kerb and locked the bike. The Astra drove past, into the side street. I stowed my helmet in the box on the back, then walked in a slow and controlled manner through the old-fashioned lobby and onto the almost deserted concourse.

It was just as I remembered it from when I came as a child with my auntie, and I wished I was five again, visiting the one woman in my family, other than my sister, who had ever shown me any real love. There was the old wooden newsagent's kiosk, the high vaulted roof, and even the pigeons we used to feed. But there were additions too, and they looked out of place: the new shops and cafés – and the modern travel centre. I glanced nervously around, looking for my tail, still praying I'd somehow made a mistake and there had been no one in particular, just another blue Astra going the same way as me.

And when I looked around the concourse, there was hardly anyone about. An old man was drinking from a bottle of cider on one of the benches; a group of young people were checking the train times and joking with each other; a man was holding onto a woman with a suitcase, kissing, saying goodbye.

I swallowed hard. He must be somewhere, watching me and wondering if I was going to make a run for it. The lights were still on in the travel centre, so I went in and walked up to the counter, asking for details of train times. Whilst the clerk talked to me, I took out my purse and made as if paying for tickets, then walked out. As I turned the corner, I glimpsed him leaning against a pillar in the shadows. He was the same size as the knifeman, the same build.

The memory of the morning flooded back. The fog. The MGB. Her screams. Her blood. The man in the black raincoat.

Maybe a near-deserted railway station wasn't the best place for this. But maybe I didn't have much choice any more.

I headed for the platforms, looking like I was leaving. I walked casually, but with my heart in my mouth, around the travel centre and out of his line of vision. Then I sprinted through the gates onto the deserted platform and slipped behind the waiting room, pressing my body against the wall, out of sight of the platform entrance. I tried to breathe quietly and ignore the thumping of my heart, the panic bubbling up inside me. I knew he must be right behind. I hoped he would want to know where I was. I hoped he would come and look for me.

He did. And when he walked past, I was ready for him.

"Who are you?" I yelled at the back of his head, ready to run if I had to.

He spun round aggressively, his fists out in front of him. Then, as he took me in, his face broke into a broad smile and he swaggered towards me, laughing.

I stepped back, holding up my hand, and he stopped. I didn't want him near me.

He looked like a down-and-out at first glance. His clothes were shabby and not too clean – a grubby khaki jacket and faded, torn denims. A pair of old, stained trainers were on his feet. He could have been a user, or a traveller, or just homeless. But when I looked at his face, I saw something different. His head and face were smoothly shaven and he looked like he took rather more care of himself than his clothes. He was in his forties, fit and well nourished, with eyes that were bright and alert. And now, as he watched me, he looked friendlier, relaxed. This was someone who, clothes apart, didn't look like a thug. And he didn't look like he was going to kill me.

I stood back, arms folded, my heart settling back to normal, the sweat on the back of my neck growing cold.

"You're following me!" I said, refusing to be seduced by his smile.

He shook his head, pleasure and recognition in his eyes. "It is you, isn't it? McGill? Cameron McGill." Then he leant forward and took my hand. This was bizarre.

"You don't remember me, do you?"

I shook my head. I'd never seen the guy in my life before.

"Bernie!" he said, gesticulating excitedly. "Bernie Marton! About six years ago. You must remember!" He sighed heavily in animated frustration. "I was on heroin, you helped me off it, got me probation... Yeah?"

"No," I replied, shaking my head, searching my memory, "I can't have, I've only been doing that job for five years."

"Well, it must be five years, then. I've got a lousy memory."

I shook my head. "Sorry... No, I still don't remember..."

He laughed and then slapped his own head theatrically. "Hah! I'm bloody stupid aren't I? Sorry, Cameron. I had long hair and a beard when I last saw you. And, shit, you must have dealt with loads of smack-heads since then! It's not surprising that you can't remember all of us."

I smiled weakly. I hate it when ex-clients reappear with their life stories – especially on a day like today, especially when they stalk me. I wanted to tell him to go away and leave me alone. That was my job, this is my personal space – now get the fuck out of it!

"I'm sorry, er, Bernie, I don't remember you." I stared at him coldly, remembering how scared he'd made me. "But I do know that you've been following me, and I don't like that very much."

He laughed again, more nervously this time. "Ahh. I'm sorry, Cameron. I wasn't too sure it was you. I saw your mug-shot in the local rag and then, when I was on my way past the Infirmary, I thought I saw you come out of the car park. I thought it was you, but I wasn't totally certain – you've changed a bit... Anyways, I followed you for a while just to make sure... Then you went into that woman's house and I thought I shouldn't intrude. Sorry, it was a bit thoughtless." He looked down at the platform for a moment. "It's just that... Well, to be honest, I was worried when I saw you'd been arrested and... y'know... I thought I might be able to help in some way... repay the favour, as it were. You helped me a lot, back then in York." He put his head on one side and looked at me, a bit like a cornered rabbit. "Sorry, girl, didn't mean to frighten you!"

"You didn't frighten me, Bernie." I shook my head in dismay. "You scared the fucking shit out of me. Have you any inkling of what I've been through today? The last thing I needed was some guy stalking me in the shadows."

He grinned sheepishly. The orange station lights reflected off his head making him look like a stand-in for a Tango ad.

"Well... I'm glad you're still clean," I conceded. "You look good. I'm pleased about that."

"Yeah." He looked down and kicked a cigarette butt, sending it skittling off the edge of the platform. "Yeah, I'm grateful, man. I never got the chance to tell you. You did a good job, you were there when I needed you."

He walked around the side of the waiting room and sat on one of the bright red benches that faced the lines. I followed and sat next to him. In truth, there *was* something strangely familiar about him. And it's true, I have counselled a lot of users in the last few years. Even so, I could remember most of them. Even racking my brains, I couldn't place him.

He offered me a Marlboro. From the way he dressed, I would have expected roll-ups. Or a cheaper brand at least. Then again, his car looked nearly new as well. There was a paradox between the way this man dressed and the rest of his style.

"No thanks. Gave up years ago."

"Yeah, suppose I should as well. But, oh I dunno, it's not such a bad habit compared to the other stuff, is it?" He lit the cigarette and took a long drag, resting his arms on his knees, then turned to look at me, smiling. "God, Cameron, it's really nice to see you again... So... are you OK? With the stabbing, I mean. I wouldn't want to see you in shit with the pigs."

"I'm fine," I reassured him. In spite of my earlier anger, I was touched by his concern. "They have no real evidence against me. Just wishful thinking. You know what they're like."

"Yeah, tell me about it! That's why it sounds like such bad shit, love – being held for knifing her. Fuck! You wanna talk about it?"

I shook my head. "No. Not at all. I'm sick to death of talking about it, today. I've done little else. What I want to do, right now, is get to bed and then, sometime soon, go home. Just as soon as I've fulfilled a promise."

"To do with the stabbing?"

Why should he think I meant that? "No, Bernie, my mother. She's in a nursing home at Barton. I promised to pay her a visit," I answered easily. "And don't worry about me, please, everything will be fine once the forensic reports are through."

"Yeah, well, I hope so, Cameron, I wouldn't want to see you in any trouble. You're a special sort of lady, y'know, and I owe you. Just shout if you need any help – y'know, a good lawyer or some bread."

"Thanks Bernie, that's good of you. But what about you, what are you doing now – you don't exactly look like you've gone all respectable."

"Came into some money, didn't I?" He smiled to himself, enjoying some private irony. "So now I do a bit of this, bit of that. Great to have that sort of freedom – to do the things you want and not to have to take the shit that life doles out."

"Yeah, I can imagine."

He lit another cigarette. The platform was deserted except for the late-night cleaning crews boarding the trains on the far platform, chatting and laughing amongst themselves as they caught up on each other's day.

"At the moment I'm indulging my passion for animals..." He looked at me, waiting for a reaction.

"You working at a zoo or something?" I said, stupidly.

He guffawed and threw his empty cigarette packet onto the railway lines. "No Cameron, I'm not working at a zoo. I'm with the protest, over at Barton. We're trying to stop the tests on animals at a place called GME Technologies."

I turned and looked at him. Like I say, I'm never too sure about co-incidence.

"That's where the woman who was stabbed worked. I was there earlier," I blurted out.

"Yeah, I know, it's a pisser, Cameron. The police are giving us hell."

"Yeah, they told me. Usual pattern, Bernie. Go for anyone who's different – we're easy targets, aren't we?"

"Too true. Hey, if you're over that side seeing your mum tomorrow, you will come over and see me again, won't you?"

"Yeah well, I don't think so. I've already been, and the others were pretty hostile."

"Ahh, don't worry about that lot, they're a bit strange sometimes, but they mean well." He put his hand on my shoulder. "Come and see me there, tomorrow, I'd like that."

I shook my head, but really I didn't have a lot of choice. I still needed help. I still needed to find Joanna Whittling. And I had to take every option offered.

Besides, like Bernie said, he owed me.

## Eleven

I'm on a narrow rope bridge that sways high above a black chasm. It's stormy and I'm hanging onto the sides for dear life, straining to pull myself along the ramshackle footway towards a woman in a mauve jacket with soaking, matted hair. She screams hysterically, pointing towards the shadow that descends towards her. "It's all right," I keep yelling, "I'm coming." But she can't hear above the howling wind and the driving rain. "I'm coming!" I stretch out my arm to her, again and again. But she's always just beyond my reach.

Then he's towering above her, in black from head to foot, with a white hole where his face should be. He raises his arm far above his head, clenching a long-bladed dagger.

"No!" I scream, struggling frantically; flying into the air as the gale sweeps my feet off the ground; clinging to the rope handrail; pulling myself along its length, lunging for his wrist... But the bridge pitches violently. I'm back where I started, on my back too far away, watching his hand falling slowly, horribly, into her belly. Over and over, gouging. She turns her head towards me. The big eyes are reproachful. Blood runs from the corners of her mouth, down her neck onto her coat.

Then it is perfectly quiet. The deep, eerie silence of death. He's gone. I pick myself up. The ground beneath me is solid again. There are just the two of us. And she smiles and turns her back on me, unharmed.

When I reach out and touch her shoulder, she is naked and I step back in astonishment at the sight of her body. She's painfully thin, her skin a dead white membrane covering pink bones. She twists her head and looks into my eyes... Angel. For God's sake, it's Angel. She's smiling through a bloody face, licking her lips. I try and look away, my stomach heaving. But when I turn back, it's Hellen, crying, holding her head. And pointing at me, as if possessed.

"Ice 'em... Ice 'em..." she hisses. And I cover my ears in terror at the sound. I'm running, stumbling, falling through a tunnel of trees. But her voice follows in my wake: a swarm of insects, wrapping itself around my head, buzzing through my ears. "Ice 'em... Ice 'em..."

I spin round in panic, beating the air, driving them off. But they multiply as they fall back, growing into a furious mob that snaps at my heels, baying for blood: a big man with a noose in his hand, blinking, saliva falling from his lips; a man with no hair, wielding a knife; an old woman screaming abuse... A raggle-taggle mob howling my name. Becky's desperate voice is wailing through the treetops: "Save yourself, Cameron. Get away..."

But my legs won't work any more. I fall to the ground, exhausted. I fight them off with my arms as their hands maul me... dragging my jacket from my back, tearing at my boots... Now I'm high up in the air. Their hands are beneath me, passing my body over the heads of a chanting, screaming rabble... I'm at the edge, then, helpless, tumbling into a deep chasm... falling... spiralling... diving into the flames of hell...

Fire engines; I hear fire engines. Their sirens cut through the smoke and the heat. They're tuneful... playing a melody... bleeping...

I shook my head. I could see curtains. Daylight. I screwed up my eyes. The bleeping went on, incessantly... And I groaned, turning in the big bed and adjusting to reality, before reaching out for the mobile.

"Hello," I croaked, trying to figure out where the hell I was.

There was a second's silence. "Hello Cameron, it's Hellen."

I struggled to sit up and focus my brain. We'd parted two days ago in anger. Now her voice was here in bed with me, and my emotional defences weren't even switched on yet.

"Hello Hellen," I managed, after a pause.

"Cameron... lievling... Are you all right?" she asked, her voice loaded with concern.

"Yes... I'm fine... you woke me up." I ran my fingers through my hair and shut my eyes. My stomach was still jumping through hoops; my head still spinning from the terror of the endlessly replaying dreams. Her voice took me back there. *"Ice... 'em..."*

"Cam, I'm really sorry we fought the other day. It's not what I intended, honestly."

"Huh." I still couldn't think straight.

"Cameron, talk to me. I don't want it to be this way. Please." She sounded sensible and grown-up. Just like always.

I closed my eyes. She was the last person I wanted to speak to right now.

"You chose the rules, not me, Hellen," I blurted out. "I just wanted a holiday with you, remember? It was you who said your work had to come first."

"I didn't say that, Cameron," she answered patiently. "All I said was my career was important to me. I realise now that you maybe don't want the same things as me. But we can work it out, darling. I'm sorry I got angry. I didn't want you to leave..."

"Well, I'd hate to come between you and the Politie, Hellen," I snapped.

"Oh, Cameron! It had nothing to do with that, you know it hadn't." Her voice was full of regret and for some reason that made me even angrier. "I'm sorry that you reacted the way you did. I thought you'd be pleased."

"About you going back on duty? Why would I be pleased about that?" I gasped, trying to keep my voice steady.

"Cameron, it isn't about that, is it? All this anger and recrimination." She sighed. "We had a really nice few days together. It was only when I asked you to come and live with me that everything started falling apart. I thought it was what you wanted as well."

For a moment I couldn't talk. Thoughts were milling around in my head like fish in a pond, randomly bumping into each other, as I tried to sort them into some kind of coherence. I knew how I felt. I just couldn't put it into words, that's all.

"Cameron? Are you still there?"

I did the best I could, trying to keep the bitterness out of my voice. "Like I said, Hellen. It'll never work. Your career will always come first."

"Oh darling, that's just not true. It is important to me and some-times I have to give it priority. Sometimes I have no choice. That doesn't mean we can't be happy together."

"There's always a choice, Hellen," I snapped back. "You just took the wrong one, that's all."

Silence.

Then her patient reply: "I did what I had to do, Cameron, that's all. I'm a senior police officer. I've been investigating Langstein's Dutch connections for months, you know that. I had to be there. You know that his rallies were illegal. He's been doing this all over Europe. Really, Cameron. For you, of all people, to complain about me helping to stop a mob of neo-Nazis..."

"But you didn't stop them, did you?" I retorted, wounded by the truth in her words.

"We contained them, Cameron, that's all that we could hope to do," she explained calmly. "If we hadn't been there, they would have gone on the rampage. We had to let them go ahead in the end, to maintain order. There were just too many of them."

Silence.

"Cameron, look, I don't want to argue. But what is more important – us spending an extra day together, or me helping to restrain a dan-gerous bigot, who's obsessed with power? You're usually so aware. What's wrong with you? Can't you see that Langstein and his cronies need stopping? He might have a better line in PR, but the man's no better than Hitler! Can't you understand that I had to go back on duty and help?"

"I'm not arguing just about that, Hellen." We'd been through all this two days ago. There was no point in recycling it again. "I'm not talking just about Langstein. There'll always be something, won't there? Last time it was a big diamond fraud, this time it was him, next time it will be something else. You expect me to come and live with you and be the good little wife? To sit at home and keep house, whilst you go chasing criminals and bent politicians?"

"You just can't cope with it, can you?

"I've told you. You're a cop. You'll always be tied up in your work."

"I don't mean that, Cameron. You just can't take affection, can you? You were perfectly all right until I asked you to come and live with me. Until I said that I wanted us to be together always. That's when it all started, isn't it?"

"I can't come and live with you, Hellen. I've got my job to think of."

"You said you were fed up with your job and wanted a change. A new start. Lievling, I wouldn't have asked you otherwise."

I leant back against the headboard. Part of me desperately wanted to see her again. Part of me never wanted any contact, ever. I pulled the duvet around me and stared at the light flooding in through the curtains, trying to rein in the panic that was coursing through my body. It would be easier if she would just lose her temper.

"I didn't mean I wanted to move in with you. I never said anything about getting married!"

I could see her, sitting there in her dressing gown, curled up on the settee. Blonde hair still tousled from sleep. Her bright blue eyes, her clean, soft complexion. The way she always wanted to do things for me. The way she was always trying to look after me. Keep me safe. Please me. I felt sick inside.

She was getting angry now. "That's it, isn't it? That's the problem!"

She made it all sound so simple. Like I had obligations and I was running away from them. "You said I was different from the others. You said I was special. Hell, Cameron, you kept telling me you loved me..."

"Yeah well... I thought I did," I snapped.

"And you don't any more?" She sounded tearful. Like I'd crushed all her hopes and thrown them to the wind.

"No... Yes... Oh I don't know, Hellen. Yes I do... We're different, that's all."

Silence.

"... Look, please let's try again, Cam. If you don't want commitment, then we'll carry on as we are. We can work it out, lievling. Please, I don't want to lose you."

It sounded reasonable. Yet even the idea of seeing her scared me now. "I don't know, Hellen. Maybe it's too late. Things have changed. You'll always be waiting for the day when I change my mind. And I'm not going to."

"I don't think so, Cameron. I think you want the same as me. You're just frightened, that's all. For the first time in your life you've let yourself fall in love and it feels scary. That's all it is."

"How can you know what I want?" I retorted, pushing away all the feelings except my anger. "I was happy as we were. Now it's different. Now I know that you want more than I can give you."

"Please, lievling. I love you, and I know that you love me. That's what matters. We can work round everything else. Please think about it."

Why didn't she just get angry? Tell me that I was a shit. Put the phone down. Anything.

"I'm not going to give up on you, Cameron, you know that. You're too important to me."

Silence.

"Can I write to you?" she asked, searching for a way forward.

"Yes, if you want," I answered, hoping that might get her off my back.

"You'll write back?"

"I'll try."

"Cameron…"

"Yes?"

"I do care about you…"

"I know you do, Hellen. And I care about you too. I'm sorry."

I don't know how long I sat there on the bed, staring at the phone in my hand and wondering what was wrong with me. She was a nice woman. I liked her a lot. And there was no doubt that she loved me. But, somehow, ever since we'd met, there had been something that got in the way. Maybe she was right… Huh, maybe Becky was right as well… I was scared. It just didn't seem safe any more.

I thumped the bed in frustration and anger. Why did it always have to end like this? Why did they always end up spoiling it? It happened with Becky all those years ago. Then with Jill last year. We'd been fine before she moved in. Then everything fell apart with her constant nagging about where I went and who I was with, even my friendship with Becky.

It had been OK before last week, with Hellen in Amsterdam, me in York. A relationship, at last, where I could keep my own life and go back to my own space. Now I would always see the unspoken question on her lips, the unspoken desire in her mind.

Yesterday I'd done a pretty good job of forgetting about her. Now I felt unsettled again. Angry that she'd changed the rules. Angry that she'd made me walk away… And sorry that I'd had to. I thought back to last night. My big mouth and the bad sex. When it came to it, there wasn't any comparison between her and Angel… or anyone else for that matter.

I felt like a wreck when I got out of bed. My head seemed to be stuffed with cotton wool, my whole body ached. The dream kept on returning, troubling me, aggravating my thoughts. When I stopped thinking about Hellen, I started thinking about the trouble I was still in with the police – and with Magda's message. Not to mention the fact that the real killer was still on the loose and might, at that very moment, be looking for me.

I sat on the toilet and buried my head in my hands. I couldn't go on like this. I had to make a break today – regain control. But first, I needed to clear my head and get some energy back. When Carrie had died, I'd coped by going to the gym every day, pushing myself to the limit. Maybe some exercise was what I needed now.

The pavements were still wet from the overnight rain. It was just after eight, and the city streets were already busy with traffic, but the air, blown around by the fresh breeze from sea, felt clean and fresh. It was hard at first, and my body refused to respond, but as I ran through the waking streets, my head began to clear. The blood pumped around my body again and the muscles in my legs stretched and began to feel more supple. By the time I passed City Hall, my mood wasn't quite so bleak. By the time I ran past William Wilberforce on his column, I was distracting myself with thoughts of the past.

I'd come here for the first time on a school trip when I was nine years old. We were doing a project on his fight against slavery and, for once, I was obsessed with my schoolwork, fired up by his battle to end such tyranny. We'd gone to the Wilberforce Museum and learnt about how the slave traders plundered African villages for the fittest men and women and packed them in the hold of a ship for weeks. We learnt that many of them died in the putrefying, sub-human conditions and the survivors were consigned to a life of degrading servitude, away from their families and their homelands. I suppose that was when I first began to understand the capacity of humans for cruelty and callousness. Thank God for people like Wilberforce. Without him, millions more would have died.

By the time I cut through the grounds of the College of Art, I was thinking back again over the last twenty-four hours, piecing together everything I knew.

I'd made a little progress, at least. For a start, I knew that Joanna Whittling used to work at GME until a year ago. I believed Beano when she told me Whittling was pushed out by the new owners. I knew also that the file Magda Swinson took was a confidential one, otherwise why would it be encoded? I knew that it had only been sent to her mailbox less than an hour before she was attacked; and I thought she had probably sent it there herself.

I also knew that the protesters hated them both. And it was a reasonable guess that the two women would have no affection for *them* either. Especially people like Charlie and Jean, who admitted that they hounded and threatened them at every turn.

I stopped on the bridge over the muddy old River Hull. Leaning on the side, I could see and hear the city all around me in its infinite colours and sounds. Downstream, the old harbour. The big modern swing bridge that carries one of the city's main roads and still opens to let ships come and go, causing traffic chaos every single time. And beyond it, the twin towers of the huge tidal barrier – like a giant guillotine, its blade poised to drop at high tide to prevent flooding. Over on my right, the old city and its narrow cobbled streets nestled quietly in the lee of the new city centre.

Thinking about the protesters, I couldn't get Charlie out of my mind. He was surly enough, mean enough and motivated enough to get violent if the situation arose. I hated the idea of experimenting on animals, but the violence of some animal activists struck me as little better. Violence breeds violence. How easily could fanaticism turn to murder? How easily could Charlie, or someone like him, try and kill the enemy rather than just taunt them?

I set off again and carried on running, across the bridge, through an industrial estate and out onto the main road, working my way back, thinking again about Hellen and the dream: the way she pointed, the way she'd hissed at me, the way I'd run from her. There was something about this awful image that I couldn't put my finger on.

As I ran back into Queens Gardens, I sprinted hard, stretching my legs and making my lungs work, and then began winding down, jogging easily and slowly back to the hotel.

Think, Cameron! What did Magda Swinson say?

*"Important file – mswinson – Line One. Please tell Joanna – no one else."* She'd said the password, *"Benjy 256."* She'd said it was *"urgent... Thursday."*

But there was something else. Something that I'd discounted until now, until I thought about the disturbing image of Hellen...

Before Magda passed out, it was like she almost hissed at me. Like Hellen in the nightmare. A sort of gasp. Sounding like *ice ise... ice 'em.* Spoken so softly that I'd hardly heard it. It had seemed almost like a cough, a sigh, as she struggled to breathe. But maybe it was more than that. Maybe it really meant something.

By the time I'd showered and eaten breakfast, it was nearly ten o'clock and I had a list of things to do. If I was going to get out of this unscathed, then today I needed to apply myself.

Vick was at his post in the internet café when I arrived. He smiled cagily at me when I walked through the door, probably the first customer of the day. "You're back," he enunciated clearly.

"Yeah, and your cold's better!" I retorted, pleased I wasn't going to expose myself to that again.

"Yeah, sorry about the sneezing and stuff," he said, colouring up slightly. "What can I help you with?"

"Nothing thanks, I'm flying solo today – just point me to a console."

He looked relieved.

After I'd logged onto the web, I checked Magda's e-mail, hoping that there might be some mail for her, but the inbox was empty, just like I had left it yesterday. So I logged onto the Yahoo! search engine and keyed in the words *ice em*. It was as close as I could get to the sound I'd heard. But I got nothing sensible. A long list of irrelevant, often weird sites appeared together with an Amazon advert telling me that I could get a book on ICE EM from them – but then it always did that. Huh, if you keyed in 'massive conglomerate putting small book-shops out of business', they would tell you they had a book on that too. Shit, maybe they have, who knows?

The list, though, was of no help. So I keyed in a whole load of vari-ations one by one, with similar results. I was beginning to believe that I'd been mistaken, that she really had just gasped, when I keyed *isem* into the search box. The screen produced the usual list of unwanted sites but, this time, at the bottom of the screen – item number ten – was something that finally looked like I could be right. *ISEM – The first International Symposium on the Ethics and Morality of using embryos in the genetic sciences.* I clicked on the title, my excitement rising, and the web page loaded up in seconds:

'ISEM takes place in Leeds on Thursday 20th April at the Boulevard Hotel. This unique event will see ethically minded scientists gathering from all over the world to examine stronger guidelines and laws to control the development of cloning techniques and to call for a per-manent ban on the use of human embryos in genetic research. Debates will focus on the implications for animal life and for mankind itself, and the long-term problems that such research could cause. The symposium will end with a formal representation to governments and professional organisations on the redrafting of current ethical guide-lines and laws.'

It wasn't a long document by any means and it was simply worded and designed, giving the impression that the scientific community too had its own minority protest movement. That was good. Maybe things weren't as bad as Elana and the others might have thought. I scrolled through the programme of debates and speakers, passing names that, though possibly eminent and respected in their fields, meant nothing to me.

On the second page I saw her name. Joanna Whittling. The keynote speaker in the afternoon debate on 'Genetics – Use and

Abuse'. I leant back in my seat and whistled softly. So she was speaking out in favour of ethical guidelines on Thursday – the day that Magda Swinson had mentioned.

Could it really be that Joanna Whittling, the woman branded as evil incarnate by the protesters, was speaking in favour of limiting the genetic experiment? That she too had a conscience?

And, in that case, could it be that Magda Swinson intended to get the file to her, so that she could use it to back up her argument?

If that was true, then both she and Magda were almost on the same side as Charlie and the others.

Today was Tuesday. The conference was this Thursday. I had less than thirty-six hours to find her.

# Twelve

The Polar Bear is not the first place you would expect to bump into a copper. Located on Spring Bank, in the industrial suburbs of Hull, it was built in the city's glory days when working-class pubs were ornate temples to late-Victorian style.

Sitting in the corner of the main bar on one of the well-stuffed benches, I could easily imagine how this big room would once have resounded with the voices of stevedores and warehousemen, seamen and labourers. How prostitutes, pickpockets and conmen would have plied their trades amongst the drinkers on a payday night.

Even now, the lounge had lost none of its grandeur. The long polished bar was still shiny and ornate, the glass mirror behind it still impressive. The fancy ceiling, picked out in gold, terracotta, dark green and cream, had an ornate cupola in its centre, hovering over the heads of its twenty-first century customers like a counterfeit piece of Renaissance art. And below my feet, the rich tones of the ceiling found reflection in a multicoloured carpet crowded with images of fruit.

In any other context, all the elements of the room would look kitsch, but, here, in Hull's main gay pub, they merely oozed a waggish sense of history. Even the jukebox, the fruit machine and the pool table seemed to add to the pastiche. All in all, it was a suitable backdrop for the sprinkling of gay men and dykes who were enjoying their lunchtime drinks.

Like I say, not the first place you would expect to meet a copper. But when I rang Jimmy Wilson to take him up on the drink he'd suggested on the bridge the previous day, he was very specific about meeting at the Polar Bear. Now, as he picked his Coke up off the bar, walked over and sat down next to me, I wondered why.

"I didn't know you frequented places like this, Jimmy," I probed.

"No, I don't, Cameron." He smiled wryly and set his glass down on the table. "There are good reasons for meeting you here. The biggest is that you're on bail and I'm a police officer. The last thing I want is to be seen socially with someone who is still a suspect – even you. This is the last place where I would expect to meet any of my colleagues.

"So how are you doing, current problems apart?" he asked, sipping his drink.

"Oh all right, I suppose…"

"You've finished with this Dutch copper then?"

"Yeah," I said, "I guess I have. You're all the same when it comes down to it, obsessed with your job."

He laughed lightly at me and we talked about the police, his career, what Hellen did… catching up on the years since we'd last met. It was good to relax with someone I liked. Someone who, maybe, could help a little.

"How's the investigation going, Jimmy? Am I in the clear yet?"

He pulled back, askance. "Ohh no… you can't be serious, Cameron… Look, I might be a friend but that subject's right off limits."

"You think I did it then?" I demanded.

He squirmed. "No, of course not! I wouldn't be sitting here with you if I did! Hell, Cameron, I know that you can be annoying and hotheaded sometimes, but the idea of you stabbing anyone – especially another woman – is ridiculous."

"So?" I persisted.

"So… what?"

"So, are you going to tell me what's going on?"

"No I'm not! You must know that I can't talk about it!" He turned his head away for a second and then looked back at me, rattled. "Look, Cameron, if you're innocent – and we both know you are – then your lack of guilt will be established in the normal way. Trust the system, will you? It works."

"Yeah, sure!" I exclaimed. "Tell that to the Guildford Four, or the M25 three – or all the others who've been wrongly convicted!"

"So you're going to be the Humberside One, are you?" His mouth quivered at the edges.

"Yeah, all right, all right. You might think it's fucking humorous, Jimmy, but if Warren and his sergeant have their way, that's how it could end up."

He became serious again when he saw my anger; even a little sympathetic. "Right, OK love, I can see how you might feel. But you shouldn't worry, once the forensic comes through, you'll be in the clear – I've no doubt. Besides, you're not the only suspect, so take some heart in that, at least."

"Really, who else is in the frame?"

He hesitated. "Cameron, this isn't even my case. I'm on secondment at the moment, I'm not even around the station much. I only took your statement because I was in the area when the incident happened. I shouldn't even be here talking to you like this." He looked at me wide-eyed. "Don't push it, eh?"

"Oh come on, Jimmy. Who is it?"

He sighed heavily. "All I can tell you is that someone else has been held for questioning."

I waited.

"You're out of order, Cameron."

"Oh come on, Jimmy, if someone's been arrested, the press will know anyway."

He gave me a look that said I was being difficult. But he continued, grumpily. "He's a bloke from the protest camp. Trouble-maker. With a record. GBH down south a few years ago. On a demo, he had a go at one of the lads down there."

Charlie. It was probably what I expected, and for a moment I was relieved.

"Yeah, I can see why Warren might be interested in him. What evidence have they got?"

"We know him and he's got motive. They've been questioning him all morning."

"But no evidence?" I shook my head. "All right, so he's a fanatic about animal rights, but that won't convict him, will it? It doesn't let me off the hook."

"It might do. He's got form..." He looked at me like he didn't know why he was telling me all this.

"Go on."

He sighed again, resigned to my persistence. "I'm not talking about something minor like obstruction, Cameron. He hospitalised a copper down in Huntingdon."

"Yeah, I can see Charlie doing that."

He stopped and stared at me suddenly. "You know him!"

I shook my head. "I've met him. Yesterday at the protest camp in Barton."

"Cameron, are you out of your mind? If Warren finds out..."

"Look, Jimmy. I haven't infringed any of my bail conditions, and I don't intend to. But you can't expect me to just sit back and wait for your boss to walk all over me again. I want to know who *did* attack the woman."

He sighed angrily. "Cameron, just leave it! All right?"

"No I won't," I countered defiantly. "I want to clear my name. I can't afford to 'trust the system'." I picked up my beer and took a swig.

"Please, Cameron. Go back to York. This is police work. If the guv'nor knows you're still here, sniffing around, he'll go apeshit."

I grunted derisively.

"I'm not just speaking as a copper now, Cameron. You're a friend. Whoever stabbed that woman is dangerous, love. I don't want you to get hurt!"

I screwed up my face and looked away. I hate being lectured.

"Look," he said sternly, "I know all about your escapade in Amsterdam. You were lucky then. Don't think that just because you got away with it once, you can go around playing amateur detective with impunity." He paused and shook his head reproachfully.

"Warren is the least of your worries, love. Judging by what you told me about the assault, the guy with the knife is a headcase. Either a pathological killer or a paid assassin. Don't push your luck! If he knows you're sniffing around, you'll be the next one with a knife in your guts."

He picked up his glass and took a swig, then slammed it down on the table, exasperated, no doubt, by my continued look of determination. "You're not listening to a word I say, are you?"

"Yes, I hear you, Jimmy." It pissed me off how everyone wanted me to go home and be a good little girl. "But what do you expect me to do? How can I sit back and do nothing? I know it's dangerous, but I'm being careful. Besides, I don't have any choice."

He just looked at me, incomprehension written all over his face. I wished I could explain, tell him about the message, level with him. But Jimmy was an honest cop. If I told him, friend or not, he'd feel obliged to pass it on.

We sat in silence, both of us calming down. I wanted to believe that it was Charlie. He looked like he was capable. And it would be nice to feel safe again. But somehow, that didn't add up either. They'd like it to be him, it would even up the score. It was too easy, too convenient.

We'd both nearly finished our drinks before I broke the ice again.

"OK, so if you're so concerned, how about checking up on something for me?"

"That depends on what it is."

"I just wondered about that firm Magda Swinson works for. Wondered if you knew anything about them?"

"Like what?"

"Oh, I don't know. Whether they're above board. Whether there's been any sort of trouble there like this before."

"I've told you, Cameron. I can't get involved!"

"I'm not asking you to." I shrugged, settling back into the seat. "I just want you to check up on them – nothing else. Please?"

He looked at me sideways. "I'm not promising anything, Cameron. I'll think about it. Maybe I'll ring you tomorrow."

Yeah and maybe you won't.

"So what's this job you're on then?" I asked, trying to smooth things over.

He leant back against the leather bench and rested one leg on the other, relieved at the change of topic. "It's a nasty business, love. You might have read about it in the papers. I'm on assignment with Immigration. A Home Office task force."

"Illegal immigrants? Like the ones coming in through Dover from the Balkans?"

He screwed up his face. "Yeah, sort of. But it's more complex than that..."

I sat back and waited.

"Women, love. It involves women." He took another sip of his drink before continuing. "About five months ago the unidentified body of a woman was found in the sea near the Wash. She was naked and bore no identifying features. The pathologist was inclined to think, from her bone structure, age and general condition, that she was from a poor background. The PM indicated a mid-European origin, possibly Romanian, maybe even Turkish. But the report was inconclusive – the body had been in the sea for over twenty-four hours. Cause of death: drowning.

"Well anyway, nobody made a big deal of it. The case was filed under Missing Persons and the investigating officer thought that was that. Then, two months ago, another woman was found floating in the sea just out from Grimsby. She was naked, just like the first, except she was Asian. There was a rope attached to her waist, as if she might have been weighted down. The body was badly decomposed but she too had died from drowning. Two weeks ago, there was a third. A Chinese woman, dredged up in the nets of a fishing boat, with the weights still attached."

"Somebody drowned them all?" I asked, sickened. "The same person?"

"That's what it looks like, Cameron. It makes my stomach turn. But, the worst thing is, we think this is only the tip of an iceberg. At least two of the ones we've found were intended to stay on the sea bed. How many more are there? That's what everyone's asking."

"And you think they're all illegal immigrants."

"It's likely. There's a lot of them coming in, and it's really sad. They're likely to have paid someone their life savings to get here. They're probably coming in from one of the countries in Eastern Europe – maybe the Balkans. It sickens me that someone appears to be selling them safe passage here, taking their money and then murdering them when they arrive."

"But why should they be all women? Are there any sexual angles?"

He shrugged. "There doesn't appear to be a sexual motive. There could be male victims too – maybe we just haven't found any of them yet. But there is something odd about this, Cameron…" He hesitated but he seemed to want to tell me.

"What is it, Jimmy?"

He frowned and scratched his head. "I know I can trust you, Cameron. This hasn't been made public, so it's strictly between you and me, right? I find it the worst part, and the bit which I can't even begin to understand."

He stopped again for a moment, clearly upset. "All three of the dead women had been pregnant. And every one of them had suffered either a miscarriage or, possibly, an abortion – a matter of hours before they died."

"Shit! They'd all lost a baby?"

"Yeah, it makes me want to throw up… maybe it's just coincidence, who knows? Anyway, my job at the moment –" he looked at his watch "– and I'd better get back to it… is to work with the Immigration Task Force and try and find out where these women are coming from, how they're getting into the UK and who is killing them off."

"And why they'd all been pregnant?"

"Yeah, it's a tall order. But we have to try and stop it. God knows how many of them there are."

"Well, I hope you can find out soon, before any more die…" I sighed as he made a move to go. I didn't know what else to say. It made my fight to clear my name seem almost unimportant.

"Thanks for meeting me, Jimmy. It was really nice chatting to you again after all this time."

He smiled. "Yeah, good to see you again."

"And I'd be really grateful if you can get me some background on GME."

"You don't give up, do you, Cameron? I don't know why I even listen to you! You should go home, you know. Even if you don't care about your own safety, you should think about those of us who do. I bet that friend of yours – the solicitor – doesn't know what you're up to."

"Not officially." I grinned, standing up with him. "And she doesn't approve either."

"Uh! No I don't expect she does!" He gave me the same disapproving look that she had and then hugged me anyway. "Just keep out of bother, will you? I'll maybe ring you on your mobile tomorrow. Meanwhile, if you do get into any trouble, ring me, won't you? It'll have to be on the record – but that's a damn sight better than getting yourself killed. Promise?"

"Yeah, thanks Jimmy, I promise. You're a pal."

I watched him go out, across the bar and through the big double doors. For all my dislike of the police, I was still attracted to some of them. Jimmy… huh, Hellen. There was something fascinating about what they did. The way they were always searching for answers, maybe. I suppose it was what I'd been doing all my life.

I sat down again and finished my drink, thinking of the answers I was looking for now. Thinking back to Angel last night. I still wasn't convinced she was a lesbian. She said she'd met Magda in here, about a year ago; that it was the only place they felt safe. I'd not thought about it before, but that would have been around the time Joanna Whittling had lost her job and the management of GME had changed. It seemed inconceivable that someone so tied up in her job wouldn't have talked to her lover about such a major upheaval in her working life. Yet, last night, Angel had denied all knowledge of her girlfriend's ex-boss.

I rooted around inside my jacket, pulled out the newspaper that Angel had given me at the hospital and carefully tore out the picture of Magda Swinson. If she'd been a regular visitor here, then someone might recognise her.

I started with the woman behind the bar. She shook her head. "Don't remember her at all, love. Missing person, is she?"

"Yeah," I said, "sort of." It's a real relief sometimes that people don't read newspapers. "She used to come in here regularly about a year ago. Were you here then?"

"Oh yeah," she said. "If I'm not working behind the bar then I'm usually playing pool. I nearly live here, love."

"So, if she'd been in a few times, you'd remember her?"

"Yeah. I'm brilliant wi' faces, you have to be in this job. But ask the others if you want, you never know. Those women over there, they're regulars."

I thanked her and walked over to a group of dykes in their late twenties, drinking pints and chatting at the other end of the bar. I got the same response. They'd been coming in here for years – but not one of them remembered her.

I went and sat down again, staring at her picture. Magda Swinson. She didn't look the least bit like a lesbian and, though that often doesn't mean a thing, it seemed odd that I'd thought – and felt – the same about Angel.

Sometimes you can sit and reason things out for hours and get nowhere. But sometimes you get the feeling in your gut first. Then the pieces begin to tumble into place all by themselves.

The chance meeting with Angel at the hospital. The flash of fear in her eyes when I'd shouted at her outside. The mild panic when I'd mentioned Magda's mother. Her eagerness to invite me home. The absence of her brother – away on business. Her insistence that she'd never heard of Joanna Whittling. The way she'd led me on...

And now, no one here recognised the picture of her lover – even though she'd told me that, for a few months, they both came in here all the time.

Taken alone, any one of those things looked innocent enough. But added together...

The sum of all the parts didn't quite make the whole.

## Thirteen

The wind was getting up as I crossed the bridge, and the sky had turned a dull shade of grey. The scene of crime looked like any other part of the carriageway this afternoon. The police had finished their work and the mobile incident room had been removed. To the casual observer, the bridge looked commonplace again. The stabbing might never have happened. But for me, the patch of cycle track on the other side of the road would be printed indelibly on my memory. Even at this distance, the sight of it made me shudder.

But by the time I reached the marshlands road I was shivering more with cold than with the memory of yesterday's attack. Jeans and a leather jacket were all right in summer, but in the bitter April wind, they were no substitute for full leathers. I thought about my black biking gear. It had cost me a small fortune. Unlike me, it was still in custody. I hoped I would get it back soon. On the other hand, I didn't know if I could face wearing it again.

A Volvo had preceded me all the way past the ponds, through the tunnel of trees, and now, as I pulled in to the verge close to the protest camp, it carried on over the cattle grid amidst a sea of shouting and abuse. I took a deep breath and parked my bike on the verge, under the sprawling hawthorn hedge, thinking obsessively about the warmth of the camp fire, hoping they'd at least let me warm myself up.

I'd got just over thirty hours to find Joanna Whittling and discover what was in the file and then, maybe, hand it over in time for the conference. Maybe less time than that, if the police decided to call in my bail before then. All my options were running out. If I was going to get anywhere, then I needed some help from somebody. And the only people I could think of were Elana and her friends. But if we were going to have a replay of yesterday, then I would get nowhere. Somehow I had to earn their trust and convince them I was on their side. I had to be more open.

They were still hanging around the gate, casting hostile glances down the road towards me as I locked my bike. I looked around nervously, hoping to see Bernie and get some support from him. But neither he nor his car was anywhere to be seen. I stashed my helmet and checked my mobile for messages: in case Becky was trying to get hold of me; in case Jimmy had been extra quick with his information; in case the police had been on the line to tell me I was in the clear.

There was a message, but it was none of those. The voice was cultured and polite.

"So sorry to bother you, Miss McGill," he began, "but I wondered if you might give me a ring. I'd rather like to meet you. You stopped an attack on one of our employees yesterday and, naturally, I'm concerned. I'd like to have a chat with you, if that's possible." He gave his number and then ended the message with, "Oh, when you call, just ask for me by name, will you – it's Stantonwell, Marcus Stantonwell, I'm, er, the chief executive of GME and Magda Swinson's employer."

I didn't have time to react. As I put the phone away, Beano's head appeared over the top of one of the tents and she strolled across immediately, smiling broadly. Part of me was relieved to see a friendly face but I tensed up, remembering our conversation the night before.

"Hiya Cameron." She beamed. "Good to see you again. Come over to the fire, I've got a brew going."

I smiled back and followed her, in spite of my misgivings, still thinking about the message. I was intrigued as to why the boss of

GME wanted to talk to me, mystified as to how he knew my number. And wondering how I could square that with a bunch of animal rights activists who already regarded me as a possible infiltrator.

Beano threw me a grin as she walked past the caravans and between the tents. The woman was incorrigible. Whatever happened, she just seemed to carry on in the same happy, unruffled way. Nothing seemed to bother her. I wished I could be like that, letting everything roll off me.

I was grateful for the mug of hot coffee that she handed me as we got to the fire, and even more pleased when she pulled out a small flask and added some whisky.

"Keeps the cold out." She passed it to me. "You've had second thoughts then; you want to tell me why you're looking for Joanna Whittling?"

There it was again. The same unaccountable interest. "What's your game, Beano?" I asked, looking sideways at both her and her hospitality.

She stepped back, feigning offence. But I hadn't missed her reaction. The sudden blink, the way her hand had moved to the lobe of her ear. "Game, Cameron? I'm here to protest like everyone else, to close this place down. Why else would I be here?"

"I don't know," I muttered, standing over the smouldering fire and warming my hands on the hot mug. "But everyone else lost interest when I said I was looking for Joanna Whittling. They assumed I was on the other side. You came after me and tried to find out more. What are you after?" I demanded. "Just why are you so interested?"

"Aw, come on, Cameron, don't be such a fucking drama queen." She laughed as if I was way off track. "I've been fighting for this cause for years. I just feel passionate about animal welfare, that's all." She paused. "I told you: I ask questions, I find things out because I don't let go. Come on, woman, you must realise, that – however touchy the others might be – whatever you know could be useful to our cause. If you support us, you should trust us and share."

"Yeah, well, you know I support you. It's just that I have a quandary. Something that I've been asked to pass on, that I've promised not to divulge to anyone else."

"Then tell me what it's about," she entreated, dropping her voice and glancing around to make sure we were still alone. "Trust me, Cameron. You'll never find her on your own; I can help you. Let's go back into Barton, or Hull, or wherever you want," she prodded conspiratorially. "Tell me all about it and maybe I can help you find the woman."

She was very persuasive. Maybe I would have capitulated right then, but I saw Beano's face change and she fell silent as Lou walked into the circle.

"You all right, Cameron?" she asked, curling her fingers around the orange hair by her shoulders, her eyes studying me. "I didn't think you'd be back after the way everyone walked out on you yesterday. I'm sorry about that, it's not the way we should treat visitors."

"It's OK," I replied, "Beano told me why you all reacted the way you did. I just came back to explain. I am on your side, you know."

"Well, I'm glad to hear it, Cameron!" It was Elana's voice behind me. "It's not that we don't like you, dear. But there are things that we can't accommodate – and helping the enemy is one of them."

She made herself a drink and then sat down, inviting me to do the same, as the others came back into the circle, huddling around the fire. Now they were all there, watching me. Waiting. I wondered what they'd think if they knew about Stantonwell's message.

Jean spoke first, her voice heavy with sarcasm. "Well, I expect you'll be hunky-dory now, Cameron? Now that the heat's off *you*."

"You mean, now that they've arrested Charlie? I don't think so, Jean. I'm still the one that was found leaning over the victim on the bridge. They might think Charlie has the motive but…"

"Just hang on, Cameron!" Stella interrupted. "How come you know he's been arrested? It's not been on the news. Who the fuck told you?"

I just stared back at her for a moment, thrown by my own stupidity.

"Well? Have you been talking to the police?" Her voice was unforgiving.

"'Course she bloody hasn't, Stella!" It was Beano. "I told her just now." She was talking to me with her eyes: 'See,' they said, 'you really can trust me.'

"Look." I paused, choosing my words carefully. "I realise you're suspicious after I mentioned Joanna Whittling last night, but it's not what you think. Like I told you, the police arrested me yesterday under suspicion of stabbing Magda Swinson. I might be free now, but they could call in my bail at any time." I looked around the circle of faces. Some were set, one or two looked like they didn't care, but most looked prepared to give me the benefit of the doubt. "You know what they're like. Based on the evidence they have, they think I did it. Pulling Charlie in is just routine. You said yesterday that they've been hassling you. Well, just imagine how scared I must feel. I'm really worried that I could end up in prison."

"I'm sure we all sympathise with you, love – none of us like the pigs," Stella remarked as she got up and poured herself a coffee. "But I don't see how that helps Charlie." She added sugar and came back to her seat. "Besides, you still haven't told us why you want to find that Whittling woman. If you want our trust, Cameron, you're going to have to earn it."

"I can understand how you feel, Stella…" I looked around at the still hostile faces. "I can understand why you all reacted like you did last night. That's why I've come back to explain. I need to clear my name. Maybe I can help Charlie as well…"

Beano and I exchanged glances. Maybe I could trust her after all.

"But I can't do either without your help."

Stella looked at me curiously. "All right then, Cameron, try us. What's this all about?"

I took a very deep breath and then began. "What if I told you that I'm trying to find Joanna Whittling because I have some information for her – and that this information comes from inside GME itself?" I asked. "What then? Would you still feel the same way about me?"

Beano's ears pricked up.

Jean looked up suddenly. "What information?"

"I don't know," I admitted, looking around at them, especially at Beano. "It's a bit complex. But maybe I should take you into my confidence."

Bernie's voice boomed over my shoulder. "Yeah, well, I'd like that, Cameron. The more confidential I can get with you the better." He was laughing, emerging from between the caravans with Charlie in tow. His flippancy aside, I was relieved to see him.

"Charlie, are you all right, dear?" Elana got up and gave him a hug. The man's face was wreathed in a cocky smile. The more I saw of him, the less I liked him.

"Yeah," he sneered, "the pigs just want to finger me, any way they can. But I've got a good brief, and they haven't got a shred of evidence." He looked at me. "They just let me go... I'm not even on bail, like some people."

Smart arse.

Elana got Charlie a hot drink and a few of the others fussed around him, stroking his ego. It amazed me how otherwise sensible, intelligent women could be so taken in by a thug like Charlie. I looked across at Beano and saw that she was thinking much the same.

After a few minutes, they all settled down again. Someone asked Bernie how he knew me.

He grinned, helping himself to a drink, and explained the York connection. Then he sat down next to me, casually draping an arm around my neck and pulling me towards him.

I saw Beano start with surprise. Charlie scowled in disapproval. Elana looked interested. I pulled away from him.

"Come on then," Stella demanded, "you were going to tell us about this information you had for Joanna Whittling."

Charlie sat up, interested. I'd really rather he hadn't been there. Of all of them, he was the one I trusted least. But it was too late now, I'd committed myself.

"Why are you looking for the woman?" asked Bernie, mystified. I noticed that, like Beano, he didn't look shocked either – just interested.

"I told everyone else yesterday, Bernie. I have a message for her. What I didn't say is that it came from Magda Swinson."

Bernie whistled through his teeth, and the others looked up, their eyes all agog. "Sounds heavy, Cameron – what's it about?"

"I don't know," I sighed, glancing over their heads towards the research laboratories, wondering about Stantonwell's message. "I don't know. That's part of the problem. But what I am certain about is that it involves GME and therefore, by definition, your protest."

"But if it's a message, dear, you must know what it says," Elana reasoned with indisputable logic.

"I'll get to that in a moment. But first, can I ask you if anyone saw Magda Swinson yesterday morning?"

Sandra, the woman with the hennaed hair, put her hand up, looking around uncertainly at the others to see if it was all right to talk. When nobody objected, she spoke. "Yes, I saw her. About 8.15 yesterday morning, it was. She was leaving the labs. Jean and I were on lookout and it was really quiet. I nearly missed her."

"Yeah," Jean confirmed, "we tried to slow her down, give her some grief as she came across the grid, but she was driving like a maniac. Both Sandra and me had to jump for our lives!"

Lou caught my eye from across the fire. "I saw her go in as well, Cameron. It was early – just after 6.30 am. I was out here making the fire."

I nodded. "Thanks. That's what I hoped you'd say."

I steeled myself. I was going to have to tell them everything. It was risky. But if I didn't do something fast, I'd never get the file to Joanna Whittling and, more to the point, I could still be facing a murder charge if Magda Swinson didn't make it. Anything was worth trying now.

I looked around the group. I had Charlie's undivided attention, Len looked interested, Elana was sitting cross-legged, waiting patiently. So was Lou. Bernie looked relaxed, receptive. Stella was all eyes. And Beano looked like she was going to burst. In spite of her help covering up for me, perhaps because of it, I still wondered what she was up to.

I paused, conscious of the risk I was taking. "What I'm going to tell you is confidential and it's something that, if it is too widely known, could put me in danger. So please, I'm asking you to respect that and keep it to yourselves."

They all murmured in agreement and I continued.

"Before she lost consciousness on the bridge, Magda Swinson gave me an e-mail address and the password I needed to access it from the web. I checked it yesterday as soon as I got away from the police and it contains an e-mail which was sent from GME at 7.45 am yesterday morning. Now, if Magda was in work around 6.30 and out again by about 8.15, then it seems likely that she sent the e-mail herself, from GME's computer, to her own private e-mail address, just before she left."

Charlie interrupted impatiently. "So what was on it?"

"Nothing, it was blank. But the e-mail had a file attached to it, and it was that file that she asked me to pass on to Joanna Whittling urgently – and in confidence."

"Christ, Cameron!" Stella shrieked. "Have you checked the file? What's it about? Is it stuff we can use?"

"I wish it was that easy, Stella. I've accessed the file and transferred it somewhere else for safe keeping. But it's encoded, which means it can only be opened by special software. Still, even that suggests it's probably highly confidential." A murmur of disappointment ran around the camp.

But Beano's eyes were nearly coming out of her head.

"Well, it's obvious what it is." Charlie was agitated, edgy. "They've been collecting information on the movement. How we operate, who's involved. That sort of thing. Criminal records, personal secrets – things they can use about us."

"Could be, Charlie, but I don't think it is. Magda Swinson was concerned that Joanna Whittling got the file by Thursday. That's the day she's due to speak at an international conference in favour of tighter guidelines for genetic and animal-based research..."

"Whittling?" Charlie snorted cynically. "Oh fuck off, Cameron, I don't believe it. Demanding *slacker* guidelines, maybe! The woman's a bitch, I've told you – a bloody serial killer. There's no way she'd be interested in anything that stopped her kind from killing animals!"

"Well, all I know is that she's listed as a speaker at The Boulevard Hotel, this Thursday. From what I know, it looks like Magda was trying to get it to her before then."

"That must be the conference we're going to!" Lou shouted, excitedly, waving a piece of paper at me. "We got this yesterday, from one of Bernie's contacts. We're going there, all of us. Bernie says there's a big anti-genetics protest outside the hotel..." She looked across sadly at him. He was looking like the perfect martyr. "He's the only one who's not going, he's volunteered to look after the camp whilst we're gone. You gonna come with us and support us, Cameron?"

"Or you could stay and keep me company," Bernie hinted, shuffling closer and staring directly at me without moving a muscle. I stood up and refilled my mug from the coffee pot and sat down further away from him. Some men don't seem to get the message.

"I don't know what I'm doing on Thursday," I said. "Besides, my main concern is the file. It seems to me that it could well contain sensitive material from inside GME. It looks like Magda Swinson stole it yesterday and that whoever attacked her was trying to get it back – or to kill her so no one else could get hold of it. Then I happened along and messed up the plan."

Elana came across to sit at my side. "Cameron, you are a brave woman, but I think you should keep this information very quiet. If

GME know that you have the file... If the man who knifed her finds out..." She squeezed my arm tightly. "My dear, you could be in the most terrible danger."

"Yes, I know, Elana. That's why I asked you to keep all this to yourselves."

Charlie still wasn't convinced by my theory. "Well, all that sounds very believable..." he said, looking round them all, "but I still think it's more likely to be stuff about us. Stuff for the media, you know the sort of thing."

"You could be right, Charlie," I replied, thinking it was time to make a point. "And in that case, the police would be really pleased to get their hands on it, wouldn't they?"

The colour drained from his face. "You've told them? They know about this file?"

I shook my head. Maybe he'd trust me a little more now. "No, I never said a word – and it seems that Magda Swinson didn't want them to know either."

"There you are." Bernie leant forward and peered across at Charlie. "Told you she was all right, our Cameron, didn't I?"

I smiled thinly back at him.

Elana peered at me through the wood smoke. "Thanks for that, Cameron, we appreciate your honesty. You did the right thing telling us."

"Yeah, thanks," Lou chipped in. "Thing is, what do we do now? It looks like this file might be useful." She looked around at everyone else. "Maybe we should help her find Whittling."

Charlie nearly choked on his tea. "Just hang on! We don't know that it could help us at all, you're just taking her word for it. Whittling wouldn't do anything to hold back the genetics industry. Why take the risk? Why can't we just find a way of decoding it, see what it says?"

"Oh yeah," Bernie responded derisively, "you're just going to walk into the labs and ask them what it is?"

Charlie wasn't amused. "All right, big mouth! You come up with something then."

"I think there's only one way," I interjected. "It seems to me that if Magda Swinson stole an encoded file, then she must have known that Joanna Whittling could decode it... She used to work there, so it's got to be a possibility. The only way we can find out is to ask her."

Beano had been quiet up to now, taking it all in. Now she spoke up. "I agree with Cameron. We should find her and talk to her."

There were shouts of disagreement from Charlie and Jean, but Elana agreed. "No, Beano's right. Maybe we're wrong about her, maybe she's reformed." She paused, thinking hard before continuing. "It could definitely be in our interests. And we don't have to give her the file – not straight away, at least. We could talk to her first. And Cameron's right, she may have the software to decode it. With a little bit of persuasion, we might even get to see it. Hell, there are enough of us, we should be able to handle her."

"I think that's a good idea," I said, pleased with the progress I seemed to be making. "But I have to be honest with you all. There is still the possibility that the file is not what we think. Charlie could be right. It could be something else, something to do with the attack, maybe even something that might incriminate individuals here."

Everyone looked at Charlie.

"However much you dislike Joanna Whittling," I said, "I'm not going back on my word. Provided that the file doesn't harm your protest, I still intend to pass it on to her."

"We understand, Cameron," Elana agreed, easy with what I'd said. Charlie looked less happy. "Trouble is, girl," she continued, "we don't even know where she lives now, since she moved away from Hull."

"We could see her on Thursday," Lou offered.

Bernie shot her a nervous look. "Yeah, Lou, but that doesn't leave any time. It could be something we don't want her to have. I think we should find her before then."

"Leave it to me," Beano suggested. "I'll do some checking around. Maybe I can trace her."

"I thought about going into GME and asking them," I suggested, seizing the opportunity. "They probably know where she is."

Charlie nearly jumped down my throat. "Fucking hell! Are you crazy? If they realise we know about the file then we're knackered. Whatever it is, we won't be able to either use it or destroy it."

"I'm not going to tell them about the file," I said, trying hard not to get involved in a shouting match. "What I thought of saying is that Magda was worried that she was dying when I left her on the bridge, and she asked me to contact Joanna for her." I shrugged. "Innocent enough."

"Yeah, that sounds pretty good," Stella agreed. "They could have been friends. Besides, none of us has ever been inside. It could be really useful. Who you gonna ask to see?"

"Stantonwell," I replied. "He's their top man, isn't he? His name was in last night's paper."

"Hang on, Cameron, just think about this!" Beano cautioned. "If the file was stolen from GME, it might have been one of them who tried to kill Magda Swinson. Best leave it, love."

"Yes, exactly, Beano. That's the other reason I'd like to talk to them. Maybe I can see what their hang-ups are. What they think about the attack. Maybe they'll let something slip."

Beano looked appalled. "They'd never let you in!"

"Oh, I think they will," I replied, noticing the slight panic that had crept into her eyes. "It was me who stopped Magda from being murdered, remember. They'd probably be pleased to see me, especially if they think she stole a file from them, especially if they were involved in the attack."

Beano stood up, a little too suddenly. "No! Charlie's right. It's not a good idea at all. For a start, they might know the file has been copied... or... they might suspect you have it... or, I don't know... anything. It's too dangerous, Cameron!"

"It's all right, Beano," I soothed, surprised at her panic. "They won't know. Even if they knew she'd copied the file, why should they suspect that I know anything about it?"

"Well if she goes, I want to go with her." This time it was Jean. I thought she'd relaxed now, but maybe I was wrong. "That way we can make sure nothing goes wrong."

"No, no. That will never work," Elana cautioned. "They know you too well, Jean; they know all of us – they'd never let any of us in in a month of Sundays. We have to trust her. They have to think that Cameron is unconnected with us or they'd never let her near the place." She turned to me. "They don't know you, do they, dear? They won't guess that you've been talking to us?"

"I don't think so, Elana. They might have caught sight of me this morning when I came in. But if they have, I'll just have to deal with it."

Nearly everyone sat back looking pleased that a decision had been made. I was relieved. But Beano swallowed hard. For some reason, she was very uncomfortable with the idea.

The phone was answered almost immediately. "Hello, this is GME Technologies, how may I help you?" The voice was female, pleasant and soothing. I wondered how she managed to deal with all the abusive calls she must take, and still sound so relaxed.

I'd walked down the road to my bike before I made the call. I definitely didn't want an audience and I didn't want Beano trying to stop me. Everyone else had come round to the idea. It made sense to them, and it enabled me to agree to meet Stantonwell without making them suspicious of my motives. If I played my cards right, he might actually give me Joanna's address or get her to contact me. If nothing else, it gave me a chance to find out who I was dealing with. Then, I could make my own judgement as to whether GME were involved or not.

"I'd like to speak to Mr Stantonwell, please," I said, raising my voice, as an old lorry rolled noisily past me and up over the hill. Its rancid smell spilled out all around it, even on a cool day like today.

"May I ask who's calling and what it's in connection with?"

"My name's Cameron McGill, I'm returning his call."

"Hold the line please, Miss McGill." There was a short pause. I could hear the protesters in full cry again by the cattle grid, and the sound of the truck as it rattled over the metal grill.

"Miss McGill? Mr Stantonwell is engaged at present, but he'll give you a ring as soon as he's free."

I thanked her politely, then sat on my bike and waited.

I still couldn't work Beano out. She didn't want me to go in there. I still got the impression that she wanted to deal with this herself. That she wanted some control over what I did, who I saw, and when. I put the inescapable conclusion to the back of my mind for now. I didn't want to believe that this outgoing, likeable woman was any more than that. I didn't want to believe that she had anything to do with the vicious attack on the bridge. But, right now, when I did think about it…

As I glanced up the road, I saw her walking hurriedly towards me. When she saw the phone in my hand, she broke into a run, waving her arms in the air. "Fuck, Cameron, you haven't rung already?"

"Just done it, Beano," I said coldly, not wanting any argument. "I'm waiting for them to ring back… What *is* the matter with you?"

The big woman shuffled her feet in panic. I'd been wrong earlier when I thought she was never ruffled; now there was desperation in her eyes.

"Cameron, don't do this – please!" she begged. "Give the file to me, I can sort it all out for you. I'm sure I can find Joanna Whittling if you let me."

"What is it with you?" I demanded, finally losing my cool. "You want to know all about what I'm doing. You expect me to just hand over a confidential file. But when I ask you to tell me what the fuck you're up to, you give me a load of bullshit. Beano, you may have fooled the others back there, but I know you're up to something."

"I'm not 'up to something', Cameron!" she shrieked. "I just don't think you should go in there. It's too dangerous."

"Why?" I was angry. "I'm only going to ask them if they can put me in touch with an ex-employee."

"Yes, but..." The phone rang and she lunged at it, trying to grab it out of my hand. I spun away before she could get it, and walked off down the hill.

"Cameron, don't!" she shouted, running after me.

"Look!" I said, turning on her. "I'm doing this, whether you like it or not."

She froze as I answered, then took off down the road, shouting angrily over her shoulder, close to tears: "Well, fuck you, Cameron! You can go to hell!"

## Fourteen

A light drizzle had begun and, as I walked back past them and over the cattle grid towards the Land Rover, the people in the camp were re-arranging themselves under makeshift canopies, their coat hoods pulled up against the gusty wind, hats pulled down. But Beano wasn't amongst them. She'd gone, striding off down the road to who knows where.

One of the guards had got down from the Land Rover and was resting languidly against the bonnet, studying me, as I approached. He was a middle-aged man, slightly overweight, with a florid complexion and a big nose. As I got closer, he stirred and pulled himself upright. "You'll be Miss McGill, I suppose?" he asked, puffing up his chest. Big man.

"I gather you're going in to see Mr Stantonwell?"

"Yes, that's right."

"You been talking to them?" He nodded towards the camp, eying me up suspiciously. "Earlier on, I thought I saw you. You know them, do you?"

"What me? Ooh, not bloody likely!" I replied, as if butter wouldn't melt in my mouth. "Just making sure this was the right place. And try-ing to be sociable. They weren't exactly friendly though, especially when I said I was coming here."

"No, they wouldn't be," he muttered cheerlessly, looking me up and down like I might be a major security threat. "They're bloody weird, if you ask me."

I bit my tongue. Look who's talking.

"Now, if you'd just take off your jacket, and stand with your legs apart... Nothing personal, we just have to be careful, that's all. Specially wi' nutters like them around."

I did as I was told and he checked eagerly through my jacket for any bombs, hand-grenades, knives and guns I might be hiding. He looked a bit downcast when all he could find was a couple of snotty paper hankies, my purse and a mobile phone. But he enjoyed frisking me all the same. I could tell.

"You're all right, you're in the clear." He stepped back, giving me the blackest of looks. "I can let you go in – just walk down the track and wait by the gates."

I fixed him with my eyes, saying nothing. When he began to shuffle awkwardly, I felt better and turned to walk down the long track towards the walls.

When I finally got there, the entrance was even more formidable close up. Big, solid wooden doors, about eight feet high, set into a brick wall that was a couple of feet higher still, and topped with razor wire. As I approached, a small door set in the gate swung open and a man beckoned me inside. I stepped through it, feeling like Alice as she stepped into the rabbit hole. Weird.

But the man who offered me a plump well-manicured hand was normality itself. He could have been a banker, a solicitor or the chief executive of a cuddly toys business.

"Miss McGill, I presume," he said politely, his accent impeccable. "Pleased to meet you. I'm Marcus Stantonwell. Thank you so much for coming to see me."

I nodded, innocence written all over my face. "That's all right, I wanted to talk to you as well. I just wasn't sure how to go about it."

He smiled back charmingly.

"One thing though – how did you get my mobile number?"

"Oh, that's a secret, my dear." He laughed, tapping his nose. "But there are ways."

Yes, I suppose there are. Probably some bootleg website... or a friend that works in the phone industry... All sorts of ways, if you know the right people.

Stantonwell was a big man, large-framed and solid – though not in a muscular way. He looked like he enjoyed the good life: an expensive light-grey suit, a respectable-looking tie, polished brogues. His face was self-assured and comfortable too. His well-groomed, thick black hair was receding only slightly, even in his late forties. He had a deep forehead above eyes set a little too far apart, a hook nose ending just above a military-style moustache – a public-school face, pleasant enough, but tinged with just enough arrogance to leave you in no doubt that he knew he was superior.

He looked me up and down, playing with the small mobile phone in his hand as he took in my jeans and leather jacket, my short salt and pepper hair, my DMs. And, though he hid it well, in amongst his oily charm it was clear he had been expecting a more conventional woman. Someone wearing a frock and make-up, no doubt. A woman he could relate to, a woman he could charm. Behind the sugary smile, I saw disappointment – and disapproval – sweep across his face. But he recovered quickly.

"So you're the brave woman who says she foiled the attack on Miss Swinson?" He spoke slowly, easily, hands in pockets. But I noticed what he said more than the way he said it. The paper and the local news had only said that I was a suspect. They hadn't mentioned that I might have saved the woman's life. I wondered how he knew.

"Mmm, well done. Important asset, our Miss Swinson, we wouldn't want to lose her."

He was saying all the right things. But his manner was too smooth, too polite. It made me distinctly uneasy.

"Well, we'd better go inside, hadn't we?" He smiled courteously and stood back to let me go ahead, directing me towards the small security building.

We walked across a car park with maybe twenty cars. If the walls from the outside had seemed cold and high, inside they were no different. All along the inside was a stretch of open ground, some twenty yards wide, with CCTV cameras and floodlights every ten yards. Then another eight-foot mesh fence, topped with more razor wire, surrounding the site itself. It was a fortress from the outside; more of a prison on the inside.

He stopped at the security post just through the mesh fence, where the guard produced a book for him to sign, and then made up a visitor's tag with my details and stuck a special barcode on it, before encapsulating the whole thing in clear plastic. Behind him, another guard was sitting in front of a bank of monitors, watching the ever changing pictures, as the CCTV cameras scanned the whole of the perimeter inside the wall.

I hung the tag around my neck and followed Stantonwell through into the main compound. It was a large site, the size of a football pitch, with a two-storey complex of newly built offices and laboratories to my left and two rows of modern single-storey farm sheds on my right which presumably housed the unfortunate animals. A road separated the two distinct halves, at the end of which were a number of smaller brick buildings that looked like housing. Mature trees and shrubs were growing freely around the office building and along the road, softening the area and providing some cover from the eyes beyond the wall.

"I'm sorry about all the security, Miss McGill," he oozed. "It's a real nuisance, but in our business, I'm afraid, a necessity."

I smiled back, muttering that it was no problem, but struggling inside to hide my revulsion as we walked past the knacker's wagon, now parked up against one of the sheds and flanked by two security men. Another two men, wearing rubber gloves, were operating a noisy hydraulic lift which was hauling a large plastic bin into the air. When it reached the back of the lorry, they tipped it over and hundreds of small animals, their coats caked in dirt and blood – mice, rabbits, dogs, monkeys – fell out onto the back of the lorry.

Stantonwell turned left quickly, towards the offices, shepherding me away from the sight. But as I looked back over my shoulder, I saw one of the men throwing the body of a ginger tomcat up onto the pile of pathetic corpses. I shuddered, thinking of Tibby and how much I loved him. Wondering how human beings could be so callous.

When we reached the main door to the offices, he passed first his and then my security card under the in-built scanner and led me into a small entrance lobby. There were three more glass-fronted doors leading off from there – two of them leading to tiled corridors, the third opening to stairs clad in thick Wilton which led to the offices above – and Stantonwell's large and airy room on the front corner of the building.

The savagery by the animal sheds was in stark contrast to the civilised comfort inside. The room was decorated in a traditional style with upholstered furniture and a deep maroon carpet. Stantonwell sat down behind a curved birch desk, with a single pile of papers positioned neatly at one side, and motioned for me to take a seat in one of the comfortable armchairs before it.

"Would you like a coffee?" he asked, putting his mobile down on the desk and pushing a button on his intercom. I said yes, and he ordered two cups and then sat back and smiled greasily at me.

"So, I wanted to see you. And you wanted to see me." He waved his hand courteously towards me. "Ladies first."

I cringed inside at his patronising tone – this arrogant politeness that, I was sure, hid a well of dislike. I prefer people to speak their prejudices, but Stantonwell was acting in one way and thinking in another. There was nothing to get hold of, nothing solid to object to, no foothold from which to fight the concealed disapproval. He made me want to shake him. He made me want to let my anger show. But I just smiled and tried to be equally charming in return.

"Oh, it's nothing much," I said, playing down the importance of what I wanted to ask. "It's just a favour really – well, not for me, but for your employee."

He nodded, hanging on my every word.

"Yesterday morning on the bridge, before she passed out, she said something to me about a friend – a woman, it sounded like her name was Joanna Whittling." I watched his eyes for a reaction and got none. "She was confused and frightened at the time, as anyone would be of course, so the message was garbled.

"But the gist was, I think, that they'd been good friends and had lost contact. Magda seemed to want Joanna to know what had happened to her. I think she probably thought she was dying." I shrugged. "It sounded like she wanted to heal some rift between them... I'm a stranger in these parts but I understand that Joanna Whittling used to work here... I just wondered if you could help me get in touch with her, so that I can pass the message on..."

The mobile on the desk chirped out a melody and Stantonwell picked it up, walking across to the window and staring out. He didn't say much, possibly because I was there: just "Yes," "Good," "Thank you" and "I'll be in touch," all delivered curtly with no hint of feeling. He stayed there for a moment, gazing out across the field. There was a knock on the door. He turned, preoccupied, then, focussing again, shouted, "Come!" and a young woman entered with the drinks. With a sharp, sweeping gesture, he instructed her to put the cups on the desk.

I smiled at her, but she dropped her eyes as soon as they met mine and asked him if there was anything else. He said nothing, just dismissed her with a wave, and she crept out, closing the door quietly behind her. A woman who knew her place and was frightened of her boss. So much for his courtesy. I was right – the man was being too nice to me. I wondered what he wanted.

He watched her closely until she left. Then he considered me for a few more seconds before inviting me over to the window, still studiously ignoring my request regarding Joanna Whittling.

"You see, over there, where you came in, the collection of tents?"

The view across the field was partly obscured by several large sycamores which, in full leaf, would shield the office from the world outside, but the buds were barely open, so I could see through them to the field beyond the wall, and the tents huddled by the gate.

"Yes," I said, weighing my words. "I saw them when I came in – a protest group or something?"

"Yes, as you say, a protest group." He spoke the words like they were poison. "If you could stand in my shoes, my dear, you would be amazed at what we have to put up with. And it isn't just those so-called animal rights protesters.

"I realise that as far as people like that are concerned – and some of the media, even a few other scientists – organisations like ours are the devil incarnate. We are cast as evil. Strange, when in the same breath, they accuse us of playing God. Yet all we are doing here is for the good of mankind, Cameron. Life-giving medical research."

His show of humility almost made me applaud.

"All we are doing is developing medicines and vaccines which are desperately needed by sick people all over the world. Would Louis Pasteur have been hounded so much when he discovered penicillin? Was Christiaan Barnard censured for giving dying people a chance with a new heart?"

"Perhaps they didn't hurt quite so many animals whilst they were doing their work?" I asked a little caustically. I couldn't help myself.

He raised his eyebrows and continued unperturbed. "Oh, yes, of course we make use of animals, Cameron. I know some people find that repellent, but what other way is there? Would they rather we experimented on people? Eh?"

He looked out across the field to the distant camp before continuing in the same patronising tone. "No, my dear, there isn't an alternative. We care for them and make their suffering as minimal as possible, but in the end they are our only means of research. And though it may seem distasteful, there is a greater good, you know. Ultimately our research will prevent a great deal of human pain and suffering.

"Miss Swinson was working on a project which was very close to completion and will, very soon, make it possible to detect breast cancer long before any growth develops. She was –" he corrected himself "– she *is* a very dedicated scientist. One of our best. Now she's unconscious, even close to death, after that vicious attack."

"And I suppose you believe it was the animal rights protesters who attacked her."

"I don't know, Cameron." He stroked his chin. "If I'm honest, I have to say it is a distinct possibility, and one which I know the police are looking into. They're violent, sick people. I'm sure they would stop at nothing to further their cause."

"You said it was one possibility?" I bit my tongue, keeping my own opinions to myself this time. "That means there must be another."

He smiled again. "Let's sit down. Have a drink of your coffee before it goes cold."

I walked back to the chair. "Is it possible for you to put me in touch with Mrs Whittling?" I asked again, as he sat casually on the desk in front of me.

"All in good time, my dear. All in good time," he counselled, taking a sip of coffee from the fine china cup and wiping the sides of his moustache with a tissue.

"The thing is, Cameron, that our ethos here is about relieving suffering. But we are a business. We need to patent our discoveries and make modest profits on them in order to pay for, and continue with, our important work. However, unfortunately, we live in a very hostile and competitive world. There are people out there who will take any measures they can, either to stop us – as in the case of the terrorist element – or to steal from us for their own profit." He stopped.

"This is a little difficult, my dear. Can I be frank with you?"

I nodded. Be as frank as you like. Just tell me where I can find Joanna Whittling.

"Magda was extremely conscientious. Too conscientious, in fact. She came in yesterday to work on her report – the final draft outlining her research on the breast cancer project. But it appears that, instead of working in her office, she decided to work on it at home." He looked at me dolefully. "Commendable, Cameron, but not something we approve of. All our files are highly confidential. As I say, there are unprincipled people out there just waiting to steal them. Nearly all of our work would fetch a very high price on the black market."

"So are you suggesting that whoever attacked her was after the report?" I asked.

He *was* worried about the file.

He took another sip of coffee and smiled. "You're a bright woman, my dear. Yes, that is exactly it. We believe there was – there is – a dealer, possibly with an associate posing as an animal rights activist. He – or she – may be acting freelance, or working for a client. But we believe they have been watching Magda for some time. And that it is someone she knew well and trusted."

"And did they manage to get the report off her?" I asked, remembering the way Beano had tried to stop me coming in here.

He shook his head. "Oh no, I don't think so. Magda was quite naughty sometimes and she'd break the rules and copy her work onto a disk to take home. But on this particular occasion we know that she didn't." He smiled to himself. "I think she probably heard me coming into the offices and was worried I might tell her off. So she sent it to her private e-mail address instead – presumably with the intention of picking it up when she got home and working on it there. We can tell that from the computer.

"However, the point is this, my dear. We think the person who was after the file believed she would have it with her on disk. And that is why they attacked her."

"Why did she have to copy files at all? Couldn't she access your computer from home?" It was a question I'd already asked myself. If you're going to work on a file – or steal it – why not do it the easy way?

"Ah, yes. In any normal business, that would be the way. But you have to appreciate our situation, my dear. Security. That word again. We don't have an open system. Too risky, you see. Anyone could hack into it and steal our secrets, however secure it might be." He smiled. "That's why we so strongly disapprove of anyone – including Miss Swinson – making copies onto disks or even e-mailing their work."

"But whoever attacked her can't have stolen the file, if she e-mailed it like you said." I frowned. "So what's the problem? And why are you telling me all this?"

He paused, savouring the moment. "You told me that Miss Swinson mentioned Joanna Whittling's name."

"Yes."

He looked at me as if I was an interesting specimen. I shuddered inside. Like the ginger cat, maybe.

"I'm telling you all this, Cameron, because we have a small problem." He lowered his voice as if he was about to pass on a confidence, leant towards me and smiled nastily. "… And so, I gather, have you."

I looked at him blankly. "I don't understand."

He observed me. "Oh come, come, my dear. We can be honest with each other, can't we?"

"I am being honest," I lied. "I don't know what you mean."

He shook his head reproachfully. "Oh, but I think you do. I think you know very well what I mean."

I gazed at him like I didn't know what he was talking about. But thinking back to his comment about my phone number, it began to dawn on me that I'd walked straight into his trap.

"Let us assume," he began, smiling knowingly, "that the statement you gave to the police was a little different to the version you've just given me."

"You don't know that!" I countered. How could he possibly know that?

"Ah!" His lips drew back into a smart-Alec smile. "I've already told you, my dear, there are ways – if you have friends in the right places, they keep you informed."

So that's how he knew my phone number, that's how he knew about my statement. He knew one of the cops.

He got up and walked across the room to the window again, letting his words sink in. Then he turned back, looking grim. "I know exactly what you told the police, Cameron. I know you told them that Miss Swinson said nothing at all to you on the bridge. That you said she passed out straight away, without saying a word..."

He walked casually back, stopping right behind my chair and hissing in my ear: "But if Miss Swinson really said nothing – then how could she have asked you to find Joanna Whittling for her? How could she have told you that she wanted her 'friend' to know what had happened?"

He came round the side of the chair and took hold of my face in his big, fleshy hands and pulled my head round until I was looking directly into his eyes, our faces almost touching. So close that I could feel his warm breath skimming over my face, smell the sweetness of his expensive aftershave. His polite manner was gone.

"Cameron," he snapped, "I think that you lied to them and that you're lying again to me now. That just won't do, my dear." He let go of me and stepped back, leaning against his desk, trying to intimidate me. And succeeding.

"I'm sure that Superintendent Warren would be very pleased to hear your new version of events. Maybe I should tell him."

"Even if I did say something different, you could never prove it!" I retorted angrily, thrown by the accuracy of his information.

He watched me for a few seconds, then languidly removed the top few papers from the neat pile on his desk, revealing a small tape recorder. He pressed one button, then another: *"Even if I did say something different, you could never prove it!"* My voice was distorted but anyone could tell who it was.

He leant back against the desk, looking pleased with himself as he removed the tiny cassette from the machine and held it in the air. "If the police knew you'd been here, asking about Mrs Whittling, if they knew what you'd said, then, Cameron, they might feel they have all the evidence they need to convict you."

"You're threatening me!" Suddenly I felt very hot.

"Oh, tut, tut. Such an ugly word… Let's just say that we could help each other. That I could help you. Your problem and ours are not so dissimilar, after all." He paused, grooming the sides of his hair with his hand.

"As you know, Mrs Whittling used to work here. In fact, she and her late husband ran the business. When he died suddenly, the future of GME was put in great jeopardy. They were in dire straits – no money, no backers. If my partners and I hadn't stepped in, then the business would have closed for good. But we did. And was she grateful? No, my dear, she wasn't at all happy. She was very bitter about the whole affair."

"And how exactly does that concern me?" What was I thinking of, letting myself walk into all this?

He sighed theatrically, running his fingers across his moustache. "Well, Cameron, it concerns you a lot, I'm afraid. You see, the thing is, Mrs Whittling has wanted to take her revenge on us ever since. And to cut a long story short, we believe she used her past association with Miss Swinson to worm her way into the girl's confidence. We believe she knew that our employee was taking the file home with her and that she planned to steal it – with the help of a male accomplice of course… What better way to get back at us than by stealing and selling details of our most valuable project?"

"But you said yourself that Miss Swinson didn't have a copy of the file with her when she was attacked." I floundered, guessing now what was coming next.

"No, of course not. But think back to your statement, my dear. You said quite clearly that the man who attacked Magda seemed to be threatening her when you arrived on the scene. Is it not likely that he was attempting to find out what had happened to the file?"

"Maybe he was." I shrugged, keeping up the pretence. "But how could that possibly affect me?"

He looked at me as if I was a recalcitrant child, and breathed out heavily. "I've already said that Miss Swinson was a very committed employee, Cameron. She was proud of her research project. She knew it was going to save thousands of lives. The last thing she would want is to knowingly let it fall into the wrong hands. So she would have kept her mouth shut when she was threatened. However, for just the same reasons, she might also be worried that, once her assailant had left, he might well go to her house, retrieve her personal computer and download the e-mail file himself."

"But how could he? He wouldn't know the password."

"Oh come along, my dear. If you use e-mail, then you will know that most people have the password already entered in their home computer. The police have told me this was the case with Magda's computer."

"So?"

"So, logic tells me she would want to protect the file somehow, wouldn't she? And just then, in the middle of the Humber Bridge, in the fog, there was only one person who could possibly help her do that, wasn't there?"

He stared at me, as if trying to hypnotise me with the logic of it all. He needn't have bothered, I was already three steps ahead of him.

He stabbed a finger in my direction. "There was only one person who could help – and that was you, Cameron. I think that in the circumstances it is very likely she would have told you all the details and asked you to get them to someone she trusted. Someone like me... or... perhaps... Mrs Whittling." He paused, watching me intently. "And since you did not come to see me yesterday and you did mention Mrs Whittling's name this afternoon, I can only assume it was the latter."

"Well, you're wrong!" I protested. "She said nothing to me about a file. In any case, how do you know her attacker didn't go straight to her home anyway, get the computer and retrieve the file?"

"Because Cameron, the police were at her flat within thirty minutes of the attack. Her computer was untouched and when they tried to download her mail later that day, there wasn't any." He paused and smiled thinly. "Somebody got to the file first, you see, Cameron. And it could only have been you."

He paused a while to let his clever reasoning sink in. But it didn't quite add up. It was after two o'clock when I downloaded that file. That would have given the police a full five hours to check Magda Swinson's computer; to download her mail and the attachment – and stop me accessing it directly from the server. So, they had either been very slow – or Stantonwell was lying.

I thought back to last night and Angel's insistence that I tell her everything. I thought back to what I'd said at the camp less than an hour before. I thought back to the telephone call Stantonwell had taken just a few minutes ago. His logic was very neat, and his argument about Magda's motives very plausible, but how could he be so certain?

"You're just guessing."

He looked at me levelly. "Maybe I am, my dear. But, just for a moment, let us imagine I'm right.

"If I am right, Cameron, then the problem you have is this. Through no fault of your own, you have come into possession of a valuable, highly confidential file. It's no longer on Miss Swinson's e-mail server, we know that. So it is perhaps on your own, or maybe you've even downloaded it already, onto disk. It's of no value to you, as I'm sure you know, because it's encoded. But the point I'm making is that it is still of great value to a dealer... Worth millions of pounds on the black market.

"Now, Cameron, we come to the nub of the matter. Since the local tabloid has done such a good job of publicising your involvement, by now Joanna Whittling and her associate – the man who tried to kill

Miss Swinson – will almost certainly have guessed that you have the file too.

"So you have a big problem, my dear. Either the police are going to lock you up because you lied to them. Or the man who stabbed Magda Swinson is going to come after you for the information, get it out of you by whatever means are necessary, and then kill you." He picked up his cup and took a last sip of the coffee, then casually wiped his moustache.

"So you can see that, however you look at your situation, you are in the most terrible predicament, Cameron…"

"So you're offering me a chance…" I looked back at him without any show of emotion, but my spirits were plummeting.

"I'm a fair man, my dear. I would hate to see you spending your life in some women's jail." He pursed his lips and looked me up and down again. "Even though you might… er, how shall I put this… enjoy some of the company in there." He smiled insipidly at his own cleverness and then turned deadly serious again.

"Equally, I would be very distressed if I heard, in a day or two, that the police had dredged your body out of the river."

"I'm touched by your concern," I answered drily. "What's your solution?"

"The deal is this, Cameron…" He filled his lungs, puffed out his chest and looked down on me. I stared straight back, squirming in disbelief at the way I'd walked into his trap.

"I need to know what you've done with that file. And I need to make sure that, wherever it is, it is destroyed. That's the only way I can secure the safety and confidentiality of that project information.

"In return I will use my influence to ensure that no further charges are brought against you, and you may have this," he held up the cassette, "and do what you will with it. Additionally, once the file has been deleted, you will guarantee your personal safety with regard to Mrs Whittling and the man who is helping her."

It all sounded so neat. But I didn't trust him. If the file I'd forwarded to the new e-mail box was just a project file, then why did Joanna Whittling want it to use at a conference demanding tighter restrictions on research? And, come to that, if Joanna was a dealer like he said, why was she speaking in a debate on ethics anyway? Before I did anything, I needed to hear her version of the story.

"That all sounds very convincing, Stantonwell, but I'm afraid you're wrong. I don't know where your file is. I don't know anything about it."

He shook his head in disappointment. "Then might I suggest you think very hard, Cameron? Maybe something has slipped your mind." Then he leant towards me threateningly until I was looking straight into his eyes.

"You look like a nice woman," he said, picking up a paper knife and running his fingers gently, suggestively, up and down the blade. "You look like someone who has a life, people who love you. I want you to be very sensible about this. The missing file is extremely valuable. We can't afford to lose it." He looked down at the knife, then pointed at me with it. "And neither can you. Do you understand?"

"I have nothing to tell you," I insisted, stony-faced, standing up and turning to go.

"Well, I suggest you find something very quickly, my dear."

"I'll think about it," I said, inferring quite clearly that I wouldn't. I didn't like him. I didn't trust him. And I didn't like his threats.

But this man was not playing games.

"You do that, Cameron. Think *very* hard – and, for your own safety, make sure you are back here by 9 am tomorrow with the details."

## Fifteen

'Know Thine Enemy', someone had once said.

As I walked back up the track towards the Land Rover, I wondered just who my enemies were. There was a long enough list to choose from.

For all his oily rhetoric, Stantonwell wasn't a friend, that was for sure. Self-seeking and two-faced, he was offering me a way out, but even if I helped him, there was no guarantee that he would keep his word. And now that I'd spoken to him, I was sure there were others I couldn't trust either.

There was Angel, for a start. I'd already had my doubts, sitting in the Polar Bear earlier today. Now I wondered if it had been her who got the information out of me and passed it on to Stantonwell. Or maybe he was just fishing when he left the message on my mobile and hadn't found out the details until I was in his office. The phone call he took there could have been from any one of the protesters. They knew all the details too, word for word.

Then there was Beano: a woman who had acted strangely from the minute we met and had seemed terrified of me going in to see Stantonwell. She knew more than she admitted, that was for sure.

And Bernie. He'd followed me that first night; he had an uncomfortable interest in me. He said he'd once been a client of mine, but however hard I tried, I couldn't remember him.

As for Charlie, he definitely didn't like me and I knew from Jimmy that he was capable of violence. Then there was his friend Jean who was almost equally unfriendly. Not to mention the rest of the camp – Elana, Lou, Stella, Len and the others. Was it one of them who had betrayed me?

Finally, there were the police. I couldn't believe Stantonwell had access to their confidential information. But he knew the details of my statement and he'd got my phone number from somewhere. Still, however credible he'd made it sound, his version of events didn't add up. If the police had wanted to check Magda's email, I couldn't believe they would have waited more than five hours to do it. I couldn't believe they'd done it at all. If they had, there would have been more questions they wanted to ask me, giving them just the excuse they needed to pull me in again.

The protesters were waiting for me as I walked back across the cattle grid, no longer concerned whether the security men saw me talking to them or not. Curious and eager, their questions were hovering, unspoken, in the wet mid-afternoon air. Only Beano was missing.

I looked at their faces as I approached, feeling shaken. They would want to know what had been said and whether Stantonwell had been willing to help. Charlie was at the front as I approached the small group.

"So what happened, then, Cameron?" he asked cynically, almost willing me to give them bad news.

I shook my head. "Nothing, he wouldn't tell me where I could find her. He didn't even offer to help put her in touch with me," I answered. Sometimes just not telling the truth is easier than lying.

Despondent and unsure how to deal with this new situation, I walked through the group to the fire. Someone had put green wood on it and the flames were dancing in shades of red, orange and blue as the heat bit into the sap-filled branches. I wondered fleetingly if they had taken to pulling their fuel straight off the trees.

I went through the details of my visit with them, leaving out most of the conversation with Stantonwell and concentrating instead on a description of the compound and the offices. I noticed Bernie staring at me as I gave them as much detail about the site as I could, describing the layout of the place, the cameras, the lights, the security post, the knacker's wagon – everything that might be of practical help.

I looked around as I talked. Jean and Charlie were clearly fascinated by what I was saying, Elana a little bemused by the scale of it all. Lou was sitting in the entrance to her tent, taking a passing interest. Len was concentrating hard. Stella was preparing the evening meal whilst she listened. Any one of them might have made a phone call to Stantonwell. I could hardly ask them.

I talked with one half of my brain, whilst the other continued to sift through the conversation inside GME, digging over Stantonwell's words, his certainty that I knew Magda's e-mail address and the password that would open it. I tried to reassure myself, but I seemed to be digging myself deeper and deeper into an ever more dangerous hole.

Now I was caught between three factions: the police, who wanted to lock me up; Stantonwell, who wanted his file found and deleted; and Joanna Whittling – who was either a vindictive woman on the make, like he'd said, or just another scientist concerned with a fight for ethical research.

Once I'd finished, Bernie came across and sat next to me, trying to monopolise me.

"You OK, Cameron?" he asked. "You look stressed out."

"Yeah," I replied, as casually as I could. "Wouldn't you be? It's not every day I walk into a place like that... Anyway, what happened to Beano?" I asked, to no one in particular, changing the subject as quickly as I could. "She seemed really angry about me going in there. Does anyone know where she's gone?"

Elana shook her head sadly. "We don't know, Cameron. We can't fathom her. When she came at the weekend, we all liked her. She seemed like a kindred spirit. But then I suppose you can't get to know someone in a few days. I dunno. Maybe she's just in a mood. Maybe it's PMT."

"You've not met her before, then? I mean at any other animal rights demos? She told me she'd been to them all."

Elana shook her head. "No, she's like you, and Bernie – new to the movement. Enthusiastic enough, though, never stopped asking questions about GME and its history, the people who work there and the issues involved in the protest. But no, I don't think any of us have met her before. We're still quite a tight-knit community in the protest movement. There aren't that many of us, unfortunately, so we all travel around quite a bit, supporting each other at special vigils and the like. To be honest, dear, it worries me when someone you think is on your side walks off like that."

"Oh, she was probably just in a mood," I suggested. "I'm sure she'll be back." I tried to sound positive but I couldn't forget how she'd made a big thing about being a long-term activist. It was yet another question mark.

"I never trusted the woman," Charlie grunted.

"Charlie, you never trust anyone," Lou remarked good-naturedly.

"So what are your plans now, Cameron?" Stella asked. "Seeing as Stantonwell was so unhelpful."

"I don't know." I really didn't. "Without Joanna Whittling I can't do a thing. I guess I'll ask around the area a little, see if I can find her some other way. Otherwise we'll have to try and see her at the conference, won't we?"

"Well, we can't give up on you now, Cameron," Elana said. "Not when the file might be so useful to us. I'll ring around, if you like. There might be activists somewhere else who've come across her – she must still be working in the industry."

"Thanks," I said. "That would be really helpful." But I wasn't sure I wanted any help. Maybe my safest bet was to steer clear.

Elana asked me to stay for supper, but I couldn't face the thought of food and I wanted to get away from there. Magda Swinson, Stantonwell, Beano, Angel, Charlie, Joanna Whittling, ISEM, the police... I couldn't connect anything to anything. Yesterday I'd witnessed a vicious, cold-blooded attack. Today I'd been threatened by the head of a multinational research company. There were so many people, all following different agendas – and every one of them seemed to revolve around the message that the woman on the bridge had given me.

I was beginning to feel desperate. It was tempting to go back into GME and give Stantonwell the details he wanted; to sit down at his computer, access the e-mail server and delete the file in front of his eyes. So very easy. But I still didn't know what I'd be deleting. I only had Stantonwell's word that it was a valuable research file with a dealer after it. And he'd acted like a manipulative liar, which meant Joanna Whittling could, conceivably, be above board. Magda Swinson could have taken the file because she wanted the contents exposed at the conference. And the file itself might be something that would move the animal rights protest into the front line.

I needed time and space to think.

So I used my mother. I made the excuse that I'd promised to go and see her. It was already gone three. I needed to get there before teatime. Sorry to rush. I had to go. Yes, I would be back. Maybe tomorrow.

I noticed Bernie watching me as I walked down the road to my bike. He made no effort to hide his interest.

It took less than ten minutes to get there.

The Oaklands Retirement Home was the sort of place you'd want to be, if you had to be consigned to the prison of a nursing home. It was set in parkland, with mature trees and extensive grounds, so that you could get well away from all the other residents. When I'm old – if I make it that long – the last place I want to be is among other old people. I know it's ageist, but nursing homes make me squirm.

I pulled into one of the parking bays and locked the bike. The main entrance was in a large mock-Elizabethan house, built in Victorian times on the edge of the estate. The rest of the complex had been added on in the sixties. It didn't go together well at all. The newer, brick-built, flat-roofed buildings would be hard pushed to complement an army camp, let alone a stylish half-timbered house.

It had seemed like a good idea when I needed an excuse to leave the camp. Now, as I stuffed my rucksack into one of the bike's panniers, I wasn't so sure. She was in there somewhere, depressed and senile. Waiting to die. We had nothing to say to each other. I couldn't think why I was putting myself through this. Or why I should feel so bad about feeling bad.

I sat on a bench under a horse chestnut tree, in the middle of the extensive lawns. Above me, the sticky buds were swelling, getting ready to release their big green leaves. Around me, the daffodils were in full bloom and the newly mown grass smelt fresh and clean.

I felt anxious about seeing her. Huh, I felt anxious about nearly everything at the moment. Every nerve ending in my body seemed to be keyed up and exposed. Even my head felt like it was bursting. Was I really going to do this? Could I do it?

Sitting there, under that tree, I felt desolate. I was still sore over Hellen. I was angry that I'd had to walk out on her like that. I was missing my home and my cat. I was missing Becky. I was all alone, with no one I could trust, and the threat of prison – or worse – dangling by a thread above my head. There didn't seem any way out. If I went back to the police now, the fact that I'd withheld evidence would almost certainly result in me being charged. And if it didn't, then Stantonwell's corrupt influence probably would. If I took the easy way out and levelled with the boss of GME, like he wanted me to, then I still had no guarantee I would be safe, either. The man was a mean-hearted bastard. Whatever he'd said, I still had no evidence that he wasn't involved in the attack on Magda Swinson himself. And, if he was, then he would have no compunction in taking the information and getting rid of me as well.

I looked across at the nursing home. I wished it was safe to be with my mother, that I could just walk in and let her hold me. I wanted

someone to tell me that everything was all right. Shit, I wanted someone to *make* it all all right.

I fumbled around in my pocket for the mobile and pulled it out,
wiping a tear from my eye before dialling. Becky's receptionist answered and put me through to her at once.

"Hello Cam!" she said. "How are you? How's your mother? Have
you delivered that blooming message yet?"

"I'm outside the home now," I said, faltering at the sound of her
familiar voice and ignoring the bit about the message. "I... don't know
if I can do it, Becky. I..." But my throat was dry with all the sorrow and
fear inside me.

"Oh Cameron," she breathed, "I know it's hard, flower. But it will
be fine, I promise you. Just go in. She's an old lady, she's not going to
harm you."

"I know... I know... but... Becky, I'm so scared."

"It's all right, love. You're bound to be. You haven't seen her for
years. But do it, please. She's all alone and she hasn't got long. Just
think of her. Just think how pleased she'll be to know you're all right.
She could pass away any time. You might not have the chance again."

"Yeah..." I mumbled, fighting back the tears. It's funny how someone you love can make you fall apart inside. "I know. I know, Becky."

She was right. It might be my last chance. But not for the reason
she was thinking.

"You'll be fine, Cam. You know you will. You're a strong, courag-
eous woman. You can do anything you set your mind to. You know
that."

"Yeah." I sniffed, wiping my eyes with the back of my hand, wishing it was true.

"Just do it, love. Do it now."

"Yeah, OK Becks. I will. I just needed to hear you say it. Thanks,
I'm sorry to ring you like this."

"It's all right, darling. I love you. I want everything to be all right."

"Thanks."

"Cameron, what about that message, have you delivered it yet?"

"I'm working on it, Becky."

"Well, take care, love... You sure you're all right?"

"Yes, I'm fine, Becky. Just fine. It's just seeing my mother that's worrying me."

I put the phone back in my pocket and blew my nose. I wanted to get it over with. Maybe it would make me feel better. At least it would be one worry out of the way.

I got up from the bench and tidied myself up, breathing deeply, trying to quell the tightness in my chest. Then, my head down, I began to walk across the grass, towards the front of the home.

I didn't register the noise at first. I was buried so deep inside myself that it took a few seconds to take in the black Jeep that came screaming across the car park.

But when I did look up, my heart dropped down into my boots and Stantonwell's warning about Joanna Whittling and her 'associate' rang in my ears.

The big ugly vehicle was riding high off the ground, no more than thirty yards away. It left the parking area, taking off as it bumped over the kerb, landing with a thud on the grass. Then it swerved in my direction, the wheels ploughing into the soft ground, shards of grass and earth spewing from them. I could see the driver leaning menacingly over the steering wheel. The big fender with its cattle bars was hurtling straight for me. I stood transfixed in disbelief. Then I spun round looking for an escape. But there was nowhere to go and he was closing in, accelerating hard.

I stood my ground until the last moment and threw myself hard over to the left, tumbling out of the way. The Jeep shot past and I stumbled to my feet, covered in wet grass, frightened out of my mind.

Then it skidded round, tearing up the lawn with its big wheels and coming at me again. I ran with every ounce of strength I had, this time, stumbling and panting across the grass, towards the safety of a belt of trees. My feet were slipping and sliding on the wet lawn. Twenty yards, and they wouldn't be able to follow me.

But I could hear the beast right behind me. I could smell the engine. I could feel the vibration beneath my feet. I glanced over my shoulder and zigzagged wildly. Only ten yards to the trees.

Ten yards too many.

The open door belted me hard across the shoulders, as the four-by-four tore past, throwing me painfully forward, first onto my knees, then head over heels across the grass.

I scrambled to my feet, stunned and aching, ready to run again, but before I could move a step, the Jeep was by my side and a man was twisting my arm behind my back, holding a gun to my head.

"Get in!" he barked. "Get in the fucking car!"

## Sixteen

He grabbed my collar and flung me headlong into the back of the Jeep, sending me crashing across the seat and onto the floor. My heart was slamming in my chest. I could hardly breathe. Paralysed with terror, I struggled to turn around. He leapt in after me, slamming my head down hard against the floor, then holding me there, the gun pressed against my temple, as the Jeep lurched forward under me.

I swallowed hard, catching my breath, sick with fear and shock.

"What the fuck's going on?" I screamed tearfully, my head throbbing with pain.

"You shut the fuck up, McGill!" he bawled in my face, spit spraying my cheeks. "You talk when I say, OK?"

Then I felt the four-by-four lurch forward over the kerb, back across the car park and out onto the road. I could hear two more voices in the front as it squealed and lurched round another corner. They were laughing loudly, high on adrenalin. Overdosing on testosterone.

Through the haze of fear and panic, I became aware that one of them was shouting at me over the front seat. "Hiya dyke! Welcome aboard! You're going for a little ride, you lucky bitch!"

"Yeah, maybe *three* little rides if you're very lucky," a second voice added, without a hint of humour.

The guy with the gun looked down on me with a sickly, terrifying leer. He was tall, muscular and mean-looking, in his thirties, with a shaved head and big, sticky-out ears. His knee was on my ribs, and his full weight was pinning me painfully to the floor. His blue jeans were dirty, his white T-shirt stained with fresh sweat. I stared back at him for minutes that seemed to turn into hours, struggling to breathe, wondering who the fuck they were. They knew my name. Maybe Stantonwell hadn't been lying after all.

I was beginning to feel dizzy, my lungs constricted by the weight from his knee. As they drove on I thought I was going to pass out. But eventually, the Jeep turned sharply left, rattling and jolting over rougher ground, and all three of them began to laugh and whoop. Like they were having a party. Like they were drunk.

"Get her up, Raz," said a voice from the driving seat. "Let's see the bitch! Let's see the fucking goods, man."

The guy with the gun and the big ears grabbed me by the jacket and hauled me up onto the seat, pinning me by the neck against the side of the vehicle. "Don't try anything, McGill," he warned, waving the gun with his free hand. "I just love topping dykes."

The front passenger turned round and leant on the back of his seat. He was shorter and younger than the one in the back. Overweight too, with close cropped hair and big cod-like eyes, shining out from a face that was sagging at the chin. "Hey, Jonno," he bellowed at the driver, "she's quite sweet for a lezzie." Then he leant over and stroked my cheek with the back of his hand, chuckling to himself. "Specially for a butch one."

The driver glanced back at me, unsmiling. He was older than the others, wearing a thick grey jumper and sporting greasy black hair. His lips parted in a sneer, revealing dirty teeth and a long knife scar on his cheek which turned white when his skin stretched.

I tried hard not to react. Nothing I could do or say would help in here. My only chance was if we stopped. I just prayed I would get that chance.

We were driving up an overgrown track, bumping and slewing in and out of the deep ruts, heading for what looked like a farm, maybe half a mile away, isolated amongst the green fields of the North Lincolnshire countryside. The tiny knot of buildings grew more derelict as we got closer. A farmhouse, with its roof caved in; old sheds; abandoned machinery; rotting bales of straw piled high, steaming in the afternoon sun. And, everywhere, thistles and nettles, black and deadened by the frosts of winter, suffocating everything around them.

The Jeep pulled in next to a long, brick-built shed with a rusting, corrugated iron roof, and I braced myself. I didn't know how I was going to do it. But this was my only chance. Somehow I had to get away.

Cod Eyes jumped down first and opened the rear door. "Get out, bitch!" he bellowed, as Big Ears shoved me from behind, sending me toppling out, so that I fell, stumbling and disoriented, amongst the rubble and weeds around me. I got up, ready to run, but he grabbed my wrist and yanked me towards him.

"Get off me, you big ape," I yelled, scared witless, struggling to break free, bringing my knee up into his groin. He screamed in pain and lashed out with his free hand, bringing it down hard across my face, making my cheek sting and my head reel.

Big Ears grabbed me roughly and pinned an arm behind me. "I fucking told you, shut it, woman!" he barked, as he shoved me across the yard, through some double doors and into the inky darkness of the shed.

Coming from the brightness of the day, I could see nothing. But I could smell the cold and damp; the fusty, shitty, animal smell that you get in abandoned cowsheds. And the smell of dereliction and decay. I twisted and jerked as he pushed me down the shed, but with every step he pulled my arm higher up my back until the pain was exploding around me and my arm felt like it was breaking. Halfway along, he stopped and threw me down onto the cold hard floor. I lay there, adjusting to the darkness, sick and despondent, knowing full well what my fate was likely to be.

The cowshed was about fifty yards long, divided into byres, two cows wide, separated by shoulder-high rails. I was lying on the filthy, straw-caked floor. They were standing across the entrance to the byre, on the channel designed to gather up all the shit and piss. How appropriate.

I could almost see the saliva on their mouths. They looked like wild animals, cornering their prey; enjoying the thrill of what was to come; anticipating their own pleasure.

The thug who'd been driving, Scarface, walked slowly towards me, his face contorted into a sadistic smile. He looked wiry and hard. And he acted like he was the one in charge. He grunted and motioned for me to get up, and as I started to rise, he grabbed me by the neck and slammed me against the wall, knocking the air from my lungs, leaving me slumped breathless and wild-eyed.

They know your name, Cameron. This is no casual assault.

Then he pulled me away from the wall into the centre of the byre and the three of them surrounded me. Cats and mouse. They were playing with their victim. They wanted me to fight. They wanted it to last.

But they knew my name, I kept thinking, as I turned around and around. Watching their faces, trying to figure a way out. They knew my name. They must want the file.

"So here we are, lads," Scarface smirked, his voice echoing back at me off the corrugated metal roof. "All alone with a LESBIAN." He moved towards me, a sickly grin on his face. I backed off, bumping into Big Ears, who pushed me back towards Cod Eyes. I spun round, my arms out in front of me, threatening retaliation.

But they laughed at me.

Scarface sneered at my futile attempts to defend myself. "We don't like LESBIANS, do we lads?" The other two howled in agreement, their faces displaying a mixture of disgust, excitement, and hate. Like I say, the human face...

"And we all know what LESBIANS need – don't we?"

"Yeah, we fucking do," Big Ears mocked, grabbing me suddenly with his dirty hands and squeezing my breasts.

I lashed out with my boot, catching him on the shin, turning his mockery to pain. And to anger. He lunged at me, grabbing my collar and throwing me backwards across the byre, into the arms of Scarface.

The dirty bastard grabbed me and pulled me forcibly back, close into his body, one hand on my breasts, the other between my legs. I retched as I felt him behind me, big and excited. And I lifted my boot high into the air and slammed it down on his trainer-clad foot.

He howled with pain and fell back as Big Ears came for me, lashing out with his fists. I grabbed his arm with both hands, twisting it hard and propelling him away from me.

"Get your filthy hands off me!" I screamed, spinning round and going for Cod Eyes.

But I never made it. Suddenly they all fell on me, grabbing my limbs and clutching me so that I could hardly move. Then there were ropes around my wrists and I was being shoved backwards against the wall and secured, spread-eagled, to metal rings. I twisted my body and let fly with my feet. It was all I could do now. But Cod Eyes and Big Ears grabbed one leg each, and no matter how I struggled, they held me tight. I was at their mercy.

They all stared at me, breathing heavily. I screamed and struggled again as Scarface grabbed the waistband of my jeans and pulled at the zip, tugging at it until my belly and my briefs were exposed.

Then he calmly stood back and looked into my face.

He was aroused. They all were. But, despite the excitement in his crotch, his eyes were cold and hard. And his words were slow and measured.

"There's nothing more we'd like to do than to fuck you, McGill. Me and the lads. But, right now... there's something a friend of ours wants even more badly. You know what it is, don't you, bitch?" He breathed all over me, fixing me with evil eyes, his dirty teeth opening and closing just inches from my face.

I shook my head and glared back.

"Yes you fuckin' do!" he shouted, going for my chin and pushing my head painfully back over my shoulders, stretching my windpipe so that I had to gasp for breath. "The file, McGill! The file that Magda Swinson copied yesterday. The one she e-mailed from the laboratories. You got it. We want it." He snarled. "Where the fuck is it, bitch?"

"I don't know what you're talking about!" I coughed, hardly able to breathe.

He pushed harder and harder. My neck felt like it was going to break. "Don't give me that shit, bitch! You've been shootin' yer mouth off. So don't try and fuckin' deny it." He leant against me, between my legs, with the full weight of his body, and brought his face down close to mine. "Spit it out, dyke!" he hissed. "Tell me, and maybe you'll get off lightly."

However scared I was at that moment, however desperate I was to keep them off me, my brain was still functioning. It didn't take a genius to work it out. The information they wanted was all I had going for me, the only thing that would keep me alive. Whatever they did, whatever they said, I had to keep it to myself. The minute I gave them what they wanted, I would be dead.

"Well?" he barked. "You gonna tell us?" He loosened his grip and let my head come forward, so that I could speak. "Or are we gonna fuck you and throw your body away?"

I looked him in the eyes. "If you kill me, you'll never get it," I croaked.

He stepped back, his face grim and angry, and turned to the other two. "Take her boots off," he ordered.

I kicked and twisted but they were holding me too tightly. First one and then the other boot came off. Scarface tore at my jeans and slowly, inevitably, worked them down my flailing legs until I was exposed.

"OK Gaz," he said coldly. "You have her first. Maybe some fucking will revive her memory."

I looked at Cod Eyes. His trousers were open and his face was full of anticipation.

I shuddered in disgust and closed my eyes.

"It doesn't matter what you do. I'm not telling you!" I screamed, bracing myself for the pain as one of them ripped my briefs away. I kept my eyes tightly shut, shaking inside, falling apart... Preparing myself for the one thing I feared more than anything else.

"Leave her!" The new voice boomed all along the shed, echoing off the roof, reverberating around the rafters.

Everything froze.

I opened my eyes and all three of them were standing stock still, their heads turned towards the silhouette of another man standing by the door.

"I said, *leave her!*" the shape commanded, walking slowly and confidently towards us, a handgun stretched out in front of him – a big man who looked like he could handle himself.

Suddenly the odds had changed and the three men looked at each other, unsure how to deal with this new situation. Cod Eyes fastened his jeans, extreme disappointment on his face. Scarface took a hesitant step towards the shadow as it approached.

"Get away from her, or you're all dead meat," said the shadow. It was a strong voice, resonating with anger; a strangely familiar voice. In my terror, I couldn't work out where or when I had heard it before.

Big Ears grabbed my face, squeezing my cheeks until they hurt. "All right, McGill," he said quietly, menacingly, "you've been lucky this time. Your knight in shining fucking armour is here to save you. But we'll be after you. You're gonna tell us where that file is, sooner or later..."

He pushed my head back and let go.

The shadow stepped into one of the bays, leaving the way clear to the door. "Now get the fuck out!" he ordered, brandishing the gun at them, "before I lose my temper. *Now!*"

The three of them stood for less than a second, before running out of the shed and back to their car. I heard the roar of the Jeep's engine and the squeal of its tyres as they took off, away from the farm, away from me, and I fell against the wall, trembling with relief, shaking with cold.

The man came up to me, undid the ropes around my wrists, put his coat over my shoulders and held me close. "It's all right now, Cameron. They've gone. You're safe."

I still didn't remember him from the counselling but, Christ, was I relieved to see Bernie!

## Seventeen

I felt better when I got my jeans back on. Bernie put the car heating on full and I let the waves of hot air cascade over me. I was warmer now, but that didn't stop the shaking as my mind relived the horror of the last hour. As he drove, I scanned the open countryside, half expecting to see the Jeep reappear from behind a hedge. But there was no one around. They'd gone – at least for now.

"Lucky I found you, eh, Cameron? If I hadn't decided to come after you to ask you out for a drink, I would never have seen them take you. Then who knows what would have happened?"

"I know very well what would have happened," I snapped unkindly, a chill running down my back, and a tear down my face. Then, more evenly: "Thanks Bernie, I can't tell you how grateful I am."

I sat quietly for a while, thinking how lucky I was that he'd been able to scare them away.

"Where did you get the gun?" I asked.

He laughed. "Replica, Cameron. Some people collect stamps, I collect replica handguns. It doesn't fire, of course, but they weren't to know that. I kind of like the look and feel of the guns. I'm a great fan of the American PIs – you know, Marlowe, Mike Hammer..."

"Oh, well... thanks again."

"It's OK, Cameron. I owed you one. I guess we're about square now." He was pleased with himself, watching over me but not quite connecting with my pain or the terror of the situation. Just a man, I guess. How the fuck could he know how I felt?

I was still glancing around the open countryside, unable to quite believe they'd gone. And this man from the past, this man whom I hadn't the grace to remember, was the reason. And I didn't even like him very much.

"You want to come back to the camp, stay the night there?" he asked. "You need looking after. You can use my tent."

"Thanks Bernie," I replied, my stomach retching, trying hard to stay civil. "I'm really grateful, but I think I'd rather be somewhere a bit more comfortable, a bit more private, at the moment. I don't feel so good."

That was an understatement. I felt sick and unclean. I needed a shower and a warm bed. Some space. I closed my eyes and wished that Hellen could be with me. For all my anger at her sudden need for commitment, I wished I could lose myself in her soft warm body and cry until all the pain had gone.

"Oh come on, Cameron, you can't just go off on your own! You need to be with someone. Come back with me."

He tried hard to persuade me. He went on and on about the danger I was in, as if I didn't fucking realise it myself. But however grateful I was, I didn't want to be around Bernie, or any man. And that apart, I didn't want to go back to the camp. I couldn't stand the thought of being amongst people, especially when I wasn't sure I could trust them. That made me think about Angel again.

"Look Bernie, I'll be all right," I answered. "I have a friend in Hessle. I'm sure I can spend the night at her house." I'd no intention of staying with her either, but it might just make him lay off.

He turned to me and smirked. "The cottage where I saw you last night? Yeah, OK. I'll take you there."

"No," I replied, as firmly as I could. "It's OK. Just drop me back at the nursing home. I'll take the bike."

He looked across at me sharply and I gave him the stare. He

seemed to give in then, thank goodness, and we drove in silence for a while, back onto the main road towards Barton.

"Cameron," he said carefully, after a few more minutes, "I never thought I'd hear myself say this, but you have to be sensible. You have to tell them where the file is. I might not be around the next time – and there's no way they're going to leave you alone."

I wished he'd shut up. I was already confused and disoriented and he was making it worse. My mouth was dry; my mind was numb. I looked away, out across the bare rolling countryside, as Bernie over-took a tractor hauling a load of sweet-smelling silage. I felt strangely troubled. Sitting here in this car felt unreal, like I was an actor on a film set. Shit, I was so relieved he'd turned up when he did... Yet something was making me uneasy.

"So, you gonna hand it over, then?" he persisted.

"How the fuck can I?" I snapped, exasperated by his persistence. "They'll kill me once I've told them where it is. Besides, I don't know what's in the file – it could be something important. It could be evidence against you lot; it could be anything."

"I don't think any of that matters, Cameron," he said, like he really cared. "Not when your life's at stake, it doesn't. All I know is that they nearly killed you just then and, if you don't tell them, they're bound to come after you and finish the job." He shook his head. "I don't know what's in that file, girl – but, for certain, someone out there wants it very badly."

"Yeah, I know. But so long as I'm the only one who knows where it is, they daren't kill me, dare they? It's the only insurance I have, Bernie, can't you see that? Once I tell them, there's no reason to keep me alive – and every reason to shut me up."

His voice was edgy. "Look, Cameron, let me help you. Let me protect you. Give the details to me and get the fuck out of here. I'll find those guys somehow and pass it on. Do it, please! For God's sake, woman, make yourself safe. Let me get you out of this mess."

I looked at him sharply. "Why are you so keen to help?" I asked.

He sighed in exasperation. "I want to help you because I like you, Cameron. I really like you! Can't you tell? Shit, I've been dropping plenty of hints!"

"Yeah, well... Thanks, but no thanks, Bernie. I can look after myself."

He opened his mouth to say something and I glared at him. "No! Just let it drop, will you? I'll be OK," I said tetchily. "I know now to watch my back. They won't get me so easily again."

"OK, OK! Don't get so fucking wound up. I'm on your side, re-member?" He shifted in his seat and said nothing for a while. Then he started again. "It's your decision, love. But they'll be following you tonight – you can bet on it." Then he put his hand on my leg. "You're gonna have to give it to them anyway. Why not do it through me and make sure they can't get you again? Please, Cameron, I don't want you to get harmed."

I removed his hand from my thigh. "No, Bernie! No. I'm really grateful, but that's where it ends. I'll be all right."

As we drove into the outskirts of Barton, he gave me a look that said, 'You stupid bitch – why won't you listen, why won't you accept help when it's offered?' But I didn't care much by then. Something in my mind had just snapped.

However stupid it might seem, however reckless, I knew then that there was no way I was going to let a bunch of thugs, or a guy who claimed to be an ex-client, force me into doing something I didn't want to do. I was going to hang on to the file, until I found out what was going on. I was going to find Joanna Whittling and see what she said about it. And the harder anyone – the thugs, Beano, Stantonwell, Charlie or Bernie – tried to dissuade me, the more determined I would become. I glared back at him, my face set now, my mind made up. Fuck you! Fuck all of you!

It was starting to get dark as Bernie drove into the nursing home grounds. "You sure you won't change your mind?"

I shook my head.

"Please?" he appealed. "Be sensible, I can sort it for you."

"I've never been sensible, Bernie," I answered dispassionately.

He looked at me grimly. "Some people just don't know when to call it quits," he grunted, giving me a weird look as I got out.

I could feel him watching as I walked across the car park. For all his apparent concern, he was making me uneasy. Getting back in his car at the farm, I'd felt really lucky to escape. But now that I was calmer...

## Eighteen

I breathed deeply as I reached my bike, stretching my arms, trying to ease the stiffness across my back and in my limbs. I felt dirty. My head ached and a small clot of blood hung to my hair where they'd slammed me against the Jeep floor. My cheek felt sore as well, but otherwise, I seemed to be all in one piece.

When I glanced over my shoulder, Bernie was still there, loath to let me go. The sodium lights were coming on across the car park, and around the perimeter, in the half-light, every shrub, every tree took on a dark shape. The sound of every car that went past on the road became the roar of that black Jeep. Over to my right, by the big tree, there were thick scars across the lawn, thrown into a ghastly relief by the fading evening light.

Sitting on my bike, staring at the lights of the nursing home and trying to ignore the man in the car, I thought again of Becky's words about my mother. I was tired of strangers and would-be friends. I needed family. I gazed at the light spilling out from behind the nursing home curtains. It was hardly the best of timing. But I had a pressing need to be with the one woman who owed me some kind of sanctuary.

Bernie gave up and drove away as I walked through the door. I hadn't any idea what I was going to say to her. I only knew that, perhaps for the first time in my adult life, she was in the right place at the right time. It wasn't that I expected her to talk to me, or to offer me any comfort. When they last rang me, the nurse had confirmed that she was becoming increasingly senile, and that moments of lucidity, already short when I last saw her, were becoming rarer. I didn't care. For once it would be nice just to sit with someone who, however remote, was family. Someone who wouldn't ask questions.

She was sitting in the high-backed chair next to her bed, gazing vacantly ahead, when I went through the door. I felt a rush of panic as the faint smell of stale urine and scent met me at the threshold. For a moment, insecurity washed over me and I wished I hadn't come. What if she turned on me? What then?

But I went in anyway, without speaking, and she moved her head to look at me as I sat down on the bed. She was much smaller than the last time I saw her. Her face and her body had shrivelled. Her fine grey hair was thinner, and her hands, resting on her lap, were shaking rhythmically. The buttons on her dress were done up wrongly and down the front were various food stains: fresh ones which nobody had taken the time to wash away. She looked comfortable but uncared for, and, for the first time in my life, I felt sorry for her.

No trace of recognition or surprise crossed her face. Her wet lips moved up and down, as if she were trying to talk, but she wasn't. It was just another mannerism, like the shaking hands, just another symptom of a human being falling apart on the road to death.

"Mother," I coaxed gently, feeling a mixture of disgust, anger and affection for the frail figure sitting opposite me. "Mum, do you know who I am?"

She focussed on me for a few seconds and then her eyes turned away, glazing over again. On impulse, I got up from the bed and knelt beside her, taking her bony hands in mine. "Mum, it's Cameron, your daughter," I said, the tears welling up inside me.

She looked into my face. "Carrie," she breathed, "when is Carrie coming?" She studied me, puzzlement rippling across the lines of her face. "You're not Carrie!" she muttered scratchily, sinking back into her reverie.

"Carrie can't come and see you any more, Mum," I sobbed, scared now of her reaction to me; scared that she still hadn't registered my sister's death. "I'm your other daughter, Cameron. I know we never got on, but I'm all you have left."

She screwed up her eyes, trying to focus her mind. "You've cut your hair... lost weight. You look different."

I fell forward, burying my head on her hands, sobbing openly now, believing she'd recognised me. She pulled a hand away and began to stroke my head. Then, shakily, she put the other hand under my chin and lifted up my head. "Why are you crying, Carrie? Tell Mummy, love."

After a lifetime of resentment from this woman, after years of estrangement, I could bear it no longer. I was supposed to be here to make her feel better. But all I could think about were my own pathetic feelings of lovelessness and isolation; the memory of the Jeep and the three thugs, the helplessness, the violence, the threats.

And all my mother could see or think about was my dead sister.

"I'm crying because I need you," I shouted angrily, and then, shocked at my own lack of control, I lowered my voice. "I'm crying, Mum, because I'm the daughter you never wanted to know. I've nearly been raped, Mum... and I need you. Why won't you recognise me?"

She stirred and her dull eyes flickered.

"Rape?" she mouthed silently, a light coming on in her eyes. "Yes... Oh yes... Nasty man... Bad! ... Horrible!"

"What?" I asked.

She looked back at me, her body straightening and fire burning in her eyes. "Promenade concerts... Philharmonic... London Symphony Orchestra..." she whispered, to herself rather than me.

"Mum? What are you talking about?"

"I was the best, Carrie. You said so. Everyone did," she mumbled, saliva dribbling down her chin.

I wiped it off with a tissue. "Mum... Who was a nasty man?"

She knitted her brow again. "Forced me," she muttered resentfully, clearly upset by some old memory.

"Forced you? Who forced you?"

"Wanted a boy..."

"Who, Mum?"

She closed her eyes, and a tear dropped onto her cheek. "Your father..." she hissed.

"My father?" I gasped, beginning to comprehend.

"Concert tours," she mumbled, tearfully. "Royal Festival Hall... so good."

"My father forced you to have sex?"

"Another child... Wanted a boy..." she cried. "Hated my Carrie."

"My father wanted a boy?" My stomach was churning and my eyes burning.

Her whole face was trembling now and her hands were fidgeting wildly. I lifted her chin gently so she was looking at me.

"My father raped you because he wanted a son?"

"Poor Cameron..." she mumbled, stroking my hair. "Didn't want her... not her fault. Mean to her, Carrie... bad mother... Poor Cameron."

"I'm Cameron, Mum! It's me, not Carrie." I was breaking up inside.

She looked confused and stared at me for several seconds. "Cameron?" Then her eyes flickered as a hint of recognition crossed her face and the tears began to trickle down her cheeks.

I sat with her for a while, holding her hand, feeling numb and unable to take in what she'd said. I occupied myself by rebuttoning her dress properly and wiping the stains away. They were small enough tokens of love, but they meant something to me just then. She didn't speak again but I replayed her words over and over in my head, letting the awful truth about my conception sink in.

When the nurse came to shepherd Mum to the dining room for supper, I held her briefly and promised to return again. I don't know whether she understood, or if she even heard me, but there was a faint flickering in her eyes as I left the room and walked out to my bike.

The car park was empty: no Bernie, no Jeep, just the orange glow of the lights reflecting off the wet tarmac and the cars of a few other visitors.

I felt wasted. I was shocked and appalled by her revelation, but somehow I was relieved too. Neither of my parents had ever wanted me around, and I'd always thought it was my fault. I didn't care about my father – none of us had liked him much – but I'd never understood about my mother. And that had always mattered.

Carrie had told me of my mother's sparkling career as a musician: the best cellist of her generation, she'd said. But no one had ever told me why she stopped playing. Now I knew the reason her career had been cut short. And I understood the slide into depression that had followed in my early years and worsened all through my childhood.

I was pleased that she'd said it wasn't my fault. I realised now that it wasn't hers either. But however much I understood, however sorry I felt for her, it still didn't make it all right.

Sitting on my bike in the car park, I made a real attempt to gather my forces. At least I knew now, and that helped. But it made me feel deprived of something that should have been mine. Born because of a violent episode between my parents that was none of my making; isolated from my father because I wasn't a boy; unloved by my mother because I'd ruined her career; I was wanted by neither of them.

Now, as I started my bike, I knew I had to see this through. Life throws shit in your face all the time, and there's not a thing you can do about it – except fight back. I'd been in difficult situations before. Just because I'd been threatened didn't mean I was going to be harmed. I knew how to look after myself. At least I'd survived today unscathed, which was more than could be said for my mother, all those years ago.

My legs felt like they weren't mine any more as I changed gear. My whole body was buzzing. So many emotions had coursed through my veins in the last two days that I could no longer tell what was coming from where. But the driving helped. It gave me something to focus on – something to take my mind off the dirt and smell that were clinging to my skin and clothes; something to distract me from the image of the man in black pushing the knife into Magda's belly, the thugs touching me, the sickness of Bernie's unwanted advances, my father violently forcing my mother to have sex...

There was no sign of the Jeep as I drove back down the hill to the Humber Bridge. They weren't hovering by the toll booths when I reached the other side. And when I got to the big roundabout and turned left onto Boothferry Road, I was still on my own.

I began to relax a little then, and as I wondered where I could go to shower and sleep, Angel's face kept coming back to me. I thought back to the hospital, the coincidence of our meeting, and how I'd stupidly gone along with her when she plied me with alcohol and dope till I blurted out my secret. I thought of how no one had remembered Magda Swinson in the Polar Bear, even though Angel had talked about going there together.

One, maybe two people had betrayed me: first to Stantonwell, then to the thugs in the Jeep. It could have been any one of them at the camp. But, equally, it could have been her.

I took a right down Swanland Road and headed for Hessle village, feeling upset that I'd let myself go so far with her. There were too many questions running through my mind now and, before I called it a day, I needed some answers.

The lights were on and the curtains drawn when I reached the cottage on May Blossom Road. The big metal gates were open, so I drove straight in and across the gravel, then noisily down the narrow path beside the house, cutting the engine at the end and pulling the bike in behind the garage, out of sight of the road.

The light came on outside the front door before I even reached the corner, and I braced myself. But when Angel's voice called out, it wasn't the confident, embittered voice of the woman I had fallen out with last night. This Angel sounded timid and frightened.

"Hello, who's there? Who is it?"

She looked at me round the half-open door, without saying a word. Then the shock on her face was echoed by the shock in my voice.

"Angel! Who, in God's name, has been hitting you?"

## Nineteen

She let me in. From the moment I saw her, my heart sank and my anger eased. There was an angry red mark on the side of her face, the beginnings of a large bruise. Her eyes were glazed, her movements slow. She looked desolate.

"Pour yourself a drink," she said without feeling, hiding away inside herself.

I went and got a beer from the fridge and levered off the metal cap. "You want a whisky?" I asked, treading on eggshells.

She looked away. She was curled up on the settee now, shivering, hugging her legs. The room was freezing.

"What's the matter, Angel?" I asked as gently as I could. "What's happened to you? Who did this?"

She shook her head wildly, her eyes dry and her face set. I poured her a drink anyway and set it down on the table beside her. Then I lit the fire and went to turn on the table lamps. One of them was on the floor. I picked it up and switched it on.

Whatever had happened between us, whatever lies she might have told me, I couldn't leave her like this. Besides, she wasn't in any condition to give me answers just then, and I wasn't going to leave until I got them. So I went upstairs and took the duvet from the bed to drape around her shoulders. Then I turned on the radio and found some soft music, before sitting quietly beside her, trying to figure out how involved she was – if she was involved at all.

Rigid and trembling, she stared into space, a big no-go zone all around her. When I started to talk, she didn't react. Either she didn't hear me or she didn't want to. She was hiding inside herself, frightened to come out. Then, as time passed, her body thawed and she began to lean into me and I put my arm around her shoulders. Eventually the shivering abated and I felt the slight convulsions as she started to cry.

"Who did it, Angel?" I asked. "Who hit you?"

She didn't reply, just buried herself into my breasts, sobbing inconsolably.

It took a while, but eventually she became still and began to breathe more steadily. I stayed there, holding her, for perhaps half an hour and, when I was sure she was asleep, laid her back against the settee and took a look around the lounge and kitchen. A few ornaments lay broken on the floor and a small chair was lying on its side. But everything else looked normal – there was no sign of a break-in or a major struggle.

Upstairs though, there was an empty syringe on the side of the sink. The blood in the needle was still uncongealed. She'd scored not long before I arrived. Whatever had happened, it looked bad – her mood, even after the heroin, was deep and dark. I went back into the bedroom, turning on the light this time. On the floor at the other side of the bed, a large suitcase lay open – half-packed. And both the large wardrobe and the drawers in the chest by the window were empty. I turned off the light and drew the curtains, checking the street outside. It was reassuring, suburban calm out there. There was no sign of anyone looking for me: no Jeep, no abuser. For the moment, anyway, we were both safe.

I came back down the steep, stone stairs and closed the door at the bottom. She was fast asleep, so I went across to the sideboard and checked the right-hand drawer. It was empty, all the oddments and foreign tobacco gone. And some of the books – the ones about real crime – were missing too. Whoever she lived with had gone and, by the look of it, Angel would soon be on her way as well.

She stirred in her sleep, curling up into a small, still bundle. She looked like she would be asleep for some time, so, conscious of my own pressing needs, I went outside and collected my rucksack, then headed for the bathroom again.

I turned the shower on hot, letting the scalding water cascade over me, burning my skin, finally cleansing it from the stench of the cow-shed and the filth of their hands. I played the water onto my back until the heat had penetrated through, deep into my skin, and the ache from the bruises had eased. Then I washed my hair and sponged the cut on my scalp.

I put on the clean jeans, T-shirt, sweatshirt and underwear out of my bag, took the old ones downstairs and stuffed them in the bin. Then, all I had left from the day was my leather jacket and boots. Somehow I'd have to cope with wearing them.

Angel was still asleep when I sat down in one of the easy chairs opposite her. Last night, she'd looked like she was upset over the attack on Magda, but otherwise she'd been acting as if everything else in her life was fine. But, as I suspected by the time I left, her reality was quite different. Now, as I sat watching her sleep, I wondered how she'd got into this.

It was a common enough story, and one that I'd tasted myself. Drugs: beginning as recreation, then developing into a habit, escalating from snorting and pill-popping to mainlining. Drugs: taken as a refuge from feelings that were too hard to handle. Then even more, to cope with the worsening downers that followed each hit. Then running out of money, struggling for supplies, getting in debt with your pusher...

It was fifteen years ago. I'd got myself in deeper and deeper, with acid, then cocaine and finally smack; once a day to begin with, then two, three, sometimes four shots. I was angry and lost. I virtually stopped eating, I became anorexic, and I slept with anyone – men or women – insulating myself from my real feelings, living for whatever highs I could get, finding the lows unendurable; borrowing and scrounging money wherever I could. I lost most of my friends. Only Becky and my sister, Carrie, stood by me. If it hadn't been for them, I could have been like Angel. I knew it.

But, however much I identified with her, however sorry I was to see her like this, I couldn't trust her now. I only had her word that she knew Magda Swinson and, however much I wanted to believe otherwise, I knew I had told her too much.

Angel stirred in her sleep. She was so slight, so thin. She must feel like I did, taking what passes as love wherever she could get it: urgent, unaffectionate, addictive – sometimes violent. No, it wasn't love, it was raw sex – physical contact that was safe because it promised nothing and gave even less. And me? I'd colluded with her last night, because I was desperate too. I'd told her my secret because I was in a mess and her affection was better than nothing.

As I sat thinking about these things, the music on the radio stopped. It was nine o'clock. The news headlines from the Humberside station were the usual mixture of world disasters, politics and local trivia. But my ears pricked up at the last item.

*"… And finally, Magda Swinson, the young research scientist who was stabbed on the Humber Bridge three days ago and has been in a coma ever since, is beginning to show signs of recovery. Doctors say she moved her eyes this afternoon and they are hopeful that she will regain full consciousness very soon. The police, who still haven't charged anyone with the assault, are waiting at her bedside for a statement. Now the weather…"*

I breathed a sigh of relief. Some good news, at last. Magda would be able to tell the police what had happened, who her attacker was, and why. I was happy for her. In truth, I was even happier for me. Maybe, very soon, everything could be resolved and I would be off the hook.

Angel woke half an hour later and I sat with her for a while. She didn't speak and I didn't ask her to. There were still questions that needed to be asked, but they could wait a little longer. I warmed a can of soup and made some toast – there was precious little else in the cupboards. But it was enough.

"While you were asleep there was some good news on the radio," I said, passing her the mug of hot mushroom soup and sitting down beside her.

She looked at me hazily, as if trying to focus her mind.

"It was about Magda, she's recovering; she's going to be all right."

"Oh." She pulled the duvet round her shoulders and cupped her hands around the hot drink, sipping.

I hoped she would be elated. But she just stared numbly at first – as if she was finding the news difficult to comprehend.

"I hope she'll be OK." Her voice was breaking and her eyes filling with tears. "But what if they try and get her again...?" She trembled, looking up at me. "Cameron, what if they get you?"

"She'll be all right," I reassured her. "There's a police guard and, besides, she's right in the middle of the hospital."

"What about you though?" she asked, looking pitiful. "You saw the attack. She told you something... Cameron, I was thinking... That file she told you about. Maybe that's why he tried to kill her."

"Yes, I know." I tried to sound matter of fact. There was no way I was going to tell her anything else. "But don't worry. I can take care of myself. Besides, that won't matter once she's talked to the police."

She nodded but she didn't look convinced. Her body was tense again, and her breathing erratic. She was holding onto the mug of soup as if it was a lifeline.

"I'm going away," she said unhappily.

"With Martin?"

She nodded, resigned. "He left half an hour before you arrived. He was angry, something's going wrong with his work. He took it out on me like always."

"Your brother did this to you?" I said, examining the mark on her face which was already turning a dark shade of red.

She shook her head, catching her breath as she spoke. "He's not my brother... He's not my brother... he's my lover. I'm sorry, Cameron, I lied to you. Please don't hate me."

"I don't hate you," I said. "But I do want to know why you lied about him."

She shuffled in her seat and looked up at me with those big, wet, emerald eyes. This time they didn't work quite so well. "I was lonely, Cameron. I wanted you to stay. If you'd known I had a man, you would have left straight away."

She was right. "So what about Magda?"

She looked at me, puzzled. "What about her?"

"Were you lying about her as well?"

She shook her head and began to sob again. "No, I did have an affair with her... honestly. Just like I said." But she looked away as she said it.

"Angel, I was in the Polar Bear today and nobody recognised Magda's picture."

She sort of shrivelled a little. "No... We did used to meet there. Honestly." She stuttered. "But it was a year ago... and... we usually went on one of the nights when a group was playing. That way we could hide amongst all the people. And... Not everyone was gay anyway, so it didn't feel so dangerous."

She sounded convincing, but when she turned back, behind the tears was something else – something very close to fear.

Maybe she saw the doubt on my face, because she put the mug down and started to move in close again. But I moved back slightly. However appealing she might look, this time I was going to resist the temptation to hold her tight and tell her everything would be all right.

"You say Martin was angry about his work, something that was going wrong... What does he do?"

"I don't know. He never talks about it. I never know where he is or what he does. He just leaves and I hardly see him for days."

"Don't you ever ask him?"

A look of dread crossed her face. "I've learnt not to ask questions like that. He doesn't want me to know. His life belongs to him, he says. I'm not really important."

"But he's important to you?"

"Yeah." She looked down as if she was ashamed.

"The drugs?"

She bit her lip. "Yes... If I don't do what he says, he won't let me have any."

"And he's taking you away again? Where to?"

"I don't know. Somewhere abroad, I expect. He just told me to pack my bags and be ready." Her voice was dull and lifeless. "Says he's just finishing off his work here and he'll be ready to move on tomorrow sometime."

"And do you want to go?"

"No... No, I don't," she sobbed, trying to nuzzle into me again. "I don't want to go at all."

"Then don't."

"You don't understand," she croaked feebly. "I have to. I have to go where he tells me. He'll kill me if I don't."

I lifted her head and looked into her face. "That can't be true, Angel. You can escape, you can go to a hostel."

"It is. It is true," she wailed, letting herself go. "You don't know him. You don't know how angry he can get." Her voice and her body were shaking again. "Cameron, my life is a complete fuck-up. You just can't know what a mess I'm in."

"I know some of it, Angel. I've been there myself."

She shook her head, catching her breath between the sobs. "Ohh, you can't know all of it. It's too awful, I've done so many things I'm ashamed of."

"You want to tell me."

"No... no." She coughed and blew her nose. "I can't, I just can't. Please, don't ask me."

I gave in then and held her closer for a while. Maybe she was just screwed up, like I thought last night when I left. Maybe she and Magda had been lovers after all. Maybe she wanted to know about the stabbing because she still cared. She certainly wasn't making any attempt to manipulate me now. She was just frightened and vulnerable. And who could blame her? No woman should have to go through this.

I wanted to make her see that it could be different, that she could be different. But I knew from my own experience and my work as a drugs counsellor that the only person who could change things was her. If she wasn't ready to face up to the problems, then I couldn't do it for her.

We sat there for some time, with her clinging on to me, sobbing occasionally, and me thinking about all she'd said. I held her until she was calmer and then I pulled back, staying next to her, just listening to the music. We sat like that for maybe a half-hour, buried in our own thoughts. Then she turned to me again. There wasn't a hint of seductiveness this time, nothing sexual, just the pleading of a woman who was clearly out of her depth.

"Will you do something for me?" she asked, putting her hand on top of mine. "Will you stay here with me tonight? I'm scared, Cameron. I don't want to be in the house alone."

"You think he might come back?"

"No, I know he won't. He's already packed and left. I shan't see him until after I get picked up tomorrow."

"He's not picking you up himself?"

"No, someone else. Someone he knows. Huh," she grunted quietly to herself, "he's far too busy to run around after me."

She looked at me again. "Please?"

I nodded. There was no harm in it, was there? I'd nowhere else to go. Besides, if I went back into Hull, they could be waiting for me. And if I had to tackle them again, I would rather do it tomorrow, in the light of day. "Yes, all right," I said, removing her hand from mine.

"But I won't sleep with you, you know that."

She smiled weakly. "It's all right, Cameron. You don't have to. You can use the spare room. Just be here, so I'm not on my own. OK?"

I checked all the windows and doors to make sure they were locked, before turning off the lights and going back upstairs. Angel was lying in her room, breathing steadily and fast asleep, thanks to the help of some sleeping pills. I went across the landing into the small bedroom opposite, finding my way in the half-light from the streetlamps, scanned the quiet deserted street outside, and closed the curtains. It all looked safe enough, and I had her word that her abuser wasn't going to return. All the same, I felt uneasy and I wasn't sure I would sleep – or that I even wanted to. But I slipped beneath the duvet anyway, keeping my clothes on, and propped myself up with cushions from an easy chair in the corner.

Being with Angel, witnessing her fear and pain, had pushed my own problems out of the way for a while. Now, though, my anxiety returned. I thought about all the abuse I'd come across in one day. The bruise on Angel's face and her mental turmoil; Stantonwell's unpleasant threats; the assault at the farm; Bernie's self-seeking 'kindness'; my father's rape of my mother – and the explanation for the subsequent abuse, mental if not physical, that they had both meted out on me because of it; Jimmy's account of the women who'd been drowned in the North Sea after their babies aborted. I sighed heavily. Human nature hadn't altered much since William Wilberforce's day.

I thought about the file again. It was obviously valuable, but I still wasn't sure that it was simply the details of an important project, as Stantonwell would have me believe. It was hard to know what to think about any of it. There were so many conflicting elements.

I still didn't know what to think about Angel, either. Her story sounded convincing and the evidence of her abuse was real enough. But something wasn't quite right. It was the same feeling I'd had earlier in the car with Bernie, the same feeling I'd had with Beano and, come to that, Charlie. It was like things were happening all round me, yet I couldn't tap into any of them.

I don't know how long I lay awake, straining my ears at every tiny sound, listening for every voice on the street, checking the engine noise and progress of the few cars that drove along. And taking the last two days apart and putting them back together in every combination I could. But eventually I fell into a fitful sleep.

It was a sleep peopled with big cars, thuggish men with guns and a derelict, dangerous building that was disintegrating all around me. The three men were there, their faces staring into mine, mocking and abusive. And however I tried to escape, one of them was there, peering into my face, taunting me. Standing in the big open door were four shadows: Bernie, Stantonwell, Charlie and Beano. No matter how loud I screamed, they continued to talk amongst themselves, unhearing. I screamed Beano's name, but she was laughing with the others. I yelled louder, screaming in terror, and she finally saw me and waved casually, a smile on her face, as she turned and kissed a woman in uniform. Hellen.

I woke in a sweat, panicking at the unfamiliar surroundings. Then I focussed my eyes, remembered I was in Angel's house and pushed away the lingering images, reclaiming some sort of reality in the semi-darkness of that room.

As I lay there, I thought I heard a slight noise. It could have been the nocturnal settling of an old house, or perhaps the remnants of the dream. But whatever it was, suddenly all my senses were alert and buzzing.

I slipped quietly out of bed and across the small landing, trying to avoid the creaking floorboards. Angel was still asleep in her room. The noise hadn't been her. Yet there was something... I stood there for some minutes, listening nervously, allowing my eyes to become accustomed to the dark. The only sound was the gentle ticking of the casement clock on the stairs.

Someone else was in the house. I could sense the presence rather than hear it. Maybe it was the breathing of another body, maybe the warmth, or the smell of an intruder. But the longer I stood there, the more sure I was that there was someone, downstairs, in the lounge.

I thought of going back into the bedroom and locking the door. If it was the men from the Jeep, here to get me, then I wouldn't stand a chance. If it was Angel's abusive lover, then I was going to have to do some fast talking. I could escape from the back window, but that would mean leaving her to whoever it was. And whatever I might think of her, I wasn't going to do that. So I grabbed a heavy, cut-glass vase off the windowsill and crept carefully down the stone steps to the bottom door, my heart pounding in my ears, the blood pumping round my head. My legs and arms were trembling with fear and anticipation.

I stopped behind the door and listened. There was still no sound. Maybe it was my imagination after all, fired by the horrific events of the last two days. Perhaps it was just the unfamiliar creaking of an old house that had woken me. Shit. Whatever it might be, I couldn't wait there for the rest of the night. There was only one way to find out. Quietly, I lifted the sneck and pushed open the door.

The room was bathed in orange light, seeping through the curtains from the street beyond. And in the far corner, by the sideboard, a dark shadow was bent over in a chair, searching through the drawers by the light of a torch.

My shock soon turned to bewilderment. This didn't look like a burglar; it certainly wasn't one of the thugs. In fact, the hair and the legs and the feet were all too familiar. I put down the vase and tiptoed across until I was standing within inches of the curious figure.

"Beano!" I shouted. "What the hell are you doing?"

She jumped several inches in the air, spun round in her seat and gasped.

"Fuck, Cameron. Don't do that! You scared the holy shit out of me!"

## Twenty

"What's going on?" Angel was standing at the bottom of the stairs, wrapped in her robe, half asleep. "... And who the hell are you?" she shrieked, her eyes widening with fear as she saw the stranger standing next to me.

Beano beamed back at her, an interested smile playing on her lips. "It's all right, love." She grinned. "I'm a friend of Cameron's."

"She's using the term in its loosest sense," I said ruefully, walking across to take hold of Angel's hand. "But don't be scared, she's quite safe."

Beano's smile disappeared. "I've got a real big problem that I need your help with, Cam."

"You certainly have, Beano. It's called breaking and entering."

"No," she carried on, unfazed. "It's a lot bigger than that. I'll tell you about it, honest. But first we've got to get away from here!" She looked at Angel and then at me and drew me close, whispering in my ear. "Cameron, you've got to get out, the fucking house is being watched!"

I went to the window, peering through the curtains. There was nobody outside, but just up the street, in the shadows between the lights, I could see the big black Jeep. I stepped back, gulping, trying to control the panic that was threatening to overwhelm me. How the hell did they know I was here?

Jenny Roberts

Angel froze in the centre of the room, her mouth open. "What is it, Cameron? What's the matter?"

I couldn't believe it. I'd watched out for them all the way here. I was sure I hadn't been followed.

"It's all right, Angel," I said as calmly as I could. "This is my problem. There's some guys out there and I think they're waiting to talk to me. We're going to have to leave."

She brought her hands up to her mouth and gasped in horror.

I closed my eyes and tried to take it all in. What the fuck was happening? The Jeep outside... Beano in here with us... Shit. It was still only five o'clock and my brain wasn't working properly yet. Steady. One thing at a time.

"Beano, can we just go back to the beginning, please? How did you know where I was? How did you get in, for Christ's sake?"

She produced a small wallet from her back pocket, waving it in the air. "My pick-locks," she said proudly, "they'll open nearly everything. And Bernie told me you'd be here – and what happened to you yesterday. Said you'd probably appreciate some help."

"Bernie? You've been back to the camp?"

"Yeah, last night. Huh, just to collect my things... Anyhow," she looked across at Angel and smiled wickedly, "he said not to disturb you two last night – if you know what I mean."

I ignored the inference. "And where did you get to yesterday?"

"I've told you, I've got a problem," she retorted urgently. "Come on, Cam. We've got to leave now!"

Angel threw her arms around me for a moment, then pushed me in the direction of the kitchen. After the initial shock, there was something different about her this morning. "Cameron, go, please..." she ordered, more controlled than I'd ever seen her. "Please. Get away now, whilst you still can!"

"I'm going," I said, pulling my leather jacket off the back of a chair and pointing a finger at Beano. "But I want to know what you're up to, Beano, and why you're here in the middle of the night." I looked at the window and then back at her. "I don't know whether I trust you any more than I do them."

She held her hands out in front of her and whispered theatrically. "It's all right, Cam. I'm on your side, love. Shit! You think I'd be here if I wasn't?" She shot a glance at the curtains. "Look, I promise I'll tell you everything, but please, let's get out of here!"

Angel was biting her lip and there were tears of anxiety in her eyes. "Go on. Go on!" she cried as she pushed me into the kitchen.

"What about you?" I asked her. "You've got to come with us."

Beano whispered loudly from the window: "Cameron, they look as if they're getting ready to move!"

"No... I can't," Angel sobbed. "It's you they're after, not me. Go on, get out!"

"But they might hurt you..."

"Cameron, please!" She took a deep breath and wiped her eyes. "It's all right. I'm quite safe. It's you they want, not me. I'll just tell them you left. Trust me, I'm all right." She pushed me towards the back door. "Go... Please!"

"Angel..." I wanted to ask how she was so sure they wouldn't hurt her.

"I can't come," she whispered again, "even if I wanted to. I'm leaving later. I have to."

"You're still going with him, then?"

She didn't look happy about it but, this morning, she looked less like a victim. There was something close to resolution in her eyes.

On impulse I took her in my arms and hugged her. She kissed me on the lips and stroked the back of my head. "Don't worry about me, Cam. You were kind to me last night. You've no idea what that meant. Whatever happens now, you've made it easier."

"They're out of the Jeep!" Beano hissed, grabbing my arm and pulling us apart as she propelled me towards the door.

"Take care, Cam." Angel touched my arm as I stepped outside. "Go home, get away from him! If you don't, he'll try and kill you too!"

I glanced back at her as Beano pulled me across the garden, and, as I turned and ran, I felt certain she knew more than she'd admitted.

It was still dark as we climbed over the wall into next door's garden and then cut through a hedge at the other side, before slithering over a low larch-lap fence into one of the gardens adjoining the back of May Blossom Road. A dog began to bark nearby and we both froze. I looked back towards the cottage, wishing I could have had five more minutes with Angel.

*'Get away from him! If you don't, he'll try and kill you too!'* So Angel was involved: maybe through fear of violence or because of her dependence, but involved nonetheless. And, as I'd left – when there was no chance of my asking questions – she'd warned me off.

Beano pulled me on, across another wet lawn, and up towards the back of another house. In the trees around us, the birdsong of the early morning was broken as a helicopter passed noisily overhead, its navigation lights winking and its rotor blades drumming through the sleeping suburbs.

Then, just before we reached the top of the garden, a halogen light on the back of the house illuminated everything with its bright white glare. We dived into the cover of some shrubs, and ploughed on through the scratchy undergrowth until we were at the side of the house. I glanced back over my shoulder. The dog was still making a fuss but otherwise the gardens were quiet. No one seemed to be following us.

When we emerged it was into a small cul-de-sac of post-war semis, bathing in the dull glow of the street lamps. We slipped over a low wall and down one of the drives, across two more sets of gardens, finally creeping along the side of a bungalow. We were about to emerge into the street beyond when Beano held a finger to her lips and waved me back. I heard footsteps and flattened myself against the side of the wall next to her, holding my breath as the shadow approached, wondering why I was trusting this strange woman, who still hadn't explained why she was here.

Then we heard the clink of glass on glass as a milkman deposited two bottles on the front doorstep, and I breathed again. When he walked back to his float, further down the road, we strolled out through the garden gate and up the road.

"Beano, where are you taking me?" I hissed as I caught her up. She turned and beamed back at me silently, pumped up by the excitement of our escape.

"Aw, relax, Cameron!" she protested, patting me on the back and nodding towards a slightly decrepit cream-coloured Escort van, parked across the road.

"That's yours?" I asked, suspiciously. "You haven't nicked it, have you?"

"No, 'course I haven't *nicked* it," she moaned, her pride wounded. "It's mine! This is Daisy."

"But you didn't have a van back at the camp."

"Yeah, 'course I did! But I kept her in one of the fishing car parks nearby. Better than a grass verge." She stroked the bonnet lovingly. "You like her, Cameron?"

"She's... all right." I shrugged, studying the vehicle. It was the best I could manage. It was about five years old and already the rust marks were showing around the wheel arches and on the bonnet. But the most striking thing was the faded, chipped lettering on its side: 'J BENSON – HIGH QUALITY PAINTING AND DECORATING.'

"You're a painter and decorator?" I said, gobsmacked.

"Nooo." She rolled her eyeballs. "It's my surveillance vehicle."

"Surveillance vehicle?"

"Yeah," she said, a little self-consciously, "I'm a private detective and Joanna Whittling is my client."

## Twenty-one

Getting into the van, I still didn't quite believe her. She neither looked nor acted like a private investigator – though, thinking about it, I'd no idea what a PI did look like. I'd never met one. I thought they only existed in books. At first I was sure this was just another of her stories, a cover-up to distract me from the real reason for her hanging on to me. My mind went into search mode as I sorted through the events of the last two days again: what she'd said to me in the pub; how she had reacted when I decided to visit GME; her disappearance; and now, her all-too-timely reappearance to rescue me from the hands of the thugs outside Angel's house.

Sometimes it's hard to know who you can really trust. It would be great if there were some solid rules to follow, or a computer programme that you could log in to, to see if someone is lying. But that's too complicated even for modern technology. Liars are often believable because they're practised; non-liars culpable because they seem clumsy in their honesty. I thought about the Native American story – was Beano a lying Blackfoot posing as an honest Whitefoot, or was she really what she seemed: an honest Whitefoot being just an honest Whitefoot? I wanted to believe her, but I couldn't understand why she hadn't told me earlier. If she had, then I could have passed on the file and been done with it. She'd lied to me before. It wasn't inconceivable that she was lying now.

We were driving along the main road into the city centre before I recovered my composure.

"You're a private investigator," I repeated. "And you're working for Joanna Whittling."

"Yep!" she said, happily crunching the gears of her heap at the roundabout.

"Well that's great!" I protested. "Why the hell didn't you tell me before, when I first met you? If I'd known you were working for her, then we both could have saved ourselves a lot of trouble."

"It wasn't just me!" she responded indignantly. "You wouldn't tell me a bloody thing in the pub. Just swallowed your drink and pissed off."

"Yeah, well, I didn't know if I could trust you," I admitted, shifting uncomfortably in my seat as the van rattled and bumped along the empty dual carriageway.

"And you think *I* knew I could trust *you*?" she snapped back. "Bloody hell, Cameron, I'd only just met you, remember. I knew nothing about you. You appeared out of the blue asking questions about my client. I didn't know whether you were a friend or an enemy. Then, when it became obvious that you and Bernie were as thick as thieves..."

She dropped down a gear as she pulled the van round the big city centre roundabout and headed for the docks – towards the terminal where I used to catch the ferry on my way to Hellen's. I pushed the thought away as quickly as it came.

"Where are we going?" I asked, anxiety gripping my chest.

"We're going somewhere safe." She scowled back at me. "To get some breakfast! I'm fucking starving."

"Oh," I said, relieved. We sat in silence for a while. "You were saying...?"

"Yeah... when it became obvious that you and Bernie were friends of some kind, I didn't dare say anything. Cameron, you saw how they reacted when you asked them about Joanna Whittling. How d'ya think they would have treated me if they knew she was my client?"

She had a point. "Yeah, well, maybe it wasn't your fault or mine. Just circumstances," I replied, more conciliatory. "At least we can sort it out now if you take me to her."

She looked distinctly uneasy as we crossed the big swing bridge over the River Hull and out on the road towards the docks. When she spoke again, I could see despair in her eyes.

"Well?" I persisted.

"A meeting with her would be a very good idea –" she sighed "– except for one thing..."

"And what's that?"

"I don't know where she is any more. She's disappeared."

"What!" I shrieked. "What do you mean? Where is she?"

"That's the little problem I mentioned." She grunted irritably. "If I knew, I'd be doing something a bit more constructive than looking for breakfast."

I sighed and glared out of the window. "I think we'd better talk," I said.

"You're damn right we'd better," she replied.


It didn't take us long to find the dock café. Its lights shone out like a welcoming beacon across the lorry park. Dawn was breaking and the place was filling up with lorry drivers, taking a break from their overnight journeys to the port, or waking from a cold night's sleep in their cabs. The air was thick with the smell of bacon and cigarette smoke, and the windows were running with condensation from the cooking and the people inside, eating their breakfasts, reading their papers, chatting amicably. Beano was right, it seemed as safe a place as anywhere right now.

She was the first to the counter, grumpily ordering a full English with fried bread and extra toast. For the thousandth time, I was sorely tempted to break with my principles, the bacon smelled so nice. She had no such qualms and, as I tucked into my eggs, veggie sausage and beans, I watched with envy as she shovelled great forkfuls of bacon and sausage into her mouth. Not a delicate eater. But at least her mood seemed to be improving.

"Right! From the beginning, Beano."

She nodded, pushed another forkful of food into her mouth, took a big swig of coffee from the pint mug, sighed and then began:

"Joanna rang me just over a week ago at my office in Manchester. Said she'd heard about me from someone she knew. She was concerned about what might be happening at her old business and asked me to investigate them. Huh, that's what she said, anyway. But when I met her, she seemed really bitter about being pushed out without a penny when her husband died. Seemed to think she was entitled to a big pay-off – several millions, she said.

"Anyhow, apparently there were some covenants in the contract of sale – something to do with the past research, and undertakings on future projects. The long and short of it was that she thought they were breaking the agreement, so she wanted me to ask around, see if I could find out about the new owners and what they were up to. She seemed convinced that their integrity was suspect…"

"From what they said about her at the camp, that sounds a bit like the pot calling the kettle."

She dipped a piece of bacon in her egg and coated it with the thick yellow yolk. "Yeah, that's what I thought, but she was really insistent that there was something important. She wanted me to listen to the gossip, try and find out what sort of work they were doing. But the funny thing is, the last time I spoke to her – Saturday night, it was – she'd changed her tune a bit and kept rattling on about that conference that Lou mentioned in the camp today."

"ISEM."

She dipped a forkful of sausage into her egg and waved it at me. "You should do something about that cold, Cameron, it's nasty."

"It's the International Symposium on Ethics and Morality in Science, in Leeds, at the Boulevard Hotel," I said, trying to ignore her joke. "I looked it up on the web. Joanna's speaking at it tomorrow."

She looked at me as she chomped on her food, impressed.

"This isn't the sort of work I normally do. I'm more of a DAD operator really..."

I looked bemused.

"DAD," she mumbled, her mouth full of food, "Debts, Alimony and Divorce... Pretty boring really. Anyhow, business has been slow lately, and she gave me this big cash advance – a thousand friggin' pounds! Shit, I can tell you it was a godsend. And she promised more. In spite of her being kicked out without a bean, the woman's loaded. The money's not a problem, as long as she gets what she wants." She looked at me as she chewed, her elbows on the table, her knife and fork in mid-air. "And when that woman wants something, she fucking wants it."

"So have you found anything out?" I asked, chewing on the veggie sausage and thinking how much I liked her.

She shrugged. "Bits and pieces, that's all. I found out that Stantonwell – however much he seems like English public school – is actually Austrian; and that the principal shareholders, who, incidentally, are from all over the place, have invested millions into what was a very small, struggling business. And, Magda Swinson apart, all the other people who work there are new, some of them foreign."

"How do you know that?"

"Friend in the tax office, went through their PAYE records." She stuffed the last piece of bacon into her mouth. "All the original employees left within a few months with big ex-gratia payments – all except Magda, like I said. According to Joanna, Magda had a contract and she was sticking to it. It seems she couldn't be persuaded by money and they couldn't legally fire her. Joanna said that she was dedicated to her work. And, though they obviously wanted rid of her, she was determined to stay and finish her project."

"Which was?"

She shrugged. "Something to do with breast cancer, I think."

"Go on." At least Stantonwell hadn't been lying about that.

"Well, that was about it. I couldn't find anything out of the ordinary. They seem to be squeaky clean, even building houses inside the site, so their key people don't need to face the protest at the gate every day." She wiped up the juice off her plate with a piece of toast and washed it down with some more coffee.

"So I decided I should come up and take a look at GME myself last weekend, pretend I was joining the protest, ask around the camp, see if I could pick up some lead. Then, just after I arrive, Magda Swinson gets herself stabbed, you turn up with a story about some weird file, and everything starts moving too fucking fast!"

"So did you know about the file? When you followed me to the pub in Barton that first day?"

"No, not exactly. Joanna rang me that morning, almost hysterical. She said Magda Swinson had promised to deliver something important to her – some information from GME – that she was on her way with it when she was attacked. Said it was something to do with their activities that she needed for the conference.

"But she sounded scared out of her brains, Cam. She was sure it was one of Stantonwell's men who'd attacked Magda – because she'd found out something about them. Joanna was terrified that he'd realise she was involved as well, and told me to back off. Then you arrived at the camp and started asking about her. Well, I just put two and two together."

She stopped and gave me a funny look. "But I didn't know who the fuck you were, what your angle was or who you might be working for. So I didn't dare say anything... Then, when you did spill the beans yesterday, you took the whole fucking lid off the can at once, and nothing I could do was gonna stop you."

"You mean when I went to see Stantonwell? You were worried about me mentioning Joanna's name to him – because he might link the stolen file to her?"

"Yeah, of course!" She screwed up her face in frustration and plunged her knife into the marmalade jar, spreading it thickly on the remains of her toast. "Still, you weren't to know. I should have trusted you. But I was outnumbered. Shit, I thought that if I came clean, you might tell 'em. If I didn't, you'd go and talk to Stantonwell anyway. Either way, I was sunk."

"Well, it's a pity you didn't you say something."

"I bloody tried, didn't I?" She took a swig of coffee and pushed her plate away. "Let's go somewhere and talk, I said. But oh no, you had to tell the whole bloody camp, and all they could think of was getting you to go in and suss the place out for them!"

She rubbed the back of her neck, agitated. I looked suitably chastened.

"Yeah... well... you weren't to know," she continued, more conciliatory. "But I knew that if you mentioned Joanna's name to Stantonwell, he'd be on to her. There's no love lost between them two. I left suddenly because I had to warn her. I rang and told her straight away, then I drove to her house in Anlaby. It took me less than half an hour, but I was too late. Someone had already been there when I arrived. The house was ransacked and she'd gone."

"You think she's been kidnapped or something?"

"Naw, she's OK, I think. I got a text message from her last night saying not to worry, she was safe. I've rung her mobile half a dozen times since, but it's always on answering service. I've left messages asking her to contact me... but, so far, nothing." She sighed in dismay. "She's probably OK. But I wish she'd bloody ring."

"Yeah, well, don't feel too bad about it, Beano. It would have happened anyway, whether I'd seen Stantonwell or not."

She leant back in her chair and pulled out the tin from her pouch, took out a packet of tobacco and began rolling a cigarette. "How come?"

Before I could answer, my phone rang and I pulled it out and looked at the screen. It was Becky, ringing from home. I put it back in my pocket and it stopped after a few more rings.

"Aren't you going to answer it?"

"No, it's all right. It's a friend. I'll ring her back when we've finished breakfast. What were you saying?"

"*You* were just saying, Cameron, that Stantonwell would have found out anyway – what do you mean?"

"Stantonwell already knew I had the file. And those guys in the Jeep knew about it as well. Somebody had told them. Huh, I thought it was probably you!"

"Me? Shit, Cameron, what do you take me for?"

I liked Beano. I was inclined to trust her now. I just hoped my judgement wasn't suspect this time.

"You've lied to me before," I said, narrowing my eyes. "How do I know you're telling the truth now? I thought private investigators only happened in books."

"No, honest, that's my job. No shit." She put the newly rolled cigarette on the table and fumbled around in her waist bag, producing a card which she handed across to me. I took it off her and read the neat, stylish printing:

BEATRICE NOLAN

PRIVATE INVESTIGATOR

"Beatrice? Beatrice Nolan!" I shrieked. "That's you?"

"Oh come on, Cameron." She was clearly embarrassed to her roots. "It's not much of a name, but it's the only one I have!"

"But... Beatrice! ... You?"

"Well I couldn't use Beano, could I? That wouldn't sound very professional would it?" She coloured up as she defended herself, her pride cut to the quick.

"Sorry," I said, stifling a laugh and trying to be kinder. "It's just that... Well, Beatrice conjures up flowery frocks and big hats. I don't think they'd suit you."

"Well, ha fucking ha, Cameron!"

"Why didn't you use Bea, or Beatty?" I suggested, trying hard to be constructive. "Or better still, why didn't you change your name?"

"It was my great-aunt's name," she explained, crushed. "I liked her. I think she was a dyke, though no one ever talked about it."

She stared at me and sighed heavily. "Well, do you fucking believe me or not?"

"Yes!" I laughed. "I believe you, *Beatrice* – nobody would invent a name like that!"

I smiled at her across the table and she wriggled in her chair, uncomfortable. "So what now?" I asked.

She lit her cigarette, blowing the smoke across the room. "I think you should tell me all you know. Maybe we can help each other."

I took a last sip of coffee, leant back in my chair and went carefully over all the events of the last two days with her: starting with the attack on the bridge, my visit to the Infirmary, the meeting with Angel and then the episode with Bernie at the station, Stantonwell's threats, my abduction by the thugs, Bernie's timely rescue and the state Angel was in when I'd found her the night before. Beano sat quietly, making no comment, but once I'd finished the questions came.

"So you think that the guys in the Jeep are working for Stantonwell – or someone else?"

"I don't know, Beano. But it seems strange that they came after me straight away, when he'd given me until this morning to give him the details. He did warn me though, like I told you. According to what he said, it would follow that they were working for Joanna Whittling."

"Christ!" She exploded. "You don't believe the creep, do you? Why would Joanna set a bunch of thugs on you, when all she has to do is ask you for the file?"

"Yeah, I know, I thought that too. But if they're not working for Stantonwell, and they're not working for her, who the hell are they?"

She shrugged. "It's got to be Stantonwell, hasn't it?"

We discussed it for ages, trying to weigh up all the facts, fill in between the lines and come to a conclusion. But however much we talked, we couldn't agree. Beano was adamant that the villain was Stantonwell – period – and that Joanna Whittling was as clean as driven snow. I wasn't so sure. We were just going round in circles.

"Look, Beano, this is pointless," I said in the end. "We're never going to get anywhere arguing like this. Let's look at what we actually know, bit by bit."

I checked the points off on my fingers, one by one. "*Fact:* Magda was in work early on Monday morning and she copied a document off GME's computer. *Fact:* she left the site around 8.15 am and was intercepted by a man who appeared to be threatening her. *Fact:* when he saw me, he tried to kill her. *Fact:* she gave me the location of the file and asked me to get it to your client, before she passed out."

Beano thought for a moment. "Yeah. And Joanna told me she wanted the information to use at this conference tomorrow – ISEM – to back up her call for tighter guidelines in the genetics industry."

"Check. And that's confirmed by what Magda said to me on the bridge and by the conference information on the web."

She leant back in her chair and stared at me belligerently. "See! It's dead simple. It's got to be! Magda must have come across a highly sensitive file about GME and she told Joanna – because she was the only person she trusted. Joanna realised immediately that the file would help back up her speech at the conference, so she asked Magda to make a copy of it and take it to her on Monday. Magda copied it to her own e-mail address on Monday morning, with the intention of picking it up later, a safe distance away from GME. But Stantonwell must have realised what she was doing, and got one of his men to intercept her. So, when you saw them on the bridge, he was trying to get the password off her so the file could be deleted. Then he was going to dump her in the river. But, when he saw you, he gave up and tried to finish her off."

She leant forward and peered into my face, as if there couldn't possibly be any other explanation. "Simple, see!"

I shook my head at her. It was too simple. Somehow, I knew

there was more to it. And some of it concerned the woman the file was intended for.

"What about Joanna?" I asked. "After what Stantonwell and the people at the camp said, I'm beginning to wonder if I can trust her."

Beano sat up, suddenly animated. "Oh, come on, Cam, you're way out of order. Joanna might be a cantankerous old sod, but she's no crook! What about this conference? Whatever anyone at the camp says, she seems to have reformed. She's stopped working in genetics, and however bitter she might be, she seems determined to expose GME. Admittedly she's probably trying to get back some of the money she lost, but she seems to be interested in the ethics just as much. Stantonwell was just trying to undermine her character, and frighten you. Huh, it looks like he succeeded."

"Well, if it's so simple, Beano, where does Angel fit into all this?"

"Angel... The woman you spent the night with? Christ, Cameron! You think she's involved?"

"... I don't know! ... I've got the impression she's been leading me on – that maybe she was one of the people who betrayed me yesterday. And this morning... she said something odd. Just as we left. It sounded like a warning. Something like, *'If you don't get away from him, he'll try and kill you too.'* She could just have been talking about the guy I saw stabbing Magda." I frowned. "But I dunno, there was something about her eyes when she said it. It was almost like she was implying that this Martin – you know, the one who's knocked her about – was the one who was after me."

Beano scratched her head and then buried it in her hands, groaning. "This is doing my fucking head in, Cameron. Can we just stop? As far as I can see, it's dead simple – Magda found something out about GME that Joanna could use. Stantonwell found out and tried to kill her. End of story!

"And, if that's the case," she leant across the table, speaking slowly so I didn't miss a word, "all we have to do is find Joanna. You give her the file. She publishes the contents. And bingo, we're both home and dry!"

She leant back in her chair and began to roll another cigarette, emptying the last dregs out of the packet of Drum tobacco and throwing it on the table.

I watched, thinking I wouldn't mind one myself right now. Beano might be certain about it all, but I wasn't convinced. There were so many elements, and none of them quite seemed to fit together... Still, if the news last night had been right, then maybe it didn't matter.

"Well, I hope it's all academic," I said, feeling more cheerful at the thought. "It said on the radio last night that Magda was showing signs of recovery. Maybe she'll come round today, then everything will be resolved one way or another – and we'll have the answers to all our questions."

"Yeah, well I hope you're right..."

The mobile rang again. I ignored it.

"... As I was saying, I hope you're right. But on the other hand, she might not come round for days, and Joanna needs that file for tomorrow." Beano paused and looked at me appealingly. "Cam, if I can find her, will you at least meet her?"

"Yeah, of course. I have big reservations, but if she'll let me see the content of the file, then maybe I'll be open to persuasion."

"Good." She grunted. "Thank fuck for that. I'm going to have another coffee and a slice of toast. You want some more?"

"Just a coffee," I replied, smiling at her as she got up. But, before she was halfway there, I heard her mobile phone ring and she turned quickly, pulling it off her belt and making for the door, as she punched the answer button.

I paid the bill and followed her out, wondering how long it would be before Jimmy rang me with the information I'd asked for yesterday. Beano was standing at the edge of the lorry park, her face set, alternately talking, then listening intently to the caller. When she finally ended the call, I walked over.

"It was Joanna," she told me. "She's OK. She's on her way here now. She wants to meet you to talk about the file."

I waited, expecting her to be pleased that her client had rung. But Beano just stood there, her face white with shock.

"Well?" I asked. "What's in the file, then?"

She shuddered, closing her eyes, talking quietly. "She won't say over the phone."

"So what's the problem, Beano? You look like you've seen a ghost."

"Maybe I have, Cameron… Joanna just told me that Magda Swinson was shot dead in her hospital bed this morning."

## Twenty-two

Just a few minutes ago, I'd been telling myself that Magda was going to recover and everything would be all right. Now, I felt like the whole world had been pulled out from beneath my feet.

"No! She can't be dead!" I protested.

Beano held my gaze, her big moon face steady but grim. "She is, Cam. Joanna heard it on Radio 4. Two armed men broke into the intensive care unit just before six this morning and killed both her and the police officer who was guarding her – in cold blood."

"But... how?" I stuttered in disbelief.

Beano was clearly in shock as well. "Apparently one of them held the staff at gunpoint, the other burst into the unit and shot them dead. Then they escaped from the roof in a helicopter. Joanna sounds very frightened."

I wasn't surprised she was frightened – so was I. Attempted murder in the fog on the Humber Bridge was bad enough, but cold-blooded assassination in a public hospital added a different dimension. Such a callous act wasn't the work of rational people – whatever they were protecting. It was like terrorism. I stared out across the lorry park. What would Superintendent Warren do now? What would happen to my bail?

Beano took hold of my arm and squeezed it, lowering her voice. "Cameron, you realise what this means, don't you?"

"Yes," I said, the inferences slotting painfully into place. "They killed her because of the file. Because she knew what was in it."

"And you're the only other person who knows where that file is."

"Yes. But if they're so hell-bent on protecting that information, why haven't they killed me as well?"

"You don't know the contents, Cam. Besides, only you know where the file is. But if I'm right, whoever has killed her is going to want to retrieve it more than ever now. Just be careful, it's your only insurance."

"Shit, Beano! Who would do such a thing?" My mouth was dry and the words had to fight their way out.

"Stantonwell," she said, without hesitation. "It has to be, hasn't it? And, if it is him, Joanna's likely to be next."

"But it doesn't make sense. How could a guy who runs a research laboratory have access to killers and a fucking helicopter, for God's sake?"

She shrugged her shoulders and exhaled heavily. "Shit, Cameron, don't ask me. I only serve writs and follow cheating husbands. It's way out of my league."

My head was spinning. I didn't really believe it could be the guys in the Jeep, they were just small-time crooks. And if there was a dealer involved, why would they be interested in killing Magda? It was me they would be after.

I shook my head. "I'm not sure, Beano. Your theory is too simple. There's got to be something else. Something we've missed."

"What?"

"If I knew that, we wouldn't have fucking missed it, would we!" I shrieked. "It's just a feeling I have, that's all."

Beano put her hand on my shoulder, calming me down. "It's all right, Cam, I'm sure we can sort it. It'll be OK. Honest."

I ran my fingers through my hair and looked at my watch. Stantonwell's deadline had already passed. Not that it mattered. I hadn't trusted him before, and I certainly didn't trust him now.

"I don't know what to do, Beano." My heart was beating wildly and, standing there in the middle of the lorry park, I felt helpless and vulnerable.

"You could always eat humble pie and admit everything to the police."

"Oh sure!" I grunted angrily. "And get myself locked up for good. It's murder now, Beano. They already suspect me. Now that Magda's dead, they're bound to want to call my bail in. If Stantonwell's told them that I withheld evidence as well, then I'm really sunk."

"Then you'd better give the file details to Joanna, hadn't you?"

"Are you serious?" I exclaimed. "You just said yourself that the information I had was my only insurance. How do I know I can trust her?"

Beano looked at me like she couldn't believe what I was saying. "Because I'm telling you that you can."

Oh well, that's all right then!

"Look, I don't want to be rude, Beano, but if I'm putting my life on the line, I need to be abso-fucking-lutely sure that I trust her first. And at the moment, I'm a long way from that particular state of grace."

She put her arm round my shoulders without saying any more and led me back to the van. "Let's just see what she has to say, eh," she soothed. "Then maybe you'll feel happier."

The blue BMW Seven Series drove into the lorry park, flash and incongruous amongst the dirty wagons. It didn't look like the car of a woman who had been cheated out of millions. And, when she got out, Joanna Whittling herself – however charitable I might try to be towards her – didn't exactly look like someone on the run.

We got out of the van and waited as she locked the car and looked around. Beano waved, and the tall, rather statuesque woman raised her hand in response and began making her way across the tarmac towards us with a walk that exuded a lifetime's devotion to looking good. Her dark brown leather bag and her unfastened

Burberry raincoat flapped around her, revealing the smart olive-green suit beneath with a skirt that was perhaps a little on the short side for her age. She obviously took care of herself. Her auburn hair was stylish and well cut. Quite short, in the dykey style that many straight women wear these days. Her face was long and angular, with a prominent, though not unattractive nose; brown eyes with a little too much mascara on the lashes. That apart, she was skillfully made up, but, however expensive the foundation, it had to fight hard to cover the signs of advancing age which the rest of her style sought so eagerly to disguise.

She smiled wanly as she shook hands with Beano and then turned to me. "You must be Cameron," she said, pleasantly enough, in an impeccable accent. But the stress in her voice, and on her face, was all too apparent.

"I'm pleased to meet you, Joanna," I responded, proffering my hand. "I only wish the circumstances were different."

She looked down for an instant, as if composing herself. "Where can we talk?"

Beano looked around, and for one awful moment I thought she was going to suggest that we go back into the transport café or sit in the back of the van. I couldn't think of anything less appropriate. But, as I caught her eye, she pointed over to the BMW.

"Your car, Joanna? Maybe it's a little more comfortable than my van."

Beano and I sat in the back. Joanna ensconced herself on the edge of the front passenger seat, turning her body so she was facing us. The car's interior was just as showy as the outside: oversized seats upholstered in a beige leather that was soft and yielding to the touch. I wondered briefly what Elana or the other protesters would say if they were here. At least it was comfortable, which was more than could be said for the atmosphere between us.

We sat there for a few moments, all three of us feeling the awkwardness of the situation. Someone had to say something. So I started with the obvious.

"I'm so sorry to hear about Magda, Joanna. You must be devastated. Had you known her a long time?"

She nodded sadly. "Nearly five years." Her face was drawn and pale, as I might have expected, but there was something about the eyes – a hardness that didn't quite match. "She was one of the first employees at Gentec, as GME was then called. We worked well together and over the years we became quite close." She smiled thinly again. "Not friends exactly, but we had a very good relationship." She shook her head, faltering. "You'll have to excuse me... I'm still reeling from the news."

"I'm not surprised. It's shocked us all," Beano agreed. She was trying hard to be sympathetic but her bluff manner failed to quite meet the moment. "We were talking about it before you came. First, the attack on Magda, then the trashing of your house, now this murder. Cameron's been threatened as well, nearly killed, like I told you. Someone is really scared of that file, Joanna. What the hell's in it?"

"I don't know where to start." She pulled a tissue out of the box on the dashboard and began to dab her eyes. "All of this is my fault. Magda's death; the threats to you, Cameron... I feel so guilty about poor Magda, she was such a nice girl, so dedicated." She looked from Beano to me, hesitating. "I think I'd better start from the beginning."

She took a deep breath and composed herself. "I'm afraid I haven't told you everything, Beano, and I'm sorry – it didn't seem relevant at the time. But, actually, Magda came to see me last Saturday. She was in a terrible state, very anxious. She said she had stumbled across a document at work which worried her. She seemed certain that GME was breaking the regulations over licensing – carrying out illegal research."

"Did she say what it was?" I asked, thinking that maybe Beano hadn't been so far off the mark after all.

"No, she had no specific details. She just said she was searching around last Thursday for some information on her own project and, somehow, she accessed a confidential file on the main computer. Something to do with cloning, she said – which, of course, wasn't particularly surprising in view of the nature of their research. What frightened her, though, was the reference to cloning experiments with human embryos."

She stopped and looked at both of us, waiting for the implications to sink in.

"I don't know whether you know, but it is quite illegal to experiment with human embryos in this way. GME shouldn't even be thinking about it, let alone actually doing it."

Beano's eyes were alight now. "So, if it was revealed that GME were conducting this sort of research, they would have their other licences revoked, get shut down and get prosecuted?"

"Without doubt. There is no leeway on ethical matters of this kind."

"What exactly were they doing?" I asked, wanting to be sure I got it right.

"I can't tell you that. Magda couldn't go into detail because, when she realised the nature of what she was reading, she closed the file. It was during a normal working day and she was worried about the security there, that someone might discover she had accessed something so confidential."

I sighed and looked out of the window. I'd been hoping for another lifeline, a safe way out. It didn't look like I was going to get it.

"She worried about it all Friday and Saturday. Just typical of her. Magda was so honest and conscientious. On the one hand, she didn't want to feel she was spying on them or somehow betraying them. But, on the other, she felt that if they really were breaking the law, then she was honour bound to report them. She was right to be worried, of course. We all know what happens to whistle blowers."

"Yes, but they don't usually get murdered."

"I know." She looked down and composed herself, then continued. "I'll get to the point. We've kept in touch since I left the business. I've helped her with her research papers from time to time. I think we had a mutual sort of respect for each other. So not unnaturally, she thought of me, and came round on Saturday night to ask for advice, hoping that I could somehow solve her quandary."

"So you talked about it and then you asked her if she could make a copy of the file. When it was safe." I was way ahead of her now. "When the offices were deserted. Say, on Monday, when they were shut for Easter?"

She looked down at her hands. "Yes. I wish I hadn't now! I thought it would be quite safe. It wasn't unusual for her to work by herself on weekends and bank holidays. Like I said, she was very dedicated. And, even if she'd been caught, I thought she'd just be reprimanded or at the very worst fired. It never occurred to me that anyone might want to kill her..."

She paused as my phone rang yet again. I turned it off.

Beano shuffled in her seat, getting the drift. "So what happened?"

"I think someone must have disturbed her. She told me she'd bring the file on disk. In the end, from what you've said, Cameron, it looks like she panicked and copied it to her e-mail file instead."

"But why didn't she e-mail it straight to you?" I asked, puzzled.

"She couldn't, could she? They would have known it had been sent to me and that I was going to use it against them. I suppose she hoped that if she e-mailed it to herself, they would just think it was something she was working on. It was quite normal for her to send files to her home computer that way. She often worked from home at weekends on draft reports."

"But Stantonwell told me that wasn't allowed."

She shrugged. "No, it wasn't, but that didn't usually stop her. She lived for her work."

I kept my eyes on Joanna. "Why did you want the file? What were you going to do with it?" I asked.

"Why... I..." She faltered and dabbed her eyes with the tissue again. "If they really were breaking the law, Cameron, I thought it was important that someone should report them. Why else would I want it?" She looked directly at me, unflinching – something I'd avoided doing when I lied to Warren just forty-eight hours ago. They say that liars sometimes over-compensate in their body language.

"And it was also a chance to get back at them?" I asked, a little more sharply than I intended.

She went quiet for a moment and her face flushed. "You think that I would put a friend in danger, just to gain some personal satisfaction?"

Beano looked distinctly embarrassed, but I continued anyway. "Maybe, maybe not. I don't mean to be rude, Joanna, but I understand there is no love lost between you and the new management at GME."

She sighed heavily. "Whatever you might think of me, I wouldn't have done it just to get back at them. But, yes, if I'm honest, I don't like the people who own and run GME. We were always such a responsible organisation, before they came along. Animal testing isn't a nice business... Are you shocked that I should admit that? ... Well, just because I'm a genetic scientist, it doesn't mean I'm devoid of feelings, you know. We always tried to make life as bearable as possible for our animals – at least within the confines of our research.

"But these new people, they don't seem to have the same integrity. They treat everyone – humans as well as animals – with the same scorn. Beano may have told you that I was cheated out of a large sum of money by them, but it doesn't end there. All the old employees have been pushed out. Magda was the only one who refused to go. They've brought in a brand new team when there was a perfectly good workforce already... And then to cap it all, Magda comes along and tells me they are doing unlicensed, illegal research." She looked at us intently. Her eyes were flashing with anger now, and she was fidgeting with her hands.

"What do you expect me to do, Cameron? Apart from the fact that they've obviously broken one of the covenants in the sale agreement, by undertaking research with embryos, what they are doing is clearly wicked and immoral. Well... After all I've been through... I decided I couldn't let them get away with it. That was the breaking point. No, I thought, I can't just sit back and ignore this any longer... So, yes, I did ask Magda to copy the file and bring it to me on Monday morning. Do you really wonder that I wanted to expose them?"

"No, I guess not." I had to agree. "But, however strongly you feel, Joanna, you still have no evidence. I can give the file to you today. But it's of no use. It's just page after page of hieroglyphics."

"It's coded," she said. "GME have special encrypted software for use with all their documents. I have a copy on my laptop. Magda got it for me so I could help her with her project."

"You've got it with you?" I asked.

"It's in a safe place. Can you let me have a copy of the file to take away?"

"No, I'm sorry, Joanna, I can't."

"Well... Can you tell me where it is? Can I access it from somewhere?"

"It's on my own e-mail server," I told her, adding firmly, "but before I pass it on to anyone, I need to see what's on it. And... since it seems so important... I have to be sure of who I'm giving it to."

Her eyes flickered. And for a split second, she looked a little fazed.

"The truth is, Joanna, there is another version of what happened that morning. I've also been told that the file was a project document and that someone – possibly a friend of Magda's – knew she intended copying it to disk that morning to take home. This person, according to my source, arranged for an associate to stop her on the bridge and steal the file, so it could be sold to a competitor. From all you've said, that could have been you."

"Who told you that?" Her eyes flashed and she shifted uncomfortably on her seat.

"Stantonwell."

She grunted cynically. "Well, he would say that, wouldn't he?" She looked deeply offended. "Cameron, if I was trying to get the file off her to sell, do you think she'd have given you my name? You know Magda trusted me. She wouldn't have asked you to pass the message on if she didn't."

She had a point.

"Cameron, believe me," she implored, "I want that file for all the right reasons. Beano will tell you that." She looked across for confirmation and Beano nodded. "Whatever it is they are doing at GME, you've got to help me stop them."

She leant towards me over the back of her seat, her eyes wide with concern. "I don't have much time – I'm speaking at a conference tomorrow. It has been convened so that scientists like me, who have a conscience, can bring pressure on the government. Pressure to stop the continuous relaxation of the regulations that govern our industry. Cameron, if I have the file, I have a once-in-a-lifetime chance of exposing GME, of illustrating what some unscrupulous organisations are doing – how even the current regulations are being flouted. There is no better way of showing the need for tighter regulation. But I can't do it without that file. And I can't get that without your help.

"You will help me, won't you? Please?" She was passionate, appealing. Hell, maybe she was genuine.

Beano and I exchanged glances.

"Of course I will," I assured her. "Provided that I get to read the file first. If it's what you say it is, then you are welcome to it. Do you want us to go with you now, get your laptop and do it?"

I suppose I expected her to grab my offer with both hands, but instead she looked at her watch. "No... No, I'm sorry, but I would rather not do it now...

"The truth is that I'm frightened, Cameron. Frightened for both of us. If we decode the file too soon, then whoever killed Magda will have no reason to hold back any more. So long as we keep things as they are then you, at least, are safe for now."

"So tell me when I can meet you, and where."

She stared distractedly out of the window for a moment, before turning back, her voice stronger. "Tonight. Later on, very late, when it's quiet. Then, I can go straight to Leeds. Once I've made the file public, we will both be safe."

It sounded like a sensible plan. "OK, when exactly?"

"I need some time," she said, writing down her mobile number. "I need to pack and get ready. Ring me this evening around nine. We'll arrange everything then."

I leant against the van and watched her drive away. She sounded entirely plausible and she had known Magda well. There seemed every reason for me to believe her. But, somehow...

For all her passion about the conference, and for all her determination to expose wrong-doing at GME, I was still uneasy. Something was worrying me, something I couldn't put my finger on. Maybe it was just that I'd learnt a lot this week about not taking people at face value. I'd thought Angel was on my side the other night. I'd trusted the animal rights camp. At the other extreme, I'd also been wrong about Beano on our first meeting, whereas I trusted her implicitly now. I was sure that she was who she said she was. But I still couldn't say that about anyone else.

"Do you believe her?" I asked.

"Yes, I do," Beano replied, without hesitation, reaching into the van and pulling out a new packet of tobacco. "Like I said to you before, I don't like the woman very much. She's too fucking pushy and high falutin'. But I think she's right about Stantonwell. Everything she says adds up."

Yeah, maybe that's the problem.

Beano took a packet of Rizlas out of the tin in her pouch and pulled out a paper. "Let's face it, Stantonwell's worried sick that he's going to be exposed by her. That's why he threatened you and that's why he's badmouthing her. He wants you to think that a dealer's involved because it makes him sound like he's on the level."

"Yeah. It all sounds very convincing," I agreed, as she began to arrange the tobacco in the paper. "But where do the thugs in the Jeep fit in? And what about Angel?"

"I think you're getting paranoid." She sighed. "They're probably both working for the bastard."

I watched her, as she closed the plastic bag and started putting it back in the tin.

"Let me see that tobacco!" I demanded, grabbing her hand.

She looked up sharply, surprised, and pulled the packet out of the tin again. "I didn't know you smoked."

"I don't," I said, taking the blue plastic bag out of her hand and raising my voice. "Beano, this is BlauBerg! Where did you get it?"

She shrank back, stunned by the fierceness of my question.

"Where the fuck did you get it?"

"Erm... Bernie sold it to me last night... I... I was running out... He said he had a spare packet. It's foreign, you can't buy it here." She spluttered defensively as I grabbed it out of her hands. "It means Blue Mountain or something. It's a really nice smoke... Why...? What's the big deal?"

"Beano," I said quietly, "this is the same brand that I found in one of Angel's drawers the day before yesterday."

### Twenty-three

Beano's mouth dropped open. "Fucking hell, Cameron! D'you think Bernie knows this Angel woman?"

"More than that, Beano. There were several packets in her drawer that first night. That means he must live there. He must be the guy she refers to as Martin. The one who hit her."

I squeezed her arm and walked away, gazing out over the port, numbed by the revelation.

*'If you don't get away from him, he'll kill you too,'* Angel had said.

Bernie Marton. Now I realised what had been eating away at my mind ever since that all too convenient rescue. Suddenly it was obvious how the men in the Jeep had known where to find me in the early hours of this morning. And it explained why Angel had been so keen to find out exactly what Magda Swinson had said to me.

Coming back in Bernie's car from the farm, I'd been wary about the ease of my rescue. The thugs had made no effort to resist him when he walked in. Scarface had a gun, he could have held it to my head and used me as an hostage. But he didn't. They'd all just walked away. It had been too neat, too easy.

This also explained why Bernie had been so pushy, trying to persuade me to give the file location and password to him – so he could 'sort it'. How he'd been reluctant to let me go my own way, but had been easier about it as soon as I said I was going to Angel's.

Cats and mouse. Bernie and the three thugs working together: threaten her, then be nice to her; beat her up, then soften her up.

He must have gone back to May Blossom Road whilst I was at the nursing home and told Angel to get all the information out of me this time. But maybe she'd had enough – she hadn't gone along with him. Maybe this time he'd gone too far.

*'If you don't get away from him, he'll kill you too.'*

She'd made no attempt to trick me last night. And, more than ever, her final words to me sounded like a warning from someone who knew what Bernie was really like.

Bernie Marton. I'd almost trusted him. I thought back to the night I first met him, when he followed me to the station, and I realised I'd been ignoring my instincts about him ever since. I'd been making allowances, because I was worried that I might jump to the wrong conclusion and misjudge him, just as I did with Pat in Amsterdam. But Bernie was not the friend that Pat had turned out to be – and this was not Amsterdam.

I turned and handed the tobacco back to Beano.

"So, you think he's the dealer?" she asked. "The thugs in the Jeep are working for him? You think he wants the information to sell?"

I screwed up my face. "That's what it looks like, doesn't it?"

"Fuck!" Beano shook her head. "Well, in that case, Cam, the sooner you give the bloody file to Joanna, the better. If you don't offload it fast, you're dead."

"No, Beano. Don't you see? It doesn't add up. There's something wrong. Everybody's threatening me but no one is actually doing anything. First Stantonwell. Then the men at the farm who were going to kill me. Bernie, who rescued me in the nick of time and then told you exactly where to find me. It's almost like everyone's trying to scare me."

"Shit, Cameron. 'Course they're trying to bloody scare you! They scare me as well and I haven't even fucking met the bastards... 'Course they are – they all want the file!"

"Yes, yes I know." I closed my eyes. My brain was racing but I couldn't pin anything down. "It's just that something really odd is happening. I feel like I'm a puppet and everyone else is pulling the strings."

Beano sighed heavily. "Cam! It's fucking obvious! Stantonwell wants the copy file destroyed. Bernie and those guys in the Jeep want it to sell. For Christ's sake, lie low for the rest of the day and then let's hand it over to Joanna tonight, like we've arranged."

A few minutes ago, I'd almost been prepared to go along with Joanna. But now it didn't feel right. I paced up and down, trying to unravel what was going through my head.

"No Beano," I answered eventually. "I can't do it. Not yet. It's too dangerous. I want to know what's going on at GME that is so bloody important. I want to know what's on that file, before I do anything else."

"So how the hell are you going to do that without Joanna's help?" she asked, her hands on her hips.

"I need to go in there. I need to see if the file will open on one of their computers."

Beano's face showed pure disbelief. "You are just fucking joking, Cameron. Aren't you?"

"No, I'm not, Beano. I mean it."

"So, how you gonna do it? Eh?" she scoffed. "You just gonna go through the gate and ask the nice man if you can use his computer?"

"I don't know," I snapped back. "… Maybe Charlie could help."

"Charlie!" she screeched. "Shit, you mean you'd trust that weird bastard? You told me earlier that you thought he might be Stantonwell's informer!"

"Yeah," I admitted, thinking of all the security around the site. "Just grasping at straws."

"So how you gonna do it? Eh?"

"I don't know," I responded petulantly. "I just know I have to. It's the only way I'll ever get to the bottom of this. I'll find a way."

"No you won't, Cam. At least, not on your own, you won't." She dropped her voice. One of the lorry drivers was looking across to see what all the shouting was about.

"So what choice do I have?"

She walked away, exasperated, then stood staring up into the sky with her back to me. When she came back, her voice was calmer.

"Look, there might be a way. Just give me a few hours, will you, and I'll see if I can come up with something."

"What kind of something?"

"I don't know yet!" she rejoined crabbily. Then, a little more relaxed: "Just give me a little time, that's all. I've got an idea. I know this guy in the East End."

"I don't want you to get involved." She was a nice woman and I didn't want her name adding to the list of people whose lives had suffered because of me.

She looked at me belligerently. "Cam, I *am* fucking involved! I have a client, remember, who is in just as much danger as you are. If you go off and get yourself killed, she'll never get the file. Besides, what do you know about breaking and entering?"

"I've done a bit." Once. Breaking into a rundown warehouse.

She shook her head. "There's no way you could get in there by yourself – it would be suicide."

She sighed heavily, opened her arms and folded me into a bear-like hug, letting me know that, like it or not, she was going to help. And that was that.

"Look, I'm gonna split," she said, as she pulled away, a hint of urgency in her voice. "You lie low here and take care, OK? I'll come back for you about five, then I'll take you into Hull so you can access the file and make some copies for us to take in to GME. Any problems in the meantime, you ring me, right?"

Sitting back in the café, I sipped at another mug of coffee and irritably arranged and rearranged the condiments on the table. It was still barely 11.30, which meant I had a whole day trapped in this godforsaken place.

I sat for maybe an hour watching the traffic: container lorries on their way to and from the port and, in the distance, ships plying their way up and down the Humber. The skyline at the edge of the river was punctuated with cranes reaching up into the sky, silent sentinels to the busy estuary. It was all too reminiscent of another place, another time...

The docklands of Amsterdam. The squat. Pat's broken body lying on the cobbles near the quayside. The chase across the water. The way Hellen and I had nearly got ourselves killed. I thought about all the pain, and my guilt at Pat's death. He'd tried to help, just like Beano was doing now, and I'd let him get killed.

I thought about when it was all over, and the good times that followed between Hellen and me. And quite suddenly, I missed her. I missed her friendship and her warmth, and the anticipation of seeing her again. For once, I'd felt good. Now, gazing across at the ferry terminal, I wished for the thousandth time that I could just go along with what she wanted, that I could want the same as her.

The guy from the kitchen came across and wiped the table, hinting that I should order something else or go. So I asked for another coffee and, as a distraction from my maudlin thoughts, picked up a newspaper that had been discarded on the next table.

It was full of all the usual stuff: controversy over a politician's latest attempt to capture the headlines; a story about an academic being held prisoner in her home by someone who didn't like her work; an article about genetic research (huh, I guess I knew a bit more about that now); another woman's body found in the North Sea...

I looked more closely at the last article. It didn't say much except that the woman was Chinese this time, and that the police were linking it with the previous three. I thought back to my conversation with Jimmy Wilson and wondered if she'd been pregnant too – if this unfortunate woman had also suffered a miscarriage or an abortion – and whether they were all illegal immigrants, like he suspected.

Genetic research and dead refugees...

I pulled out my phone and rang Jimmy's number. I still hadn't responded to the flashing answerphone icon, but maybe one of the calls had been from him.

"Hello, is that you, Cameron?" His voice was cautious.

"Hiya Jimmy." I tried to sound bright and casual. "I wondered if you'd found any details on GME yet?"

"Cameron, where are you?" he asked urgently.

"In Hull. Why?"

"Because I've just spoken to Superintendent Warren and he's going ballistic."

"I thought you didn't work from the station. You're on this Immigration assignment, aren't you?"

"Not now, not since this morning... Where are you, Cameron?"

"Why? What's wrong?"

"Hasn't your solicitor rung you? Hasn't she told you?"

"What... told me what?"

"Your bail. It's been rescinded. You're wanted at the station. Warren's put out an all-points search for you and police all over the city are on the lookout. Where are you? I'll come and pick you up."

"What about GME?"

"They're clean. A very reputable business... You've got to stop this stupidity. Give yourself up, then everything can be sorted out."

"Oh yeah! Like Warren charging me with murder?"

"That isn't necessarily going to happen if you co-operate. You're already in enough trouble. Don't make it any worse!"

"I don't see how I could possibly make it any worse..."

"Be sensible!"

"No, Jimmy," I said, ending the call. "There's no way I'm going to let them lock me up again."

## Twenty-four

Hull city centre was heaving with traffic as the taxi crossed the swing bridge and skirted the old town. I was more keyed up than ever now: frightened, yet focussed.

The three messages on my answerphone were all from Becky. They were variations on a theme: 'Give yourself up Cameron – It's the only way – We'll sort this out in court.' I didn't ring her back. I wasn't in the mood for arguments. A simple text message would have to do: 'I'm OK Becky. Don't worry. Be in touch.'

I slid down in my seat as two squad cars shot noisily past on the opposite side of the road, tearing over the bridge towards the docks, their sirens wailing and their lights flashing. Someone had once told me that the phone companies could trace the area that any cellular call came from. Great! Now the police were after me as well.

I stayed low as we reached the main city centre roundabout. Traffic was backing up right along Ferensway, well past Paragon Station, and two uniformed police officers were diverting everything away from the centre. Only the exit onto Hessle Road was clear and the cabbie drove onto the dual carriageway, grunting unhappily at the disruption.

"What's going on?" I asked from the depths of the back seat. Surely they couldn't be going to these lengths to catch me?

"Big demonstration, love. Some bloody foreigner." He snorted. "Politician, they say. You can't bloody move round the centre for people. All shoutin' and pushin'. There's bloody yobs everywhere. Troublemakers, I reckon. The city's crawlin' with 'em."

"Can you get me to Paragon Station?" I asked, worried that he was going the wrong way.

He glanced over his shoulder at me. "I'll get you as near as I can, love. I'm goin' round the back way, but I think you'll have to walk the last bit." He drove on a little further, then looked back again. "Look, love, this is nowt to do wi' me, but I don't think..."

"Please," I insisted. "Just take me there."

I saw him shrug as he changed down and filtered off the main carriageway. He turned right at a roundabout, taking me through the back streets, then onto Anlaby Road. By the time we passed the Infirmary, the traffic was backing up again.

"Just like I thought," he grumbled with an air of resignation. "This is as far as I can go, love. You'll 'ave to walk rest of way."

I paid him and said nothing. His eyes followed me as I got out and I saw him shake his head as he drove off.

I got away from the main road, made my way through the back streets behind the station until I emerged into the bus depot, then came out into the car park next to Paragon Station, the one I'd used on that first day.

All I'd wanted to do was to go to the internet café, access the e-mail inbox where I'd put the file, get a copy and leave the city. But now I was curious about all this activity and all the people, mostly men, teeming out from the buses and trains onto the pavement. They were pushing and jostling through the log-jam of traffic across Ferensway and then disappearing up the street opposite.

I stopped behind a van and looked around, checking for police, then, when I was sure it was safe, I ran across the road and melted into the crowd on the opposite pavement. I'd never seen so many people in the middle of Hull. It seemed almost like the exodus from a football match, but that didn't make any sense, right in the city centre on a Wednesday lunchtime. They didn't look like soccer fans either.

There was the same sense of tension in the air, but the mix was wrong.

Young men, old men, yobs – they were all there. But amongst them were men in suits and smart overcoats: business men, professional men and just a smattering of smartly dressed women – all surging and pushing past me in a vast communal hurry. The noise was extraordinary too. Groups of younger men were shouting, swearing and laughing at each other, as if they were high on something. Older men, being willingly carried along by the crowd, were chatting intensely. And packs of skinheads were looking mean.

I allowed myself to be carried along up the street, breathing the testosterone-loaded air. This didn't feel like a safe place for any woman, let alone a dyke. But I pulled my collar up around my neck and kept my head down. The group of men on my right jostled and swore at each other, pushing me off the kerb and into the side of a car. The driver looked scared and I didn't blame him. Some of the men ahead of me were banging on the stationary vehicles as they walked, knocking the wing mirrors, lifting the windscreen wipers, sneering at the occupants as if they were monkeys in cages.

By the time I reached the junction with King Edward Street, I was soaked with sweat and trying to stop the panic that was welling up inside. I swallowed hard when I saw the police ahead in riot gear, and merged back into the middle of the crowd to avoid their gaze. They were lined up on the other side of the road, batons out and shields ready, making their presence felt but standing back. 'Containment,' Hellen had called it – allowing an unauthorised rally to continue as long as it remained peaceful.

As I passed them and turned right, I could hear the noise from Victoria Square: cheering and whistling, impatient clapping, and the amplified voice of a man trying to talk to the excited crowd. A warm-up act, preparing the audience for the star turn.

When I got to the pedestrian precinct, just down from City Hall, the whole street was filled with people straining to get a view of the man on the lorry parked near Queen Victoria's statue. Up ahead, near the fountain by Queens Gardens, a parabolic aerial on top of a television van pointed into the sky. Cameramen were threading around the edges of the crowd.

Although some of the people around me looked intimidating, most looked ordinary, the sort that would serve you in your local shop, draw up your will, authorise your overdraft, deliver your milk. The scattering of women held on to the men by their sides, and a few children were being held aloft, some sitting on their fathers' shoulders.

There were no black people, no feminists, no single mothers, no gay men and, except for this one butch lesbian, no dykes. It was just like the neo-Nazi rallies in Amsterdam last week – exactly as Hellen had described them to me.

I pulled back into the shadows of a shop doorway at the edge of the crowd. Over in the square, someone came onto the makeshift platform to adjust the microphone, and an excited murmur rippled around the crowd as a tall, smartly dressed man came onto the stage. The murmur turned to cheers and people started to call out his name. It was Langstein. I knew it.

He was a clean-shaven, middle-aged man, with blond hair and a presence that even I could feel at the fringes of the crowd. He wore no coat – just a well-cut grey suit – even in the cold of the afternoon. And when he reached the microphone, he paused, waiting for the applause and the shouting to fade away, asserting his authority on his followers – a performer, preparing himself.

A hush fell over the huge gathering. But over on the other side of the square, beyond the edges of the rally, near Queens Gardens, the noise grew louder as a big anti-Nazi demonstration voiced its disapproval with whistles and cat-calls. Over the sea of heads, I could just see their placards waving in the distance. I guessed that, as in Amsterdam, there would be a thick line of riot police between the two camps.

Langstein surveyed the expectant, upturned faces in the crowd like a monarch. When he started to speak, the dissenting voices grew louder, but they were no match for the bank of loudspeakers all around him, which carried his powerful voice into the crowd.

"Ladies and gentlemen... Friends," he began, in the kind of clipped English accent that betrayed him as someone of middle-European origin. "It is so good to be here in your beautiful city – a city, like so many others in Europe, that you can be truly proud of. And it is right that you should be proud. Proud of your birthplace, proud of your heritage, proud of your national culture. Our predecessors – men and women – worked hard to create them for us. And we should thank them for their gift.

"But today I have a serious question for you. Today I want to ask you what our gift to the future will be. What our children's children will think of the legacy, which we, even now, are preparing for them."

He stood gazing down at the crowd and lowered his voice. "Sadly, my friends, I fear that our children's children will be disappointed in us.

"Yes, my friends. Disappointed. Because as we begin the new millennium, the heritage that our grandparents bequeathed to us is disappearing. Those values which we received as a gift from them are being slowly and systematically eroded by the very people you have elected to preserve them. Piece by piece, your heritage as Britons, and our common heritage as Europeans, is being taken apart, as politicians from all parties offer it up to one minority after another. Immigrants who belong in far off lands, alien religions, single mothers, drug addicts, homosexuals."

I shook my head in disbelief as I pushed my way out. Henri Langstein, extreme right-wing leader of the European People's Alliance, had been holding rallies all over Europe. Now he was bringing his poison to Britain. Hellen had told me all about him last week. I'd seen the television reports on Dutch News. I'd read the papers. I didn't want to hear any more. The crowd around me erupted in cheers and yells, as I pushed my way through them.

Langstein was a man who played to the fear of change, especially in men. Between the lines of his oh-so-moderate-language, there was an obsession with racial purity, with the traditions of white Europe.

The basic premise was that the world belonged to the white, hetero-sexual male and that it was time to take it back. Racial integration, mixed marriages, homosexuality, drugs, feminism, and other non-conforming behaviours, were evil. Now, he intimated, was the time for the white people of Europe to assert themselves again, before it was too late; before they were in a minority in Europe. But he wasn't just racist and bigoted. He was misogynist too. When he said 'white people', he meant 'white men'.

I pushed on with my head down, in the direction I came from. But I'd forgotten about the riot police, and when I finally reached the edge of the crowd, I saw them again and turned quickly back. I couldn't risk it. So I threaded my way back through the tightly packed bodies to-wards the main platform, his amplified voice falling all around me.

"So I say to you: as good Europeans, it is time for us to make a stand on immigration. It is time for us to stop giving away our jobs to people from other lands. It is time that we stopped them eroding our culture and diminishing our values."

The noise was deafening as the crowd cheered and whistled at every point he made. I felt sick inside and I pushed on harder than ever, heading for a side street to get away from his cant.

"If our society is to thrive again, then we need to honour the fam-ily. Women must return to their rightful roles as mothers and carers, society must once again respect the role of men, and homosexuality must be outlawed."

A man in front of me hoisted a child onto his shoulders so that he could see the speaker. I tried to skirt a group of skinheads nearby but one of them snatched at my jacket, shouting out to his mates and call-ing me names. They jostled me but I twisted away, sweating with fear, and pushed through another group of older men, desperate now to escape into the open and breathe clean air again.

"... And you, my friends, are the vanguard of this proud new European Movement. Join me! And together, our strength will be in-surmountable. Together we will be an unstoppable force. Together we can build a new and better future. A future, my friends, that will be a true and lasting gift to those who follow."

I worked my way through the last few people and slid into the side street, the crowd roaring behind me as he finished his speech. I felt deeply demoralised as I walked through the back streets. We'd come so far on our path to an inclusive, tolerant society, and I was shocked at the level of support Langstein could command.

When I emerged from an alley, I was a long way from the internet café I'd been heading for. I was on a main road at the other side of the square, a few hundred yards from the rally. But, looking towards the fringes of the crowd, near Princes Quay, I could see scuffles already breaking out between Langstein's supporters and the anti-Nazi protest. There were riot police everywhere up there, and police horses, toing and froing in the melee. A tear-gas canister sailed over the heads of the crowd, trailing white gas behind it, and people began to panic, running in every direction.

As I watched, a white Mercedes came shooting out of the mayhem towards me. I stepped back into the shadow of the alley, straining my eyes to see inside as it passed.

In the back were two men holding a heated conversation. One of them was Henri Langstein. The other was Marcus Stantonwell.

## Twenty-five

I was still in a state of shock when I left the computer bureau with the disks. By the time I got into the taxi at the station, I was replaying the events of the last three days yet again. It had never occurred to me that there could be a political connection with Magda Swinson's murder. But now, seeing the two men together in the car, the whole affair had been thrown into a sharp new perspective.

As the cabbie drove down Hessle Road, I caught glimpses of the estuary through the houses and recalled Jimmy's account of the bodies found in the North Sea. I remembered Langstein's carefully veiled dogma about white supremacy; Lou's detailed description of cloning, that first morning at the camp, and Elana's sad reference to eugenics. When I thought of that conversation now, it was with a new conviction – that GME were indeed involved in something illegal and immoral, just like Joanna Whittling and Magda Swinson had believed.

I slid down in the seat as we passed Hessle police station, where I'd been locked away earlier in the week. Images of the desk sergeant and the bare cell flashed through my mind and I shuddered at the thought that they were looking for me, perhaps to lock me up for good. Whatever happened now, I had to stay free. I had to give myself enough time to find the last pieces of this complicated puzzle.

The sky was heavy with dark grey clouds and, though it was only mid-afternoon, the light was fading as I got out of the taxi in Hessle village. When I walked up May Blossom Road, it looked like any other suburban street, if prettier than most. The parked cars and the people tending their gardens were the stuff of normal life. A woman was washing her car, a delivery van was making its way out, neighbours chatted over a garden wall. No Jeeps. No police. No Bernie Marton.

I walked casually down towards the cottage, eyes peeled, ready to make a run for it if I had to, but acting like I was a regular visitor. There was no sign of anyone waiting outside and the house was in darkness. Angel had left, like she said she was going to. If she'd gone with Bernie, then it was unlikely anyone would be there. But I checked the back just to make sure. The garden was clear and the house was locked. I breathed a sigh of relief, stopping by the back door, thinking about Angel and the warning she'd left me with. She may have deceived me that first night, she may have put my life in the greatest danger, but I was grateful she had let me be, last night. And in spite of everything, I still hoped she would find a way to escape. No one deserved a life like hers.

The Harley was where I had left it, leaning quietly against the back of the garage, with my rucksack and helmet in the panniers. It looked untouched but I ran my hands under the mudguards and checked all the cables to be sure.

It was just like the rescue at the farm. They must have known I'd come back for my bike, but they were letting me get away on it. It was almost as if Bernie and his thugs *wanted* me to meet Joanna tonight.

Now all I had to worry about was the police. I couldn't afford to take any more chances. If they were watching for me anywhere, it would be at the bridge, on the M62 along the estuary, or on the road out to York. So I took the back roads through to Anlaby, then picked up the country roads to the west of the city, eventually chancing the main road around the edges of the estuary, heading for Goole and the south side of the Humber.

I stopped on the way and rang Beano. She listened without

comment as I explained that I was now a fugitive. But she was guarded when I asked how she was doing. "Fine, I'll see you later," was all she would say when I suggested a time and meeting place. She was with someone, I could tell.

After I rang off, I dialled the Boulevard Hotel in Leeds and asked for the conference manager. It was a short call but it told me everything I wanted to know. And as I put the phone away, the mists in my mind began to clear. The pieces were beginning to fit at last. If I was right, then I would be safe from everyone except the police – at least until I handed over the file.

By the time I reached Barton it was nearly six o'clock. I came into the little town from the south, cold and miserable after the long journey, and drove cautiously down the marshlands road towards the camp, ready to pull in at the sight of any other vehicle. But the road was quiet and the fishing car park was empty when I pulled into its secluded, muddy space and hid the bike in some bushes.

As I walked past, the entrance to the camp was also deserted, but I could see smoke from the fire blowing in the wind over the top of the hill. They'd all be going to the demonstration outside the Boulevard Hotel tomorrow and I wondered what would happen to the tents and the caravans in their absence. It was tempting to warn them, to go up there and tell them what was happening. But, however thoughtful that might be, it was far too late now – and far too risky.

I turned and headed away from their road, along the track by the water, striding out towards the distant sea defences. It felt good to be on my own, breathing the cold, damp air deep into my lungs; stretching my legs, getting my heart beating; enjoying the sensation of warmth as my body responded.

The wind was in my face, but now the chill air felt less debilitating – clean and cold. To the right of the track, the surface of the lake was rippling with small waves and the bed of rushes on the edge vibrated noisily in the wind. A lone duck squawked in panic as I passed, flying off fussily across the water and into the grey sky. I pulled my long black scarf further up around my neck, put my gloves back on and zipped my jacket up as far as it would go.

Far off to the left, I could see the bridge, straddling the Humber, etched silver against the sky – majestic, a mighty giant demanding acknowledgement wherever you went. In spite of what had happened this week, I was still seduced by its scale, its beauty and its isolation. And after my journey right round the estuary, I was impressed too by its convenience.

It took me a good ten minutes to reach the earth embankment that stretches all along this part of the Humber, holding back the spring and autumn flood tides from Barton and the marshlands. I climbed straight up onto the path at the top and began to walk along it, down-river with the lake on my right, surveying the area around me.

To my left, a skirt of grassy wilderness led to the edge of the sea, taking in the bleak, wide vista of the estuary mouth. A few ships were making their way up and down the river: tankers, cargo boats, container ships, plying their way back and forth across the North Sea, trading goods between Hull and the continent.

On the landward side, about a half-mile away, a belt of trees almost hid the buildings of GME. I could see the security lights already, a thin strip of whiteness blinking through the firs that surrounded the high walls.

I thought back to our conversation with Joanna. She'd said that Magda had thought they were cloning human embryos. I knew nothing about genetics, but, if she'd been right, it seemed highly unlikely that they would get away with it in a research establishment that was continually monitored by government inspectors. There had to be something else; something that everyone else had missed.

I walked on, thinking about the way Langstein and Stantonwell had been looking at each other when they passed me in the big car. The politician's face was a mask of thunder, the boss of GME's a veil of abject fear.

The wind had dropped now but a fine, remorseless drizzle was wetting my face and hair. Soon my jeans were soaked through, and even my leather jacket began to feel heavy and damp.

I was about to leave the exposed path for the shelter of the lakeside when I saw what I had been looking for. About twenty yards away, just beyond the top corner of the lake, a small, mud-stained jetty clung to the edge of the estuary. The tide was turning and the waves were beginning to wash over the mud banks at the feet of the jetty, filling a dredged channel that led to it from the main expanse of water. It wouldn't take a big ship, but a small boat or a launch would easily be able to moor alongside at high tide.

I forgot my discomfort and walked onto the wooden boards, curious that there should be a mooring in such an isolated place – and elated that I'd found it. There was no road leading to it, and no sign of any boats stored inland or on the lake which might use it. Anyone who wanted to launch a boat from here would need to pull it overland across the rough terrain at the lake's edge.

The wood under my feet was green with algae, and grass was growing out through some of the boards, but there was no doubt it had been used recently. Some areas were blacker and dirtier than others, where feet had crushed the algae. And, though the two bollards on the seaward side were pretty well covered in green, the centre parts were clean, with all signs of the mould polished away by the friction of mooring ropes.

I studied the whole area and spotted a small track leading across the embankment to a path on the far side of the lake. I followed it, imagining the people who might have used it in the recent past, feeling shocked and sick at the conclusions that were going through my mind. The ground was relatively firm, but, even so, it looked well used. There were footprints – some left by large boots, others much smaller, left by people wearing ordinary shoes or even sandals.

Sure that I was onto something now, I followed the path, passing large signs warning that this was private property and entry was forbidden. Cold and wet, I kept going, in a world of my own, right down the side of the lake. Through the trees, the lights from GME were visible again and getting closer and brighter. I thought at first that the path was leading straight there but, just before I reached the wood, it veered off to the left, away from the research site and through another belt of trees.

I followed it up a rise and into a large clearing. The area was fenced with eight-foot-high wire mesh. And, where the path met the fence, a big metal gate was securely locked.

Beyond the gate, the ground was covered in rough, half-dead scrubland. Yellowed clumps of grass mixed with thickets of gorse and brambles, nettles and dead thistles. And, every so often, there was a mound of earth, perhaps twenty feet by fifty yards, with a concrete-sided entrance in each one, leading downwards. They were bunkers, left over from the war – probably ammunition bunkers, like the ones on the common in York, not far from my home. They were sited all over the fenced-in clearing, underground, well apart – built in another time to keep their contents safe from the bombs of the Luftwaffe.

But the fence was new. And the lock on the gate was shiny and well oiled.

I pushed through the scrubby grass and brambles, until I reached the end of the fence nearest to the lab site. From where I stood, I could see the lights shining over the top of the GME wall and through the small belt of trees in front of me. Looking back inside the fence, the first bunker was clearly visible too. And the distance between them was no more than a few hundred yards.

Suddenly the final pieces were falling into place. Now at last I could put it all together. Now I knew who had killed Magda Swinson and why; where Bernie fitted in; what Stantonwell was up to; and why Joanna Whittling wanted the file so badly. I knew how it all connected with the bodies in the sea; and why the e-mail attachment could be so important.

All that remained was to get the proof. And that lay over the high walls, beyond the cameras and the security lights, hidden deep in the fortress that was GME. I prayed that Beano would come up with something tonight that would enable us to get in and out without being seen. But, as I pushed my way back through the wet undergrowth alongside the wood, I couldn't imagine how that might be possible.

The rain had stopped now but large drops of water fell onto my head as I struggled along the waterlogged path, through the overhanging branches and brambles, towards the lake. As I neared fishing territory again, the track opened out and the going got easier. A couple of men passed me as I made my way back, their rods over their shoulders, chatting happily, on their way to a cold night's fishing. The way I felt just now, it amazed me how any man or woman could have fun, sitting all through the night, dangling a hook in the water.

When I reached the road and the lake, the sky was clearing and dark clouds were scudding across the moon, hiding it from view one moment and then releasing the ghostly light across the water so that it shimmered briefly with silver, before returning to its oily blackness. As I passed by, I glanced up the track I'd taken earlier, towards the sea defences and the dark sea beyond.

She was just over the water – probably at home in Willemstraat, making dinner. I thought back to our phone conversation of the day before, wishing I could ring her. I wanted to explain why I left; what stopped me from giving myself to her. But it was no good. How could I explain feelings which I didn't even understand myself?

I turned right down the earth track towards the car park. The moon went in again and I strained my eyes to see where I was going in the pitch blackness, stumbling over the rough ground and picking my way uneasily along the side of the big hawthorn hedge.

All of a sudden there was a rustling in the bushes behind me and, before I could turn round, a hand gripped my shoulder.

My heart stopped and my body went rigid, images of thugs and men in black raincoats flooding through my mind.

"Cameron, where the fuck have you been?"

I sucked in a lungful of air. Beano.

"What the hell are you doing, skulking up behind me like that?" I demanded, still trembling with shock. "I said I'd meet you at eight."

"I know," she murmured through gritted teeth, "and that was half an hour ago. I've been worried out of my fucking mind about you!"

"Sorry. I sort of lost track of time. I've been busy."

"Yeah, so have I. You still want to take a look inside GME?"

As the moon came out, I could see the smile on her face and a touch of wildness about her eyes.

"Well, you're in luck, Cameron," she said. "It's all fixed. We go in at eleven tonight."

## Twenty-six

"How can you be sure it's safe?" I asked. "What about the lights and the security cameras inside the walls? What about the internal fence, and all the guards? How the hell are we going to get past them all?"

We were sitting in her van with the windows open, alone in the anglers' car park. A few more fishermen had passed, some returning from their afternoon's sport, one or two more arriving for theirs. Over in the woods behind GME, I could hear the faint sound of owls hooting. But I was all too aware of the sophisticated security I'd seen yesterday in the security post by the fence, and I was sure the guards would be watching the perimeter on their closed-circuit TV screens.

"You told me this morning that it was crazy to even consider it – why the sudden confidence?"

"Simple." She smiled, taking a deep drag from her roll-up, cupping the red tip in her hand, blowing the smoke out of the open window. "Whilst I was bollocking you for even thinking about it, I remembered something an old lag once told me." She turned and looked at me like it was a pearl of wisdom. And in a way it was. "He said that a firm can spend thousands installing the most sophisticated security system in the world – but in the end it's always operated by people – and usually by men who are badly paid."

"So?" I asked.

"So you forget about bypassing the system. You just pay someone to turn it off. Easy, see?"

"Easy if you know someone who works there, someone you can trust."

"Ahh, well, Cam, the point is that I do. I saw him leaving on Sunday. An ex-screw, from Strangeways, bent as a two-bob note and always strapped for cash. I remembered him from way back – an acquaintance of an ex-con I used to knock about with. I didn't want to say anything to you this morning, though, 'cos I didn't know if he'd deliver, or if I could even find him. But after I left, I asked round in a few of the less select pubs in the east end. Talked to a few ex-cons. They said he was still on the game one way and another. Anyhow, to cut a long story short, I eventually found him and did a deal. No scruples at all. As long as he gets his price, he's happy."

"So you bribed him to turn off the security?"

"Yeah, and the cameras on one stretch of the walls. Simple, see? Mind you, the bastard knows how to deal – it's costing Joanna a fucking fortune."

"How much?"

Beano grunted. "Umph – a grand, with a monkey up front." She seemed to be slipping into lag-speak.

"A thousand pounds! Christ, Beano, where do you get that sort of money?"

"Told you, Joanna said she would pay all my expenses, whatever it took. I've had to raid my savings of course, but I'll get it all back."

I hope you do, Beano.

"Anyway, Eric – that's the guy's name – is on duty tonight. He's agreed to switch off the entire alarm system from the main control and also camera number five – that's the one watching the stretch of wall at the back of the site. It'll happen at eleven o'clock exactly. It's break time then, so there'll just be two of them in the control room until 11.45 and he says his mate will be up for it as well, for a cut. When it's done, he'll call my mobile – I've switched it to vibrate instead of ringing – then we can go in."

"But what about the offices?"

She smiled mischievously and produced a laminated card with a security barcode. "This is what the guards use to get in, when they need to warm up on cold nights. They're only supposed to use it in an emergency. But the sneaky bastards nip in and out all the time. It cost another two-fifty, but I reckon it's good value." She waved it in the air. "With this, we can just walk in. It'll be a breeze."

I wasn't entirely convinced by her enthusiasm. "But, Beano, if he's so bent, how do you know you can trust him?"

"The money, Cam, the money," she explained patiently. "The guy's earning peanuts – and it's common knowledge that he bets heavily. Likes the doggies a little too much, and he's run up debts with the wrong sort of people. For a grand, I can trust him, believe me!"

"OK, you can trust him, but what if something goes wrong and he can't get to the controls?"

"Then he won't ring – that's the fail-safe. No vibration, no breaking and entering." She rolled herself another fag. "You got the copy of the file?"

I produced a floppy disk and a CD from my pocket. "One of these should fit."

"Yeah, well, I hope so. This file holds the key to everything. We've got forty-five minutes tonight, that's all. But, if we can get into the offices and open their software, it's time enough to print off a hard copy of this – then, we're cooking with gas."

I leant back against the van seat, studying her. "Beano, you seem to know a lot about certain things – picking locks, bent screws, that sort of thing?"

Her look of mild triumph faded to embarrassment. "Erm... yes... I... er... spent some time in Holloway."

"Holloway!" I shrieked. "You're an ex-con!"

She shifted uncomfortably, her eyes wide, weighing up my reaction. "Only small time. Nothing much... honest! Just me and a few mates. We tried to nick a lorry full of fags. We weren't very good though. The cops caught us when we stopped at a pelican crossing to let an old woman across." She looked at me and grinned. "You've got to be ruthless to be a real criminal."

"And you've gone straight since?"

She bit her bottom lip. "A touch of freelance housebreaking," she admitted, adding quickly, "Only rich capitalists though. I never stole from people who couldn't afford it."

"Well, I'm glad about that," I replied, a little concerned. "You're not still at it, are you?"

"Fucking hell, Cameron! Here I am sitting in the middle of nowhere with a woman who's wanted for murder... And you're asking me if I'm a criminal!"

I was about to defend myself when I saw the smile playing around the edges of her mouth.

"No, don't worry. I gave it up when I was caught for the second time."

"What happened then?" I asked, unable to help myself.

She squirmed again. "I was caught by the owners at a big house in Hampstead. They had a really nice kitten... I... got distracted and started playing with it. I forgot where I was."

I looked at her all too serious face and realised she'd been winding me up. Then we both burst out laughing.

"Anyway, it's all right, I retired eight years ago now." She touched my arm reassuringly.

I shook my head. "I think you're probably the most surprising person I've ever met, Beano."

"You really think so?" She laughed. "Christ, Cameron, you should see my brother. He's a transvestite safe-breaker. The Met have been trying to catch him for years!"

I smiled, almost believing her again. "Yeah, well, to get back to the subject in hand, I'd like to take a look at another part of the site whilst you sort out the file – the south-east corner, if that's OK."

"Yeah," she said, "no problem, but why the sudden interest in that part?"

"Because, Beano, I know exactly what's going on now. All I need is to collect the evidence to prove it."

I told her about the jetty and the bunkers; about the rally in the city centre, my call to the Boulevard Hotel, Jimmy's account of the women washed up in the North Sea, and all the other loose ends that had suddenly come together. This time there was no argument. The facts were clear now. The endgame was about to begin.

Around nine o'clock, I made the call to Joanna Whittling. She sounded calm and in control. And that was exactly how we wanted her to feel. She had her laptop now. She had the GME software loaded on it. All she needed was a copy of the e-mail attachment and everything could be finalised.

We arranged to meet at 2 am, just a fifteen-minute drive from the marshlands road.


A drip of water from a tree above me fell straight down my neck. I winced as the cold water hit my skin, and pulled the collar of my jacket further up, as I shifted away from a twig that was sticking into me. It felt unreal, sitting there in the undergrowth on the edge of a wood, in the heart of North Lincolnshire, waiting to go over the high wall into the laboratories.

"It's 10.50. We should be in the shadows by the wall at spot-on eleven," Beano whispered, sorting through the contents of her rucksack, checking her kit. "You still OK with this, Cam?"

"Yes, of course," I replied, trying to keep the nervousness out of my voice and wrapping my arms around myself to stop the shaking. I didn't like it. I would rather not be here. But it had to be done. I just hoped that Beano was right about the guard – and that we would get out alive.

The next five minutes seemed like hours, but at 10.55 we slung our rucksacks on our backs and moved out. I felt sick and my heart was beating wildly, but Beano's eyes shone out from her blackened face, like she was some kind of adrenalin junkie, high on anticipation.

Once in position, we crouched and waited on the soft ground at the edge of the wall. I tried to control my breathing as I watched the dial on my watch move round from 11 to 11.01. Beano was next to me, holding the grappling iron and the rope, keyed up. I had a thick blanket in my hands, ready to throw over the razor wire on the wall top. We waited. The minute hand moved round to two, then three, then four minutes past.

At five past, I saw Beano stiffen as the noiseless call came to her mobile. She nodded to me, then stood up, backed off from the wall and tossed the iron over. When she pulled it back, it caught and she tugged hard before taking the blanket off me and throwing it over her shoulder. Then she climbed to the top, with surprising agility for a heavy woman, placed the thick blanket over the wire and disappeared over the other side.

I was straight up after her, retrieving the iron and the blanket before I jumped down on the other side, and stashing them in a small black heap at the foot of the wall, ready for our escape. Beano was already at the mesh fence, her big wire-cutters in her hand. The twenty yards of scrubby grass between us were lit as bright as day by the lights shining down from their high posts. The site was deserted: darkened houses, sheds and offices, no people. But Beano was signalling for me to hurry. I got there with only seconds to spare, just before two guards came into view, walking the inside perimeter, swinging their torches like truncheons. We both flattened ourselves in the rough grass by the fence, praying to whatever god or goddess might be listening, as the men's feet came within inches of us.

"No excitement tonight then," said one of them, kicking at the ground and sending a shower of earth cascading through the fence around our heads.

"No," the other agreed, "fucking dull. I keep looking forward to some action. After the way the boss goes on, the least I expect is a bunch of loonies from that camp spoiling for a fight."

"Yeah, bloody hippies, you can never rely on the bastards." They both laughed as they walked away.

Then Beano pushed the nose of the wire-cutters into the fence. I held my breath as she made the first cut, half expecting an alarm to go off, or a surge of security men as the fence was breached. But Beano's contact had done his stuff. The night air was still and quiet as she pulled the wires apart into a body-sized hole and we squeezed through into the compound, closing the hole behind us. We saw no one as we ran across the grass and into the shadows beneath a big tree. Then we ran from shadow to shadow across the back of the site, past some small houses, to the corner nearest the underground bunkers.

We stopped at a windowless brick building, close to the fence. The door was half covered with a sign warning that it was an inflammable liquid store and smoking was forbidden. This had to be the building I wanted: the way into the bunkers.

"Quick, Beano," I breathed, aware that time was short, "unlock the door and then leave me to it."

She took out her pick-locks and began to work on the lock. I looked around nervously. The site was quiet, but we were right out in the open and all it would take would be one guard wandering past the houses...

Beano sighed behind me, having trouble. I paced out the side of the building – roughly ten yards – then shuffled my feet and bit the ends of my fingers, whilst she fiddled interminably.

Then there was faint click and she stood upright as the door swung open. "Little bastard," she swore under her breath. "Good luck, Cam. I'm into the offices now. See you back under the big tree in twenty-five minutes exactly." She grabbed my arm. "No longer, or we're trapped, OK?"

I nodded and checked my watch. Then, as she disappeared back around the houses and out of sight, I slid through the door.

Once inside, I switched on my flashlight. The room was only about eight yards deep – a good six feet less than on the outside – and perfectly empty, apart from one bay of metal shelving on the back wall. My spirits surged. I was right, thank God. I was right.

The shelving on the back wall looked like the sort you would find in any industrial store – sturdy uprights and shelves, with a metal sheet backing. But, as I knelt to look at the base, I spotted one big difference – wheels, almost hidden by the metal skirt. And when I pulled on the right-hand side, the shelves swung away from the wall, revealing an ordinary wooden door: unlocked, but bolted securely from my side.

I pulled back the bolts and opened it, shining my flashlight into the dark void beyond. Ahead of me was a set of steep steps, leading down into a tunnel, constructed out of concrete sewer pipes and stretching straight ahead for a long way underground.

I trod carefully down the steps, holding onto the metal handrail, and started along the tunnel, checking my watch. I only had twenty minutes left and, if I was right, the tunnel would be at least a quarter of a mile long. Five minutes at a brisk walk, five minutes back. Then another ten to get safely back over the wall. It was tight. I walked quickly, my back bent, my head down in the narrow confined space. Then I began to jog into the blackness, towards who-knows-what. The smooth grey sides of the tunnel slid past, as I ran in my sphere of shifting light. The last thing I wanted was to be trapped down here when the alarms came back on.

The tunnel closed in behind me as I ran. Like a never-ending treadmill, a subterranean nightmare. My heart was thumping and my head felt like bursting as blood coursed around my brain. I was hot, so hot. Sweat was breaking out everywhere. I breathed faster, trying to keep up with my body's demand for air, but my lungs were emptying rather than filling. Caught in the grip of icy panic, my body started to give up the fight.

I stopped before I fell. Coloured pinpoints of light danced in their thousands before my eyes. My legs and arms like jelly, I was a marionette slumped against the curved side of the tunnel. If I didn't calm down and breathe properly, I would pass out. Come on, Cameron. Pull yourself together. Breathe, for God's sake, breathe. Slowly. Deeply. Calm. Calm.

I turned off the torch and tried to compose myself, bending over and breathing as slowly and deeply as I could, telling my brain that I was in the open, on a dark windless plain. That I was safe, that there was emptiness all around me. Slowly, the points of starry light gave up their dance and my legs began to feel solid again as the air reached my bloodstream.

Bit by bit I came round, and when I turned my flashlight on again and looked down the tunnel, I saw the door and stumbled the last thirty yards to stop next to it, listening for any sound. But the stillness was almost deafening. I turned off the torch and carefully slid the bolts out of their sockets one by one. And very slowly, very quietly, I opened the door.

It was pitch black again on the other side. But the air smelled different, damp and warm – the smell of living creatures, the smell of people, of women. I took in the faint sound of breathing, the light cough, the murmur of someone turning over in their sleep.

My heart in my mouth, I turned the torch full on and shone it down the room.

I knew what I expected to find. I knew what I thought was going on inside these old ammunition bunkers. But when I saw the reality it was more chilling than I could ever have imagined. Down the room – all down the long concrete wall of the bunker – were beds, around fifty of them. And in each bed was a woman. One by one, they opened their eyes, despair, confusion and panic on their faces. And as I shone the light around, some of the women sat up and looked at me, shielding their eyes from the glare.

When they realised that I must be an outsider, they got out of bed and came towards me, talking in languages I couldn't understand – pleading with their hands in the universal language of desperation.

I don't quite know how I did it, but I kept my head and took my camera out of the pouch on my waist, pointing it towards them, flashing brightly. The white glare stopped them in their tracks.

It wasn't the noise that upset me then; it wasn't the cramped, inhuman conditions; it wasn't even the severe distress that dripped from every face. In that instant, as I spun round to get out of there, I remembered again about the bodies in the sea and Elana's warning on human cloning.

And what shook me to the core, what made my guts turn and my head spin, was that all of them – every last one – was clearly pregnant.

God help me, I shut the door and locked them back in their prison. I could hear the crying and the pleadings drumming in my ears all the way back along the tunnel. But there was nothing I could do for them right now. Their best hope, and mine, was to get back to Beano, back to the fence and away from here. I checked my watch as I ran, stumbling through the darkness, my torch barely lighting the way ahead as the batteries faded. Seven minutes to get out and back to the tree.

By the time I reached the door, I had only five minutes left. I pushed the shelves back against the entrance, got out of the store, closed the door and ran like hell, across the grass, past the houses and over to the big tree. Beano came out of the shadows as I approached, a broad smile on her face.

"Got it, Cam!" she whispered, patting her coat pocket. "Now let's get the hell outta here!"

"No!" I replied. "You've got to lock that store again!"

She stopped in her tracks, astonished. "Are you fucking crazy, woman? The alarm goes back on any minute. We gotta split!"

"Don't argue," I insisted. "Just do it! There are women down there. If they know we've found them, they'll kill them!"

She looked at me for a split second, then set off at a run with me behind, back to the store. We nearly ran into two more of the guards who were making their rounds, the opposite way around the fence. I pulled Beano into the shadow of the houses, just in time, pinning her against the wall, one hand over her mouth, until they'd passed.

"You stay here," she said. "There's no point in us both taking the risk." And she was off again, running directly for the store, her pick-locks in her hand. I crept along the back of the houses, keeping her in my sight, willing her to hurry as the seconds closed in on us. A light went on in a kitchen behind me, and I could hear a man singing quietly to himself, unaware of what was happening outside. Overhead there was a flap of wings as an owl passed. Come on, Beano. For fuck's sake, come on!

She turned and started to run back, just as I saw another patrol walking towards us from the direction of the offices. We couldn't go back that way; I had to stop her before they got a clear view of the open ground she was crossing. I ran like hell across the grass, wildly signalling for her to go the other way. She saw me just in time and veered sharply to her left, following me around the front of the houses, towards the big tree.

Just then, all hell broke loose. The sirens sounded, extra lights came on all over the site and guards began to appear from everywhere, shouting and waving to each other as they spread out over the area. Beano grunted coolly and pulled me into some shrubs, taking her rucksack off her back and delving into it.

"What the hell are you doing?" I shouted above the noise.

"Contingency, Cameron," she hissed, handing me three nine-inch sticks of what looked like dynamite, keeping three for herself.

"Army thunderflashes, picked them up in Hull this afternoon. We need a diversion. When I say, pull the tabs hard and throw the bloody things as far as you can over towards the animal houses. Spread them well apart."

She waited a few seconds and then nodded at me. We pulled the tabs and lobbed the oversized bangers high into the air. The pause before detonation was less than twenty seconds but seemed like twenty minutes. There were more than a dozen guards searching behind every tree, in every bush, around the houses just behind us, closing in, getting too near for comfort.

But when the thunderflashes exploded, the noise was deafening – and the effect on the guards was instant. As one, they threw themselves to the ground and waited, lifeless, as others exploded around them.

We hurtled off in the opposite direction, straight across the open ground, taking a direct line to the gap in the fence. As Beano slid through, I looked back. The men were still running around in confusion, searching the area where the explosions had gone off. Then I heard one of them shout. By the time we got to the wall, they were closing in on us. I grabbed the grappling iron, threw it over and scrambled to the top. Beano tossed the blanket up to me and I leant over, my hand reaching down to pull her up.

It was then that I saw two men with rifles taking aim, and everything went into slow motion.

I swung my body down and to the side. The first gun flashed yellow and red. Then the second. Air rushed past my head, the report of the guns following. The smell of cordite exploded all around me. I grabbed Beano's wrist and pulled her heavy body forcibly onto the wall. She opened her mouth to speak.

But no words came out.

I just felt the warmth of her blood as it splashed onto my face. Then we tumbled headlong together down the other side.

## Twenty-seven

Instinctively I tried to save myself as I crashed towards the ground. My hands smashed into the wet grass, and a searing pain jolted up my arms as I fell heavily onto my shoulder, rolling across the ground, the impact juddering through my bones, pain screaming through my body.

Beano landed with a dull thud next to me. Groaning loudly, she curled up into a bundle and grasped her ribs.

I was up in an instant, the shock of my own fall unimportant compared to my panic over the bleeding, stricken woman by my side. Somehow I got my arms under hers, and rolled her onto her knees and then up onto her feet, holding her upright as she swayed drunkenly by my side.

"Are you all right?" I asked breathlessly, supporting nearly all of her weight.

"Don't be stupid!" She coughed as she began to stagger forward. "'Course I'm not! I've got a fucking great hole in my side."

Her face was a mask of pain as we stumbled together towards the cover of the woods, every step sending shards of pain through her shaking body and draining my strength. But I hung onto her, supporting her heavy weight, hauling her forward. The twenty yards of open ground seemed endless, but, somehow, we reached the blackness of the wood before our pursuers came over the top of the wall.

We pushed on in desperation, staggering noisily through the undergrowth.

I glanced round. Through the trees, silhouetted against the security lights, more shadows were leaping down from the walls before spreading out. They were moving stealthily our way. I tripped over a fallen branch in the blackness, jolting Beano as she lurched forward, screaming with the pain.

"Leave me, Cameron!" she pleaded, gasping for air. "Save yourself. Get the fuck out!"

I knew she was right, that there was no way we could outrun them like this. But if my bearings were correct, my bike was only yards away now, at the other side of the wood on the rough, overgrown path that I'd walked on earlier.

"Keep going, Beano. We're nearly there!" I gasped. "Keep going! For Christ's sake keep going!"

I could hear the dead wood snapping under their feet as they entered the trees, could see the beams from their powerful torches sweeping through the damp firs. I scanned the way ahead in the darkness, looking desperately for the edge of the wood. The Harley must be here somewhere. Where in God's name was it? I hitched Beano further up onto my shoulder and dragged her through the firs, praying for a little more time. A few more minutes and they would be upon us.

Their voices were echoing through the trees all around us now. "You can't get away! Give up! Stop, and you'll come to no harm."

Yeah, tell me another.

Then I saw the bike. She was standing where I had left her, as close as I could to our escape point: my beautiful Harley Sportster. The sight of her faint outline, nestling just inside the woods, had never been so sweet. With one last massive effort, I hauled Beano onto the seat and squeezed myself in front of her, turning the ignition as I mounted, pushing the bike off its stand.

"Hold on!" I screamed. "Hold onto me!"

The engine roared to life and I shoved her into gear, gunning the motor and releasing the clutch at the same time. The bike shot forward, its back wheel spinning on the pine needles, then we were out of the trees and onto the path – just as the rifles flashed and the bullets started to fly.

But they were too late. We were down the track now, lurching and bumping along, Beano holding onto me around the waist, swaying dangerously as we cut through the branches and brambles. The tyres slid on the wet, muddy ground. I drove down the hill and out onto the road, accelerating wildly past the camp entrance and up the marshlands road.

I slowed down once we were halfway along, turning my head to shout to my passenger: "I'll stop soon – hang on!"

She lurched from left to right, squeezing my ribs in response. When I reached the end, I slowed right down, taking the bends into Barton carefully.

I could feel her grip getting lighter as we reached Whitecross Street. "I've got... to talk... to you." She coughed painfully as I drove ever more carefully up the hill, her body slumped into my back, her voice hardly audible above the noise of the engine.

"It's OK, I know what you're going to tell me," I yelled back, holding her wrist tightly and steering with one hand. "I've seen it."

"You can't... you can't know!" she gasped, as I turned in to the nursing home.

I doused my lights and cut the engine, coasting down the path to the main entrance. I jumped off and supported her as she painfully lowered herself to lie on the ground.

"The file..." she gasped, fighting for air.

"I know, Beano, I know," I said, taking off her rucksack and putting it under her head. "It's about cloning. Cloning humans."

"Yeah... but... there's more," she gasped, grabbing my arm urgently. "You were right... GME is... owned... by Nazis... the first page... it's addressed... to... Langstein."

I held her head in my hands and kissed her on the cheek as her eyes began to flicker. I was remembering Pat, remembering Magda Swinson just before she passed out.

"We know it all now, don't we," I said grimly as she opened her eyes again and looked up at me. I wanted to stay, to make sure she was all right. But there was nothing I could do for her. And, if I was going to stop them, if I was going to clear my name, then I needed to get away.

"I have to go, Beano," I said, my heart thumping, tears running down my cheeks. "I have to go. I've got to stop them."

She grabbed my arm. "Don't, Cameron... For God's... sake don't go... and meet... Joanna now."

"I have to!" I wailed as a light came on in the office. "We can't let them get away with it!"

"Then let me come... Please!"

I shook my head. "You need help, you're losing blood, fast."

"Fuck you," she croaked. "You just don't know when to give up, do you?"

"I guess not," I replied, putting my camera into her hand. "Give this to the police, tell them everything. Give them the printout of the file. Tell them to raid the place before daylight, before they kill the women I saw in the bunker."

I stood up as the night orderly came to the door.

"You just take care, Beano."

She pulled a face at me, as the worried figure peered out at us through the glass.

"Be careful, Cameron," she coughed. "You're... very... special."

I looked down at this woman who had just been through so much with me, and swallowed hard. Images of Pat flashed through my mind again. She mustn't die. I couldn't bear it. I gulped in the cold night air and pushed the thought away.

"Yeah, Beano... well, you're special too."

"What is it?" The scared voice crackled through the security intercom and I suddenly remembered the mud on our faces.

"Help her!" I yelled, coming back to life. "Get her inside and lock the doors. Get an ambulance!" Then, jumping onto my bike, "Get the police!"

I stopped at the gate and looked back: at two women in the pool of light by the door, bending over my friend; then across to the annex and my mother's bedroom. My heart felt like it was breaking.

It was nearly 12.30 am when I pulled in to the kerbside down the hill in Whitecross Street. I stopped and breathed deeply, trying to banish the image of Beano from my mind. If I was going to make this work then I would need all the concentration I had.

Now I knew that I was right about GME, Langstein, Joanna Whittling and, most of all, the man on the bridge – the man in black who had started all this with his vicious attack on Magda Swinson. And I also knew how all the events of the last few days added together.

Langstein's party were the owners of GME. And the research was funded by them. It was, as I had suspected, some kind of fanatical att-empt to breed a super-race of white Europeans. Human clones were being manufactured like Lou had said, using eggs emptied of their genetic material and injected with the cells of the most eminent of Langstein's party members. They were raised as embryos in laboratory conditions and finally inserted into the wombs of illegal immigrants – women who had come from all over the world with hope in their hearts. They had been split from their loved ones with the promise of a better life and brought in by sea to the small jetty on the side of the estuary. Imprisoned in the bunkers, they were the human incubators for Langstein and his new elite.

And the bodies in the sea? Stella had said that every success in-volved many failures, that the surrogate mothers and the failed foet-uses had to be expendable. And the chilling truth was that the women in the sea were Stantonwell's failures. The foetuses were aborted, so that the evidence was removed. Then the women were consigned to a cold, watery grave because they were a liability.

It was the new eugenics: a sick, science fiction version of Hitler's dream; cloned babies imbued with the selected qualities of the white supremacists. Then, when they had grown for a few years, the most perfect children would be cloned again. Clones of clones of clones. Generations of super-beings to infiltrate the highest offices of Europe, reclaiming the white, middle-class, heterosexual supremacy that Langstein spoke about today. The new eugenics. The Master Race.

I wiped all the dirt off my face and checked my watch. It was nearly one. I was about to become the decoy in the most chilling of finales. But this was the only chance I would have to get the man who killed Magda Swinson. I had to take it.

But if I was going to survive, I needed back-up. I pulled the mobile out of my pocket. They would have an hour before the meeting with Joanna. An hour for them to ensure my safety. It wasn't long, but it was all I the time I had to give.

As the phone rang, I prayed that I wouldn't get his answering service – that Sergeant Williams' phone would be switched on, ringing by the side of his bed. My heart stopped beating as I waited in the deserted, amber-lit streets of Barton.

"Yes?" Jimmy William's voice snapped in my ear and I breathed again.

"Jimmy, it's Cameron," I said urgently.

"Cameron? What? Where are you?"

"I've no time to explain. But, if you want the man who killed Magda Swinson, then be at the big quarry on the Barton to Barrow road at 2 am exactly and wait around the quarry edge."

"Cameron, what the hell are you talking about? It's the middle of the fucking night!"

"You know what I'm talking about, Jimmy!" I snapped back. "I know who killed Magda Swinson. He'll be down on the floor of the quarry some time after two. Please be there. No lights. No noise. Just wait and watch. When he comes you'll know. Don't move in until he does."

"Cameron...!"

"Jimmy, I haven't got time to discuss it. Just get some officers there, preferably some marksmen, around the quarry edge. There'll be a few of them – and they'll be armed. But I repeat, come quietly, keep a low profile – no lights, no noise, or you'll lose him."

"OK, OK! I hear you. But an hour is tight, Cameron. Hang back, will you? Don't, whatever you do, go down there by yourself. Wait for us!"

"I can't, Jimmy. I need to be on the quarry floor before you move in. It's the only way to flush him out. If I'm not there, you won't get him."

I ended the call before he could argue any more, and got back on my bike, heading for the Barrow Road. I was taking a massive risk and I knew it – walking into the depths of that quarry by myself to meet Joanna Whittling. There wouldn't be any second chances.

But I had to do it. If they were going to use me as bait, I wanted to make damn sure that I caught the big fish.

## Twenty-eight

I pulled my bike behind a hedge and walked the last half mile, leaving the deserted country road and making my way across the fields towards the quarry. The moon had set now and the clouds had thickened. But the air still felt damp and wet, and the mud from the field clung to the soles of my boots as I ploughed across the last patch of ground leading to the quarry.

When I reached the chain-link fence, I pulled myself over and then crawled on my stomach across the last few yards of scrubby grass to the quarry edge. There was a drop of nearly a hundred feet to the dark quarry floor. The sheer walls on three sides blocked out any light. The fourth side was a long gentle slope, giving access to a wide tarmac road that wound its way down to the vast open arena; down to the big silos below me. During the day, long queues of lorries would be lining up there to pick up their heavy loads and then trundle back and forth to whatever new road was being built.

But right now it was deserted. Except, that is, for the silhouette of a single car, parked a few yards from the silos. It wasn't my idea of a safe meeting place: out in the middle of nowhere, boxed in on all sides, with only one exit. It was a very good place for an ambush. More than ever, Joanna's choice of meeting place convinced me that I was right.

I glanced back over my shoulder, scanning the empty Lincolnshire countryside. It was nearly 2 am, and still there was no sign of the police officers who would soon, I hoped, be creeping into position. The roads around me were all in darkness and I couldn't leave it much longer. By five minutes past, my trust in Jimmy Williams all I had left, I took my life in my hands and started to walk down the road into the quarry, towards Joanna's car.

She got out as I approached and waited for me as I made my way cautiously towards her, scanning the silos on her right and the two Portakabins behind them for signs of anyone else. I was walking into the lion's den, and my body knew it. My legs felt weak and my chest was tight with fear. I could hardly breathe for the panic inside me fighting to get out. But, if this was to work, I had to keep calm. I needed to appear normal. Not easy, when I was possibly doing the last thing I would ever do.

But the smile on *her* face betrayed no fear. This was what she had been working for, these last few months. This was her chance to get back at the people who had taken over her business and discarded her; her chance to shine again. But all the same, I saw her move nervously as I approached. She was, after all, taking a massive risk herself. And for all her apparent composure, she too must be shaking inside.

"Where's Beano?" she demanded, concerned.

I was glad she was safe, back at the nursing home, with the evidence. At least one of us would survive to tell the story.

"She's indisposed," I answered.

"But where is she? I wanted to see her." Panic in her eyes. Good.

"Well, you can't. She's not here."

"Have you got the disk?" she asked, her breath swirling around her in the icy air of the subterranean rendezvous.

"Yes."

"Give it to me then." Her eyes moved around nervously as she held out her hand. "Then we can expose the illegal practices at GME."

I ignored her and kept my hands firmly in my pockets. "I want to see what's on the file, Joanna," I told her forcefully. "Like I said earlier,

I can't let you keep the disk until I'm sure of what it says." I needed to stall her awhile.

"Of course." She held my gaze. Her eyes were the same as this morning – steady and full of self-interest. "Quickly, Cameron. Give me the disk, then I can open the file and we can get out of here. I'm worried that someone may see us."

She was good, very good.

"How do I know I can trust you?"

"Because I was Magda's friend," she said without blinking an eye.

Some friend.

I paused for as long as I could, then handed her both disks. "Take your pick, Joanna, there's a floppy and a CD."

"Good." She nodded in satisfaction. "Thank you, Cameron, thank you so much. You have no idea how much this means to me." She smiled, greedy, excited, as she took it to her car.

"You're still going to present the file at ISEM tomorrow?" I asked as she took out her laptop and balanced it on the bonnet of the car. "You're going to expose the activities of GME to the world?"

"Of course!" she breathed. "That's what all this is about."

I wished, just then, that I could believe she was driven by idealism and integrity. But as she booted up the computer and slipped the disk into the drive, I knew that I was right about her.

She opened the software and, as it came onscreen, loaded the file. I perused it for a minute or two. It was just as extreme as I expected. The research was already over; the propagation of Langstein's super-Nazis already underway. It was Hitler Youth all over again – but with a deadly new twist.

"Are you satisfied?" she asked.

"It's wicked and immoral," I said, stepping back as she removed the disk, connected her mobile to the laptop and logged onto the web.

"Now, one more thing, Cameron, and then we've finished." She smiled, pleased with herself, inviting me to step up to the computer again.

"You want me to wipe the file off the e-mail server."

"Yes, of course. You've been through so much to get it. The least I can do is make sure that you are safe. Once that's gone, no one will have any reason to pursue you."

Yeah, and the moon is made of cheese.

I did as I was asked, keying in the Line One address and *u.n.known* – the user name I'd set up specially on Monday. Then I entered my password, and when the file came up, I wiped it in front of her eyes. I'd given it all up now, every bit of my insurance was gone. I hoped to God that the police would be here soon, otherwise everything would be lost.

Then she stepped back and smiled at me. A smile of triumph. The depraved smile of a bitter woman on the make.

"You're not going to ISEM, are you?" I asked bluntly, as I saw the first signs of movement in the shadows around the silo.

"No, Cameron. I'm not… How did you know?" she asked, stepping back from me.

"Because ISEM doesn't exist, does it? I checked with the Boulevard Hotel this afternoon. You invented the whole thing. You designed the website yourself. It was an elaborate ploy to make me believe that you were driven by idealism, rather than greed.

"And the trashing of your house. That was faked as well, wasn't it? To impress Beano, and to convince us both that you were under threat."

"Well," she purred, as the three thugs surrounded me, "it worked, didn't it?"

Almost Joanna, but not quite.

Cod Eyes grabbed me roughly by the arms. "Hello again, dyke!" he breathed, straight into my face, as one of the others pulled my wrists together behind my back. "Nice to meet you again. Maybe we can get better acquainted this time."

Scarface appeared out of the shadows with a radio and began talking hurriedly into it.

"So, you're going to sell the file to the highest bidder after all, Joanna. So much for Magda's trust."

She leant back against the car. "She was a fool, Cameron. Just like you. A stupid, idealistic fool, who thought that she could stop scientific progress. Huh!" She snorted sarcastically. "The information on this file is worth millions of dollars to certain countries – not to mention Henri Langstein. You really think I would give up that opportunity just for a warm feeling?

"Oh yes, it would have been nice to expose Stantonwell and the people who own GME. But this way is much better. I still get my revenge – but I also get the money they cheated me out of."

"Money that you will have to split with your partner," I said, wincing as Big Ears pulled the rope tight across my wrists. "When can I expect to meet him again?"

"Oh, you are clever, Cameron," she sneered. "Very soon. Very soon indeed. But I'm sorry, I'm afraid it will be a brief meeting. I rather think he will kill you shortly after he arrives."

The thug with the cod eyes stroked my face and pursed his lips in a grotesque imitation of a kiss. "Yeah, but maybe this time, butch, he'll let us have some fun with you first."

I kicked out at him, catching him hard on his shin, making him cry out with pain.

"Bitch!" He brought his hand hard across my face.

I glared at him defiantly. "Just keep the fuck away from me!" He laughed in my face as I spoke to the woman again. "You're not going to get away with it, Joanna. You've made a big mistake... And you don't even know it, do you?"

"Oh I don't think so, Cameron," she snorted, looking up into the sky, as the powerful throbbing of rotor blades filled the air. "It's you who has made a mistake. Very soon you'll be dead and we'll be on our way out of here."

The quarry lit up with the glare of the helicopter's landing lights as it skimmed over the edge and hovered high above us, blowing small tornadoes of dust around our faces and drowning out any other sound.

I seized the opportunity and ran as fast as I was able, struggling to keep my balance with my arms behind my back, weaving and dodging across the quarry floor. They were after me instantly, running hard, screaming at me to stop. Then they grabbed for my arms and my shoulders, bringing me down onto the sharp stony ground. Big Ears kicked me hard in the ribs and then hauled me roughly to my feet, pushing me ahead of him until I was back by Joanna's car and under Joanna's smug gaze.

By now the helicopter had set itself down in the wide open space of the quarry and, as the rotors rattled and whooshed to a standstill, a solitary figure emerged, running from the cockpit across the rough ground towards us.

It was just who I had expected it to be: the man who I couldn't remember, the man who had been in the right place at the right time, the man who didn't want to leave me alone. But now, he was dressed differently. Gone were the shabby denims and the old jacket, replaced by a dark, flat cap and a long black raincoat.

"Well, what a surprise!" I jeered, as he approached. "I don't suppose, by any chance, you're here to save me this time. Are you, Bernie?"

He threw me a look of pure contempt, and turned straight to Joanna.

"You got the file?" he demanded.

"Yes." She turned to smirk at me. "Your little friend delivered the goods just like you said she would."

"Where's the other one? The big woman?" he snapped.

"Somewhere you can't get her," I replied. "Somewhere safe."

His face coloured up in anger, and the cool dispassionate eyes flashed hotly. He pointed his finger at me, his voice loaded with malice. "I'll deal with you later, dyke!"

Then, turning to Joanna, "You deleted the original copy, like I asked?"

"Yes Bernie, it's all done. Just like you asked. Have you got the money?"

"You saw her do it?" he asked Scarface.

"Yes, boss. And she's got two disks."

"Let me have them," he demanded. He was cold and unemotional – just like he had been on the bridge, when he drove the knife into Magda Swinson's belly. "Let me have the disk."

Joanna hesitated, her look of satisfaction flickering for the first time. Then she took the disk out of her bag and started to walk towards him.

"No, stay where you are!" he commanded, walking up and taking it out of her hand. "... And the computer. Give it to me!"

"Have you got the money?" she asked again, her voice unsteady now.

"No, Joanna." He stood calmly studying her for a moment, then hurled the laptop to the ground and put his heel right through it. "There's no money."

Then he stood back from her, laughing coldly – still looking at her, but addressing his remarks to me.

"You see, Cameron, there is some justice, after all. When Magda Swinson stumbled across this file, she went to see Joanna. She went to ask her advice because she thought she could trust her." He smiled ironically. "Of course, her trust was misplaced. Once Joanna realised the big secret, the greedy bitch just wanted the money. She conned her friend as well as you with the fabricated story about the conference. So when you arrived at the camp and mentioned her name, naturally I went straight along to see her." He looked across at her, smiling wickedly. "Didn't I, Joanna?"

"You bastard!" she spat, at last getting the drift and making for him. But Scarface and Big Ears grabbed her and held her still, one either side.

"I told her that I was a dealer, Cameron, and that I would buy the file off her if she got it off you – and, of course, she believed me." He sneered, taking out his gun and raising it level with her chest, then talking directly to her.

"But I'm not a dealer, Joanna. I never was. I lied to you. Just as you lied to Magda Swinson." He turned to look at me as if vindicated. "See, Cameron, natural justice at work."

Joanna's eyes opened wide and she tried to step back, a look of nausea on her face, her body trembling as the horrible truth dawned on her.

The report from the handgun reverberated all around the quarry, echoing off the high cliffs and ringing in my ears. A neat hole appeared in the Burberry raincoat, between her breasts. Her upper body convulsed violently with the impact, so that she staggered backwards, dancing absurdly as her legs fought to keep up with her. Then her mouth dropped open, as if she was about to speak. But there were no words, just two big over-mascara'd eyes that said all that was needed: betrayal by someone she thought she could trust, incredulity that it should end like this.

As she fell to the ground and lay quite still, Bernie knelt down, checked her pulse and nodded to himself. Then he looked up at me. "See Cameron, I'm a professional."

"Yeah, I can see that, Bernie. I can hardly hold back my admiration for you. Always in the right place at the right time."

He came close and spoke quietly in my ear. "Shut the fuck up, bitch."

I'd hit a nerve at last. Maybe in the few seconds I had left, I could work on it. Where the fuck were the police? Where was Jimmy Wilson?

"Like the farm. You set that up to scare me, didn't you?"

"Of course, Cameron, when you weren't persuaded by Marcus Stantonwell's charm, we had to do something. We knew you were too clever to just tell us. You knew we'd kill you as soon as we had the information. We knew you'd only give it up for the right reasons. So I told Beano where you were, knowing that she'd innocently help us to scare you right into the arms of the late Mrs Whittling. And, of course, you fell for it."

"For a while I did, Bernie. I almost trusted you. But you were too good, too attentive. Always happy to oblige. And you made two big mistakes."

"And what were they?" he asked mockingly.

"The first was that you left some packets of foreign rolling tobacco in the drawer at the cottage. The second was when you gave one of them to Beano. When I realised they were yours, I knew it must have been you who told Stantonwell about my conversation with Magda, told him I had the file. I knew that these thugs were your men; that the trashing of Joanna's house was a set-up and that it had to be you who was pulling her strings. It was only a short step from there to realising that it must have been you and one of your thugs who murdered Magda Swinson at the Infirmary. However you dress it up, Bernie, you're nothing more than a liar and a killer."

He grabbed my collar and brought his face close to mine. "I'm a professional. A freelance fixer. I tie up loose ends for people. I'm incorruptible, Cameron. And I'm scrupulously fair. I only kill those people who I am contracted to kill."

"So that's why you let me go, on the bridge... Huh, impressive!" I sneered. "A code of conduct for killers."

He smiled grimly and let go, lifting his gun and holding it to my head. "Yeah, maybe. But like I say, I always deliver – and right now, dyke, the contract is out on you. But first, you're gonna tell me where your friend is. Hold her, boys!" he barked.

The three of them moved towards me, their faces contorted with hate.

"It's too late, Bernie. It's over," I said, sensing movement, at long last, far above us. "She's safe. Safe with enough evidence to put you, Stantonwell and Langstein away for good."

He smirked. "No she isn't, Cameron. We'll get her. Dead women can't give evidence. This isn't over yet."

"Oh, but I think it is," I smiled, as the metallic voice from the Tannoy began to fill the air around us.

"Stay where you are! This is the police!"

The blades on the helicopter started to turn again. Shards of stone flew into the air around us, splintering in all directions as the warning shot from a marksman ricocheted off the hard ground, whining away into the night air. Bernie grabbed me violently, holding the gun to my neck and dragging me in front of him. He spun me erratically around, using me as a human shield. Clouds of white dust engulfed us. The rotor blades picked up speed.

The thugs drew guns and leapt back into the cover of the silos but, when they saw the three police cars tearing down the quarry road, blue lights flashing through the clouds of white quarry dust, they turned and ran after us.

Bernie backed up the steps and into the cabin, hauling me through the door, then pushing me headlong across the floor by the back seats as he yelled to the pilot: "Go! Go! Go!"

The cabin started to vibrate and the air became thick with the powerful thunder of an engine on full power, lifting us off the ground and out of the quarry, leaving the three thugs scrambling around in the vacuum below us.

Lying there in the darkness, convinced that I was finished, I felt something soft against my face – something warm, something human. And as Bernie slid the door shut and the noise abated, I twisted my head round.

"Angel!" I gasped, looking up into her bruised, unhappy face.

"Hello Cameron," she murmured, her voice breaking. Then she took hold of my arm, pulling me up onto my knees as the helicopter banked, making a wide arc over the countryside, heading for the coast.

"Leave her!" Bernie yelled, turning round from his seat and grabbing me under the chin, pulling my face up towards his own.

"You bitch! First you interfere on the bridge – now, this!" he spat, hurling me back onto the floor. "Well, you won't interfere again, McGill. This time you're going for a swim – a long cold swim in the North Sea."

He yanked open the cabin door, as the pilot swung the helicopter out over the coast. And as the wind howled around the small cabin, I looked out towards the Humber Bridge twinkling across the estuary, the lights of Hull shining next to it. Ahead of us was blackness and cold, icy sea.

"Martin, you can't!" Angel screamed above the wind and noise.

Bernie pointed a finger at her angrily, his voice seething. "You shut the fuck up, bitch! Or you'll be next. I've had enough of you and your lousy help!"

I looked up at her. "I guessed that you tricked me, Angel."

"He made me, Cameron, I had no choice." Her voice was nearly hysterical.

"You slag," he snarled, "you know you enjoyed fucking the dyke."

Angel turned to look at me, her emerald eyes wet and distressed, her face pleading for forgiveness. "Don't take any more." I mouthed the words slowly behind Bernie's back. "Break free, Angel. Break free."

She looked from me to him and I saw her eyes flash with anger.

We were out over the open sea now, so close to the surface that I could see the white horses on the waves as we skimmed close to them, keeping under the radar. The wind howled through the cabin from the open door, the smell of spent fuel soaked the air, and the noise from the rotors above drummed through my head.

Angel leant forward, shouting above the noise. "Last night, Cameron, I felt so safe with you. I'm sorry. I'm so sorry!"

Bernie half stood and turned around, grabbed her and brought his hand down across her face. She fell back dazed and hurt into her seat.

Then he grabbed me by the collar, bawling in my ear: "This is it, Cameron, you're going out."

He hauled me helplessly to my feet and pulled me past the edge of his seat until my head was outside, the wind whipping around me as

I struggled to stay on board. I looked back at Bernie's hard, expressionless face and at the figure of the pilot beyond him, calmly flying the plane, his eyes on the instruments, his hands on the controls. All I could do was hang on. I wrapped my feet around the back of Bernie's seat and held on for all I was worth, jamming myself between the cabin wall and his seat.

Then suddenly the helicopter lurched wildly. The pilot, taken off-guard, wrestled with the controls, and an RAF Harrier thundered past to our left, rocking its wings from side to side before turning away.

The chopper's pilot looked across at Bernie with panic in his eyes, just as a second Harrier, bristling with air-to-air missiles, settled in on our left, just feet away, flying in close formation with us.

"Christ Almighty!" the pilot screamed, struggling with the controls. "They're intercepting us!"

I looked across at the Harrier. He was right. The figure in the cockpit was clearly visible, pointing first at us and then down at the water.

"Keep going, you idiot!" Bernie screamed back at the top of his voice. He was pulling at my arms, lifting me up and, little by little, forcing me forward.

The radio crackled to life as the pilot switched channel. "I say again: intercepted helicopter – you are using this airspace illegally. Return to land under our direction. Acknowledge."

The helicopter pilot slowed, glancing nervously from Bernie to the Harrier, uncertain of what to do. But Bernie seemed oblivious to it all. He grabbed my head with one hand and pulled at my jeans with the other, jerking me forward. I'd almost given up. My feet were losing their grip on the back of his seat. One more yank and I would be gone.

And, as he gripped me hard under the arms with both hands, I braced myself for the fall.

But it never came. Instead, his grip suddenly relaxed and an angry noise filled the cabin – the sound of someone gasping for air. I twisted my body to look back. Bernie was reeling in his seat, his hand on his neck, grasping at a syringe that Angel had buried deep in his neck.

I pulled myself back in with my feet, scrambling away from the open door, as Angel grabbed the gun from Bernie's hand. She held it with both hands and pointed it first at him, then at our pilot. "Keep your hands on the controls!" she yelled.

"You won't use that on me, Angel," Bernie croaked, grimacing as he pulled the needle free. "You're in too deep now. You need me."

"Don't count on it, Martin," she shouted back. "I've had as much of you as I can take."

"Don't, Angel!" I yelled.

But she wasn't listening. As Bernie went for her, she pulled the trigger, hitting him in the shoulder, the force of the blast sending him rocketing towards space. He was left clinging, half inside, half outside the cabin, his one good hand desperately gripping the edge of the door.

"Angel!" I yelled again. "Don't! Don't kill him!"

"I'm sorry, Cameron," she said quite calmly, "you were right. I have to be free." Then she pulled the trigger again, sending him crashing out of the door, screaming as he hurtled down to the freezing water below.

The radio crackled to life again: "We repeat. You are using this airspace illegally. Return to land under our direction. Acknowledge."

The pilot looked at the Harrier, then back at Angel, his face white.

"Acknowledge!" she yelled.

He paused for just an instant and then clicked the radio control switch. "Acknowledged. We're making a turn now. We will follow you."

## Twenty-nine

I laid the spray of lilies and irises on the newly finished grave and stood back. The old cemetery had a fresh, simple beauty: the smell of newly mown grass, the blaze of butterflies on the old buddleia bush, the birdsong, the warmth of the sunlight shining through the trees, and the pealing bells of York Minster cascading out across the still sleepy city.

Four months on, the evil at GME was over. Langstein, Stantonwell and the others had been stopped, the women from the bunkers were safe, the protest camp had achieved the permanent closure of the laboratories. And Angel would soon know her fate.

Looking at the grave, I wished my mother's memory could be as easily laid to rest.

I'd always imagined that I would feel nothing for her when she died, but three weeks ago, at the simple funeral, I had felt a real loss. In the last few months of her life, I'd visited her a lot, and though we hadn't talked much, she'd begun to recognise me, and smiled whenever I appeared. After thirty-five years of bitterness, we'd finally achieved an understanding. If only that had been enough.

Becky came up behind me and laid a hand on my arm. "You did the best you could, Cameron. Don't blame yourself."

I sighed and turned to face her, feeling inadequate. "Becky... If only we'd had a little longer..."

A little longer. A lifetime. For ever. Deep down I knew that no amount of time would have made any difference. It had taken me all my life to understand what had come between us. Now that I knew, the hard bit was facing up to the truth about myself. If my father hadn't raped her, she would have been happier. If I hadn't been born, she would have tasted the joy of doing what she loved, being who she was. However I looked at it, the chilling truth was that I messed up her life and there was nothing I could ever do to put that right.

Becky must have read my thoughts, because she linked arms, pulling me close and smiling at me as we walked back along the path and out of the gates. Sunlight shimmered through her spiky blonde hair, her eyes shone a bright blue, her cheeks were flushed with the pleasure of friendship. Whatever I might feel about my past, I shouldn't forget the good things in the present. As I looked at her, it felt like a light had come on.

"So Cam," she said, her voice bright and positive, "it's a brand new start now, eh?"

I smiled back, pushing away my morbid thoughts. I had to live with the past, but the future was mine. And it was a future that, just now, looked both thrilling and scary.

"Yeah, I'm just about set up," I replied. "Mum left me enough to buy all the essentials and there's a little left over to keep me going for a few months, whilst the work builds up."

"Well, like I told you last week, I'm sure you'll pick up jobs from all over the place, once word gets round." Becky squeezed my arm encouragingly. "Everyone I know has to use the big firms in Leeds. It'll be really nice to have someone local – and a woman too! I bet you'll be busy a lot sooner than you think."

I hoped so. For all my excitement at starting out on my own, I couldn't help wondering if I could make it pay. But as we walked across the Selby road towards the grey Renault Clio, I was looking forward to the challenge.

"You did well." Becky ran her hand admiringly along the clean, shiny body of the car.

"Yeah. It's the right colour – not too noticeable – and it's in good nick for a two-year-old. It'll do me fine."

"But you're keeping your bike?" Becky's smile slipped a little as she got into the passenger seat.

After I got back from Hull, she'd given me a lecture about calming down, keeping out of trouble from now on. The new business had been my idea, and it worried her at first. Eventually she'd agreed to help on condition I stuck to routine work, but I knew she would rather I'd sold the bike – that potent symbol of my wild side.

"Yep. I'm keeping the Harley, Becks," I replied brightly. I wasn't ready to grow old just yet. "The car's for work. The bike's for me. There's just no substitute for two wheels. Besides, if this venture doesn't work and I have to choose, then it'll be the car that goes. Me and the bike... Well, we've been through a lot together."

She snorted and threw me a disapproving look as we drove off. "Mmm, well, just don't get into any more brushes with violent criminals. You've had more than enough for one lifetime."

I could feel her staring across at me, so I kept my eyes firmly on the road, staying quiet as we headed back towards the city centre.

But her censure didn't last long. "By the way, Cam, good news!" she sang after a few moments. "I had a call from Anne Smithson on Friday – you know, the solicitor who's handling the immigration appeals for the women at Barton. It's going well, she says. The ones who wanted to go back to their families have all returned now, expenses paid, and it looks increasingly like she's going to be able to swing it for those who want to stay. She said it was very much on compassionate grounds but, for once, the Home Office have been very sympathetic."

"Well, I should bloody well think so!" I declared. Sometimes the machinations of bureaucracy were beyond me. "For God's sake! Those poor women came out of one prison only to be sidelined into another by the authorities. It's about time their appeals were heard and they were given their lives back. How could they even think about forced repatriation? After all they've been through!"

Becky shrugged. "Well, you know how it is, Cam: procedures have to be followed. Anyway, they've been fortunate. It looks like their ordeal is nearly over."

Then she asked, "You still happy about your evidence for the trial?"

I nodded, dropping down a gear and pulling to a stop at the lights. "Yes, Becks. You know I am."

I'd had a choice with Angel's trial. I could have been the prime witness for the prosecution and helped to lock her up for a long time. But that wasn't what I wanted. She may have misled me but, in the end, the woman had saved my life. Now all I wanted to do was repay the favour, perhaps help her make a start on some kind of a life, even if that start was in prison.

"Well, I would reckon that I'll need to call you some time next Wednesday," said Becks. "The prosecution will cross-examine you afterwards, of course. They'll do all they can to get you to incriminate her, Cam. You know that, don't you?"

I glanced back at her earnestly as the lights changed, and then pulled forward across the junction before continuing. "Don't worry, Becks, I can take all they throw at me. The fact is that Angel only helped Bernie under severe duress. She wasn't party to any of the killings, I'm sure of that. And even shooting him was justifiable on grounds of self-defence, surely? Shit, he was trying to kill me, remember?"

"Yes, Cam," she replied, looking at her watch. "But the other side will do all they can to twist your words, so you'll have to be on your guard, flower. It's a fine line you have to tread. And the outcome will mostly turn on your evidence."

"I know," I admitted, my stomach churning with anxiety. "But she's got you as her lawyer and a really good barrister. I'll do all I can to help. I'm just hoping she comes out of it all right. You still think they'll put her away?"

"I'm sure they will. Drugs; assisting a criminal; manslaughter. The prosecution will ask for the maximum sentence. So we have to try and mitigate. She's pleading guilty, so that helps; and if you do your bit well, then maybe we can limit her sentence. We'll have to see."

She laid her hand on my arm as I indicated to turn right. "Aren't you going to show me your office?"

"Yeah, if you're interested and if you've got time." I shrugged. "It's just a room, nothing special."

"Well, Cameron –" she stuck her head on one side, mock-stroppy, and held me with those big blue eyes "– if I'm going to be one of your biggest clients, I need to see your set-up to make sure it's acceptable."

I stuck my tongue out at her and changed lanes. I was beginning to think she'd never ask.

I turned left towards the city centre and up into one of the side streets, looking for a parking space and thinking back to that early morning in April and my feeling of relief as the Harrier led us back to the airstrip. The police were waiting when we landed and both the pilot and Angel were taken into custody at once. I never got the chance to see her again, and I felt sad about that. I wanted to thank her and tell her she could make it.

But I was taken in a separate car to Hessle police station for a chat with Superintendent Warren, who was not the least bit grateful for my efforts. Instead of thanks, I got a caution for withholding evidence and the threat that if I ever stepped out of line again, I would be charged. Unfair, I thought, and I told him so – especially since the information from Beano had resulted in an early morning search of GME and the arrest of Stantonwell and most of his staff. Still, despite Warren's lack of grace, it felt satisfying to hear the next day that Langstein and the other owners of the business had been arrested too.

Becky smiled tentatively at me as we got out of the car, glancing at her watch again and ignoring my enquiring look. "Have you heard from Hellen lately?" she said, casually enough, as we strolled up through the Shambles towards Newgate Market. She knew as well as anyone that it was still a touchy subject.

"Actually, I spoke to her on the phone last night, Becks." She put her head on one side, waiting for my reaction. "It was all right. A bit strained and awkward, though. We've been writing to each other for months, but that's the first time we've actually spoken since she rang me in Hull."

"And?"

"Well, I was OK, really. I didn't panic or anything like the last time. In fact I was quite calm. She seems to have got used to the idea that we're just going to be friends and I suppose I feel better knowing that. She's coming to York for a few days in September. It scares me a bit..." I closed my eyes for a moment, composing myself. "We'll have to see how it goes."

She smiled knowingly and let the subject drop. "So you've got your office, you've bought all your equipment, you've got transport and you've done the training course," she said, looking at her watch yet again as we walked into Newgate Market.

"Yep. I know all about surveillance, serving writs, finding missing persons, interviewing witnesses, debt collection and all the other stuff. All I need now is enough work... Becky, why do you keep looking at your watch?"

"Oh... no reason," she said innocently, peering along the row of old buildings that lined the marketplace. "Where is it, Cam? Is it one of these?"

I stopped near the centre of the medieval terrace of shops and studied her for a second. She was up to something, I just knew it. "It's this one," I said, indicating a small door between two shops, but keeping my eyes firmly on her face.

Her expression of innocence didn't budge an inch, so I unlocked the door and led the way up the steep stairway onto a small landing with a stripped-pine door leading off on each side.

"This is it," I announced, going up to the door on the right, fumbling with the keys. "I really wanted one of those glass-panelled doors that you see in the old Bogart films – you know, with my name hand-painted in big letters on it."

"I think the brass plate probably has more class," she offered, putting on her glasses to read it. "Cameron McGill, Private Investigator," she announced grandly. "Mmm, it's good. I just hope you can keep to routine work."

So did I. But, as I unlocked the door and swept it open, I wasn't at all convinced that serving writs and taking statements was all I wanted to do. Still, it was a start and – for now at any rate – it would keep Becky happy.

Inside, it wasn't what you might call impressive. The room was a small one with plain magnolia walls and a low uneven ceiling, with a single lightbulb hanging from the centre. The floor sloped rather dramatically to one end and through the small window you could look out over the busy open market. I'd added a cheap carpet; a new birchwood desk with a computer on it; a telephone, fax machine, filing cabinet; and three office chairs upholstered in a nice quiet grey. Just a room, but it was mine.

"It's great, Cam!" Becky enthused, sneaking a look at her watch again and glancing towards the door. "Really cosy and in just the right place. You'll be able to do your shopping in the market and there's a great sandwich shop just round the corner."

I looked at her in disbelief. "Becky, I got it because it's cheap and central. I just hope it works, or I won't have any money to buy sandwiches with."

"I'm sure you'll do just fine." She was peering out of the window. "Like I told you, I've got some research I need doing, some witnesses for you to interview and there's a couple of people I'm trying to locate, so that's a good start. And I'm sure word will soon get round. In a few weeks you won't know which way to turn." She stood up straight and turned back to me as I heard the outside door slam.

"Who's that?" I asked, puzzled, walking across to the office door.

"It's Sunday... Besides, no one else knows I'm here..."

But before I even got to the landing, there was an almighty scream and the sound of someone collapsing noisily on the stairs. A formless body, dressed in a grey suit, was lying in a heap halfway up, one arm stretched up the stairs as if in supplication. I froze momentarily, my heart beating wildly.

Then I saw Becky's reproachful look and the grey heap lifted up its face and croaked at me dramatically.

"Help me! You've got to help me! I'm looking for the famous detective... Cameron McGill..." it said, before apparently passing out.

"Beano, just get up, will you!" I laughed.

She picked herself up, grinning broadly, and came the rest of the way up the stairs, a bottle of champagne in her hand, to give both me and Becky a bear hug.

"What the hell are you doing here?" I asked, amazed and delighted.

"I've come to help launch the new business, of course!" she replied, brushing down the smart grey trouser suit and adjusting her tie as she looked across mischievously at Becky. "Hell, Cam, we couldn't let you start in the PI business without a fucking celebration, now could we? So we'll have a drink first, then off to the pub round the corner for a slap-up meal on me!"

I shook my head and hugged her again. She looked well – really well. "God, you're so smart, Beano. Shit, you almost look respectable!"

"Hey," she cautioned, darkly, "that's enough. I wouldn't have made the effort if I knew you were going to insult me."

"Yeah, OK," I laughed, "but you've got to let me pay – I know you must be hard up after all that time off work."

"Ahhh, I'm doing all right!" she said offhandedly, walking round the room, opening drawers and poking about at the computer. "Hey you've got a good set-up here, Cam." She sat in one of the chairs and leant back, her feet on the desk.

Becky handed her a cup. "Make yourself at home, why don't you?"

Beano grinned and jumped up, tearing the wrapper off the bottle, popping the cork to the sound of our cheers and then pouring the fizzy liquid until it cascaded over the edge of the cups.

"Here's to you – Cameron McGill, Private Investigator!" She held the cup high in the air, then clinked it against mine and Becky's. "I just know you'll enjoy it, love. Right up your street, it is. Some routine to make money. Some excitement to lift the spirits…"

"Just hold on, Beatrice!" Becky held up her hand at Beano. "I don't want you leading Cam astray. She's promised me she's going to keep out of trouble in future!"

"Me, lead someone astray?" Beano gasped, stepping back, like butter wouldn't melt in her mouth. "Me? I wouldn't do that, Rebecca!"

Becky looked at her critically then back at me. "You promised to stick to interviewing witnesses, finding missing persons, serving writs. That sort of thing, remember? I don't want you to let this woman get you into serious trouble again, Cam – OK?"

Beano feigned offence, glancing across at me out of the corner of her eye. "Don't look at me like that, Becky! You think I want to try and get myself killed again?" She shook her head energetically. "No fucking way! Give me the boring routine sort of work any time!"

Becky looked from her to me, uncertainly. "Yeah, well… OK then… You promise you'll avoid anything heavy, Cam? Like we agreed?"

"Yeah. Of course, Becks."

She looked far from convinced.

I glanced across at Beano, hoping for some support. But I could see it in her eyes… She didn't believe me either.

## *Have you read the first thrilling Cameron McGill mystery?*

**Needle Point**
*Jenny Roberts*

**"Completely enthralling"** Amy Lamé,
***Entertainment Zone***, BBC London Live

"The bruising and the torn skin were worse than I had ever seen before – even the most hardened users protect their veins."

Cameron McGill is on a mission: to find out why her sister, who never touched drugs, was fished from a canal with needle marks all down her arm. Riding through Amsterdam on her Harley-Davidson, Cam encounters radical squatters, evasive drug agencies and a particularly alluring policewoman. But it's hard to know who to trust in a quest that could claim her life as gruesomely as it took her sister's.

**"An excellently paced, well-plotted thriller"** *Guardian*

**"A fast-moving tale of revenge and retribution"** *Time Out*

**"Riveting and well observed. Recommended!"** *Gscene*

**"A pacy, energetic thriller told in a crisp, direct style"** Manda Scott

**"An impressive debut... hugely believable characters and bright-as-a-button prose"** Alma Fritchley

RRP £8.95  ISBN 1-873741-42-1

**Hearts & Minds**
*Jay Taverner*

**"A vividly satisfying adventure story about the things
desperate women do for love"
Emma Donoghue**

When Hope and Bell are parted by family duty, both women find their separation hard to bear. Enter Lucy: frightened, impoverished and used to being cursed for her dark skin. It won't be long before charges of witchcraft lead to a series of tragedies and close escapes.

Like Jay Taverner's popular first novel, *Rebellion* (Onlywomen Press), Hearts & Minds sucks us in to England's hidden past: its teeming markets, where quack doctors and travelling players converge; its inns and its ironworks; its filthy gaols, rolling countryside and secret loves.

The story picks up where *Rebellion* left off but is complete in itself.

**"Excels in its depiction of the filthy cold miserable reality of life,
especially for autonomous women, in our not-so-glorious past"
*Time Out***

RRP £8.95  ISBN 1-873741-59-6

**DIVA Book of Short Stories**
*edited by Helen Sandler*

**Includes a brand new story from Jenny Roberts:
'Making the Horse Laugh'**

"This wonderful collection presents fresh work from familiar names –
including Emma Donoghue, Stella Duffy and Jackie Kay – alongside
the best from a new generation of British talent. In tales of pride and
jealousy, cruelty and community, the characters find themselves eating passports, healing horses and running for cover when the gossip
gets out of control. The selection and originality of the work makes a
refreshing change, with situations that the majority of lesbians can relate to – there are plenty of characters here that you'll think are based
on people you know or at least recognise from the scene.
Recommended!" **Gay's the Word website**

**"Look out for the DIVA Book of Short Stories"**
*Observer Magazine*

**"Good value"**
*Time Out*

**"A brilliant collection"**
**Rainbow Network**

RRP £8.95   ISBN 1-873741-47-2

**It's a Family Affair:**
**The complete lesbian parenting book**
*Lisa Saffron*

**Indispensable help with the littlest big decision of your life**

Are you planning a baby by yourself or with your lesbian partner? Or perhaps you have a more conventional family but now it's time to come out to your husband and children about your 'other life'?

What will life be like after your big decision? How does self-insemination work? How do children cope with being part of a non-conventional family? What will your mother say? Will things change between you and your lover?

All these questions and much more are explored in this thorough and readable book by a leading authority in the field. Lisa Saffron has run parenting workshops for many years and writes a regular column in DIVA magazine about lesbian families.

In this unique volume, she uses interviews with parents and their kids to bring alive the issues. Gay donors and fathers are also interviewed to find out how they fit in to the lesbian family.

NEW   June 2001   RRP £15   ISBN 1-873741-62-6

DIVA Books are available from all good bookshops, including Waterstone's, Borders, Libertas!, Gay's The Word, Silver Moon and Prowler.

DIVA also has a mail order service on freephone 0800 45 45 66 (international: +44 20 8340 8644). Please quote the following codes: Hearts & Minds HEA596, Diva Book of Short Stories DVB472, Breaking Point BRE588, Needle Point DVB421, It's a Family Affair ITS626

For a year's subscription to DIVA magazine, call 020 8348 9967 (international: +44 20 8348 9967). UK £24, Europe £50, rest of world £60.